MYRA-HATI

CROSSED PATHS

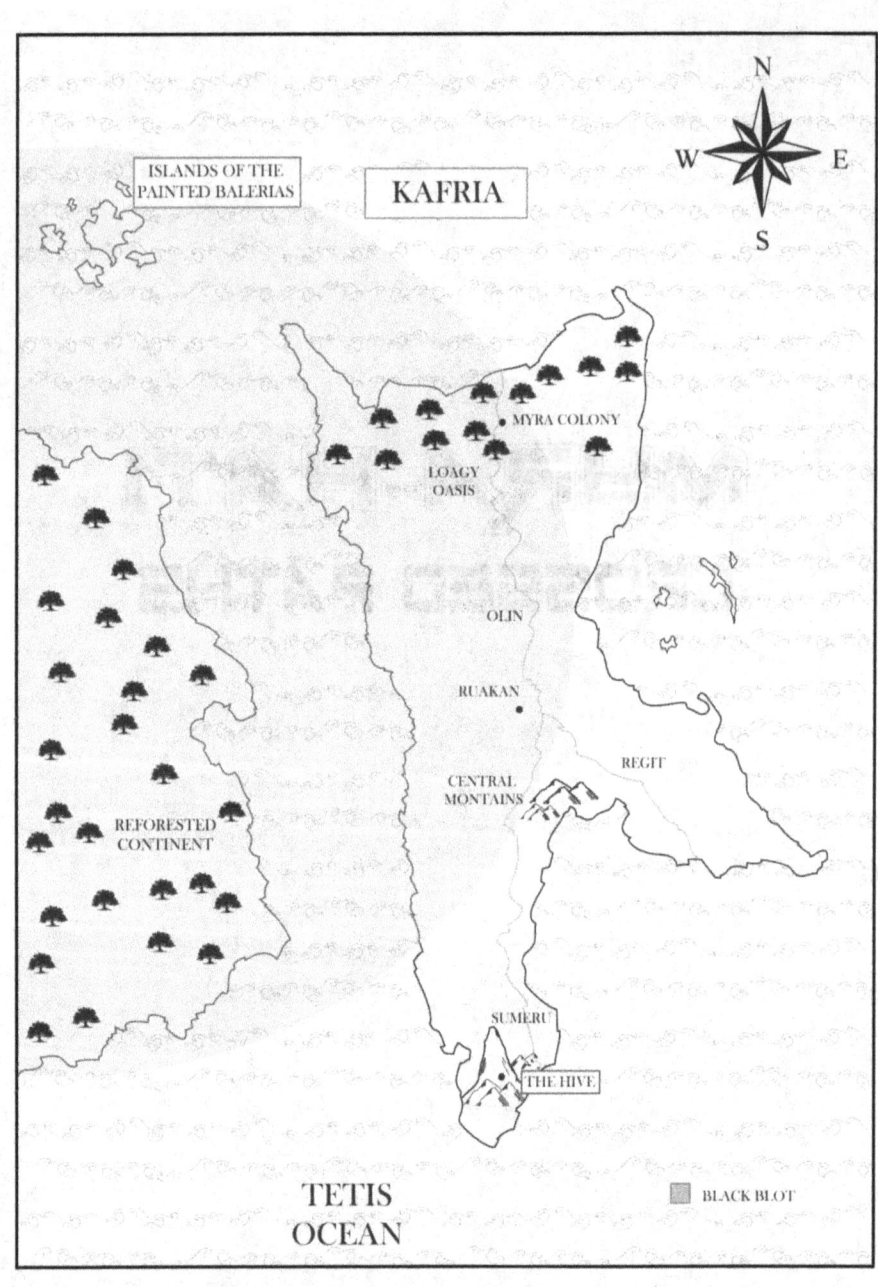

ISLANDS OF THE
PAINTED BALERIAS

KAFRIA

N
W E
S

MYRA COLONY

LOAGY
OASIS

OLIN

RUAKAN

REGIT

CENTRAL
MONTAINS

REFORESTED
CONTINENT

SUMERU

THE HIVE

TETIS
OCEAN

BLACK BLOT

MYRA-HATI
CROSSED PATHS

BY

FABIO EVANGELISTA

Translated from the Portuguese by Lenita Rimoli Esteves and John Milton – professors of Translation Studies at USP - University of São Paulo - Brazil.

Donnalnk Publications, L.L.C.
4405 S. Kirkman Rd. Suite #B208, Orlando, FL 32811
Visit our website at www.donnaink.org

Editorial Team: Donnalnk Publications, L.L.C., Mr. Philip Bartholomew, Mr. Quante Bryan, Ms. Shelby Catalano; Layout and Design: ZenCon an Art of Zen Consultancy, Ms. Dana Queen.

First Paperback Edition: December 2014. First Electronic Edition: January 2014.

Library of Congress Cataloging in Publication Data:
Fabio Evangelista, 2014 -
    MYRA-HATI: Crossed Paths / Evangelista, Fabio. - 1st ed.
                        ISBN: 978-1-939425-67-6 (print aka)
    480 p.cm.

Summary: "In the second half of the 21st century, the world witnesses the creation of plugs. These are devices created by Japanese scientists, which record the five human senses. With the help of these devices people record their own life experiences in order to relive them at any time and they can share them with others. When shared with a friend or acquaintance, the receiving mind feels the experiences as if they were their own. In a short time, these devices become a worldwide phenomenon and that is where trouble begins. Entertaining and illusive novel." ~ Summary provided by the author.

[1. Literature - Fiction, 2. Fantasy - Fiction, 3. Relationships - Fiction, 4. Futuristic - Fiction, 5. Science Fiction - Fiction, 6. Social Issues – Fiction, 7. Brazil – Fiction, 8. South American – Fiction, 9. Men's Adventure – Fiction, 10. United States - Fiction.]
I. Title. II. Title: MYRA-HATI: Crossed Paths
Dewey Classification: 813
10 9 8 7 6 5 4 3 2 1

2013936138

TABLE OF CONTENTS

TABLE OF CONTENTS

PREFACE

AUTHOR'S NOTES

The argument is a link between our reality and the imaginary world created in the book. Four specialists assessed the book, and although all agreed its content could be classified into fantasy and science fiction, each contributed his/her own definition. It is a novel, since it revolves around the psychology, acts and thoughts of the several characters. It is an adventure, for the characters travel and face many challenges. It is also science fiction, for the story is set in a post-apocalyptic future where technologies are still non-existent.

As an author, I believe I have accomplished my objective in writing this book. My intention was to write a book that had a little bit of all these literary genres, as well as some mystery, so that the reader would be enthralled all through the story.

It took me seven years locked on my room to complete the first book, writing it at least 10 hours daily as I was learning how to write. It was a struggle and I had to abdicate all my others things in order to do it exclusively. When the book was finished after I'd rewritten it for about six or seven times, I left my room and I glazed myself through the mirror.

My first though when I saw my beard was –Oh my God, I'm Kliver all throughout coming from his cave.

Anyway, now I am less amateur about the writing process and I make the promise that the second book will be finished soon. Enjoy.

ACKNOWLEDGEMENT

I would like to thank mainly to my family, who supported me through my decisions and also to all the people who believed in this book.

DEDICATION

For Maria Teresa Sabia, my wife and my main teacher, and for the journey we follow together.

MYRA-HATI

CROSSED PATHS

PROLOGUE

Judis raised his large head. Two visitors were asking him for something which was beyond his telepathic skills. One of them, a young Myra-Hati called Tork, who had long hair and a look of curiosity in his eye, was carrying a golden sword, stamped with a serpent dragon carved in jade. The other was an autotrophic mutant called Flouts.

Tork was insisting that Judis revealed the secrets contained in the sword. Despite its mystical appearance, it seemed to be an ordinary sword, a golden katana with nothing else special about it. "According to Hanara", he said, kneeling down to offer it to him, "it represents knowledge and courage and has the power to change the Era in which we live."

Flouts had also knelt down, but kept silent.

"How could a simple sword change the world?" asked Judis.

"I don't know either" replied Tork. "But my master insisted, before he was captured, that I should find it."

Tork hesitated before continuing:

"I have now had it for some time, and I offer it out of gratitude to the man who helped me and my brothers when we were in such great difficulty."

"I had told you never to come back here" Judis reminded him. "You gave me a lot of problems. I only allowed you to see me at the time because you were a mixed group of young people, and because you are a Myra-Hati, something very unusual today."

"I agree" replied Tork. "But if the war spreads, your people will also be affected."

"This will not happen" guaranteed the Guardian. "The Reforested Continent is a place which brings fear, and, in addition, they don't know of our existence. We are only here to observe. Nobody, except my people, knows the true history of the world. Where do you think we are?"

"I'm not sure. As far as the truth is concerned, maybe the Hati Emperor also knows it. Take us to your people, I implore you. Give us food and shelter. In exchange, Flouts and I will be your faithful serfs".

"I can't take you. My people would not understand."

"I am not worried about what they will do to us as long as you reveal the secrets of the sword."

The herberist guardian thought for a moment, looking at the strange appearance of Flouts and the gold gilding the sword, which was half way out of its sheath.

"You're speaking courageously and have a pure mind. I'll take you, but I don't know what the reaction will be. Don't expect a welcome. I'll cover your faces so you won't memorize the route, and I'll introduce you as invaders."

"Do what is necessary" said Tork, in agreement. "But before this, give me your word that you will look after the sword."

PROLOGUE

"You have it" replied Judis. "By the way, how did you get it?"

"It's a long story . . ."

CHAPTER 1

iNVASION

The North Wind whistled through the cliffs along the large mountain ridge. The atmosphere, hot and dry, prevented ice formation even on the highest peaks. A gentle draft of air moved the fog around the mountaintops, swallowed by darkness. At some site in that unfriendly place, the continuous cry of a child could be heard.

The silhouette of a man was crouching on the high rock, and he gazed into the immense blackness of the moonless night. Leo Kliver had the appearance of a primitive man, but the wisdom brought by experience showed in his eyes. His beard was long and bushy, with mixed brown dust, hanging from his face as if petrified, and in it families of ticks and fleas had their nests.

His hands perspired, and he was unable to decide whether to thank or curse his gods. The high-pitched cry that had awakened him and echoed on and on in the cave behind him had the meaning of a blessing. Finally the child had been born, and he was a father for the second time. He had gone through the same anxiety he had felt when his first son, Aron, had been born. Still in his mind, he could see the image of Jill, his first wife, drawing her last breath as she gave birth to their child. Miku's childbirth had been equally difficult, and in the mountains, there were neither doctors nor midwives to comfort her. But now, after fifteen hours of labor, mother and son rested safe inside the darkness of the cave, and Kliver, feeling the wind on his face as if it were divine providence itself, was thankful.

He stood up and returned to the interior of the cave. Despite the cold, Miku was sweating on the pile of straw. During labor, she had twisted and writhed in pain, hitting her head against the rocky ground, hurting her arm, her back, and her nape. The bruises were insignificant, however, if compared to the joy of having the newborn on her lap, the small rosy hand clutching her finger, the little mouth searching for her breast.

Kliver did not have a scale, but holding the child in his arms, he would guess it weighed about six pounds. Makuro, his stepson, and little Aron looked amazed at their newborn brother crying. They could not understand how that small child had emerged from the woman's body. Soon the baby stopped crying, and Kliver huddled close to his wife, giving her a smile and a kiss on the forehead. Miku closed her eyes and smiled back at him. Aron and Makuro got closer, and the straw mattress became small for all of them in their embrace. The cold disappeared as if it had never existed, and the five people soon fell asleep, hearing the crickets' symphony outside.

Morning broke suddenly. The sun slowly expelled the shadows. It was past seven, and Kliver, already up, was making his morning prayer and getting prepared for another ordinary day. He stood up and observed his wife sleeping beside the baby. The baby was warm in its mother's arms, wrapped in coarse cotton cover.

Kliver picked a piece of rock and marked one more stroke on the damp wall that, little by little, received more light. They had lived there for exactly two years, and Kliver knew he had to do something about it. They could not live in the mountains forever, but for the time being, life did not offer them any other option.

At this moment, the baby stretched his little arms and yawned but continued sleeping. The father smiled, full of pride, and crouched to pass through the tight exit of the cave. It was already bright enough outside. Over a red background, a yellow light shone through the greenish clouds. Kliver approached the edge of the cliff and sat down, fixing his eyes on the precipice. The morning breeze brought the smell of a new day and the hopes that came with it. He remained there for some time, gazing at the sands of the large desert that met the sky in the horizon.

Then, he stood up.

He had many tasks to do, and the first was to fix a nice breakfast. Leaving the edge of the cliff, he climbed down the mountain to get to the grass patches, carrying a rope and a jug, and approached Misha, the bigbug his friends in the army had given him.

Bigbugs were mammals. Their milk was naturally sweet and creamy, rich in calcium and all the proteins needed by humans. They looked like gigantic insects with their distinct heads, thoraxes and abdomens. From their mouths grew three sucking-trunks through which they sucked leaves and moss that served as food for them. Bigbugs had no teeth. Their esophagus was thin, and their digestion was made only through chemical processes. They grinded their food and were able to digest grains and small stones. Most of them were hermaphrodite and bred without having to mate. They were half blind and had nocturnal habits. Used mainly for transporttation, they could also help humans as pack and draft animals. When they became old and nonproductive, they were killed and their skins were used in workmanship while their meat was consumed as food.

Kliver tightened the rope around Misha's neck and pushed her bigbuglets back so as to bring it near the shade of a cogus, and he sat on a low stone that he always used as a chair. Observing Misha's bigbuglets moving about was rewarding after Misha's sixteen-month-long pregnancy. They were six months old now, but surely they would not wean before they reached the age of one year.

The man tied the bigbug to the roots of the cogus and started to fill the jug with the milk from her udders. The milk was thick and yellowish, did not produce much froth and took small pressure to collect. With the jug filled, he unfastened the animal and she could go back to the grass patches where she was before. Kliver climbed up the slope to make his habitual fire and boil the milk. He realized that Makuro, his stepson who was only two years of age, was already awake.

"What's up, son?" he asked with a calm voice. "Cannot sleep anymore?"

He used the Myra language, a neo-anglo speech originated in the old world. Rubbing his little eyes, Makuro answered that his new brother had started crying, and he could not get back to sleep.

"You stay put and behave yourself," said the man. "I need to go up to the lake. I forgot to bring water for the tea."

A few meters away from the grass patches, there was a small pond encircled by tall trees and some coguses, which were mushroom-shaped gigantic clusters of fungi. Kliver kneeled down and saw his face on the surface of the water.

"You are old," he said with some melancholy to his own reflection, "old and ugly."

At that moment, he felt something lightly touching his hand. An ant was moving towards a nettle leaf full of dew. When the tiny insect approached the leaf to quench its thirst, a bee alighted beside it with the same purpose. It was a black bee, long and equally small, distinguishing itself from the ant only for its translucent wings.

The bee considered the ant as an enemy and attacked it. The two insects stung each other for about thirty seconds. The bee's poison was stronger; the ant could not resist and died, its body becoming entirely shrunken. Observing the scene, Kliver could not help but shed a tear. What was the use of the bee's winning of the battle? It left its stinger inside the enemy's body, so it would soon die, too, he thought.

It was almost midday, and the yellow blot of the sun was near the middle of the sky. Aron and Makuro, the two boys who lived like brothers, had already had their breakfast and were now playing around the cave. They were virtually the same age, Aron being only four months and some days older than Makuro. They were too young to understand that now they had a common brother. Although they were very small, much was demanded of them. Makuro had just turned two and was already learning to speak two different languages and, also, to scratch some letters both of the Myra and the Hati alphabets. During the last few hours, however, their parents had concentrated their attention on the newborn, leaving them to themselves. They could play freely and do things for which, in general, they would be scolded, like playing with Misha's bigbuglets, for example.

In the drier corner of the cave, lying on a layer of straw, Miku was breast-feeding the still unnamed baby. Kliver went to talk to her.

"What a gluttonous baby!" he scoffed, trying to coax a smile from her. "Look at him. So small and defenseless . . . it reminds me of when I first saw Aron."

The woman tried to avoid his look. She lowered her eyes to the straw and was still for an instant. She knew her husband approached her for something other than an endearing talk.

Kliver did not hesitate.

"Darling, I think this is the moment for us to talk about that old issue," he said, changing his expression.

She contracted her body and held her baby tighter. She found a comfortable position and focused her attention on her husband. Kliver continued:

"What will happen to us?" he asked in a worried tone. "What will we do? The boys are playing. They are happy . . . but for how long? We cannot allow them to grow up here. Now, with the baby, we have three hungry mouths to feed. We cannot go on living in these mountains."

Having said this, he lay down beside his wife and was silent. They were speechless for some time, looking at the stalactites that threatened to fall from the high ceiling. The only sound to be heard was that of the boys having fun outside, but then Miku spoke.

"And what can we do? Returning is unacceptable. We simply can't go back. We will be convicted and shall pay with our lives and the lives of our children," she said, speaking in Hati because she could not speak Kliver's language.

"I know that," he answered, also in Hati. "It never crossed my mind to go back. I was thinking of moving on to another place, a place where life could be more dignifying."

"And where could that place be?" she asked, her voice a little tense. "There is no hope for us. We are runaways. Here, at least we have water and food for a long time. And soon, Misha's brood will grow up, and they will give us milk and meat."

"We cannot go on living like savages," said the man. "I have made my decision. Soon after you have recovered, we will pick up our children and head on to the desert. We can find an oasis with trees and water. We can tame animals and live as farmers. We can make tents and have a little more civilized life, instead of living in a damned cave," he continued, try-ing to calm down.

He kissed his wife and stood up, walking to the entrance of the cave. As he passed through the opening between the rocks, he heard her agreeing with him.

Kliver went back.

"You are right," said Miku. "We really have to go. Here, there is no future for us, and we won't be able to raise our children as they deserve to be. But let's wait for the big buglets to grow and for the little one to take his first steps."

Kliver looked at the newborn, sound asleep, huddling tog-ether with his mother.

"I agree," he said, "let's wait a little longer. Some months more will not make a great difference."

The man knew that it would really be better to wait for the animals to grow. The journey would be long and they would need them to carry their belongings. Moreover, with Makuro and Aron a little bigger, they would avoid many difficulties. The best thing to do was to let time pass. After all, despite the other difficulties, hunger and thirst would not be a problem. There were natural wells along the hillsides as well as many edible plants on the margins of the lake.

The sun was going down, and the sky was getting a violet hue. Kliver was finishing his monotonous daily task: to cut firewood for the next day's fire and, once more, tie the bigbugs to the trunks of the trees to prevent them from escaping during the night. He was against building fences around the grass patches. "Bigbugs are half blind, and enclose-ing them could cause some inconvenient accidents," he thought.

The position of the sun revealed it was past 6 o'clock. Miku was still lying inside the cave.

"Today, she has not moved from the spot," Kliver said to himself.

He knew she was weak, owing to the complicated child-birth, but he believed some exercise could do her good.

The man finished his work and sat silently on the cliff edge. Despite the wind, his beard did not move. From that spot, he had a wide view of the world around him, and that was, in his opinion, the best place to collect his thoughts. He was pleasurably swinging his feet back and forth in the air, thinking how he missed that last cigarette he had smoked months before.

Aron came close to him slowly, silently as a snake and kneeled down next to his father.

"Watch out or you will fall, young man. Go back and stay with your mother. It's dangerous here."

The boy did not heed his words. He sat beside his father and observed the beautiful scenery spread in front of him. It consisted of dry, arid lands cracked by the old world's sun, and not a desert with dunes and fluffy sand.

Kliver breathed in the cold air of the afternoon.

"Looking from up here, don't you feel like a god?" he asked his son.

Aron just nodded, his little blue eyes roaming the land-scape till they caught something that seemed different.

"Daddy, what's that?"

"What, son?" asked Kliver, looking in the direction the boy pointed.

"That dash, far away, making a lot of smoke in the sand. What's that?"

The man strained his eyes to see more clearly. Suddenly his expression was tense and his fingers started trembling. His heart was pounding, and he could not salivate.

"Aron, go into the cave and get me my binoculars," he asked, agitating his hands nervously.

"Daddy, what is a binocar?"

"Binoculars," corrected Kliver. "I will pick them up myself. You won't be able to find them."

Kliver picked up Aron in his arms and ran to the cave, leaving the child near his mother, telling Makuro to stay beside her, too. He opened an old backpack that was in one of the corners and picked a pair of high power binoculars out of it.

"What's the matter?" asked Miku, worried, "Why are you in a hurry? What's happening?"

"Take the children to the hiding-place," he commanded. "Quickly!"

"I'm not doing anything before you tell me what's happening," she insisted.

"There's something coming very fast in our direction. It is much too fast to be an animal or a sand storm. I suppose it is a Hati military vehicle."

Miku's eyes were wide open. "Are you sure?"

"Yes. Do as you're told, please. Take the children and go to the hiding place."

He reached out his hand to help her stand up, which she did with difficulty. When she was finally standing, she dropped a small round metallic object on the straw. A faint light shone in its center.

"What's that? It fell from your dress." Kliver crouched to pick it up, showing it to his wife.

Miku took it into in her hands, looking confused, trying to understand what it was.

She touched her nape and felt the three holes of the connector, completely unobstructed, and concluded in amazement:

"Heavens! It's my signal blocker! It got loose from the connector. It must have happened while I was having the contractions. I beat my head against the floor several times and . . ."

"What is this device for?" asked Kliver, cutting her short.

"It is used as an anti-diffuser. It blocks the signals that are sent from my internal transmitter. Without it, the transmitter must be working again. These signals indicate my position in the continent, and they can be detected from far away by the Hati trackers."

"What are you saying?" cried Kliver, snatching the device from her hands. "So that's why there is a Hati vehicle coming our way. You have been detected. The vehicle is coming very fast. Soon they will find us."

He got out of the cave and almost threw the object away down the slope when Miku's voice stopped him.

"Don't throw it away" she said, still inside the cave. "The device must be connected to me. It is the only way for us to be safe from the Hati trackers."

Kliver went back and gave the object to his wife. Miku lifted her long black hair and pressed the pin against the holes in her nape, connecting the device.

"While this is connected to me," she said, "the Hatis won't be able to find us. However, the vehicle must be near enough for them to have calculated my position. Let's go to the hiding place before it's too late. We will stay there till they give up the search.

Kliver obeyed. He did not have to look again to be sure that what he and his son had seen was a Hati vehicle. He tucked away the binoculars and put the backpack on, leading his family to the hiding place.

It was located right beyond the grass patches, only a few meters from the lake. It was a hole, deep in the ground, dug by Kliver himself, under a big purple cogus. He had always been a wary man, and he knew that things like that could have happened a long time ago. That's why he had made the hole. It was a dirty and uncomfortable place, but it was the perfect hiding place for, under the shade, the cogus roots provided an effective camouflage for the entrance.

Kliver led his wife and three children through the narrow passage and settled in the corner that was left for him. He covered the entrance with roots and watched through the empty spaces between them.

In the middle of the desert there was a cactus. It was alive, green and vigorous, despite being the only living thing in the middle of hundreds of miles of desert. Suddenly, a low cloud passed at the speed of sound. The wind, mingled with dust, blew strong. The cactus tree was torn away violently along with its deepest roots.

It was a military vehicle. It had neither tracks nor crawlers. It moved on a cushion of air that was impelled by powerful atomic turbines. In design, it was similar to a racing bobsled, with seats for four people. That vehicle in particular was occupied only by the conductor.

The external parts on both sides of the motor were chromium plated, and the body had a golden metallic color. The machine was flying low, sliding towards a mountain ridge. Its radar had just lost the tracking signal, which a moment earlier shone brightly on the screen, pointing to a spot amongst the rocky peaks.

When the vehicle approached the spot indicated by the radar, the turbines entered reverse mode, and pressurized air was released from the front jet nozzles, decreasing the speed almost instantly. The vehicle came to a stop when it reached the foot of one of the mountains that rose as a vertical wall.

A man of average height got out of the vehicle. He was wearing a flexible yellow armor and a helmet with two radio aerials. He stretched his neck and backbone, relieving the stress of the long trip. Holding his hands around his waist, he bent his head back, trying to see something up the cliff.

The sky was turning dark very fast, making it difficult for him to see. The man put down the shield of the helmet and turned on the infrared vision device. He pulled an energy capsule from his belt and fit it between the two 20mm guns fixed to his right wrist. Three small red lights went on between the guns, warning that the guns were now charged and ready to fire off. They were laser-guns, and just one shot would be enough to eliminate any living being within its range.

The soldier touched his nape, searching for the button of his connected plug. A small red light indicated it was on then he spoke something in an order tone and two titanium wings opened behind his shoulders, with embedded flat turbines. The compartments in the belt moved, giving rise to two levers by his hips.

The soldier started moving around in his vehicle, his eyes fixed on the top of the cliff. He pressed the button on his belt lever, and blasts of wind blew at his back, raising him from the ground. He pulled the lever back, and the power of the turbines grew stronger, taking him higher and higher till he reached the mountaintop.

He landed on the cliff plateau. The turbines went off and the titanium wings lowered, closing like the blades of a pair of scissors. He examined the place with the help of the night vision device in his helmet and saw a cave hewn in the mountain; he stretched his right arm, pointing the guns on his wrist to the entrance. For a moment he stood on the alert and then moved his eyes towards the ashes of what in the morning had been a fire. He crouched and picked up a remaining piece of coal and smashed it between his thumb and his index finger. He sniffed it and once again spoke to himself, turning on the heat sensor in the helmet shield but could not detect any high temperature spot; he then switched it back to the night vision mode.

At this moment, in the middle of the dark in the hiding place, Kliver felt an adrenaline rush through his body. He whispered into Miku's ear:

"We're lost! I have not unfastened Misha and her bigbuglets."

"And what's the problem?" she asked, already expecting a certain answer.

"If someone finds them tied up, he will be sure their master lives around here. If I don't release Misha before they find her, they will never give up their search and will wait a week, if necessary, till we go back to rescue the animals." Kliver said that as he dragged on the ground to get out of the hiding place.

"Take care," she said.

"Don't worry. If I'm not back, remember . . . I love you."

Kliver was expecting something like "me, too," but he heard a "hurry up," not without a touch of acrimony.

The man got out of the hiding place and crawled towards the grass patches. His bigbug was calmly grazing, tied to the trees, while her bigbuglets kept poking their muzzles, searching for her udders.

At the top of the slope, Kliver spotted a human figure entering the cave. He quickly dropped his backpack onto the ground. He opened it and took out an unassembled crossbow, its parts dusty and oxidized. He held some arrows between his teeth while he assembled the weapon with professional skill.

With the crossbow ready to shoot, Kliver dusted it and loaded it with two arrows. Generally, this kind of arrow had poisoned or explosive points, but the poison or the gunpowder had probably lost their power over time.

Kliver stood up, put on the backpack, released Misha and the bigbuglets. He crouched between two big stones and waited, aiming the arrows at the top of the slope and the entrance of the cave, which was at a right angle to the spot where he stood.

Minutes later, the human figure got out of the cave and came slowly in Kliver's direction. The arm holding the crossbow trembled, following every move of the other man, aiming the weapon at him. When the man trodded on the grass patches, the last sunrays faced him and Kliver could recognize him.

"As I suspected," Kliver thought, staring at the golden armor shining in the twilight, "a Hati soldier." He kneeled down and propped the crossbow on his shoulder, lowering his eyes to the weapon sight. He searched for the best spot to hit the man so that one shot would be fatal, which was difficult since the man's vital organs were protected by the apparently impervious armor.

The soldier approached Misha and stood there looking at her bigbuglets. The animals acted naturally, ignoring the intruder, which showed they were tame.

The man once more spoke to himself and then he stretched his right arm, pointing the laser gun at Misha. He coldly fired three quickly double shots, all at the animal's head.

Misha uttered no cry of pain. Her legs faltered and she dropped dead on the green grass. Merciless and not yet satisfied, the soldier also slaughtered her bigbuglets, which, one by one, fell beside their mother's body.

After that, the man walked cautiously to the lake.

Kliver witnessed the dreadful extermination of his little herd in silence. And now he watched the killer going to where his family was. He had to kill him somehow. He drew a deep breath and tried to calm down. He had to aim perfectly before shooting an arrow.

The soldier approached the margin of the lake and remained there for some moments, looking at the clear water then checking his mini-radar on his wrist, trying to locate the tracking signal he had lost. While he was doing that, Kliver hit him from behind with an arrow thrust deep into his nape, a little below the helmet and a little above the plug fixed to the connector. That was a lethal spot left un-shielded. The soldier uttered a muffled cry and fell into the water.

Kliver ran in that same direction to make sure the man was really dead. He pulled the senseless body out of the water and plucked the arrow from his nape, shouting to his wife that they could now come out from the hiding place. The woman picked up the kids and got out, holding on to a root for support.

Kliver turned the body up and took off the man's helmet. The soldier was very young and had typical Hati features: straight hair, fair complexion and tiny eyes. Kliver removed the guns from his wrist and threw them into the lake, knowing that, if they were laser weapons, they would be ruined by water.

"Stand back," he said when he sensed his wife's presence.

"Check if he is plugged," asked Miku.

Kliver once more turned over the body and examined the pin-shaped black device fixed to his nape.

"Yes, he is plugged," he said to his wife. "How can I disconnect it? You must know."

"Try to press the main button and pull it," suggested Miku.

The man did as advised but could not remove the plug.

"It's not working. I can't do it."

"That's strange," Miku said. "I think we'd better leave him there and go away. Let's get away from here before other soldiers come. I am still weak because of the birth of the baby, but I can stand a journey of some days. It's for the sake of our family."

"There's no way of leaving," retorted Kliver. "We don't have a means of transportation. Misha and her bigbuglets have been killed. We have to—"

He could not finish his sentence. The soldier woke up from his short period of unconsciousness and jumped to his feet. He turned around and seized Kliver's neck with both hands. Aron opened his eyes wide when he saw his father fall to the ground. The soldier climbed over him, smothering him with both hands. Kliver let go of the crossbow and gripped the man's hands trying to release his neck. The weapon slipped and fell into the lake.

Miku took the initiative to pick up a large piece of wood that was nearby and banged it on the soldier's head. The Hati's body rolled and fell on the ground again, beside his helmet. His body contorted and jerked, but soon was parlayzed, and on his nape the plug made a strange sound.

Miku understood what had happened.

"Are you all right?" she asked her husband, still terror-stricken.

"Yes," he answered, holding his neck and still feeling the pressure of the soldier's hand. "What will we do with the body? We have do disconnect the plug."

"It's impossible," Miku said. "The plug is clogged. There's no use in trying to disconnect it."

"And what can we do?" asked Kliver, sitting on the sand. He reached out his arm and lightly touched the body, but soon shrank back. He received a high voltage charge.

"Stand up and get away from the body," Miku said. "Let's go away from here before his companions arrive. We will leave in the Hati vehicle. The Empire will know it all the same; we have to be far away when this happens. Let's go before it's too late. We can search for an oasis in the desert or we can go to another continent.

Kliver was 36 years of age and knew some things about the Era in which he lived. He knew that in the calendar the year was 213 A.E. and that it was impossible to move to another continent because it meant crossing the endless ocean called Tétis. And even if they could do that, he learned that the lands of the other continents were either flooded or contaminated with radiation from the last wars. Not even bacteria could survive away from Kafria—that was what the books said. But at that very moment, all he wanted was to flee from those mountains. Kliver agreed with his wife only because of that.

They abandoned the body and started to prepare for the journey.

With a rope, Kliver dragged Misha's heavy body to the foot of the mountain, on the spot the man had parked the vehicle. But he did not do the same with the bigbuglets. They were too small and would not be enough for more than two or three meals before the sun rotted their flesh.

He collected some vegetables, cut some more firewood, filled a jug and a bottle with water, gathered some straws in a piece of cloth and put some belongings in his backpack. The night made the operation difficult. The sky was dark and always moonless, and it was never possible to see the lumenosity of the stars.

He tried to find his crossbow that had sunken into the lake but did not succeed. He drew a last deep breath of the rarefied air of the mountains, asked for the protection of his god and, together with his family, climbed down the less steep hillside towards the desert. Aron and Makuro held on to their mother's legs. They felt fear but were too young to understand what was happening.

When he looked at the complex golden vehicle, Kliver was confused. He was not acquainted with the Hati technology, which was much more advanced than that of his people. He could not even figure out the use of those mysterious plugs, and now he had a complicated atomic-propulsion machine in front of him. He would have a short time to learn how to operate it, and he had no idea of where to start.

"Let me drive," Miku said with a tired expression. "Put those things at the back while I start up the engine. Sit and put the children on your lap."

Kliver had not imagined that Miku would be able to operate the vehicle. She was a member of the Hati society and, as such, understood its technology. She was 24 years old, an idealist and an unsubmissive young woman. For the last two years, she had been hunted as a fugitive from the Empire.

Miku sat on the front seat, taking control of the directional levers, executing several commands. Soon the turbines started working, echoing a heavy sound through the valleys.

"I'll turn off some instruments and the on-board radar to keep them from tracking us," she said, turning her head back to look at him. "We will travel at about 100 knots. If we run at supersonic speed, I won't be able to keep the steering wheel stabilized, and certainly we will turn over if we hit something. Hold on to the boys and let the spirit of Sakyamuni bring us hope and protection."

Kliver admired his wife's determination. Observing her effort to keep her family safe in the painful beginning of her childbirth recovery was really rewarding. They shared an affectionate smile, breathed deeply and set off, leaving the mountains behind.

CHAPTER 2

THE RITUAL

The vehicle floated over a ground that was fairly level, a vastness of dry land partially covered with creeping vegetation and one or two trees scattered about. The silhouettes of the cacti in the distance looked like sentinels waiting in ambush, and Kliver had the impression that one of them had moved. Miku thought her husband was losing control of his mind, but she also knew that, in the heat of the desert, exhausted minds could have hallucinations.

They had been traveling for 36 hours, with a few short stops to relieve themselves and for Miku to feed the baby. And after facing the previous night's terrible cold, with strong chill winds, now they fought against the unbearable heat of the afternoon. Even with its rays rigorously filtered by the new world's atmosphere, the sun was hot enough to make them soak with sweat.

"Let's make a stop. We have to eat, and the baby seems to have a fever," suggested Kliver, feeling the newborn's forehead with the back of his hand. The baby was really hot, but he did not seem to feel uncomfortable.

Miku dried her face with the sleeve of her dress and stopped the overheated vehicle under the shade of a coconut tree, lost in the middle of nowhere.

Kliver got out of the machine and spread a cloth on the ground. He tied a strap to his waist and started climbing up the tree in order to pick some coconuts. Miku sat on the cloth and stretched her legs; then she started nursing the baby.

"Pick up the firewood next to the straw mattress," she said, pressing the baby against her bosom. "Let's roast the big-bug before the meat rots."

With the coconuts in his hands, the man was prepared to climb down when he spotted something in the distance. He seemed puzzled. He protected his forehead against the sun and strained his eyes to make sure that that was not a mirage.

"Miku, Miku," he cried from up the tree.

The woman raised her head.

"What's up? Do you want to startle the baby?"

Kliver did not answer immediately. He wanted to make sure that it was not an illusion.

"Darling, from where I am I can see a village far away. It seems to be made of stone, and must be in ruins. It is probably also abandoned," he said as he came down.

"Would it be one of the fortifications of the enemy?" asked Miku, cautiously.

"I doubt that," he said, putting the coconuts on the ground. "As I said, nobody seems to be there. It would be a good place for us to hide for some days."

"Dad, I am hungry and thirsty," said Aron.

"Me, too," added Makuro.

With a smile, Kliver caressed their hair. From the car, he brought some fruit and water.

"Don't waste our water," Miku said "give them only the necessary."

"We are safe, Miku. We don't have to save our food. We are near a village. Certainly, the people that built it chose a place near some water source."

"But if the village is forsaken, as you say, these water sources may have gone dry."

Kliver interrupted the conversation. Seeing the children eating, he could not control himself. Hunger was stronger than reason. They had been traveling for more than thirty hours at a speed between 70 and 100 knots. He was more than 3000 miles away from the cave, and since they started the journey, he hadn't eaten anything.

He then decided to roast Misha for lunch. He felt some affection for the animal, but her death would be in vain if he allowed the meat to rot.

He picked up the firewood from the car and brought it near the coconut tree. He struck two flints together and lit a fire. The dry wind helped to flare it up, and soon, it started to crackle. Kliver pulled an old knife from his backpack and sliced a big chunk of Misha's back and put it on the fire.

The inviting smell spread in the air. Miku did not resist the temptation and accepted a slice. When all were satisfied, the man stored away the meat leftovers, and once again, they got into the vehicle. Miku took over the command, and they set off towards the village, leaving a little heap of garbage under the coconut tree.

A blinking light in the control panel indicated that they were running out of energy. The woman was on the alert, but she thought there was enough for them to get to the village.

Unfortunately, Miku was wrong. When they were near a steep ravine, just some miles from the first buildings of the village, the engine started to falter. The control panel went off several times, the turbines stopped, and the machine landed on the hot sand, motionless.

"We will have go to on foot from here," Miku said, getting out of the vehicle. "The machine is useless now. There is no way to recharge it. It is propelled by uranium. We don't have the capsules."

"There must be some extra capsules in one of the compartments," supposed Kliver. "That soldier would not travel without fuel."

"I don't think so," answered Miku. "He came with one single objective. The energy should be enough for him to go to the mountains and return . . ."

"And what shall we do with our things?"

"Leave everything here. Later, we can come back for them and take them to the village in some kind of cart. Bring Aron and Makuro. I will carry the baby. We have a long way to walk."

Makuro walked on his own feet, moving them faster to catch up with the adults while Aron asked to be carried by his father. Along the ravine, it was possible to see, even from the ground, the highest roofs of the village.

Miku walked with difficulty. For her, walking was a torture. Step by step she felt a searing pain between her legs. A thread of blood trickled down and wet her dress.

"I don't think I will be able to walk much longer."

Kliver tore the sleeve of his old T-shirt off and wiped his wife's blood. As he was doing this, she felt a twinge of conscience.

"Oh, Kliver," she said, moved. "We've got everything wrong. All this was a mistake. We should not have had this baby; we should not have stayed together. It was an error to leave our societies. You should have taken me as a prisoner to the hole from where you came and not have fallen in love with me. At least, Makuro would be safe and I could see him grow up, even though it would have been through the prison bars."

"Darling, don't let the pain take you over," answered Kliver. "We are safe, can't you see? Finding this village was our salvation. CaTand, the son of God, would not have forsaken us at this hour."

"Stop preaching Catandism," said the woman in an irritated tone. "You know that my people don't worship CaTand. I accepted to get married in the Catandist system because I was desperate. Don't talk religion to me. I will never accept Ca-Tand as the son of God".

"Forget our differences, Miku," said Kliver in a soothing voice. "The beliefs we follow do not matter, not any more than our backgrounds. We have promised not to talk about the past. The important thing is that we are together, and this is enough. Together we are a family and should act as such."

Miku held her tongue. They had been together for two years, and he had never asked anything about her people. And every time she wanted to know something about the Myras, he changed the subject. Was it possible that Kliver, the man who lived with her, considered her capable of betraying him and handing him over to the empire's authorities?

"Do you need help?" he asked, slowing his pace. "Do you want me to carry you?"

"It's not necessary. We are not far away," she answered, feeling hurt. "I'm lucky to be alive. If I have not died during childbirth, a long walk will not kill me."

"Are you sure? We are halfway there . . ."

"Yes, I'm sure," she answered curtly.

"All right, then . . ."

After some more steps, Kliver stopped suddenly and asked his wife to be quiet. He thought he had heard a whistle coming from somewhere in the ravine. He stretched his neck, looking cautiously in all directions. He put Aron on the ground and asked the children to crouch.

It could be some trick played by a worn-out mind, or some bird. He bent his head back and confirmed his suspicion: there were really some birds among the clouds, flying in the deep red sky.

Miku started to get worried.

"Why are you acting like a crazy person? You are frightening me."

Kliver laughed at his own childishness.

"Forget it."

Just after speaking he heard another whistle. The sound seemed to be much nearer than those birds in the sky. Aron and Makuro were already getting up when their father made them stay where they were.

"What's up?" asked Miku. "What is it now?"

"Be quiet," whispered Kliver. "Listen!"

The woman crouched, still carrying the baby. Suddenly there was a third whistle. This time it was so near that it seemed to be just beside them. Miku also heard it. They froze and did not speak a word.

A fourth whistle and Kliver moved his shoulder abruptly and gave a loud cry in pain.

"What was that?" Miku was distressed.

Kliver touched his back and felt an object buried in his flesh.

"Miku, tell me what you see," he asked, turning around and showing her his wound. "What is this thing thrust into my back?"

"It looks like a thorn," she answered, frightened.

"A thorn?" he said, surprised. "Would it not be a kind of dart? I hope it is not poiso—"

The man could not finish the sentence. His eyes rolled back in his head and he collapsed on the ground, raising the dust.

Miku got desperate. She fell over her husband's body and broke down crying. Her anguish did not last long, though. A little later another dart hit her on the neck, and she fell plumply beside him.

Minutes later Kliver opened his eyes. A trickle of saliva seeped from one corner of his mouth, and white luminous particles exploded before his eyes. He felt that he was moving, for the cliff was slowly drawing back from him. His heels carved long trenches on the ground, as if he was being dragged. Someone was pulling him by the arms. He bent his head to one side and saw a pair of strong dark legs, adorned with bones and teeth. Soon the image faded, and when he opened his eyes again, Miku was beside him.

The couple woke up almost at the same time, both upside down, suspended by their feet. Their hands were tied at their backs with a very tight knot.

They were in a small room made of stone, illuminated only by the light beams that entered through the breaches of a single window. There were red-dyed curtains and an entire human skeleton on the sandy ground. The door was made of heavy wood.

In the opposite corner, a bonded animal observed them. It was strange. His body was entirely covered with long brown hair, and only his reddish eyes could be descried. Outside the room people were talking, but it was not possible to understand their words. They spoke a different idiom: neither Myra, nor Hati.

"Miku, are you awake?"

"Yes, where are we?"

"I don't have the faintest idea. But those who captured us are neither Myra nor Hati," he answered.

"Are you sure?"

"Yes, they speak neither of the two languages."

They were interrupted. The animal shook its hair and started walking in their direction, as if attracted by the sound of their voices. The bonds restrained it, and it could not come nearer. It uttered a loud cry, like a howl.

"What kind of animal is this?" whispered Miku, a little tense.

"I've heard about them. This is a hitie, a carnivorous animal entirely covered with hair. Though small, they are very dangerous. In the Colony, these animals are used in interrogations. Be quiet and don't move. This kind of animal is attracted by sounds and abrupt movements."

The animal would not stop howling, though. The talk outside was interrupted, and soon the door was opened. Some people entered, but the couple could only see their feet, which were covered with a leathery material.

"Where are my children?" cried Miku in a mix of anger and despair.

The strangers did not say a word. They drew knives from their loincloths and cut the ropes. The couple fell on the floor. They gagged Miku's mouth with some rags.

Amazed at what he was seeing, just before being himself gagged, Kliver shouted:

"Savages!"

Kliver and his wife were thrust out of the room. Outside, Kliver squinted his eyes because of the bright sun. Neither of them could understand what was happening. Since childhood they had been told that the savages and their descendants had been extinguished from the planet more than four centuries before, due to several wars. The primitive Indians they saw contradicted what they knew, and they had the sensation of being in contact with people from another world.

And they were tall, strong, stout Indians. They paraded their dyed bodies, adorned with chains, earrings and necklaces. All of them held long spears. Some had bows and arrows and others carried darts and blowpipes. Kliver supposed they had perhaps run away from the attacks of the last war and had taken refuge in the village. Probably they had been living there in secret for a long time . . .

Two Indian guards led the couple through the ruins of the only accessible street. The village was small and dirty and its structure was completely ruined. There were several houses with destroyed walls and roofs full of holes. There was a library in a very bad condition; in the holes of its walls small sparrows made their nests.

Old black women interrupted their task of hanging washed clothes to look at the couple. Naked children walked along with the prisoners with curious eyes. An old Indian said something in protest and threw a stone at Kliver's back. Vultures flew in low circles in the sky, anticipating some sacrifice or execution. Chickens scratched the ground.

They walked down a blind alley that led to a square in front of an old abandoned temple where a crowd of savages laughed, sang and danced to the sound of drums and flutes. The men drank a dark liquid from clay pitchers, and the younger women swayed their hips sensuously.

At the center of the square, surrounded by the throng, stood a scaffold on which there were four poles with ropes at their ends, generally used in sacred rituals . . .hanging rituals.

Miku's bladder failed her. Despite being strong, she was a woman, and could not face what was ahead of her.

When the crowd spotted them, the uproar stopped and the people stood up, making room for them to walk through. The guards goaded them with their spears, forcing Kliver and Miku to climb up the scaffold. As they went up the stairs, the crowd threw rotten eggs, tomatoes, cabbages and oranges at them, shouting offensive words that they could not understand.

Miku started wondering whether all that she had believed in and fought for had been in vain. Fate seemed to say so. They had nowhere to run to. Death was certain.

Kliver kept in silence. As a soldier, he had been trained to face pain and torture. Accepting death seemed easier to him. He only hoped it would be quick and painless. The one thing he regretted was to have failed his children. He could not die like that. His task as a father was just beginning; he had to fulfill it. And what worried him most was that he did not know if they were still alive.

One of the guards pressed his spear against Kliver's arm, speeding him up. The couple climbed up the scaffold and their backs were propped against the poles. The ropes were placed around their necks.

Kliver noticed he was stepping on a wood trapdoor. Probably, it would collapse under his weight, and gravity would be his main executioner.

Miku was concentrated, her eyes shut. Her heartbeat was bumpy and fast as she awaited her fate. One of the warriors tried to take advantage of the situation. He stretched out his arm and put his hand under her dress. The woman reacted aggressively, hitting his testicles with her right knee. The savage groaned in pain, bending forward. After coming to himself again, he slapped her face twice, leaving on it the imprint of his fingers.

Miku frowned, looking furiously at him. The savage caressed her face, wiping away her tears and then spat on her. He whispered some words of his strange tongue in her left ear.

The guard assumed a grave expression and uttered something in a low voice, as a hangman condemning the soul of the person he was going to slaughter. He drew a handmade knife from his loincloth and slashed Miku's forehead and cheek. She trembled and salivated because of the gag on her mouth, while the dark blood dripped onto her breasts.

Quite surprisingly, the savage licked the gash on her face from end to end, spitting the blood onto the applauding crowd.

Tied to the pole beside her, Kliver struggled to free himself from the ropes. Thick veins stood out on his forehead. Somehow he wanted to tear away with his own teeth the heart of that coward who was harassing his wife.

The savage turned his eyes towards Kliver and noticed his anger. He walked up to him with short steps, and the audience roared with excitement, realizing the white man would also be spanked. At each blow Kliver received, the Indians shouted in tune with the beat of the drums.

However, to the crowd's disappointment, the spanking did not last long. It was interrupted when one of the savages, standing at the top of the temple's tower, struck the alarm gong, announcing the coming of the leader.

The leader came, escorted by four warriors as big as giants. He walked with his eyes fixed on the ground and his arms crossed over his chest. His face was hidden under a straw hat shaped like a basket. The crowd became absolutely silent and opened for him to pass.

The leader approached the scaffold and climbed the stairs, walking up to the couple. He said something to the warrior beside them, who immediately put down his weapons and drew back. Then, the leader bent his hat backwards and revealed his face.

Though he did not show it, he was old, around 70 years of age. He wore a white garment that covered most of his body and had a pouch tied to his waist. He seemed superior to the others and, to the couple's surprise, was not a savage, not even a descendant of the tribe.

The old man was thin, of medium height and had tiny eyes. His hair was white and long, just as the beard flowing down his chest. His skin was fair and wrinkled, a little tanned by the sun. He had a typical Hati face.

Kliver drew a deep breath, relieved. Perhaps the leader was an equitable and wise man that would be willing to negotiate his and his wife's freedom. Perhaps the misunderstanding could be explained, and Kliver would be allowed to apologize and continue his journey in peace.

The leader turned to the white man and started scrutinizing him, as if he were searching for something. He noticed Kliver's thick and filthy beard, the grime covering his skin and the bruises caused by the recent spanking. When he lowered his eyes to Kliver's left triceps, the old man seemed to have found what he was searching for. Kliver's muscle, grown weak by lack of exercise, exhibited a tattooed coat of arms in two colors. On it there was the representation of two bigbugs, facing each other, reared up in positions of combat. Under the animals one could read the number 64748-2.

The leader looked pensively at the numbers, trying to decipher them. He came up to Miku and started to examine her. He bent her head without any courtesy and raised her hair to look at her nape.

He saw a strange metallic device in it connected to a three-hole socket. He considered disconnecting it but thought better and stopped. The old man turned to the crowd and raised his arms, shouting to everyone:

"MYRA-HATI!"

Kliver was surprised but calm. At least he was beside someone who knew something of the present world.

The leader stared at him again. He walked up to him and removed the gag from his mouth.

Kliver immediately spoke:

"Where are my children?" he asked in a tone that was more supplicant than authoritarian.

The old man crossed his arms.

"I don't speak your language," he said in Hati. "But I know that you speak mine. So, repeat what you've just said in my language or in the tribe's native language."

"Where are my children?"

"Your children are fine," the man assured him. "They are safe and sound. Now shut up your big mouth and let me question you. What can a white man with a military tattoo and a woman that has a plug connector in her nape be doing here? By any chance, are you married?"

"Yes, we're married," said Kliver. "Why are you asking?"

"How did you meet?"

"I prefer not to tell," spoke Kliver after some seconds.

The leader gave him a harsh look and warned him, saying, "Listen, my friend. I'm not the one who's tied to a pole, soon to be hanged. If you want to live, I suggest that you cooperate and answer what is asked of you. I will ask just one more time. Where did you meet?"

Kliver decided to obey him.

"I . . ." he gasped for some breath. "I used to live in a cave . . . high up a mountain. I'd lived a solitary life for many years. One day I saw her near . . ."

"Don't lie to me," growled the old man, interrupting him. "I know that you belong to the Myras and that she is a Hati. Tell me the true story."

"Sir, the Myras don't exist anymore," revealed Kliver. "I've always been a lonely man, till the day I met her."

"I repeat that you are lying," insisted the man. "Your tattoo contradicts you. The Myras still exist."

"My tattoo? My father made it. He and I were the only surviving Myras. Unfortunately, he died some years ago. Today, my son Aron and I . . ."

"Tell me your name," interrupted the man one more time.

"My name? Leo . . . Leo Kliver."

"Well, Mr. Kliver, as you may imagine, I am an old Hati. Perhaps you are curious to know how a Hati at my age is the leader of such a well-structured society of banjins. This is irelevant. The important thing is that I am here, and by the power conferred upon me, I can negotiate your freedom. The crowd is eager to watch an execution, and I'm the only person who can frustrate them. I'm against the laws that rule the world, so I don't condemn you for being a white Myra. My interest is not to discover the whereabouts of the Myra colony, if there is really a Myra colony. I personally consider all this an enormous aimless stupidity. I abandoned the Hati society a long time ago and do not intend to return. However, I will condemn you for lying. From now on, if you don't tell me the truth, I will give the command, and they will hang you. I advise you to answer sincerely what I ask, for if you are lying, I will know it. Am I clear enough?"

Kliver was convinced.

"I realize I have no choice," said Kliver. "The Myras still exist, it's true, and we have a hidden city-colony. But I will never tell you where it is located. You may hang me for that if you wish."

According to the Myra oath to the clan's flag, Kliver should never reveal the location of the Myra colony. He would rather risk his life than betray the regent's confidence.

"You are a brave man, Mr. Kliver," said the old man. "I admire such attitude in a man who has a rope around his neck."

Kliver nodded lightly.

"If you're satisfied," he said, "bring my children, release my wife and me and allow us to go in peace."

"Not yet," objected the old man. "You have not told me how you met her".

Kliver breathed deeply, turning his eyes to Miku. She seemed frightened, trembling in front of the pole. The bleeding wound on her face made it look like she was crying blood tears. She lowered her eyes, resentful. Kliver turned to the old man and started speaking.

"About two years ago, I was a soldier in the Myra army. I was a sergeant instructor of shooting, an expert in precision weapons. I was fairly satisfied with my life. I was happy, as it were, for I had become a father for the first time. My son was given the name Aron, Aron Kliver, in the beautiful, though sad, Catandist ceremony. Catandism is our dominant religion. Jill, my first wife, had a serious bleeding during delivery. She could not resist and died. The pain of the loss made me desperate. I could not live without her; I would not be able to raise a child alone.

"I decided I should spend some time in seclusion, trying to find peace in loneliness. I volunteered for a task in a new spying program whose aim was to locate and photograph the enemy's city. My colleagues in the army gave me an animal as a farewell gift. It was a bigbug called Misha and would be my means of transportation, also carrying my belongings.

"I left Aron to the care of the government. I rode Misha for some weeks, along the waters of the Olin, always camping in the evening. On one of those solitary nights, I lay down under the sky and rolled a cigarette. My only company was a chorus of crickets. In the distance, I heard the sound of murmurs coming from somewhere in the woods along the Great River. I quickly put on my uniform, grabbed my gun and set out in the direction of the sound.

"It was very dark, and I didn't want to be noticed and so I didn't light the lantern. Amid the high grass near a marsh, I found a woman lying on the ground, almost senseless, urgently in need of help. She was frightened when she saw me and drew back, but I put away my weapon and made a sign to calm her down. Thus, I found Miku. She was some months pregnant. She was suffering, hungry and cold.

"At that moment I completely forgot my mission. I'd never seen a Hati woman. To me, she was a heaven-sent angel to make me forget the death of my first wife.

"I took her to my tent, fed her and protected her from the cold. I remember we spent several nights getting to know each other under the moonless sky. Little by little, she made me feel like a man again. I found out she belonged to the Hati society and had fled due to her pregnancy. The child she bore was not allowed to be born, and to prevent the authorities from submitting her to an abortion, Miku had challenged the laws of the empire and left for the desert. For some days ago she had been hunted as a traitor because of that.

"We forgot our differences and decided to live together. I proposed to her, and she said yes. I suggested that we should go to a distant place and live together, away from the world and the laws that forbid our union.

"I tied my equipment onto Misha's back and we returned to the Myra colony, for I had to rescue my son. I asked for the help of a Catandist pastor—an old friend of mine who worked at an orphanage where my son had been sent to—and we got married with his blessing, unbeknown to the Myra authorities. I picked up Aron, and we left for the desert. Some months later, her son was born and I adopted him, giving him my surname. His name is Makuro Kliver.

"I believe that by now the Myras don't even imagine that I'm still alive . . ." Kliver finished his account, amazed at having told the whole story to a stranger.

"Can you untie us now?"

"Not yet," spoke the old man. "You have not told me how you came here, to these ruins. Why have you invaded this place?"

"After riding for several weeks, Miku and I found a place in a cave in a mountain, where Makuro was born. There we have spent these last two years, living as a family. Recently we had a child and . . ."

"What was that?" asked the man, getting near Kliver. "A Myra, a Hati . . . so that newborn is a . . .? A . . .?"

The old man could not hold back his emotion. After staring at the couple silently for a minute, he threw his arms in the air and broke out in a roar of laughter in front of the crowd that was already impatient with the delay of the execution.

"The sacred scrolls were right," he shouted at the top of his old lungs. "O great Sakyamuni, I've never doubted his prophecy. After many years of waiting, at last comes to the world a Myra-Hati half-cast, the one who will strike a balance between the two worlds."

CHAPTER 3

SEPARATION

Kliver could not understand what the old man was saying. Miku, on the other hand, knew all the legends and prophecies announced by the latest incarnation of Sakyamuni. Knowing them was almost an obligation; after all, she was a Hati and had inherited the Buddhist teachings.

Miku was moved. The old man reminded her of a legend she had forgotten a long time before, and she felt proud to imagine that all would consider her son to be the new world's Messiah. He would bring hope to his people and, one day, perhaps, peace.

The legend of Sakyamuni—the historic Buddha, born on the earth—said that a half-cast in the new times would put an end to the threats of the brooding war, establishing a balance between the remaining nations. Having the blood of both races, he represented their union.

The old man started untying Miku. "Go and rest, my daughter," he said, kissing the wound on her forehead. "You are the mother of the one who will bring us eternal peace. If you allow me, I will assume all responsibility for the precious one. I will teach him the good principles and do for him everything I can. At the right moment, when he is ready, we will fight for the eternal union of the races."

"Nothing is eternal," retorted Miku, casting off the muzzle, holding her left wrist marked by the ropes. "Prove that you are a Hati, and tell me your name."

The old man turned his back to her, smiling. He took off his straw hat, raised his long white hair, and exposed his wrinkled nape, where a four-hole connector was inserted. He turned his head towards her and said:

"In my time, the plugs had four pins. My name is Yoshi Hanara."

Miku stared at him, surprised. Her face showed clearly that she had recognized him or, at least, had already heard about him.

"Are you Yoshi Hanara? Really? I thought you were dead. You were much admired by the Hati people . . . and also much hated by the empire. As far as I know, you were a general for many years, you've studied mechatronic engineering and genetics, you have a hu-tae-mui purple belt, you were imprisoned as a traitor, and you were then freed after winning the first Battle of the Convicts. You were also the only Hati to be expelled from . . ."

"Slower, my darling," interrupted Hanara. "From now on, you are welcome to the ruins of Ruakan. You, your husband and your children will live with us for many years, and we will have plenty of time to talk about the past. If one day you win my confidence, I will let you know the real reason for my being expelled from the empire. As for now, go and do what I've told you. Have a rest. And take care of this wound on your forehead."

Once more, the old man raised his arms to the Indian crowd and made a gesture meaning that, from that moment on, the prisoners should be considered welcome guests and that the hanging was called off.

The savages were disappointed at the leader's attitude. They wanted him to continue the ritual. For them, seeing those who represented their oppressors being hanged would be quite a show. However, the word of the leader would be respected. Without discussing or arguing, little by little they left the square before the temple, resuming, downcast, the tasks each one of them carried out in the tribe.

The tasks in the tribe were very simple, subdivided according to the physical characteristics and abilities of each person: the more nimble hunted, the stronger protected the entrances to the village. Some had a little trade based on exchanges, and the women cooked or worked in the fields. Up the road, following a shallow creek that moved a mill, one could see several plantations near the bigbug herds. There were cogus, coffee, corn, wheat and several other species.

Raising bigbugs had always been a common activity among the less developed nations of the new world, for they relied on these animals for field labor. The Myras had developed and enhanced their techniques for raising bigbugs while the Hatis had substituted machines for animals.

The Indians of Ruakan, called Kuata-Noans in the tribe language, an expression meaning the "Harvest Masters," lived performing their routine tasks related to the survival of the group. The Myras called them "rough savages," and the Hatis called them "banjins" (barbarian people). But though the other clans had a name for them, they were remembered only as a historical people, and nobody imagined that some of them were still alive.

On a lace hammock, strong hospitable women with their breasts exposed carefully carried Miku to a room that they considered luxurious.

Kliver and Hanara were still on the scaffold. The white man spoke to the elderly leader, starting a long conversation in the Hati language.

"And what about me?" he asked. "Aren't you going to untie me and remove this rope around my neck?"

"Not yet," answered the old man. "You have not finished telling how you arrived here. Please, go on with your report . . ."

"You prevented me from doing so. By the way, I would like to know how an old Hati like you has become the leader of such a well-organized tribe of savages."

Hanara changed his mood. He suddenly put on his straw hat again and warned Kliver.

"I will refresh your memory just one more time. I am the one who asks questions here. You are not to be trusted. You are a foul Myra coming from a foul civilization. Thank your wife for being alive. If it weren't for her, my hities would be feasting on your corpse. However, I will make an exception and answer your question, if you really want to know about this.

"When I was expelled from the Hati civilization, I walked for several weeks in the desert before finding these ruins. Just as you must have been surprised, I was amazed at meeting banjins, or 'savages,' as you call them among the Myras. Anyone would have. The banjins arrested me and also tried to hang me. At the moment the former leader ordered my execution, I had managed to untie the ropes around my wrists. With my hands untied, I released the gibbet's rope and killed the five warriors who were keeping guard over me, and then I stabbed the former banjin leader with his own spear. I therefore became the new leader and have been living here for twenty years already. In the beginning they feared me, but little by little I won their trust, and today I am respected and revered. Satisfied?"

Kliver seemed incredulous. If all that was true, that man must be a great man or even a hero for the Hatis. What had been the reason for his expulsion? What had he done that was so serious for him to be considered a traitor? A general, who had studied engineering and genetics . . .perhaps also an expert in several martial arts since he had defeated, bare-handed, five armed warriors.

If Kliver really knew what the rules were for the choice of a new emperor, in his opinion, Hanara would be a strong candidate. He wondered if that had not been one of the reasons for his expulsion.

"You don't have to believe me, Mr. Kliver," said Hanara. "The pain I feel is stronger than my desire to impress you. Now, don't make me wait any longer. Tell me how you arrived here," he asked for the third time.

"Ah, yes," said the white man, shaking his head. "As I said, Miku and I have been living in a cave these last two years. Two days ago our son was born. Miku had a difficult childbirth that lasted almost 15 hours. During the contractions, her signal blocker got loose from the connector in her nape. As she lost the device, her internal transmitter started working again. The Hati Command detected her signals and sent a soldier on a solo mission to rescue her. Luckily, I noticed him in time. I hid my family and prepared to face him. The soldier landed on the mountain and killed all my bigbugs, preventing us from running away. He wasted some time looking at the lake; I hit him from behind with an arrow. Miku and I were afraid to continue there. We picked up our children and fled to the desert. That was when we found the ruins" summarized Kliver, making a short break.

Hanara pressed his arm violently. "Did you allow the soldier to see you or your wife, or any of your children?"

Kliver was surprised at the question.

"It is possible. I think he saw me, a little before Miku hit him from behind," he remembered. "But if you're worried about the plugs, I inform you that the soldier was plugged. Miku and I tried to disconnect him, but it was not possible.

After his death, the plug clogged. And when I touched the soldier's body, I got a shock that made me draw back."

"The plugs don't have any importance," stated Hanara. "What worries me is the 'Inter-plug'."

"What the heck is this?"

"Forget it," pondered the old man. "You don't understand the plug technology. Speaking of the Inter-plug would be a waste of time. If you are sure the soldier saw only you, calm down. Your family is safe."

"He saw only me," asserted Kliver. "And besides, we are very far from the mountains. The Hatis will never find these ruins. There's no need to worry."

"You may be right," agreed the old man, picking up a pipe from his pouch. "By the way," he said after lighting it, "how did you get here, if the bigbugs were killed?"

"We took possession of the vehicle in which the soldier had come," he said with a clever expression on his face. "Miku knew how to operate it."

The man turned pale.

"And where is that vehicle now?" he asked, holding Kliver's shoulder and puffing smoke in his face.

"Not far away. We left the car at the entrance of the ravine. It had run out of energy. It must be parked around 2 miles from here."

Hanara shook his head in distress, clutching the pipe between his fingers.

"We are lost!" the man said.

"Don't worry," Kliver said. "Miku knew that machine very well. Before we left, she turned off the whole tracking system, as well as some devices in the on-board radar. They cannot track down the vehicle."

Hanara looked him in the eye.

"It's impossible to turn off the tracking system of any Hati vehicle," he shouted, "especially if it's a military rescue vehicle. I know that. I've worked as the head of the air-engineering department for many years. I was the main deviser of the track-ing system. It is a hidden device. It apparently turns off but remains active. Believe me, Mr. Kliver, we are being tracked since you arrived here."

Kliver's face showed his affliction.

"Are you sure? And what can we do?"

"The only way to prevent the Hatis from finding us is to go back to the place where the vehicle is parked and melt it over the fire. Fire destroys the transmitters and blocks their pulses. Remember, if the Hatis find these ruins—and they must be near—all the hope for peace is over. We don't have any means of fighting against their forces. We will all die, and the last banjins on the planet will be exterminated. You don't want that to happen, do you? It all depends on you. After all, it was you who showed yourself to the soldier, and, through the Inter-plug, to the officials of the Hati high command. You are the one who should set fire to that machine. To you I ascribe the responsibility. Now it's up to you. Think of your children."

Hanara touched Kliver's weak point by mentioning his children. He started thinking in silence.

"What if, on my way, I see a Hati platoon coming in my direction?" he asked.

"You will have to run the risk," said the man. "Trust me and do as I say. If this happens, the only way to survive will be to surrender to them and let them capture you."

"What?" asked Kliver, now taken by panic. "Are you crazy? If I surrender, they'll kill me. This must be a plot you have con-trived. You still must be in touch with the Hati Command. Your expulsion must have been a sham, just an excuse for some secret reconnaissance mission. You want me away from this place to do what whatever you wish with my wife and children." Kliver would have pointed a warning finger to the old man if his hands weren't tied to the pole.

"Think it over, my friend. This is not possible. You were a soldier and must know that the Command would never send an ex-general on a reconnaissance mission. Moreover, I've lived here for twenty years . . . what kind of mission would take so long?"

Kliver was quiet and lowered his eyes to his feet, supported by the trapdoor. Hanara continued:

"As for what I ask of you, be aware that it's not my interest to have you arrested. Your people should not hate the Hati authorities more than I myself hate them, and I wish with all my heart for the end of the threats that surround us. However, I can't have you here with us if there is an invasion. That would be too risky for the banjins and for your family. But if this happens, try to keep calm. I assure you that if you are captured, the Hatis will not kill you. Your tattoo will keep you alive. It's evidence that the Myras still exist."

"My tattoo?" asked Kliver.

"Well, don't pretend you don't get my meaning. This coat of arms represents the Myra Legion, or do you think that I know nothing about your race? And this number is a statistical record. It means that you belonged to an army or to some military group. If there is a Myra army, then certainly there is a Myra colony."

"I understand what you say," Kliver said. "The Hatis will not kill me but will force me to reveal the location of the Colony."

"Exactly. If at any moment this comes to happen, don't be weak. You should never reveal the place where your people live; otherwise there will be an invasion and the war will be inevitable."

Kliver turned his face away in confusion.

"This doesn't make any sense," he said. "The Hati technology is highly developed. There must be several satellites in orbit, capturing images of the whole continent. Why does the empire need me to reach the Myras?"

"The truth is that our satellites are useless," explained Hanara. "A great fraction of the Kafria territory is now in the shade of a black circular blot that obstructs the view from the sky. Nobody knows for sure the origin of this blot, but it is believed to be a toxic gas curtain covering our atmosphere, highly contaminated by the radiation of the last wars. The region of Ruakan is constantly shaded by this blot, and therefore protected from any Hati satellites. This is why these banjins have never been discovered during the years of their existence. I believe that what happens to the Myras is the same . . ."

Kliver breathed silently, thinking to himself.

"My civilization has been hiding for more than 200 years," he said. "How come? Do the Hatis know about the Myras and our Colony?"

The man intertwined his fingers.

"This is simply a hypothesis," he said. "The Empire never believed to have exterminated your race completely. We suppose you must have a hidden city. The tattoo on your arm confirms the thesis. Without the help of our satellites, our troops had to search every corner of the continent after survivors. But they have not found anything, which leads to the supposition that you have a hidden city built underground. The Empire has to know the location of the city, so that our strategists know what to do.

"This explains why the Hatis need a guide," said Kliver. "But what about the name? How do you know the name of my race?"

"That's easy," answered the old man. "The great Sakya-muni revealed that to the Emperor. As you said, your people follow a religion called Catandism, don't they? The word 'Myra,' in the language of the Catandist prophet, means 'ant.' Ants live in colonies underground, just as your people."

"So," concluded Kliver, "the Hatis, with their equipment, are able to fly individually. In your language, 'Hati' means 'bee.'[1]"

"Exactly," confirmed Hanara.

Some things started to make sense to Kliver.

Hanara raised his head, observing the greenish clouds gliding in the red sky.

"It's getting late," he said. "We have to act quickly. I will untie you now and . . ."

His phrase was interrupted. A watchman in the temple's tower struck the alarm gong. The vibrations were worrying, for they meant that someone or something could be seen approaching the village. From the top of the tower it was possible to see 40 kilometers beyond the plains to the east. The savages had not had a turbulent day like that for a long time.

Soon the square in front of the temple was again crowded with tense Indians, and they squeezed around the scaffold.

"How many are there?" cried Hanara from the ground, in the tri be language, already foreseeing what was happening.

"I cannot see well, sir," answered the sentinel from the tower, pressing his eye against a telescope. "They are very far . . . they seem to be group of fifteen, at most. They come all together, and very fast."

"How long will it take for them to get here?"

"Fifteen minutes, I think."

"Everybody knows what to do, right?" the old man asked his people. Let's go all to the chapel underground chamber.

Hospitable women, bring Miku and the three children care-fully." And turning to Kliver, he said: "Kliver, forget that about setting fire to the vehicle. They are already after you, and I have to watch over the banjins. I'm sorry to be forced to hand you over. Go walking towards the platoon and do not resist capture. For the sake of your wife and children, never reveal the location of our hiding-place."

Kliver swallowed his feelings. It was difficult because of the rope around his neck. Hanara untied his hands and neck. The old man opened his pouch and picked up a tiny round black object, very similar to a flat button, though smaller than, as small as the head of a nail.

The old man asked Kliver to open his mouth and fixed the object behind one of his teeth, saying, "I will assemble your family and the banjins, and we all are going to the chapel's underground chamber." He made a gesture with his head, pointing to the temple in ruins. "I want the Hatis to think that the village is abandoned, and confirm this idea when they check it out. You, as I said, will be arrested for some time but soon will be released. Resist any form of interrogation; don't let any information leak, not even under torture."

"The Command will eventually think they are wasting their time with the interrogation and will adopt another strategy. The Hatis will drug you and plug you. But you will not realize it, because this will be an internal plug — it will be inserted under your skin. After that they will leave you behind in the desert, hoping that you return to the Myra colony. However, once you are plugged, your senses will be available to the Inter-plug, and the Hatis will be able to detect you from far away, which means they will be able to know the way to get to the Myras if you return. Therefore, you should never return to the Colony, do you understand?"

Exercising his hands to recover his movements, Kliver nodded.

Hanara continued: "When they release you, the Hatis will give you food and a bigbug, or some other animal for transportation. Now, take heed to my words, yours and your people's future will depend on this," he turned to Kliver and stretched both hands towards the other man's face. "When you are free, you shall ride during two or three days in the desert. When you are far away from the Hive, camp for a night and swallow the small device I've fixed to your tooth."

"The Hive?" asked Kliver, confused.

"Hive is the name of our imperial city. It's a city totally fenced and covered, located at the southern end of the continent, on top of the great Sumeru, the highest mountain of the present world. In Buddhist language, 'Sumeru' means 'great sacred mountain.' When you see it in the distance, you will see something similar to a swarm of bees near their nest at the top . . . has your wife ever told you about the Hive?"

"She has only told me some details about its laws . . . though she has never given me names," confessed Kliver, a little embarrassed. "We avoid speaking of the past when we're together."

"But you should. You would learn a lot from each other."

"What's the use of this little button I will have to swallow?" asked Kliver to avoid the subject while pressing the device against his tooth.

"Don't press it," warned Hanara. "You'll dislodge it . . . this 'little button,' as you call it, is in fact a micro-transmitter. I've stolen it from the espionage department a long time ago and have saved it for a special occasion. Its diffusion ray is wide, covering almost the entire area of Kafria. I've altered its frequency so that no one can detect it. I am the only one who has the radar capable of tracking its signals — which means only I will know where and when to find you. Few people know this kind of device. If you maintain it glued to your tooth, they will never find it."

Hanara paused a little before continuing.

"The outer layer of the device is made of a fiber that is highly resistant; it can withstand mouth acidity for a long time. After swallowing it, your gastric juice will melt this protection layer, and the device will start emitting its pulses so that I can locate you. But before that, put a bandage over your eyes, and don't remove it till I am beside you. This way your vision will be protected from the effects of the Inter-plug . . . have you understood what to do?"

"I think so: travel for three days, camp for a night and swallow the button," said Kliver counting on his fingers.

"Great," praised Hanara. "Now, hurry up. Go and fulfill your destiny, and may the spirit of Sakyamuni bring you luck and protection." And he then made a gesture with his hand that looked like a greeting or a Buddhist blessing.

Kliver had no choice. He drew a deep breath, turned his back to the old man and started walking in the opposite direction. The white man climbed down the stairs of the scaffold and headed towards the east exit of the village while Hanara organized the crowd so that everybody entered the temple without commotion.

The old man was the last to cross the large entrance to the hiding place, in the catacombs just under the chapel. The Indians waited for him in the dark. Then they blocked the entrance with a tall marble sculpture, which slid on tracks that were embedded in the floor. They had nothing to do besides hope and expect that Kliver would not tell on them.

After some moments inside the hiding place, Miku missed her husband and decided to go out as fast as she could. Hanara tried to calm her down, saying that Kliver would be all right and that his courage would assure her and her sons' survival. But the woman was too nervous to hear him. She started struggling and shoving everyone in her way, trying to find the exit in the midst of darkness.

One of the Indians warned another that the woman's reaction would put the whole community in danger. The noise she was making might be heard by anyone who entered the temple.

One warrior took advice from Hanara and asked permission to subtly shoot a tranquilizer dart at her and put her to sleep for the necessary time.

"You have my permission," whispered Hanara in the language that Miku certainly would not understand.

And with a quick movement, the warrior shot the painless dart at the woman's arm, making her tumble in a few seconds. Hanara held her before she fell to the ground.

The sun was sinking in the horizon, and Kliver walked carefully on the road east of the village towards the place where he had left the vehicle. The Ruakan ruins had already been left behind, and now he walked along the ravine where hours before he had heard the whistles. He was treading the same ground. The sand still showed his footprints and also the tracks left when he had been dragged along, unconscious. Up to that moment, he had not seen his children again and feared he might not see them so soon.

He took short steps, looking at each side of the ravine. A cloud of dust could be seen in the distance. Within some minutes, the cloud assumed the form of nine golden vehicles coming very quickly toward him. They were similar to the vehicle he had abandoned, though smaller, with seats for just two people.

The moment of exposing himself to the Hati military was coming. He had to do something to signalize his surrender. He knelt down and lowered his head, sitting on his heels, and then bringing his hands to his nape.

Soon the nine vehicles were positioned around him. The heavy sound of the turbines being turned off echoed through the rocky walls. The highest-ranking soldier in the platoon, a middle-aged first-lieutenant, got off his vehicle.

Kliver remained still, and a kick in his ribs was necessary to make him raise his head.

"You!" said the lieutenant, recognizing him. "You're the man who killed our scout-soldier. Tell me your name, and take us to your leader."

Kliver showed he had not understood. He wanted to avoid an interrogation, so he tried to convince the soldiers that he could not communicate in Hati.

"Where is Miku?" asked the lieutenant. "What have you done to her?"

"What do you want to know?" asked Kliver in Myra, praying that they would not understand.

"He cannot speak our language, Sir," said one of the soldiers.

"I know," answered the lieutenant. "I'm not deaf . . . look, soldiers, he has a statistic record," he said, pointing to the tattoo with the coat of arms and numbers. "Shackle him and lock him in my vehicle. Sergeant, you stay here, watching the entrance. Communicate with me through the radio if anything happens. I'm going with the soldiers to explore the village in search of Miku. I leave the prisoner under your full responsibility," he said finally, charging the laser guns on his wrist.

The military turned their plugs on and followed the track through the ravine.

The last lights of the day were fading when the heavily armed men crossed the east entrance of Ruakan, scrutinizing carefully every corner of the ruins. The soldiers entered each house, each monument, each tent and each building in the village, searching for somebody hidden, or at least for a clue that Kliver had not been alone there.

Some of them turned on the turbines of their titanium wings and explored the village from the air, looking into the broken roofs of the houses and the temple tower. They searched the scaffold at the central square, the aviary, the library hall and the inner temple.

In the dark hiding place, the Indians were completely silent when they heard steps on the floor above them. At each step the soldier took, a little dust fell from the ceiling of their underground shelter. One child, allergic to powder, could not help sneezing. The sound was muffled, but it could be heard anyway and put the soldier up there on the alert.

Stepping on the wooden floor, the soldier turned on the heat sensor in his helmet so that it could detect high temperature spots below the seats and the plaster sculptures. He soon calmed down, though, when he heard his companion, who was entering the temple, also sneezing. "Ah, it was you!" he said to himself.

The Indians felt relieved when the soldiers left the place.

They went away taking the north road and invaded the pastures breaking down the fence. They approached the barn and opened its doors. They saw the bigbugs sleeping on the hay. The place stank of animal dung. There were leather saddles and harnesses hanging from hooks on the walls. They checked the two floors of the shelter and soon came back to the village.

On their way back they entered the plantations. They had the sensors in their helmets turned on, searching for signs of life or some refuge amidst the trees and orchards. They were disappointed, however, at finding only rodents' burrows and wild birds' nests.

It was very dark and past midnight when the Hati first-lieutenant decided to call an end to the mission. Ruakan seemed to be abandoned, but the plantations, the bigbugs inside a fenced pasture, the aviary with hundreds of birds and some bonded hities aroused their suspicion. The evidences of abandonment were strange, but they could not find anybody.

"Soldiers, assemble," shouted the lieutenant. "We're departing now".

Back to the ravine's entrance, the military were preparing to leave. One of the soldiers came before the lieutenant and volunteered.

"Sir, I ask your leave to keep guard over the entrances to the village," he said. "I may stay at night and watch the surroundings, if you want me to."

"That's not necessary," said the lieutenant. "Our mission is completed. We have the Myra assassin, and we know for sure that he is the only one involved in the killing of our scout-soldier . . ."

"We can install sensors inside the houses," suggested the sergeant, "so that we will know if someone has been here."

"And worry every time an animal crosses its range of action?" asked the lieutenant. "Let's go away, men. We have nothing more to do here. The issue is now in the hands of the Command."

Kliver continued quiet, locked in the lieutenant's vehicle, listening to the conversation.

The military got into their vehicles and positioned them in a row. The turbines went on, and the soldiers set off at high speed back to the city known as Hive.

When they passed close to the vehicle that was abandoned by lack of energy, one of the soldiers asked through the plug's audio system. "What are we going to do with this BT-304 model, Sir? Leave it here?"

"Leave it there." answered the lieutenant. "We'll use it as a bait. It is well tracked. If someone steals it or if it moves, we will know there are people living in the village and its surroundings. Moreover, the vehicle is useless without energy, and we have not brought extra capsules. Nobody in the Hive would use a vehicle that was used by a soldier killed by a Myra. Let the desert consume its metal.

And so they left the ravine and went on into the desert, the turbines at full power.

CHAPTER 4

MIKU'S STORY

In the silence of the cold dark night, the Hati squad were traveling at top speed. The nights were always dark. No stars or any other body in the sky were visible, and nothing could be seen ahead without the help of a light. Continuing during the night without at least a torch would be something no one would risk. They would certainly lose their way in addition to becoming easy prey for the animals that wandered around the desert at night.

But the Hati soldiers did not have this kind of problem. The technology of their transport allowed them to float over an air cushion without the slightest risk of collision. Their laser mapping system would warn them when there was danger of hitting something, sending a signal to the direction chip which would deviate the vehicle away from any obstacle. Thus, the pilots could take some sleep during the journey as they would be in complete safety, while the navigation system would do all the piloting.

Kliver, handcuffed in the middle vehicle and escorted by another eight vehicles, forming an octagon around him, held on firmly in order not to fall. He was feeling sick and his stomach was upset. He was not used to traveling so fast. He thought of his wife, who he had not even said goodbye to, and his children, who he had left with strangers.

The night was long, and when dawn broke, Kliver realized that the vehicles were always heading south. He was not able to sleep during the journey, and fear and anxiety prevented him from sleeping.

The vehicles went up a hill, and on reaching the top, the horizon opened out before them, showing in a distance the fascinating meeting of the Olin with the Tetis Ocean, its waves breaking furiously against the huge rocks. This was an unusual sight which could only be seen in the present geography of Kafria:

According to History books, as a result of flood many years before, Tetis, the only ocean, had swallowed up a large part of Africa, flooding nearly sixty percent of its territory. The size of the continent had shrunk, giving rise to Kafria, and the distance between the borders of the Olin, the main river formed by the floods which spread all over the continent, increased considerably, so much so, that at the points where certain tributaries entered the river, there was a distance of almost thirty kilometers between its banks.

The view from the top of the hill was amazing. A dry arid desert met the green banks of the Great River. The sun rose behind the Rocky Mountains to the south, its beams like arrows of white light, making the air red as it slowly brightened.

And beyond the hills, a huge mountain reached the clouds of the sky, rising like a gigantic cold and inactive volcano. The crater on top of the mountain was surrounded by sharp rocks, and its peak was lost in the mist. It was so huge and high that Kliver thought he might see the entire world from its peak.

"Sumeru sighted. Decrease speed to a hundred knots" ordered the lieutenant on the plug's audio system, without realizing that behind him the prisoner was alert and understanding every single word he said.

The vehicles slowed down, broke up the octagon and formed rows. In a single movement the squad went down the hill and approached the green areas to the east. They flew over them and then went down to the bed of the Olin, making a trail of water as they went down to the sea. Kliver was sitting with his back to the driver, so that he had to twist his neck if he wanted to see anything ahead of him. But neither fear nor the pain in his neck which was beginning to hurt prevented him from admiring what he could see:

On the top of Great Sumeru, rising above the rocks and fitting almost perfectly inside its crater, there was a base city. It was totally surrounded and fenced and had a rounded roof, flattened at the center. Around it there was considerable air traffic in every direction, entering and leaving the large number of openings around the base of a huge bluish dome which was in the center of the structure.

"Hanara was right" though Kliver. "From a distance it looks like a huge swarm near the nest!"

However, this was just the air traffic, hundreds of aircraft which helped the city to live up to its name. The city in itself did not look like a real hive. If Kliver had not heard anything about it, he could have easily thought that the construction was a UFO, a gigantic yellow flying saucer which had apparently landed on top of the mountain.

In the center of the city, the translucent dome was made up of various interlinking hexagonal plates. This gave them greater resistance, in the same way that the interlinking of carbon atoms makes up the structure of a diamond. But Kliver could not avoid comparing the way in which their plates were connected together to the structure of a beehive.

On the cover of the Hive there were enormous defense cannons, ready to shoot laser beams at any threat of invasion, anti-air artillery and a large number of towers to receive signals. Three thick tubes came out of the large central dome and went out towards the sea. These tubes sucked in water and stored it in large filters, after which would then be desalinated to make it drinkable.

Kliver gave in to curiosity and tried to imagine what the inside of the city would be like while the vehicles glided quietly over the crystalline mirror of the Olin, with the turbines furiously disturbing its waters behind.

A single gesture from the commander was all that was needed for the squad to line up, turn on their air jets, and change from semi-land vehicles to flying machines. They rose in a straight line, towards the entrances of the Hive, and the other vehicles gave way to them. And then they entered through the conventional gates, which were fixed onto a rectangular ring going right around the base of the dome.

The lights of the city went out as the sun rose. Kliver was immediately taken to the Hati headquarters, where he would be interrogated by the high command officers. He would then be sent to the military law court, where he would be given a fair trial.

Far away, in the ruins of Ruakan, Miku woke up from her forced sleep to find herself lying on the bed of a guest room, the cut on her face clean and free from infection. Hanara was waiting at her side. When he saw that she was opening her eyes, the old man told the nurses to give her a cup of tea. Miku looked right around her, wondering where she was.

"You have been sleeping since yesterday, my dear" said Hanara, smiling. "It is now morning. I took advantage while you were unconscious and melted the transmitters in your internal tracking system. You no longer need the anti-diffusing device to block the signals from the tracking system. Your connector is now free, even then the Hatis will not be able to find you.

Miku lifted her head, touched the back of her neck, feeling the free entrances of her connector. She began to feel a slight anxiety.

"Are you sure it is safe?" she asked, taking the cup of tea that was offered her.

"Perfectly safe." assured Hanara.

"How did you manage to melt my transmitters?"

"I used high temperature filaments", explained the old man. "But don't worry. I left the contact receivers intact. You will still be able to connect with the plugs. This will not prevent you from being a user . . ."

Miku did not look at all relaxed.

"Where is Kliver?" she asked, and Hanara looked seriously at her.

"He needed to leave us", he said. "Unfortunately the Hatis took him. However, I think that they will free him soon, let's wait . . . Luckily they did not take the abandoned vehicle."

Miku was not going to make a scene. The old man was sure that Miku would accept the loss of her husband.

"What do you intend to do with the vehicle?"

"I spent the night taking the transmitters out of its tracking system. I buried them in the ground, in the same place where the vehicle was, in order to avoid tracking of movements. I fueled the vehicle up and put it in a safe place. One day it may come in handy."

Miku sat up and began to drink the tea, its hot steam pleasantly tickling her nostrils. Hanara brought the chair near to the bed.

"Tell me your story", he asked. "What made you escape from the Hive? How did you get through security, and how did you meet Kliver?"

Miku was not ready to open up to the old man. However, this mysterious man, who had been part of the history of the civilization which she had left, and who had been imprisoned and expelled for some secret reason to become leader of a complex community of Banjins, suddenly began to inspire confidence. If her subsequent years were going to depend on the leadership of this man, this exchange of information would be crucial for some empathy to appear between them.

She remained quiet, wondering about the experiences she had been through. She was tired, in spite of having slept well, and remembering all that had happened to her would be painful.

"Where are my children?" she asked. "I have to see them."

"They are in the next room."

"Bring them to me. I must feed the baby. He hasn't been fed for a whole day."

"If you want my advice, I think it is best not to disturb them at the moment", said Hanara. "They are resting . . . I will send someone to get them. For now tell me your story, please do. I need to hear it."

Miku nodded. She adjusted her position on the feather mattress and began:

"The years I lived in the Hive were not easy. The requirements and repression women went through inside that imperial cloister are memories I want to forget forever."

"Like all Hatis, I was obliged to have my plug connector implanted when I was twelve years old. And you know that, according to the laws to prevent crime and escapes, all the connectors have a built-in tracking system which locates any user in the continent."

Hanara nodded.

"I know this", he said. "I also have a connector. It is an old apparatus, perhaps older than me. But it is still useful to me and it is still working. Tell me something about your life."

Miku continued:

"I got married early, at seventeen, a marriage arranged by my parents and those of Tadashi Ozarra, my first husband. But I was never in love with him. Tadashi was a hard and severe man . . . But he managed to fulfill the womanly side of me."

"I always wanted to be a mother, but control is very strict in the Hive. The law allows only one child per couple, and if couples decide to have children, they need to go on a waiting list as the population cannot exceed exactly a hundred thousand people."

"So, according to the rules, if three Hatis die, three babies may be born in order to replace the losses, privileging the next couple on the list. If four die, so another four may be born and so on. The number born never exceeding the number of deaths . . . it is simply a question of space. The Hive is crowded!"

"When I was twenty, my turn to be a mother finally came. It made me very happy. My husband and I went to the laboratory in order to collect our zygotes, so we could create a fetus which would be genetically perfect to be implanted in my womb. Tadashi wanted a boy, and in order not to contradict him, I accepted."

"In the Hive, even the sex of new babies is controlled by the Empire. If in a certain period there is a lack of women, then only the birth of girls is authorized, and vice versa. If the parents want to have a boy in a period when they are not allowed, there are two possibilities: either they wait until permission comes, giving up their place on the list to the next couple who want a girl, or they take advantage of their turn and have a girl."

"This problem happened to us. When my turn to become a mother came, only the birth of girls was allowed. Tadashi was mad. He was a respected soldier and tried to use his authority to make the geneticists make an exception. It took me a lot of effort to convince him to accept the condition, but in the end he decided that we should have a girl."

"Nine months later my daughter was born. Tadashi and I chose the name 'Yuka' to register her — Yuka Ozarra."

"By law, every woman who gives birth must have a tubal ligation, a small cut in the tubes, to prevent any accidental second pregnancy. But this operation did not take place when I gave birth. Something went wrong."

"For some reason the geneticists could not explain, Yuka was born with a serious bone marrow problem. Her body did not produce enough immune antibodies, and she became seriously ill with asthma. Believing that Yuka could die, the surgeon decided to put off my tubal ligation. If it came to the worst, I would be able to have a second child."

"After six months, Yuka improved. Her problem was corrected and my tubal ligation was arranged for the following week."

"But when the routine pre-operation tests were made, we had a surprise: I was once again pregnant! This time, it had been a natural pregnancy without the intervention of the geneticists. But it was an illegal pregnancy. As Yuka was alive, I had no permission to have a second child."

"The Empire gave me two alternatives. The first was that of the abortion, in which my womb would be removed with the fetus. The second was to keep the fetus until the birth of the child. But when it was born, the baby would belong to the Empire and would live in the research laboratories. God knows what would be done to my child. They might use it as a guinea pig in genetic experiments . . . I could never allow this to happen."

"I chose to keep the fetus until the end of my pregnancy and legally give it to the Empire. This choice would give me time to plan to escape."

"As I was married to Tadashi, I was lucky to live in the sector five shelters. Tadashi was a proud man and had used his influence to be admitted to the Faculty of Medicine, just to have the right to live in the most comfortable sector of the Hive. I thus became a neighbor of Meling, the woman to whom I owe the life of my son."

"Meling was a recently qualified doctor and worked in the clinical center examining the children who would go through the operation to implant connectors."

"I walked to the doctor's cell and asked her if there was a way of taking out the internal tracking system of my connector. Meling looked at me in a strange way, and I noticed that she was suspicious of something. She asked me if I was intending to escape, whether this was my intention, and she said that I should immediately give up."

"It is impossible to take out the internal tracking system from the connector, she said, without resulting in the death of the user. Even if you manage to escape, the Empire will soon find you and will imprison you for the rest of your life. Tadashi will also be judged by the laws of marital dishonor, and your daughter will grow up an orphan. Think seriously before doing something so crazy, my dear. Do you think it is worth it?"

"These words made me think. And in an act of desperation, which I never thought I would be capable of, I fell to my knees and grabbed her feet, desperately imploring for help.

This was my maternal instinct coming out. I loved Makuro even before he was born, and I wanted to have him at any cost!"

"I let everything out to the doctor. I held her hands and told her everything about my relationship with Tadashi. I told her about our quarrels and the fact that he was hitting me because I had not chosen to have an abortion; his excessive strictness in bringing up Yuka; his constant threats; and his repressed hatred for not receiving the authorization to have a boy at the time he could be a father. This softened the heart of the young lady with curly hair, my savior."

"I told her that Tadashi and I were getting a divorce and that he would have permanent custody of the girl. Tadashi was a first lieutenant at the time and also a medical student. This gave him the right to receive certain fringe benefits which I did not receive. With the separation, I would lose the right to live in my cell in sector five, and would soon be sent to an ordinary sector."

"I was alone. I was sure that it would be a long time before I saw Yuka again. If I tried to obtain custody of her, I would have no chance of winning. In spite of the various witnesses who said I was a good mother, I was illegally pregnant, and this would put me at a great disadvantage in the eyes of Hati law."

"Little by little, I convinced the doctor to help me. It was equally risky for her. If they discovered that she was helping me, Meling would be a considered accomplice to my escape and would be imprisoned and possibly put to death."

"The doctor excused herself and went into her cell. But before this, she promised that she would talk to a friend who lived in our shelter, a worker called Miazatsu, married to a doctor, and he might be able to help me. Miazatsu loaded the goods of a factory and had access to the cargo aircrafts which picked up raw material in the Kafria countryside."

"And as for the tracking system, she added, I will see what I can do."

"I ran to my cell and immediately plugged myself in and turned on the sleep programmer as this was the only way I would be able to sleep."

"The next day, Meling visited me, carrying a medical kit in one of her hands. She took her plug out and put it on my bed, telling me to do the same. She said that we needed to talk and asked me how long it would be before Tadashi came. I locked the door of the cell and told her not to worry — Tadashi was busy training the new group of cadets and would only return three hours later."

"The doctor opened the medical kit and took out a round metallic object which gave off a weak light in its center. It was an apparatus similar to a plug, but with a very different function. It was a signal anti-diffuser, a secret apparatus used by the command to block the signals of the tracking devices of their spies, when they were on secret missions. Its energy came from the body warmth of the user himself so that its power would never be used up while the user was alive."

"Keep it in a safe place" she told me. "You will need it when the time comes. In order to use it, you just need to put the pins it in, as if it were an ordinary plug. The device will block the signals from your internal tracking device. After connecting it, you will have to use it for the rest of your life. If you ever take it out of the connector, the Hatis will be able to locate you. This means that you will never be able to use a plug. This is a condition you will have to accept."

"I accept" I told her. "I will destroy my plug before leaving."

"Do so."

"Soon after, Meling told me that she had talked to Miazatsu, who agreed to help me."

"We have already set up everything" she said. "On Tuesday morning, connect the anti-diffuser and go to the central sector. Don't use the jetpack, as they are also tracked. Go over one of the connecting bridges. The factory where Miazatsu works is on the sixty-fifth floor of the sector. Don't use the main entrance, look for the external lifts. The cargo hangars are at the back, around the other side of the building. Miazatsu will be waiting for you in hangar 21. He will look after everything. You must be quick, my dear, as the hangars will be locked at five-thirty, at the end of the last shift."

"I thanked the doctor for her help, and she returned to her cell. I lay down on my bed full of hope and once again programmed my sleep."

"I needed to wait four days before putting the plan into practice. During this time, Tadashi showed me the conclusion of the divorce suit and a letter of recommendation signed by the general, advising the judge not to allow me to see Yuka."

"At that moment, any anxiety I had to carry out the plan disappeared. But I attempted to keep calm. I was fighting for the life of my son, and to see him taken away from me to become a guinea pig was the worst of all possible punishments. I had lost Yuka, but I could not lose Makuro."

"Early Tuesday morning I turned off my internal alarm a minute before it would go off. I had remained hours in bed awake, lying beside Tadashi, thinking of the worst things that could happen to me. I got up and rushed to the bathroom. Tadashi was still under the effect of his sleep program, and Yuka was in her grandparents' shelter."

"I closed the glass window of the bathroom from the inside in order to muffle the noise. I disconnected my plug and threw it at the floor. The device rebounded a number of times and did not break up, but I could see it was cracked on the outside. I hurled it once again, and the crack increased. The third time, the device shattered into a thousand pieces."

"I picked up the memory chip and threw it into the toilet bowl, flushing it immediately; then I gathered the remaining broken pieces, hiding them in a secret drawer in the cupboard together with two letters: one for the Hati authorities, telling them Doctor Meling was innocent, and the other for my daughter to read one day."

"The fact that I was almost five months pregnant limited my movements. And I needed to be agile. I firmly plugged the anti-diffuser into the back of my neck, put on a hood and walked to the exit of the shelter on the twenty-first floor of the sector."

"A young couple were embracing in front of the entrance to the nearest connection bridge, looking at the distant city lights. I passed them in silence, unrecognizable under my hood and thought that they did not even notice my presence."

"I needed to walk nearly two kilometers to arrive in the central sector. A patrolman was flying around it. I tried to hide in the shadows, but on one of his rounds he saw me and accelerated his jetpack in my direction. He asked me to take off my hood and show him my identification. I showed my pregnancy certificate and said that I was feeling sick and needed to get some air."

"Are you a worker in this sector? he asked me"

"Not really. No. I replied. I left the workers class when I married Lieutenant Tadashi."

"I thought that the mere mention of the name of my husband would intimidate him, but it didn't seem to bother him much."

"I'm sorry, but I will have to ask you to return to your own sector. This area is restricted at this time."

"At this moment I thought that everything had now finished. I would not be able to arrive in time for my meeting with Miazatsu."

"Hiding my desperation, I tried something which I will always be ashamed of. I went up to the patrol man and said, quietly:"

"Can you see that couple?" I pointed to the young people who were embracing on the other side of the bridge"

"The soldier couldn't see them, so he lowered the visor on his helmet and increased the zoom of his vision."

"Yes, I can see them" he said. "Any problem?"

"Yes. I don't want to tell you, but you don't give me any choice . . . I've been observing the couple at the request of the secret service." I invented. "They have no authorization to be together. The girl is betrothed to the son of the advisor of our Prime Minister."

"Do you really work for the secret service?"

"Yes" I replied.

"Can I see your papers?"

"At this moment I hesitated, and I tried the use the tactic of threatening which I had learned from my husband (or rather, my ex-husband)"

"Do you think the secret service uses personal papers? I asked, firmly".

"The patrolman was not threatened by the tone of my voice."

"Please, wait here" he ordered. "I'll go and ask the couple to show me their authorizations. If there is no irregularity, I will be obliged to hold you."

"You can go, if you wish. But it will hold up my investigation, and I'll have to mention it in my report. What is your name and which unit do you belong to?"

The patrolman thought a bit and reconsidered.

"You can carry on" he told me, finally feeling intimidated. "This time I will let you go. I realize that our conversation has been registered in my plug. If I find you walking around here again at this time, I'll have to take you to the High Command."

"It is only your job, patrolman" I said. "I also recorded our conversation in my plug. Have a good shift."

"The man did not say anything else. He turned around, turned on his jetpack and took off, disappearing from sight high above the sector."

"I put my hood back on and continued walking towards the central building. I went into one of the external lifts and went up to the sixty-fifth floor. Then I went around the back of the building, where the hangars of the stocks of raw material were. I looked for hangar number 21. I knocked twice on the entrance and then it opened. A man was there, behind the gate."

"Miku? he asked."

"Yes. I said."

"My name is Miazatsu. he bowed, and I returned the bow."

"I apologized for being late, and he took me by the arm, taking me to one of the aircrafts, an enormous machine, which took up a large amount of space at the back of the hangar."

"This is a cargo collector" he explained to me, opening the back compartment. "It collects and stocks a large amount of raw material. Today it will be used in the rice harvest. The aircraft will leave at eight in the morning for a Hati settlement in the West of the continent, near the junction of the Olin with the River Regit. You are lucky. Rice only grows near a river."

"You should stay hidden here, inside the cargo compartment." he continued, tying an almost invisible thread in the lock of the door. "Hold firmly onto this thread inside. I will leave the compartment unlocked, but the door can only be opened from outside. When the aircraft reaches its destination, pull the thread and push the door with your feet. You can pull the thread strongly, as it's made of aramid, which does not break."

"I tied the other end of the thread to my finger and went into the compartment. Before closing it, Miazatsu gave me a rucksack with a number of utensils and ten kilos of food."

"When you reach the settlement" he told me, "run to the river and hide in the woods. Don't leave the banks as you may run out of water."

"Thank you" I said, while I settled down in the compartment."

"Thank doctor Meling. She insisted I helped you. Now hurry up. Take care not to be seen. You'll have to be hidden for at least four hours. Try to stay awake and keep alert."

"Miazatsu closed the door and went to finish his shift, and I kept still in the darkness, avoiding making any noise. Almost two hours later, I heard two men talking, the sound of their voices getting nearer and nearer. They entered the control cabin of the aircraft and turned on the engines, making the compartment shake."

"At the beginning, the aircraft made a number of curves and varied its speed, and I was there in the back, trying to balance myself in order not to be thrown against the walls. But soon the aircraft followed a straight line, and everything was calm."

"A number of hours later I felt that the turbines were getting slower, and the aircraft began to descend. There was a jerk. The engines were turned off and I was certain we were on the ground."

"I must have waited some twenty minutes before leaving the compartment, listening for any noise. Apparently the pilots had not yet got out of the aircraft, or they had done so without my noticing. But I could not feel their presence, and this encouraged me to get out."

"I pulled the thread which was tied to my finger. I noticed it was taut and pulled it more strongly. The outside lock opened and I pushed the door with my feet. Light and wind came into the compartment. From far I heard the song of a number of birds, and in the background the sound of the rapids of the River Olin."

"From the half open compartment I could see what was happening outside. The aircraft had stopped near a thick forest, full of high trees, which blocked the view of the river. To the south I could see a number of men near a muddy area. They were wearing hats and rubber boots and, as they had no shirts on, I could see that their skins were brown because of the sun. At such a distance, I doubted whether they could see me."

"I left the compartment and closed the door. I untied the thread from my finger and sneaked around the side of the aircraft when I saw that one of the pilots was walking towards me. I became desperate. There was nowhere to escape to without him seeing me, and there was no more time to return to the compartment. Hardly thinking, I lay on the ground and crawled under the aircraft, pressing my stomach against the sand."

"Protected from the view, under the axel which supported the turbines, I could see the feet of the pilot coming near, stopping in front of the cargo compartment where I had been. He stayed there a while, and I didn't know what he was doing until he suddenly began to urinate."

"The stream of urine made a frothy puddle on the sand, running under the aircraft. I tried to remain still and silent, under the axel, feeling the hot liquid wet my face, my lips and my hair under the hood."

"The pilot found the thread which had been tied to the lock of the door. He took hold of one of its ends and abruptly opened the door, examining the inside of the compartment. As he didn't find anything, he closed it again and left, as the other pilot was calling him."

"While he was moving away, I heard him shouting to his co-pilot, asking him whether he had left the cargo compartment unlocked."

"After this episode, I remained a few more minutes hidden, waiting for the ideal moment to flee. When I felt sure, I crawled from under the aircraft, put the rucksack on my back and ran into the forest, making a path between the branches and leaves."

"Then my journey along the banks of the Great River began."

"I walked for many days, eating little in order to make my provisions last. I made sure I did not leave any tracks, and went upstream. I must have been very far from Sumeru, but I was not sure whether the satellites of the Empire could visualize that area. Because of this I never left the bank, thinking that its trees would protect me from being located."

"On one of these dark nights I lost hope and felt desperate. My legs were trembling, and I could not take another step forward. I realized that there was no chance of survival far from the Hive. I was weak, hungry, covered in scratches, weakened by pregnancy."

"I lay down by a bush and began to cry. I cried, I wept desperately. I even thought that I might miscarry."

"A man heard my weeping and cautiously approached. I looked up and was frightened when I saw him. That man, in front of me, contradicted everything that I knew about the new world. I could never imagine that the Myras still existed."

"Kliver was different. He was tall and strong, and his eyes were round and light. He was wearing the Myra army combat uniform, black with red stripes, and on his head a helmet hid a large part of his face. In his hands he carried a strange weapon, a type of long shotgun which shot arrows."

"A feeling of curiosity and fear went right through my body. Despite his neat appearance, I thought he might be some kind of savage. I thought he would kill me there and then, without even blinking. But instead of this, he offered me, in my language, food and shelter."

"Kliver was traveling alone. He took off his helmet, held out his hand, and I had no choice but to have confidence in him. He took me to his camp and made us a stew of roots and leaves. We spent the whole night talking, trying to keep warm."

"I told him I did not know anything about the Myras. On the other hand, he knew quite a lot about the Hatis. He knew a little about our history, our laws and also understood our language. He said that he had learned the Hati language and alphabet when he was a small boy, and this was an obligation of all the members of his colony."

"Kliver did not say much about his life, but little by little I managed to get some information out of him. I learned that the Myras are very inferior in terms of technology, but much more numerous, with a population of around a million and a half. The majority follow a strange religion called 'Ca-Tandism', whose teachings forbid the use of plugs, and, thus, the devices were totally forbidden in the Myra Colony."

"I found out that Kliver's situation was very similar to my own. His wife had died giving birth to their child Aron, and in order to forget her, he had volunteered on a solo military spying mission, whose aim was to locate and photograph the Hati city."

"I remember that we spent a week getting to know each other, camping near the river, and in this short space of time, Kliver proposed to me. He suggested that we escaped to the desert, far from the world and the repressive eyes of our societies. But before going, he needed to rescue his son Aron. And, to do this, he would need to return to his underground colony."

"I thought a little and decided to accept his proposal. I didn't really have any other choice of survival other than to join him. I didn't love him. It was much too early for this. But he had saved my life, and with a man at my side, it would be easier to bring up Makuro. I thus accepted his proposal. I told myself that love would come with time . . ."

"With Kliver's help, I got up onto his bigbug and we went towards the Colony. We rode for a number of days, always camping in the evening. Kliver could not take a Hati with him to his civilization. When we reached the Myra territory, he told me to wait on the outskirts of Loagy, the gigantic oasis situated to the north of the continent, beneath which the Colony had been built."

"Kliver disappeared into the trees, and I remained seated on a high stone, surrounded by the forest. Night came once again when he returned, wearing some rags, which made him look like a beggar. He was holding Aron in his arms, and, beside him, a man in a cassock was following him. He was a catandist preacher. He had come in order to bless our marriage. He was carrying a square crucifix at his waist, and in his hands he was holding the book of religious teachings."

"We got married without any ceremony, with few words and, after a lengthy kiss (our first), we said goodbye to the preacher and began our journey with no fixed destination through the desert."

"After two weeks riding on Misha's hard saddle, we saw from a distance a chain of mountains and tall crags. We went towards them, with the few provisions which were left. We went up one of the mountains in order to get a sight of what lay before us, hoping to see a savannah where we might stay. On top of the mountain, we found a dry safe cave, green grass and a lake, surrounded by fruit trees and a number of cogus."

"We decided to shelter there for a while and, after some months, Makuro was born."

"Unexpectedly, Kliver's bigbug became pregnant. When the Misha's young were born, I was already three months pregnant with my third child, Kliver's second. In the mountains there was no comfort, but with the fruits from the trees, the water from the lake and Misha's milk to feed us, we stayed there for two years."

"Three days ago I gave birth to another boy. But I had a complicated birth, with my labor lasting almost fifteen hours. In one of the contractions, my anti-diffusing device came off my neck, and my internal tracker began to work again. In a short time, the Empire managed to track me and sent a soldier on a solo mission to look for me. It was then that . . ."

At this moment Hanara interrupted her.

"I know the rest of the story, my dear", he said, happy with the woman's story. "You don't need to stress yourself anymore. As I had said, you and your three children are happy to live in these ruins with me and all the Banjin community. There may not be much luxury, and survival is difficult, but it is safe and is a good environment in which to bring up your children.

"That is if there is no war", contradicted Miku, serious. "The Empire will not stop. They will make Kliver tell them about us. It is very dangerous to stay here. The Hatis will invade this territory"

"Kliver will not say anything, I am sure", said Hanara. "The new laws on captured prisoners prevent them from using heavy drugs or violent torture. The Command will use the interplug as a strategy."

"The interplug?" Miku was surprised. "This is Just a rumor. The interplug does not exist. The Hatis will never be able to put this technology into practice".

Hanara did not say anything. He decided that he should not worry about threats which did not yet affect them.

"Tell me", he asked, bending over the bed. "What do you think the chances are that the Myras will win, if there is really a war between the Myras and the Hatis?"

"I don't know", Miku said, sincerely, sitting up on the mattress. "Kliver did not tell me very much about his people. I only know that there are a lot of them and they have an army which is almost five times larger than the Hati population. The Myra Regent will certainly use this advantage as he cannot fight against our fire power. The Myras have no aircraft or heavy weapons. But if the Hatis use all their destructive strength, then there will be a terrible stalemate, and the result of the battle will be, I believe, zero zero.

"It will be zero zero in any case" added Hanara. "The bee that stings kills and also dies. We cannot destroy the only continent which we still have. War is a great folly, but a necessary folly in the eyes of our leaders. Your mixed race child will open not only the eyes of our leaders, but of everyone. People will hear him. When he grows, he will balance the two rival nations and will change the world in which we live. Believe what I say. But before opening the eyes of the world, it will be necessary to open his. And this is why I humbly ask you if I can look after him. I will make him an able man in every way I can.

I will teach him to think and act. Don't worry, my dear. I'll prepare him to be good."

Miku remained thoughtful, looking into Hanara's eyes. She wanted to avoid the subject, but she now realized that it would be a good time to ask that which she wanted to know from the old man:

"I told you all of my story", she said. "It was difficult to tell so much to someone I hardly know. Now I would like you to tell me your secrets. Why were you expelled from the Hive? What were the motives that led the Emperor to imprison and expel a general who was as respected as you were?"

"Patience is the main virtue of man . . ." said Hanara, getting up from the chair and heading to the door, putting his straw hat on his head. "And also of woman! This is not the right moment to tell you about my past. There are still possibilities of a conflict. The destination of you and your children is not decided. The future is full of uncertainty, and a wrong step might change it forever. But I cannot tell you anything. Excuse me."

The old man said that he would go to the library to look for dictionaries and encyclopedias about the Myra culture, as it would be important for the children to grow up knowing its language. And if Hanara was to teach them, then he would have to learn.

"We must teach the Myra-Hati and their brothers about the different cultures", he said, leaning on the entrance to the door. "They need to know Mathematics, Philosophy, Science and Literature, in addition to the culture of the tribe. With your permission, I would like to educate them. By the way, what will be the name of the baby?"

Miku changed position on the mattress.

"I haven't yet had time to think of a suitable name", she said. "But I would like you to be his godfather and choose his name."

"Tork", said the old man without thinking twice. "A mixture of Tokyo and York. In order for the prophecy to become true, he should have a name which has Myra and Hati characteristics. It will be homage to the two cities which were once the great powers in the ancient world.

Miku smiled in surprise. Hanara once again made her remember the prophecy, and she felt honored when thinking that her son would have the name which had been stipulated in the sacred parchments.

"I agree", she said, satisfied. "My son will be called 'Tork'".

But before giving the old man permission to bring him up, she made a number of demands:

"When they are children, I want them to live in harmony with the Banjins, and I want them to think that they are the only different ones living in the tribe. I also want them to believe that the natives are a sacred people and they should never touch the young girls here. You will never tell them anything about the outside world, about the Hive or the Colony or about the Myras and the Hatis. If you agree, I'll allow you to bring them up."

"I agree" said Hanara. "But, be careful not to let the boys see your plug connector. It will make them ask questions which will not be easy to tell lies about.

"It will be difficult, but I'll try", said Miku, tapping on the holes in her neck. "I hope you will do the same."

Hanara nodded and went out. One of the nurses came in with the baby wrapped in a blanket and put it in its mother's arms. Miku uncovered her breast and brought the baby closer.

"Hello, little Tork", she said, unwrapping its blankets.

CHAPTER 5

BOYS AND MEN

The years went by, and the space within the walls of Ruakan filled up with lies. The boys grew up according to Hanara's plans. They learned the culture of the tribe, to lasso and tame wild animals, in addition to speaking, reading and writing in the three languages (Myra, Hati and Kuata-Noans). They grew up believing that Aron and Makuro were full brothers and that Aron was a year older. They believed that old Hanara was their paternal grandfather and that Miku was the real mother of the three, and that their father Kliver had died in the last war, which had exterminated all the remaining population of the world. Their own world was just a ruined city, lost in the middle of an empty desert, but they heard rumors about the existence of another faroff and inhabited continent, which was impossible to reach.

It was now the year of 229 AE. In these sixteen years little had changed in Ruakan, although security had strengthened after the last Hati invasion. The leader decided to build high observation towers, placed at six strategic points of the village, which would be able to observe a much larger area than the old tower of the temple. The warning signals were now given by bugles made of horns, used by the warriors who guarded the main entrances.

When the hunters needed to go somewhere they could not be seen from the towers, a group of warriors followed them, in case they were in danger. Sixteen years were spent in this rigid preventive regime, during which there was no threat of another invasion.

During this time there was no news from Kliver, and little was said about him in private meetings between the men of the tribe. Hanara always hoped that he was alive and would return some day. Miku also wished to believe this, but after telling the boys about the heroic way in which he died, she herself began to believe in her own lie and accept his loss.

Anyway, Hanara accepted his own mistake in foreseeing the actions of the High Command and invented various theories to explain the disappearance of a prisoner who had been for so long in the hands of the Empire. The most frightening of them was that the micro tracking device in Kliver's tooth could have come loose or could have been discovered by the Hatis. If this happened, Kliver would have no choice of survival when he was freed, other than returning to his Colony.

The war might even have begun without Hanara knowing.

The afternoon sun hid behind the clouds, relieving the tiredness of the workers who cultivated the fields. Poko, a young Negro, son of one of the nurses, stopped looking after his younger brothers and sisters at three o' clock, when his mother got back from harvesting the cogus fruit. She brought a number of full baskets, one of them balancing on the rolled-up cloth on her head. His father had gone out with some hunters and would be back at dusk.

The woman placed the baskets in a corner of the room and told Poko he could go out and do what he wanted, as she would now look after the small children.

The boy went into the street and ran to the house of the "white-skinned brothers", the largest house in the stone village. He wanted to invite one of the boys to go fishing in the stream or practice archery. He stretched his neck up and looked through the window. When he was just about to shout Aron's name, he saw an embarrassing scene, which on another occasion he would have turned away from: Miku was singing in front of the mirror, combing her long wet hair, and wearing just a towel.

Poko had enormous respect for the mother of the white-skins. He wanted to turn away, but he noticed something. When Miku lifted her hair to tie it up, Poko saw three holes inside a circular salience made of dark material, which was attached to the back of her neck, apparently encrusted in her vertebrae.

Poko thought this was very strange but decided not to bother her and turned around to look for the boys.

"Have you seen Aron or Makuro, or even Tork?" he asked the first person he saw, a tough warrior, who was carrying a spear twice his size.

"Aron has disappeared", the native warrior said. "No one knows where. Tork is on the hill, training with the Leader, and Makuro is probably in the library."

Poko thanked him and went to the library, where he saw Makuro sitting at the desk, looking at a large book with a blue cover, speaking aloud to himself:

"Ridiculous!"

"What's up, Mak?" asked Poko.

"Half the history books are missing. They are all here listed in this book, but they have disappeared from the shelves, almost as if someone had thrown them away or hidden them, afraid that they would be read."

"Why would anyone do that?"

"I don't know. Maybe they want to hide something", guessed Makuro. "Do you believe in what my grandfather teaches us about the world in which we live? Do you believe in what he says about why I and my brothers are the only ones who are different to the rest of the tribe?"

"Yes, he is the leader . . . I'm not sure. Where is Aron?" Poko tried to change the subject.

"I don't believe him. A lot of things must have been hidden from us. Secrets or facts which they don't want us to discover. The books which have disappeared prove it. They must contain proof that . . ."

Makuro noticed that Poko didn't show any interest.

"Aron is probably in the barn, watching Tork training" he said, trying to calm down.

"Is it already Wednesday? I'll see if I can find him".

"Wait" sighed Makuro, closing the reference book and putting it back in the drawer. "If you want to do something with him, I'll go with you. I must get some air and amuse myself".

They left the library and went to the road which led to the field. When they passed the north observation tower, the sentry refused to allow them to leave. But he changed his mind when they told him they were just looking for Aron.

The herd of bigbugs was less than two kilometers away from the village, along the road which passed the plantations and the fresh springs. From a certain distance it was possible to see the shape of two people who were going through skillful movements on top of the hill, practicing martial arts.

The field was totally fenced in, and, at one end, there was a wooden barn, which also gave shelter to the bigbugs. From time to time, they were woken up during the day to be used as transport for the hunters or to pull the carts, which were full of water and fruit which the women had picked in the orchards.

It was easy to find Aron on Wednesdays. Hidden on the top floor of the barn, he leaned out the window with the old binoculars which his father had left, looking at his mixed-race brother practicing hu-tae-mui with the leader. Aron was glad whenever Tork made a mistake or when Hanara surprised him with a blow.

The truth was that Aron could not believe that his younger brother could beat him in a fight. Aron was the eldest and strongest of them, and in the tribe this made him worthy of respect. But strength was not worth anything when compared to the skills that his brother was gaining from this practice.

Hu-tae-mui is a kind of martial art that was the most popular entertainment among the Hatis. You take guard by standing upright, with your clenched fists in the air, with just your forefinger and middle finger held out. The attack is based on touching the vital parts of the opponent with precision and speed. Despite his age, Hanara was still skillful and could be considered a purple belt.

When they reached the barn, Makuro and Poko did not see Aron at the window, which was unusual, as this habit of his had become almost a routine when Tork was training.

"Can you see him?" asked Poko. "I don't think he is there. Do you think he is hiding elsewhere?"

Makuro did not reply. He half-opened the doors of the barn and entered silently, followed by Poko. In the stable, there was bigbug dung and straw everywhere, mixed with the unpleasant smell of mildew. The animals were asleep, shaking their bodies to get rid of the flies, but Aron could not be seen anywhere.

They suddenly heard laughter coming from above, muffled by the floor above them.

"There's someone else here", whispered Poko.

"It seems my brother is not alone", said Makuro in the same tone of voice.

They both smiled and silently went up the ladder. They surprised Aron and a native girl, who were both totally naked, lying on the hay.

"Ah!" said Makuro, "so this is what you get up to when you disappear every day. You are up here hidden with the Noans. Wait until granddad knows about this".

The couple were taken aback, and Aron quickly covered the girl's body with the hay.

"I don't hide up here with the Noans", he said, as soon as he calmed down. "Just with my Daiara", and kissed her on the face.

Makuro and Poko sat down beside them.

"Aren't you tired of hearing your grandfather saying that native girls are forbidden?" said the Negro boy, slapping his friend's head. "Only I can do this. So, if you excuse me, wait outside while I and Daiara talk . . ."

Aron was distressed.

"I'm not interested in what that stupid old man says", he said in the Myra language, so that Daiara would not understand. "Leave us alone. Wait outside while I get dressed. I'll come down in twenty minutes."

"Twenty minutes?" laughed Makuro and Poko.

They left the barn and went back to the field. Poko put his foot on the fence.

"Your brother is going crazy, Mak" he said. "Even though I have permission to choose a Noan and get married to one, I don't show off or go near them like your brother does. He will soon have problems with the leader."

"I don't agree with you, Poko" said Makuro, serious. "My grandfather is hiding something. I'm beginning to doubt his teachings. Why did he teach us three languages if we live in a place where only one is spoken? Why is he training my brother so much if he says that the world is just a city in ruins, isolated in the middle of an empty desert?"

"Now you've said this, I'd like to tell you something" said Poko, "but I don't think I should".

Makuro's expression made it clear that Poko had no choice but to tell him what was on his mind.

"Just now, I went to look for you in your house. Your mother had just come out of her bath. She was sitting down with her back to me, and, from the window where I was, I could see the back of her neck."

"And you saw three holes in her neck", completed Makuro. "I've also seen them a number of times".

"Really?" Poko was surprised. "And what did you do?"

"I didn't worry about it. I didn't ask any questions. I pretended not to see them. Those holes are part of a lie. I bet they have something to do with the past of my mother. Her bitterness, that horrible scar she has on her face, there must be some connection. The disappearance of the history books, five people who are different, living together with hundreds of natives . . . They think we're stupid!"

At this moment, Aron came out of the barn, tying the string which held his trousers up.

"What are you two doing there?" he shouted. "Talking about me?"

"We're just discussing our brother's training", said Makuro.

"Why did you come to look for me?"

Poko answered:

"We wanted to invite you to go fishing in the river."

"Get the rods. I'll get the hooks", he said, without thinking.

At night time, the four young men, including Tork, enjoyed themselves telling stories while they roasted cogus fruit on a fire, and got drunk with two jugs of babadune, a strong fermented drink, popular with the men of the tribe. They were sitting on the slopes of the pass, five hundred meters from the eastern entrance to the village.

On the orders of Hanara, the boys were forbidden to light a fire after sunset, as the flames might attract evil spirits from the desert, but his anxiety was really that the light could show the presence of life among the ruins.

Aron was not worried about disobeying his grandfather's orders and dared to challenge his authority.

"Evil spirits!" he joked. "Let them come here so I can punch them on the nose".

They all laughed, except Tork, who told him off for joking about things he did not understand.

Soon after, tiredness overcame Tork, who had been practicing hu-tae-mui all day long, and his bed time had already passed. He got up and threw the skewer into the fire. He said goodbye to them all, and returned to the village along the pass, lighting the way with a small lantern.

When Tork had gone, Aron could not avoid saying:

"There goes Hanara's little puppet. Big-headed kid! Who is he trying to fool?"

"Leave him alone", said Makuro. "Let him fight for what he believes."

"What does he believe in? A load of lies which they think we can easily swallow?" Aron also had his suspicions. "Someone has to open our brother's eyes, Mak. For his own good. We must show reality to Tork, before he's bewitched by the old man's madness. Look at the way in which he is training, going through a marathon of physical endurance tests six days a week. It even seems as if war is coming! We must make him realize that all this effort is unnecessary, by force, if necessary."

Makuro didn't say anything, and Poko got up, his black skin reflecting the brightness of the flames.

"I have an idea" he said. "Let's play a trick on him. Let's put Tork in a difficult situation where only he will take the blame. Something that will make everyone furious, especially the leader."

"That will be worse", said Makuro. "We've got to talk to Tork. Make him understand all the contradictions around us".

"I like Poko's idea", said Aron. "If we put Tork into a difficult situation, everyone will see how naïve he is, and Granddad will have to reduce some of the tasks he's imposed on him".

"I don't agree with you", said Makuro. "Irresponsible behavior like this is not the best way to help our brother. We've got to put him against the old man, and not the old man against him".

"Granddad's teachings are false", said Aron with conviction. "The best thing to do is to show Tork they are false."

"But how can we prove they are false?" asked Makuro. "We are prisoners in these ruins".

"What do you intend to do? Steal the bigbugs and escape into the desert?"

"No. That would be stupid. In addition, if we escape, we have to make plan things so that nothing goes wrong. And if we find no proof in the desert, it will be difficult to face people when we get back. We might even suffer a serious punishment, and we'll never get our freedom back."

"Let's do the following", said Aron, standing up. "Poko will tell Tork that the evil spirits are invading the village. And Makuro and I will hide behind those rocks", pointing to a gap in the pass. "When he looks for us and doesn't find us, you suggest to him that we were captured by the spirits and . . ."

"It won't be successful", interrupted Makuro.

"It will. Tork is naïve. You just need to convince him to give the order to blow the bugles. Everyone will wake up and rush to the square. When they find out that it's a false alarm, they will want to hang him". Aron chuckled at his own plan.

"And don't you think that he will accuse us?" wondered Makuro.

"Well, we can deny it. It will be three against one", said Aron. "The Noans will think that our lovely mixed-race boy is losing his mind".

Makuro thought a bit.

"Do what you want", he said. "But if the consequences are serious, leave me out. I don't want to be an accomplice in this trick."

"Don't worry" said Aron. "If it comes down to it, I'll take the blame."

"I know you".

The plan was accepted, and Poko had to do things quickly. While Aron and Makuro hid behind the rocks, Poko rushed back to the village. He managed to reach Tork by turning the outside door knob and silently opening the door so as not to shout and wake up Miku.

"Quick, Tork. Come with me!" he panted. "Your brothers have disappeared in the middle of an explosion. The flames of the fire became dark and mysterious voices came from beyond . . ."

"Don't be stupid, Poko", doubted Tork. "Nobody disappears as they do in a magic trick".

"It wasn't magic. It was the supernatural! The evil spirits were attracted by the fire. Quick, Tork! Your brothers are in danger. They need your help. Do something!"

Tork had no doubt that Poko had been influenced by Aron. However, if that request for help was just his brother's trick, Makuro would certainly not get involved. Although he knew that the evil spirits were just stories invented by the old people to prevent the young people from leaving the ruins at night, something inside him made him believe Poko. If Poko was telling the truth, something had really happened. It was not necessarily the appearance of good or evil spirits, but perhaps something extraordinary beyond his understanding had happened

Tork also wondered whether if it was just Aron's trick, and then the victim would be Poko. He could then think that the trick was not on him and help his friend, before Poko did something stupid which could disturb the peace of the tribe.

"Let's go to the fire", said Tork. "If what you say is true, I'll tell the leader. He will know what to do."

When they got back to the pass, Tork shouted out his brothers' names. He saw that the fire was still alight and realized that nothing unusual had happened. The flames were not dark, as Poko had said.

When for the fourth time he shouted out Makuro's name, a reply came:

"We are prisoners. The evil spirits captured us", said Makuro, through a rolled up piece of grass, which made his voice deeper. "Quick, Tork, get help. They are planning to attack the village after midnight!"

"How many of them are there", asked Tork, feeling his legs tremble.

"We don't know. It's very dark. I think there are more than a hundred!"

"I'll tell grandfather", said Tork, about to run off.

"There's no time!" shouted Makuro. "Tell the Noans, before it's too late."

Tork turned around and ran back to the village, but not because he believed in spirits. He was thinking that his brothers had been captured by some unknown people wearing macabre clothes, or even by some groups of semi-intelligent animals, who knows? Desperate, his imagination ran faster than his legs.

Aron, hidden behind the rocks, could hardly prevent himself from breaking out into laughter. At his side, Makuro felt a certain discomfort and was worried about the consequences that would follow. But, as his brother had said, it would be three against one. Tork would take the blame alone.

Shortly afterwards, they heard the bugles in the distance.

"It is starting", said Aron. "Tomorrow they will all think that the half-breed they now love is crazy".

The noise of the bugles continued. The natives woke and desperately rushed into the square, blocking the temple entrance, forming a confused crowd. Women shouted, old people were pushed, and men yelled at each other. Hens were trampled underfoot, and children were separated from their parents.

Amidst the confusion, the warriors attempted to prevent the crowd from invading the temple while they waited for the arrival of their leader. "Is it an attack by animals coming from the desert to look for food?" wondered the natives. "Could it really be the evil spirits?" "Or the Myras, looking for Kliver, who had disappeared from the colony almost eighteen years before?"

However, the majority agreed that a Hati invasion was taking place. There had been at least three since the natives had occupied the ruins, and they were expecting another one to take place.

"Who ordered the bugles to be blown?" was the first question that Yoshi Hanara asked when he reached the crowd.

"I gave the order", replied Tork. "Aron and Makuro were captured in the pass."

"What's happening?" asked the old man, with his hands on his hips. "Are we being invaded?"

"I'm not sure, grandfather. I think it is some unknown people".

"Did you see them?"

"No. But I heard Makuro's voice. It sounded strange, as if he had been captured by the darkness."

"How did you know they were prisoners?"

"Poko told me."

"And where is he now?"

Tork looked everywhere and could not find him.

"He's also disappeared. He might also have been captured!"

While the natives waited apprehensively inside the temple, Hanara got six men to go with Tork to the pass. There they could only find the ashes of the fire, giving off a thread of black smoke. Aron and Makuro were nowhere there, but their footsteps were visible on the sand, going in the direction of a gap in the rocks. The warriors lifted up their torches and followed the footprints. On the ground they found a rolled up leaf of grass.

One of the warriors picked up the leaf and put it to his lips, asking Tork if the sound of his voice was not similar to that of Makuro which he had heard.

Tork agreed and then understood that he was the victim of a hoax. The leaf was handed over as proof, and soon all was explained. The natives were furious and said that if Hanara didn't severely punish the boys, they could be lynched when they returned.

But that night they did not return . . .

CHAPTER 6

PLANS

Alot happened that Wednesday, but nothing compared to Thursday, which was only just beginning . . .

Aron and his friends had spent the night out sharing a bed with two bigbugs who were sleeping in the barn. Makuro and Poko had been thrown out of the floor above (which was more comfortable as there was more hay there) when the lovely Daiara came in and threw herself into the arms of Aron. She had run away from the village after everything became quiet and went to sleep with her lover on the top floor of the old barn, as she knew that he could be there in times of difficulty.

According to Hanara's rules, relations between the couple were forbidden. Their biggest worry was that there would be a child with both Myra and Banjin genes. If the world was not yet ready to receive a Myra-Hati child, how would it react to a "Myra-Banjin" child?

Although he had been expelled more than thirty years before, Hanara still behaved as if he lived in the Hive. And even though he was in charge of a community which was outside the boundaries of the Empire, the Hati rules were strictly applied within the Ruakan walls.

When dawn came, Daiara said goodbye and went home, hoping to find her parents still asleep. She reached the window of her room and easily climbed in.

Now the girl had left, the three friends slept on the top floor.

They woke up in the early morning when they heard the noise of the hunters, choosing the best bigbugs to use as transport. The two animals which slept on the first floor were chosen, together with another three who were in the pasture. While the bigbugs were being saddled, the boys heard one of the natives say:

"If I get one of those white-skins, I'll skin him!"

"Me too!" agreed the other, while he attached the blinkers on to his bigbug.

On the top floor the three boys were now beginning to get worried. Poko suggested that they left the village for a few days, until things quietened down. Aron, according to the original plan, continued supporting the idea of saying it was all Tork's invention. On the other hand, Makuro thought that it would be better to tell the truth and admit their mistakes to the tribe, and that this would be the only way to be forgiven.

During the whole morning they planned an acceptable excuse. And at exactly ten o' clock the barn doors opened, and their names were called:

"Aron and Makuro, come down", boomed the authoritarian voice of Hanara.

Poko kept still, anxious about what could happen to him. His parents must be furious. He decided he would not climb down. Moreover, Hanara had only called the names of the two brothers, not his. But, with a threatening gesture, Aron made him accompany them.

The three of them went down the ladder and left the barn, walking towards Hanara, who was standing with his arms crossed on the green grass of the pasture, the strong wind blowing his toga. Poko and Makuro came after Aron, their heads bowed while Aron walked confidently in front of them.

"What can I do for you, grandfather?" asked Aron.

"I think you all owe an apology to everyone, especially your brother Tork".

"Why do you think so?" continued Aron, challenging him.

"Now, son of a bigbug", said Hanara. "Don't mock me. Have you forgotten all the moral values I taught you?"

"I'm sorry, Granddad . . . you haven't taught me anything for a long time".

"Ah, so that's it. Are you jealous of your brother's training? This doesn't give you the right to challenge my authority and make everyone a fool. If I'm your leader today, you must know that I was chosen to be so".

"With great effort and devotion", completed Aron. "I know that, Granddad. You don't need to go on repeating it. If you think that we were involved in everything that took place last night, you must know that we have proof that we were roasting cogus in the mountain pass. Don't believe everything Tork tells you. He's angry, and he's unfairly accusing us."

Hanara was taken aback.

"So, in addition to being liars, you also disobeyed my orders not to light a fire after sunset. How do you know about what happened last night if you were not there? I haven't said anything. If you were not involved, why did you hide the whole morning?"

Aron had no reply.

"We heard the bugles", interrupted Poko. "There was no more time to return to the village, so we decided to spend the night in the barn".

Poko became quiet as soon as Hanara gave him a look which made him shut up.

"Listen to me . . ." continued Hanara. "I don't want to waste any more time arguing with immature children like you. You don't owe explanations to me. You have until nightfall to apologize to the tribe, and if not, you'll have to answer to me." Hanara pointed his finger to them before turning around and leaving, adding, without looking behind him:

"I shall now prepare your brother's class. You three will stay here until you make it up with Tork.

Time went by, and the four of them looked at each other in an uncomfortable silence. The wind whistling through their hair and the buzz of insects could be heard. Tork was the first to speak:

"You all betrayed me" he said, looking at Makuro.

"We acted for your own good" said Makuro. "We tried to open your eyes to our grandfather's lies".

"Never show a lack of respect to the Master in my presence! For me, he is much more than a grandfather. We owe him everything we know today. Passing his knowledge on is the least he can do for us so that we can teach future generations? Grandfather does not tell lies."

"So, how can you explain the disappearance of history books from the library and the strange holes your mother has on the back of her neck?" asked Poko.

Aron stared down at Poko.

"What are you talking about?" he yelled.

Poko was now obliged to tell them that he had seen Miku's connector the previous morning, and from then on the conversation changed. What was going to be an apology slowly became a heated discussion between the boys. As Makuro told them about the books which had mysteriously disappeared from the library, Aron's body began to tremble with hatred.

Makuro also said that there was no logical motive for Hanara to have ordered the observation towers to be constructed, as his teaching stated that the desert beyond the village was empty.

"Can't you see that everything our grandfather tells us is a complete farce? A lie?" shouted Aron to Tork.

Tork began to understand and did not deny the basis of what Makuro was saying. But he continued to strongly defend Hanara:

"We must take into account everything he's done for us. Mother told us that he learned the "white men's language" just to teach us. Just think of that. Learn a complete language just so your grandchildren can know it!"

"Why?" asked Aron. "Why should he take so much trouble? If what Granddad taught us were true, then there would be no other people living in the world. And, therefore there would be no need for him to teach us a language which is no longer spoken"

"It is a question of tradition", continued Tork, defending him. "Granddad does not want the language of our ancestors to be forgotten. I can only repeat that the Master has worked so hard for us."

"But this effort does not give him the right to lie and try to control our lives. Neither does it give him the right to hide a world which also belongs to us, nor which, because of him, we are not allowed to discover. Think, Tork, Granddad does not even allow us to accompany the hunters further than wherever can be seen from the towers. He is afraid we are going to discover something. I'm sure he is hiding something from us."

"Granddad does not hide anything", repeated Tork. "If we do not have permission to leave the village, it is for our own good, to prevent us from facing the dangers in the desert".

"Look, you little obedient soldier, you even seem a miniature replica of him. Prove to me that your darling Master tells the truth", said Aron.

"Prove that what he teaches is false", replied Tork.

"You are not going to carry on with this stupid argument, are you?" asked Poko, getting bored. "If you want to prove something, why don't you go to the Forbidden Continent? Everyone knows that it is a distant and dangerous place, impossible to reach. If you manage to set foot in the Continent, then you will have proof against our leader's teaching."

"The legend says that a dense radioactive cloud totally covers the sky there. There is no way we can survive", said Makuro. "But I disagree with theses legends, and I'm ready to risk my life to disprove them. Let's leave today, when everything is quiet, or early tomorrow morning".

"And how are we going to cross the Tetis, genius? Swimming?" asked Aron. "Isn't it you who always says that something like this should be planned months before, so that nothing goes wrong?"

"You can't be serious", remarked Tork.

"Yes, we are", replied Makuro. "I want to know what is beyond these walls. But Aron is right. Crossing the Tetis Ocean would be a problem".

Poko now remembered the stories his father told him about the past and the invasions which the tribe had suffered throughout the years. His father, an ex-guerilla who had become a hunter when he got old, had told him about a vehicle which Hanara had found and kept in secret since the last invasion, exactly sixteen years before. Poko also knew through the older Noans about the existence of a hiding place under the temple. And, from his point of view, there would be no better place to hide and keep a secret.

Remembering what his father had said, Poko told his friends about the vehicle, emphasizing how it was able to move both along the ground and in water, in addition to flying. It would be the perfect way to travel over the Continent, if they were really interested in taking a risk.

"Why did you never tell us about this, Poko?" asked Aron.

"Now I understand why Granddad always prevented us from entering the temple alone", said Makuro. "He was afraid we would find the hiding place".

"And then we would find the vehicle."

"Calm down", said Tork. "You don't know whether this vehicle really exists or whether there is really a hiding place".

"But didn't you see the scared crowd running into the temple? There really must be a secret hiding place!" said Poko.

Aron took the lead.

"There is only one way to find out".

"Don't rush into it", warned Makuro. "Even if we find this vehicle, we have no idea of how we can make it work".

They carried on the discussion a little more until Tork said:

"I know . . ." he said, with his head down.

They all looked at him.

"How can you pilot a vehicle you've never seen?" asked Aron.

"I just know in theory. I learned from grandfather in one of my mechanics classes. But I've never seen or touched a machine like this. But don't worry. It can't be too difficult".

"When shall we do it?" asked Poko, restless.

"Wait!" shouted Aron. "First we must know whether Tork is on our side. We must know whether he will go together with us, or whether he will stay here holding the old man's toga". And he held out his hand to Tork, challenging him. "What do you say?"

Tork thought a little and then shook his brother's hand.

"I'll join you just to prove that our grandfather is telling the truth. If I need to risk my life for this, let it be so".

"Great! So let's begin tonight, when everyone is asleep. But before that we need to admit our guilt to the tribe for yesterday's misunderstanding, as the old man wishes". Aron turned to Makuro and Poko. "A deal?"

They put their hands on top of each other and lifted them up high to seal the agreement.

At midday the Ruakan bugles sounded once again. This time it was not the warning of a real or false invasion, but a call for everyone to see the boys apologize before the tribe. Shortly after, the natives crowded around the scaffold outside the temple. Some were there just out of curiosity, but others were there to hurl abuse at the boys.

Miku and Hanara were at the front of the crowd.

Without his losing confidence, Aron took Makuro and Poko on to the scaffold. The natives were angry, banging their saucepans in protest. They were ready to boo. Many could not wait and started booing before they began to speak.

Aron took a deep breath, trying to keep his leg, which was trembling with anxiety, still, and then he improvised a speech.

"My dear neighbors, mother, grandfather and friends, if anyone is to take the blame for last night's trick, it is I. Poko and Makuro had nothing to do with the huge lack of respect that was shown to our community. I was angry as my grandfather had given all his attention to my younger brother, and I admit I was wrong in trying to show him up in front of you. I tried to show the tribe that Tork is naïve. Now I realize that it is I who am naïve."

"I also apologize for not valuing our grandfather, who has devoted himself to teaching the young men in the village. I also apologize to my mother for being introverted and not sharing with her my moments of joy and pain, and to my brother Tork, for having betrayed him and having mocked his belief."

"I promise that, from now on, I shall try to change my behavior and think about the consequences of what I do. I apologize to you all". Aron lowered his head on finishing, trying to hide his grin.

The Noans accepted his apology. He had said little in a short speech, but if he were telling the truth, his repentance was proven, and his error was forgiven. Miku ran up to embrace him. Hanara was happy, but somewhat suspicious of his behavior. He could not believe that Aron could lose his arrogance so quickly.

Things got back to normal, and the natives went back to their houses as it was lunch time. Poko accepted the invitation to feast in the house of the white-skins and went there after being told off by his parents.

While they were sitting at the low table in the kitchen, a discussion between Miku and Aron began:

"I'm very proud of you, my son", said Miku, as she took a chicken wing. "I've always thought you were a spoiled boy, but today you showed you are a man, when you admitted it was all your fault".

Aron looked seriously from over his dish.

"Spoiled? Mother, you don't know anything about your sons. You never worried. If it hadn't been for Granddad, my brothers and I would not even know how to speak the language of the tribe. You stay here all day long lying down with the nurses at your beck and call and you tell me that I'm spoiled?".

"That was your father's wish, before he died: to give all the responsibility of bringing you up to your grandfather", said Miku.

"And the secrets you've been hiding from us? And this thing you have on the back of your neck. Do you think I've never seen it? Our father might even be alive, and we are here, unable to do anything."

Makuro and Poko looked at each other, both amazed. Aron should not have revealed his suspicions to Miku, and neither should he have said that he knew about the connector, especially today, when they were just about to set off to unknown lands.

Miku gave the impression she had not understood:

"What are you talking about?" she said, avoiding the eyes of her sons, and filling her plate for a second time.

"The black circle full of holes on the back of your neck. Are you going to tell me it's a birth mark?"

Miku became angry.

"Respect me. Keep your place. You know nothing about me or about my past."

Aron stood up, knocking over the chair and leaving his terracotta dish half full.

"This is our problem, mother. We know nothing about each other", he said, as he left the kitchen.

When she calmed down, Miku felt sorry. She had nearly revealed that she was not his real mother and was relieved she had managed to resist as this was something that should be told calmly and not in the middle of an angry argument.

"Be patient with Aron, mother", was the only thing Tork said during lunch.

Aron stayed with Daiara in their refuge at the top of the barn for the rest of the afternoon. Their fear of being discovered added spice to their relationship. Daiara was calm and understanding, the opposite of Aron, who was short-tempered and easy to anger. That very afternoon, Daiara had to listen to many complaints about the world, the leader, the community and Miku.

They were lying on the hay, Aron with his head on Daiara's lap while she caressed his hair. Her look was worried. She stared through the window at the hill beyond the pasture, anxious and indecisive. Aron realized that something was worrying her as her heart was beating fast.

"Something is wrong", he said. "Any problem?"

"Darling," she looked down. "I know you are having a lot of problems with your family, but we must talk about things".

"If you intend to go back to all that about bringing our relationship into the open, forget it. Your parents and my grand-father would never accept it, and I would have to stop seeing you."

Daiara was offended.

"We will not stop seeing each other. They must know that we like each other. Makuro and Poko already know we're together, and so does my sister Jana. They are not worried about our relationship."

"Poko is my best friend", said Aron, "and Makuro is my favorite brother. They will always support me. Their opinions don't matter".

"But it is exactly their opinions that matter", Daiara contradicted him. "We must only be worried about those that worry about us. The others can go to hell!"

Aron was surprised as he had never heard her speaking like this. And she continued:

"Ah, Aron, how I would love to tell everyone that we are together. We don't need their approval. We will stay together anyway, whether they like it or not."

"If we don't need their approval, then why should they know?"

"Because I'm sick of having to hide!"

Aron took his head from her lap and sat up.

"Look, Daiara. I can't talk about it right now. I need to straighten my thoughts out to help my brothers. Leave me alone, won't you?"

"Your brothers, your brothers, always your brothers in first place! I'm going to give you something that will straighten your thoughts out!" Daiara thought, bitterly.

"Whatever you wish", she said. "But yesterday I discovered something I must tell you about".

"If it's about me spying on Tork's training, you know it is a lie. Don't believe anything they tell you. I'm not jealous of my brother. I like to see it when he makes a mistake and my grand-father hits him on..."

"That is not it!" Daiara was getting angry. "It's something much more serious".

"Will I get angry?" Aron asked.

"I think so."

Aron began to get worried.

"What is it?"

Daiara lowered her head, not knowing whether she should tell him or not. She preferred not to hesitate. She had reached this point and could not go back. She looked at him again and confessed:

"My period is three weeks late."

"What do you mean?"

"I'm pregnant, Aron. Pregnant!"

He stopped still a while, with his eyes opened round like the full moon.

"Don't joke about this", he muttered. "I'm not ready to be a father."

"But you are going to be one."

"No, I can't be a father to this child. Let's speak to Poko's mother. We can trust her. She will know what to do. The nurses will help you to have an abortion."

"I don't want an abortion, Aron, I'm sure. I want to have this child. If we have a child, they will be obliged to accept us. A child would change everything!"

Aron did not move.

"Leave me alone. I must think."

"I'm leaving, but I will not look for you again", said Daiara, firmly. "We won't see each other until you decide. It's your decision. If you don't accept our relationship, I'll have this child alone, and everyone will know who the father is. If you wish to talk, you know where to find me. I'll be at home with my family. Knock on the door, ask to come in, and enter".

Daiara climbed down the ladder and returned to the village, preventing herself from crying. She had done something wrong, terribly wrong, but now she had begun there was no return. She had spent the previous night thinking of a way to make him accept their relationship. She had told her sister Jana, who had advised her to tell the lie. There was nothing growing in her womb, but a pregnancy would be the best way to get him to make up his mind. But this plan was too Machiavellian for her and, while she was on her way home, her conscience was hammering in her head. If Aron discovered, he would never forgive her or see her with the same eyes again. But now it was too late.

The sun had gone down, giving way to the blanket of night. It was nearly time to act. Lying down on the hay, Aron reasoned to himself. He felt that the world was disappearing under his feet. He didn't need any more worries, whatever they were. And this would be something to talk about another day, and not the very day he was ready to set off on his adventure with his brothers and friend. He could not, or *did not* want to accept Daiara as a girlfriend, but a pregnancy? "A child would really change this", he said to himself. "What would be the reaction of Hanara or Miku when it became impossible to hide?"

With conflicting thoughts, Aron left the barn and hurried along the road to return to the village, crouching behind the walls of the temple, the place he would meet Poko and the rest. The recent news had made him vulnerable, and he even thought of not setting off on the journey. "And what if Hanara is right? What if they die trying to reach the Continent? And what if his son grew up without a father, as he did?"

Suddenly Aron felt a tap which made him shiver.

"Thinking about life?" joked Poko and the brothers. "Are you ready?"

Aron looked up.

"Yes, I am", he said, trying to concentrate. "Let's go ahead".

"That's the way to speak!"

"Did you bring everything I asked?"

"It's all here", replied Poko, opening his backpack. In it there were some food, a canteen of water, the old binoculars, some home-made matches (made with fermented urine and sand), a machete, rope, an oil lantern and a number of tran-quilizing darts, which Poko had taken without his father's per-mission.

The four of them hid in the shadow and crept around the walls of the temple. When they were passing within the range of vision of the north tower, they stopped and only went on when the sentry was distracted, to reach the curving front façade.

From there, they could see the side entrance, which was closed, and protected by two warriors armed with spears, something which rarely happened.

"I think it's better to go back", whispered Aron, who was still anxious.

"Why?" asked Poko, behind him.

"Can't you see? There are two warriors protecting the temple. There is no way we can pass. Grandfather must be suspicious of something and has reinforced security. Maybe we should put off the plans to another day".

"We are not going to give up", said Poko, decided. "We can wait the whole night for a chance, if necessary".

They didn't do anything for a long time, avoiding talking as much as possible. After almost two hours waiting, one of the warriors left his position, apparently to go to the toilet, leaving his partner alone in front of the temple doors.

"Now!" whispered Aron.

Poko knelt down on one knee and took the pack from his back, taking out a tranquilizing dart and a bamboo blowpipe. He set up the blowpipe and put it between his lips. He aimed and then blew the dart at the warrior. The wind blew the dart to the side, making it hit the door jamb.

"How stupid you are, Poko!" Aron hit him on the forehead. "How can you be a hunter, if you can't hit such a big target at such a short distance?"

"I'm sorry. It was because of the wind."

The warrior protected himself under the entrance and whistled to warn the patrolmen who were on their round. The natives held out their weapons and organized themselves in pairs, releasing the hities from their chains. They began a careful search of the alleys, communicating by whistles.

"Quick!" said Tork. "Let's climb onto the roof of the temple, before they find us".

"Great idea", said Makuro.

They went around the walls once again, looking for the lowest part of the roof. They climbed up on to the tiles by getting onto the shoulders of Aron, who was the tallest. The three of them climbed up and Aron stayed on the ground, trying to reach up to Makuro's hand as he was not strong enough to climb up.

"Quick, Aron", said Makuro. "Hold my hand."

Aron was looking for a block or stump which would help him climb up when one of the patrolmen came out of the shadows and pulled his clothes. He held up his fist and threatened to hit him. But before the first blow, a dart hit him in the neck. The effect was immediate, and Aron could feel his rotten breath before he fell into the sand.

"Thank you, Poko. Your aim is getting better", Aron made a great effort to praise him, as he was still trembling. "I owe you a favor".

Tork and Makuro managed to take the rope out of their bag and pulled him up. The body of the patrolman was lying on the ground, under the effect of the tranquilizer, while the boys crawled up on to the top of the roof near the observation tower. They took off a number of tiles and went in through the hole.

Now, inside the temple, they were on top of a wooden beam, which was so old that it was a miracle that it could stand their weight and not break. Their only obstacle now was to climb down to the floor and discover the entrance to the hiding place.

It was dark inside the temple. They looked down into the deep. They seemed to be a long way from the ground. Poko got the lantern, struck a match, lighting up just a small area around the beam. Three meters to the left, Tork saw a chain hanging from the ceiling, holding an ancient looking chandelier.

Tork was agile and fit after his hu-tae-mui training, and this allowed him to find a solution. He went back in order to get more thrust. He then was able to run a short distance and jump towards the chain, managing to hold on to it and make it swing from one side to another.

With the pendulum-like movements, Tork managed to bring the chain nearer the beam, which the boys could now hold on to, and, one by one, move on to the chandelier, from where they would have a three meter fall to the ground. Poko needed to hang on to one of the branches of the chandelier to let go, as he was afraid from jumping from such a height, which made Aron laugh.

When on the ground, Makuro went on ahead, searching all over with the lantern. They looked in every corner of the room for the hiding place: the shattered stained-glass windows, the bits of glass all over the floor, the rotten chairs, the melted wax in the candlesticks and the plaster statues, which had become dark with time.

Poko found a small sharp marble idol, weighing some seven kilos, on the altar. He picked it up and examined it from all sides. It slipped from his hands and made a thud as it fell to the floor. As it reverberated on the floor, Tork suspected that the floor was hollow.

"There must be a secret room underneath", he said.

Tork approached, moved the altar aside and there it was, underneath. He found the iron trap-door, which covered the entrance to the underground chamber.

He crouched and slipped away the metal cover with his hands, revealing a spacious rectangular opening. There was a staircase going down into the darkness. Aron grabbed the

lantern from Makuro and began to go down. The rest followed him.

Down below there was a real medieval dungeon, a damp
maze full of tunnels. The light of the lantern was reflected in
the drops of water on the spider webs, making them seem like
tiny pearls. The smell of monoxide gas filled the place, and
they felt dizzy.

"I don't think I'll be able to stay here", said Poko. "This
smell is making me sick!"

The chamber was big enough for all the native community,
but it was no bigger than the temple which had been built on
top of it. Aron lifted the lantern up to his eyes and went down
one of the tunnels. But there was nothing to find as its exit
was blocked by a high stone wall.

They discovered another tunnel, which was also blocked,
but, at its end, they found a wagon on its side and what
seemed to be the remains of an iron track. They came back
again. Makuro took the lantern and lit up the ground to look
for more the track. And, before them, they found the track in
front of the entrance to the eastern tunnel.

"Let's go down here", he said. "The track must take us
somewhere".

They went through two smaller chambers and along various forking paths, always following the track, and finally
arriving in front of a large wooden door, locked by bars and
iron chains, which were joined by a large silver lock.

Makuro leaned on the bars.

"They are locked", he said.

"So what should we do?" asked Poko, losing confidence.
"What's the plan now?"

"This seems to be the end of the line, boys. I think it is better to go back", said Aron, turning around, still anxious about
Daiara's pregnancy.

Tork had not come all this way to stop. He picked up two rusty nails from the ground and put them in the hole of the lock.

"What are you doing?" asked Aron.

"One day," said Tork, "I saw Granddad opening a trunk belonging to someone who had lost her keys. He turned two pieces of wire around inside the lock and managed to open it."

"And you think you can do the same?" wondered his brother. "Let's go away. The adventure is over".

"We can't stop now", said Poko. "We must first check where the other tunnels go to".

"Forget the other tunnels!" shouted Aron. "Can't you see how secure they've made this door? It is obvious there is something important behind it".

"I've had a brainwave", said Makuro.

Makuro pushed Tork away and tried to pull the bars at with his hands. It was difficult, but they had become rusty because of the damp.

He took off his T-shirt, rolled it up in his hands, pulling one of the bars up and down. And after doing this a number of times, it broke. He put the bar inside the closed padlock and, by banging the stake with a stone for almost ten minutes, he managed to break open the lock.

"Did you see that?" he said as he took a deep breath and wiped his face with his T-shirt. "It was easier that way."

They boys looked at each other, took the chains away and opened the door.

Behind it there was a dark room. Tork held his arm out and felt the wall to find a switch. When he found it, the generator started its engines, turning on the ventilators, making the monoxide gas quickly disappear. On the ceiling, a row of phosphorescent lights turned on.

Now everything was lit up the boys could see much more than a grey room made of concrete blocks. It was a secret laboratory with glass pieces and test tubes everywhere. Around the walls, there were a large number of metal shelves full of jars with chemicals. In one corner, there was a metal locker and in another an ultracentrifuge used to enrich uranium. In the center of the room there was a large shape, covered by a dusty canvas.

Tork entertained himself with a bubbling liquid that was running through a transparent hose, feeding the generator. Aron picked up a number of unlabeled jars from the shelves, while Makuro looked at the doors of the locker and tried to open them.

Poko went to the canvas sheet in the middle of the room and lifted one of its corners. Underneath it, there was something covered in gold-colored metal. Poko pulled the cover away, producing a cloud of dust. He sneezed five times, but when the dust was sucked out by the ventilators no words could express what he saw.

There it was, on the floor of the laboratory, the Hati transport vehicle, which for him was highly sophisticated and complex.

Aron immediately put the jars down.

"My God!" he said. "Look at that!"

The vehicle was old and had not been used for a long time, but its engines must be working. Makuro was impressed by the size of the turbines. Tork leant over and read the instructions on the control panel, but did not dare to touch it. Poko fingered the barrel of the machine gun attached to the side of the panel. He supposed that it was a weapon, but Makuro prevented him from testing it.

Aron examined the synthetic material which lined the seats.

"We're lucky", He said. "The vehicle has four seats. We can travel in comfort!"

"But how are we going to take this monster up there? "asked Makuro, stroking the chrome metal surface.

"Have you forgotten that it floats?" remembered Tork.

"Tork, turn out the lantern", ordered Makuro. "You're wasting its fuel. We might need it in the *unknown lands*", these last words came out like the sound of a flute.

Aron tapped on the shoulder of his younger brother:

"Good, Tork", he said. "We have little time. Let's begin."

Tork agreed, leaned over the panel and began to study how the buttons and levers worked, while the others continued exploring the room.

In a box on the shelves, Aron found a number of shiny crystals. Makuro looked at the spiral shape of the glass tubes while Poko tried to open the locker doors, which made a grating noise.

"Stop this noise!" scolded Aron. "Do you want them to find out?"

"I can't open the locker!" explained Poko.

"So don't open it. What could there be of importance in an old locker?"

"The history books which had disappeared", asserted Makuro.

He ran out of the laboratory to get the iron bar with which he had broken the padlock. He tried to wedge it between the hinges of the locker, but it was too thick.

"Tork, see if you can open the locker with those nails, as you tried to do with the padlock".

Tork did not reply, as he was concentrating on the control panel of the machine and trying to start it up.

In one of the corners, Poko found a box of tools, full of various keys, drills, hammers, welding material, an electric drill and a small crowbar.

"We can open the locker with these tools", he said, happy to find them.

Makuro picked up the crowbar and tried to put it in the locker. However, before being able to force its hinges, a strong vibration came into the room. The turbines of the vehicle were furiously turning around, making an enormous noise and shattering various glass jars.

"All aboard!" shouted Tork, joyfully turning the hand accelerator.

"Wait!" shouted Makuro, covering his ears, trying to speak above the sound of the turbines. "We must get the lost books. We need to open the locker".

"There is no time!" said Aron, sitting down on one of the seats. "Wait until we get back".

Makuro, unwillingly got into the vehicle, fastened his seatbelt. Tork pulled the lever, and strong jets of wind were blown down, forming an air cushion which pushed the vehicle up from the ground.

When he unlocked the accelerator, the vehicle jerked violently backwards, banging into the shelves and knocking over various boxes and jars. With this abrupt movement, the boys were thrust back and hit their heads.

"Forgive me", said Tork.

The direction levers were carefully handled, allowing the vehicle to leave the laboratory. They went through the tunnels and reached the chamber. The passage to the temple was very narrow for such a big machine, but with a little care, it was possible for it to go up the staircase and through the trap door.

Now they were in the temple, the only problem would be the gates which protected the exit.

Tork discovered the triggers of the machine guns which were behind the direction levers, and on the panel he found the key for the front missile launching cannon.

He only needed to fire one missile to smash the doors through which they went to the outside square. The warriors who were protecting the temple outside had to jump away to protect themselves from the flying splinters of wood and not be seriously hurt.

The sound of the explosion woke up the community and warned the patrolmen on their round. The majority of frightened Noans rushed into the square, fearing a Hati invasion or another of Aron's tricks. This time they would not forgive him.

When Hanara appeared in the crowd, a large object with its own light quickly appeared through the hole in the temple doors. It broke through the floor at high speed and disappeared out of sight as it passed through the eastern entrance to the village.

The natives could not understand what it was, as the vehicle was so fast that no one could see who or what it was.

Hanara was worried. He looked at Miku and put a hand on her shoulder.

"They already know too much, my dear", he said. "We cannot do anything else. May the spirit of Sakyamuni protect our boys . . ."

When everything calmed down, Hanara went into the temple and climbed down into the hiding place. He saw that the generator was still working. His laboratory was now a complete mess: pieces of glass everywhere, tools all over the floor, and a number of shelves had come loose or had fallen down. His greatest worry was that the boys had seen what was inside the locker. He was happy it was still closed, but the crowbar in the doors worried him.

He closed the laboratory door from inside in order to be alone, and took out a bunch of keys from his case. He opened the locker and saw that everything was in place: the pieces of uranium were still piled up on the top, the Myra language dictionaries were in the bottom part, a number of books were in boxes and there was something long, wrapped in a piece of filthy cloth, which was standing upright.

Hanara picked up the object and closed the locker. The object protected by its dirty cloth was part of his past, and it would no longer be secure there.

Hanara managed to push the locker away with his shoulders. Behind it there was a riveted steel door, round like a hatch, and as secure as a safe. He turned the pressure valve and typed a password into the console. The door opened slowly, creaking and showing the entrance to the uranium mines.

The mines were an old Hati reserve, which had been abandoned as a result of the shortage of raw material. Nobody in the tribe knew of their existence, and few were worried about how Hanara had got the uranium. No one had been down there for a long time, but the lifts still worked, and their pulleys also seemed to be working.

Hanara turned on his flashlight and went into one of the lifts, slowly disappearing into the dark. There, the smell of sulfur was unbearable and there was no way to purify it, making him cover his nostrils with his hands.

The lift arrived. Hanara went to one of the rocky walls and hid the object behind the cracks between the salt crystals. He took off his hat and pulled out the four-pin plug which was hidden under its straw. He lifted up his long white hair, pressing the device against the holes in the back of his neck and connecting it. He turned on the plug with his first finger and clearly remembered the place with his eyes, as if he was taking a photo. And then he hid the plug once again in his hat, after having said some words in Hati.

He was turning to go back to the lift, when he decided to take one last look at the object.

He picked it up once again and took away the cloth. He proudly lifted it up high. It was a sword, a katana, which had been forged in pure gold. Its hilt was in the shape of a serpent dragon, which had been sculpted in jade and whose mouth was turned to the blade, spitting out fire all over the blade. Hanara shivered and trembled when he looked at it. It still shone brightly in the dark.

If the secrets of the sword were known, many people would give their lives for it.

Hanara dried a tear with the dirty cloth and wrapped it up once again, putting it back in its hiding place. He went back to the lift and went up out of the mine, closing the entrance with the steel door and the locker. And then he left the under-ground passageways. He now believed that the sword was protected against the curiosity of his grandsons, or anything else that might happen . . .

CHAPTER 7

EGGS IN THE NEST

For the fifth time, in almost four hours, Aron asked his brother to have a look at the map on the screen, which was generated by the on-board radar.

"It looks as if we should have been crossing the Tetis hours ago" he said.

"Don't worry" said Tork. "The map tells us that in less than fifteen minutes we will reach the west coast and see the ocean."

They crossed a number of small savannahs and went down the sierra, reaching sea level. Dawn was coming. In a distance, the never ending Tetis Ocean could be seen reflecting the first sun beams.

They reached the shore and parked near the sea. They got out of the vehicle and sat down on the beach, feeling the icy-wind in their faces. Tork put his arms behind his head and breathed in deeply.

"It seems you are right, not our grandfather" he said, amazed by the feeling of freedom.

"Why have you said this?" asked Makuro.

"This vehicle . . . This machine . . . It is so technologically advanced. A society which has a weapon like this won't easily be exterminated. It is not logical that the Noans are the only survivors."

"Maybe our tribe was not so involved in the war that it was exterminated" said Makuro. "In addition, we don't know the weapons of the rival society, or even its strategic ability . . . Damn it! If only I'd taken those books which had disappeared . . . Granddad didn't want us to find out the truth. I bet there is another hidden society . . ."

"If there is, it is in the Forbidden Continent" deduced Aron. "And we shall find it."

"You can bet on that" encouraged Poko.

Soon a large golden blob appeared on the horizon, and the boys were able to see the black sky change to red. The sun did not only bring the light and heat which they needed so much, but also a guiding point while they were on the water. The satellite receiver was not able to show a complete map in the vehicle as it was partially blurred. The only working instrument was the on-board radar, though there was also a compass, which was old and losing its magnetism.

"Get up" ordered Aron. "Let's go."

The boys were tired and overcome by sleep, but did not flag. They got up, and soon the vehicle was making a straight line over the waves of the Tetis. Soon they were on the high sea, and the waters became calmer. The Kafria coast could no longer be seen, and the birds completely disappeared from the sky.

A number of drophins and balerias came out of the deep, singing their sea shanties as if they wanted to welcome the visitors. Poko always pointed them out when he saw them spraying huge quantities of water when they swung and swayed their tails.

"According to the books I studied," said Makuro, "balerias and drophins are large aquatic mammals, which have developed from whales and dolphins.

Poko held out his arm to stroke the head of a small drophin, who was swimming near the vehicle, but he was soon told off by the angry mother drophin, who spat out a jet of water into his face, making his friends giggle. While all this was taking place, Aron forgot that he would soon become a father.

Time went by and they were now approaching nearer the unknown land. They enjoyed singing a song which they had been taught when children, called *Islands from the Topsail*, a song about journeys and acts of courage.

Some hours later, Tork turned the lights on. The sky went dark again, and he was the only one who had been awake during all of the journey. His brothers were drooling in the back seats and Poko was snoring out loud. Tork had not slept for two days and this hampered his reflexes.

He once again examined the control panel and found the automatic pilot system. After turning it on, he joined the others in a deep sleep.

But, unfortunately, Tork did not see that, when touching the commands, he accidentally turned off the laser mapping system, responsible for making the vehicle deviate from obstacles. In the sea this was not important as its waters were on a level and there were no barriers. But on land this could result in a serious accident.

Tork, without realizing his mistake, slept deeply, and during all Friday night, not even the strong gusts of wind or cold raindrops could wake them up.

Many miles on, Aron woke with a start. The sky was clear once again. It was now a new day, Saturday, and a strong vibration in the vehicle woke him up. He sat up and noticed that no one was piloting. Tork was sleeping in the front seat. The surroundings which previously had been a huge blue ocean were now a fine sand beach, and in front of them there was a huge tropical forest, surrounded by high palms and fruit trees.

There was no time for Aron to warn Tork. In a few seconds, the vehicle went into the forest, made its way through the branches and collided with the protruding roots of a fig tree. The high speed crash made the vehicle flip over various times in the air and, on falling, its front fell into the muddy waters of a swamp.

The soldering which held the front seat of Poko split. Poko was thrown a great distance, and the seat flew over him. His landing was softened by the bushes, but the metal seat fell on his leg, hitting him heavily below the thigh. Poko closed his eyes and cried out in pain.

Aron and Tork were thrown forward. Aron fell on his belly, his face against the ground, and Tork fell on top of him. They were dragged along the sand for some twenty feet, until they absorbed the impact, almost reaching the thorny branches of a rose bush.

It was Makuro who was least hurt. He was attached to the vehicle by his seatbelt and was not injured. The front of the machine was now sinking into the mud and making bubbles. Makuro unfastened his seatbelt and jumped onto dry land shortly before the vehicle sank into the swamp. And as it they sank, the turbines threw a large amount of mud into the air, making Makuro as muddy as if he had been in the swamp. He took off his dirty T-shirt and tied it to his waist. There was a purple mark on his waist, which had been caused by the pressure of the seatbelt.

Tork got up, noticing that his elder brother had softened his fall. He turned him over onto his back and was worried when he saw that Aron was unconscious and had a deep cut on his forehead, and might be seriously hurt.

But Tork left his brother when he heard the desperate shouts of Poko, who was trying to free his leg which was stuck under the seat.

"Are you okay?" Tork asked.

"Yes . . . but I think I've broken my leg" Poko replied.

"Are you all okay?" asked Makuro.

"Go and look at Aron" said Tork. "It seems that he's fainted."

"Don't worry. I'm fine" said Aron, staggering behind the rose bush, wiping the wound on his forehead with a piece of material he had torn from his clothing.

"Help me to pull Poko out" asked Tork.

Makuro spat on his hands and rubbed them. He put a piece of wood on a stone to use as a lever and, while Aron helped him to lift up the seat, Tork pulled Poko out of the pieces of broken metal.

When he saw his friend's swollen leg, Makuro decided that it was not fractured, and he was proved right when Poko stood up without needing too much help.

Tork gave him two long branches, which he could use as crutches, and they went into the forest, abandoning the vehicle in the swamp. The only compass they had was in the vehicle, so that they walked without realizing they could get lost. The forest was thick and dark and formed a green roof overhead. There were a large number of fallen trunks full of mushrooms, and butterflies flew in and out of the beams of light which came in from the sun. They walked to the north, and the oxygen filled air gave them strength to walk on.

A scab began to form on Aron's forehead, attracting a number of botflies. Poko was limping, with his swollen leg tied with the strips of cloth, which Makuro had torn off his T-shirt.

They had now walked a certain distance from the shore and were talking about the accident. Tork did not feel he was to blame, but Aron was the first to accuse him.

"It was Tork's fault. He slept while piloting."

"But before falling asleep I turned on the automatic pilot" Tork defended himself. "The vehicle is old. Its instruments could have made a mistake."

"We'd better not blame each other" said Makuro. "It's no good crying over spilt milk. The important thing is that we are all okay . . ."

"I'm not!" Poko put up his finger.

"The best thing now" continued Makuro, without listening to Poko "would be to think about we are going to get back. The vehicle has sunk into the swamp, and this must have damaged the turbines."

"We are not going to return" said Aron.

"And how are we going to live?"

"The forest will be our home. The trees will be our houses. The sky will be our roof. The animals will be our neighbors and food."

"Talking about this... What is there left to eat?" asked Poko, ignoring what Aron had said.

Tork took off his backpack and looked inside.

"Everything is finished!"

"What?" asked Aron.

"We ate it on the way."

"Impossible. We couldn't have eaten everything. This bag is so big!"

"Stop arguing, you two!" Makuro interrupted again. "Look upwards, the whole place can be eaten. There must be fruits whose name we don't even know, in any of our languages."

The group stopped talking and carried on walking. Some steps ahead, Poko had the feeling that he was being observed, and this feeling was increased by the silence. Only the insects flapping their wings, the songs of the birds, and the rustling of the dry leaves could be heard. Poko looked suspiciously to his right. Nothing could be seen, only high trees, hanging lianas and leaves and more leaves. He looked to the left and also found nothing. When he looked down, Poko could see something crawling through the dry leaves on the ground, following them.

Poko first thought it was a snake, but soon changed his mind when he realized that the thing was made up of flexible metal rings, with an optic lens at the front. This thing could only have been manufactured by human hands, and it was not a strange animal. When it noticed that Poko was looking at it, the thing quickly buried itself in the leaves and disappeared.

"Did you see it?"

"What?"

Poko shook his head.

"Forget it. Whatever it was, apparently it was not dangerous."

They had now walked a long way and it was impossible to know whether they were going to North. The path opened out and went up a steep slope full of mossy stones. They were now breathing heavily, and they realized the similarity between the air in Kafria and that in the Continent.

"Hey, we've not been walking for more than six hours and I can't see any contamination in the air here." Poko was the first to comment on this.

"Now you've noticed?" said Aron, disinterested.

Makuro looked at his brother.

"Satisfied, Tork?" he asked.

"Why?" Tork replied.

"With the proof that Granddad's teaching is false."

"What proof?"

"Look around you. Life is normal here. I can see insects, birds and some reptiles. The dense layer of radiation which everyone is afraid of is no more than a legend. I think there has never been a war here."

"Look, Mak. I think you're being naïve," said Tork. "If there was no war, then how did the blue sky of the ancient world become the red that we see now?"

"I don't know" said Makuro. "But I know it wasn't because of the supposed war, which didn't take place. Tork, look. Where did the atmospheric radiation that everyone talks about go to? We can see that this radiation does not exist. And I bet it never existed."

"Yes, it did" said Tork. "But with time it came up from the ground and went high up in the sky. It might be the origin of the red color of our atmosphere."

"This is all very strange. There must be an explanation. When we return, I'll tell our grandfather to return the books which have disappeared."

"Stop arguing, you two" said Aron severely. "You're making me lose patience. Thinking too much will not help us to understand the mysteries of our Era. In addition, we are having a unique experience. So, take advantage of it. Don't waste this moment by asking useless questions we can't find the reply to."

"Aron is right" said Poko. "This is something for you to talk about in the future with your grandfather, and not here in the forest. There are more immediate problems to worry about."

Makuro and Tork shut up and continued walking along the path, climbing the slope until they were exhausted. Poko once again complained about his hunger.

Tork climbed up a tree and went up to its highest branches, picked its fruit and threw them down to the ground for his brothers to collect. But before climbing down, he used the height of the tree to orient himself in the forest. The sea was a long way to the East, showing that they had deviated a little from the path and had gone to the West. In front of them, there was a wide valley with waterfalls coming out of the rocks. He thought that, if they continued the path, they would reach the valley in just two hours.

He climbed down and gave the news.

The boys put the leftover fruit in the backpack and carried on. They managed to walk fasted, though their speed depended on Poko's huge effort to drag his injured leg along. They walked, walked, and walked. The beams of light which came through the trees were losing their strength. It was getting dark, and there was no sign of the valley.

"Are you sure that you saw a valley?" asked Poko, suddenly sitting down and putting his crutches on the ground.

"Yes" replied Tork. "But from up above it didn't seem to be so far off . . ."

"I think we have already come a long way, boys" said Makuro, tired. "I think it's better to go back."

"Go back how?" asked Aron. "There's no way to go away. We're stuck in this place. We'll never manage to repair the vehicle or even get it out of the swamp"

"We still have the machete and the rope" remembered Makuro. "We can cut down some trees and make a raft."

"And you intend to return to Kafria on a raft?" asked Aron, amazed. "Cross the Great Tetis Ocean on a raft? You're crazy!"

"It's an idea..."

"A stupid idea! Even if we don't get lost on the high sea, it will take months. Even if we manage to fish to survive, which will be difficult, we will have to take more than a hundred liters of drinking water with us! There is no way we could store so much water. We've only brought a small canteen."

Makuro looked at Aron, admiringly.

"I can see you understand something about survival" he said.

"I just know that you can't drink sea water, but I don't know the reason."

"The reason is simple: your body dehydrates."

Poko did not find any logic in his friend's reply.

"How can your body dehydrate if you're drinking water?" he asked. "Even if it's salty, water is water, isn't it?"

"Salt harms your body" explained Makuro. "When found in large quantities, the organism needs to eliminate it in your urine. And for each liter of salty water you drink, you need two liters to eliminate all the salt. Therefore, if you drink a liter of sea water, you will lose two liters of water, and your body will dehydrate. Understand?"

Poko thought a little.

"So what can we do?" he then asked.

"At the moment, we need to find somewhere to sleep. It is getting very dark. Let's decide tomorrow."

It really was very dark, and the forest was losing its usual sounds. Only the chirp of the crickets, the warbles of the night birds, and a number of distant howls, similar to the sounds of coyotes, could be heard. They continued walking, but could soon see nothing nearby, apart from the light of an occasional glowworm.

"Tork, turn the lantern on" asked Aron. "We can't carry on in the darkness. We must find some shelter soon."

"The lantern shattered when we crashed" said Tork, feeling the broken glass at the bottom of the backpack.

"So, get the machete. We'll have to cut down some wood and make a fire."

Half an hour later a bright fire flamed up in the middle of the forest. Animals fled from its light and hid in their dens. They roasted the fruit leftover in the backpack and soon needed to get more. They talked for some time and slept on the ground covered by the leaves. The heat of the fire warmed them and kept the beasts of prey away. That night no one needed to keep guard.

The following day, Poko woke up early. He lifted his head and stretched, muffling a cry as he tried to stretch his leg. The fire had now gone out, and his friends were still asleep, except Tork, who could not be found anywhere. He could feel that something was moving under the leaves on the ground.

He stood up and swept away the leaves with his crutches, becoming surprised again when he found the long metallic thing with an optic lens at the end.

"Wake up!" he shouted, looking at Aron and Makuro.

"What's up?" groaned Aron, opening his eyes.

But when Poko looked at the thing again, it had already disappeared.

"I don't know" he said. "But it is something very strange. There has been something following us since we came into the forest. We are being spied on."

"Ah, forget it. It must be your imagination..."

"Why so much noise?" asked Makuro, rubbing his eyes with his knuckles.

Tork suddenly reappeared, exhausted.

"Let's go" he said, taking a deep breath. "You need to see it. The valley is near. We only need to walk some two miles, following the path in that direction" and he pointed to the north-west.

Tork turned on his heels and went back along the same path, slowly followed by the other boys. After walking about fifteen minutes, they could hear the distant noise of the waterfalls. The thick vegetation was slowly opening out, and in a short time, the valley was visible. Aron opened the backpack and took out the old pairs of binoculars when he was near the edge of the cliff.

A river, which was receiving the water from the waterfalls, was flowing past them sixty feet below. There was a large amount of greenery and a number of caves in the rocks; rainbows were forming in the steam, and flocks of birds were merrily bathing and warbling.

Aron took off his shoes and began to climb down the cliff, holding on to the ledges and roots, and supporting himself on his heels. Poko found it difficult to climb down, and his crutches were useless on the muddy stones. Tork and Makuro tied the ropes to his waist and held him in case he slipped.

They went down slowly, legs first, on their backs. Aron was the first to get to the bottom of the cliff and jumped onto the ground, his bare feet hurting on the stones. Down in the valley, between the cliffs, there were a number of small ponds, full of mosquito larvae and tadpoles.

Aron took off his clothes and dived into the river. The water was cold, clean, and surrounded by the twisting branches which grew along the banks. High cliffs, shrouded in mist, with their peaks covered in ice, could be seen upstream, where a number of fish struggled to swim. Aron thought it would be easy to catch them when they were hungry.

The other boys had now made their way down and were also in the river. Poko was bathing the swelling in his leg and suggested Aron did the same with the cut in his forehead. Makuro sat down in the river and let the water cover him up to his neck, while Tork went into one of the waterfalls and felt the powerful stream of water hit the back of his neck. The noise produced a continuous echo behind him. Tork went to the other side of the waterfall and disappeared for a moment. When he returned, he went to the river to find his brothers.

"There is a cave behind the waterfall" he said, enthusiastically. "It's deep and dry, and protected by the waterfall. We can shelter there tonight."

"I don't know whether it's a good idea to sleep in a cave" said Makuro.

"But we need a shelter" continued Tork. "It's dangerous to sleep in the open air. We were lucky that nothing happened to us last night. Let's see if the cave is safe. And if it is, we'll spend the night inside."

"Let's not stay here in the valley" said Aron. "It's still early. We'll have to begin walking again soon . . ."

"Where to?" asked Tork. "It's no good walking blindly. We won't get anywhere. The Noans must be worried, let alone our mother. We must think of how we can store a lot of water if we have to cross the ocean on a raft."

"We'll stay here in the valley for just a few days" added Makuro. "There are fruit, fish, and drinking water, everything we need."

Aron thought a little and agreed.

"Let's see what the cave is like."

He got out of the river and put on his trousers. He went to the waterfall and looked inside, shivering as he felt the water falling on him. The cave was deep and dark. Inside, the air did not circulate, and the echo produced by the falling water gave him a strange feeling of *déjà vu.* It was as if the image of the cave had been recorded somewhere in his memory, and wanted to show him something from the past. "The subconscious is powerful", Hanara had once told him in his teaching.

Suddenly, the figure of Kliver passed before his eyes, but Aron was not able to remember the shape of his father. He was making an enormous effort to remember when Poko interrupted him:

"Don't stay here. Let's go."

Aron shook his head and finally entered the cave, accompanied by the boys, and their heads got wet as they went through the water. Poko felt the adrenaline flowing as goose pimples came up over his body. And he enjoyed the pleasant mixture of fear and excitement. There might be a large number of forms of life in a cave of that size.

The shadows slowly swallowed them up, and, when they looked behind them, the entrance became smaller and smaller.

"Keep still" Tork whispered to them.

"I can't stop shaking" said Poko.

Some yards ahead there was total darkness. A dripping which came down from the roof was enough to make their hearts beat faster, as it produced a loud echo. They went on slowly, step by step, feeling the walls so they could situate themselves.

Aron, who was ahead of the rest, reached the end of the cave. He held out his arm and felt just rock, no entrance they could follow. He felt a warm breath on his hand and felt his fingers touching something wet and sticky. He started. His fingers were touching a tongue!

Before he could think about it, there was a loud roar, followed by a strong shout of pain. A jaw closed on his hand,

and when he took his arm out, Aron felt the skin on his finger tearing.

"Run!" he shouted, his fear stronger than his pain.

They had walked into the cave in a line, but they now rushed out, each of them trying to save their own skin. Poko, who was behind them, was trampled on by the others, who quickly reached the exit and left him behind, alone in the darkness of the cave.

Outside, in the daylight, Aron shook his finger in the air to get rid of the pain. The blood was dripping out, forming a red track on the rock, which was soon washed away by the waters.

"Where's Poko?" asked Makuro.

"He stayed behind in the cave" replied Tork.

"He can't run!" remembered Makuro.

But before thinking about doing something to help him, they could see his shape coming through the waterfall, limping on his good leg.

"You were going to leave me there?" he shouted, angrily.

Then the waters of the waterfalls behind him gushed out violently on all sides. Poko slipped on the stones, but got up immediately and, forgetting his injury, began to run.

A pack of wild animals then rushed out of the cave, sniffing and snorting all the time. The boys desperately ran to the river, but the animals ran more quickly after them as the water was too shallow to prevent them from approaching. The animals surrounded them near a high rock on the opposite bank. There was nowhere they could escape to, no trees they could climb, or long branches they could use as weapons. They were cornered.

The animals seemed to be aggressive. They were bigger than wild boars and much stronger. They had fine honey-colored fur and horns which bent back behind their heads.

Their long canines could be seen coming out of their jaws. The six animals were sniffing the boys' fear, until their leader arrived.

And if these animals made the boys afraid, this was nothing compared to their leader, who was almost double the size of the rest, with long dark gray fur and a white back. It had huge curling horns, strong paws with curving claws, and canines which were like scythes. Its back sloped up slightly, showing his front paws to be thicker and shorter than the back ones.

The leader stared at them in fury. He prepared to attack, moving towards Tork, who confronted him fearlessly. He stopped halfway, sharpening his claws on the rocks, and let out a roar. All the other beasts roared together, in an orchestra of terror.

"We're dead!" shouted Aron, pale with fear.

Makuro and Tork said nothing. They remained still near the rock. Poko was pissing himself.

Aron gave the backpack to Poko.

"Quick, Poko. Take out a dart and blow it. Make them sleep before it's too late."

But Poko could not move.

"Come on, Poko. You can do it."

The bag fell out of Poko's hands and onto the ground. Aron felt his mouth dry. The beasts gave way to the leader, who placed himself at the head, glaring at Tork.

"Stop staring at him" asked Makuro.

"I cannot show I'm afraid" said Tork.

"But by staring at him, he will think you're challenging him" he insisted.

"I know what I'm doing. Believe in me."

Another roar announced the attack. While the largest animal was sharpening his claws, the others positioned themselves so their prey would not escape. The leader gave another shout and finally jumped at Tork, who defended himself by closing his eyes and lifting his arms to protect his face.

This scene seemed to have been projected in slow motion before their eyes.

At the moment the animal was jumping, a gigantic flying reptile captured the beast in its claws, flying with it to the shallow river and tore its flesh open with its teeth. The beast attempted to struggle and free itself, but could not defend itself against this gigantic predatory reptile monster. The waters of the river became red with blood. The other beasts were now afraid and ran off to the cave, amidst desperate howls.

The enormous reptile beat its wings and took off, taking its prey towards the mountains.

Poko sat on the ground and tried to get over the fright.

"What was that?" he asked, still trembling, urine running down his legs.

Makuro knew that there was no shame in pissing yourselves in such a dangerous situation. It was something perfectly normal, a natural defense of the organism, just like pain. The brain sends stimuli to the bladder, ordering it to empty. As a natural human, or rather mammal, instinct, the brain believes that by eliminating an excess of urine, the body will become lighter and will therefore become more able to run or confront a dangerous situation.

"What was that?" Poko repeated.

"I don't know" replied Aron. "But if there are such carnivorous birds here, it's better to get out!"

"That was not a bird" contradicted Makuro. "It's a reptile. I once read about them in a science book. It's a pterosaur."

"A what?" asked Poko, still ashamed of his survival instinct.

"It's not a bird" repeated Makuro. "Did you see any feathers or a beak? Pterosaurs are like flying dinosaurs."

"I don't know about you" said Aron. "But from what I know, dinosaurs stopped existing a long time ago, in a period when not even our most ancient ancestors existed."

"I also think it is inexplicable" agreed Makuro. "Animals do not regress with time, they evolve! But I must believe my eyes and what I saw."

At this moment, Aron had what seemed to be a good idea.

"What about climbing the mountain to look for its nest?" he asked.

They all looked at each other without understanding.

"If there's a nest, there must also be eggs. And we can get some of its eggs."

They still didn't understand.

"Don't you understand? These eggs are the proof that we were looking for to show that Granddad's teaching is false."

"And how will we return to Kafria?" asked Poko.

"We can lasso one of these ptro . . . pter . . . dinosaurs . . . and we can return to the old continent riding on its back . . ."

"That's the most stupid suicidal idea I've ever heard in my whole life" said Poko.

"But it makes sense" said Tork, and everyone looked at him. "Aron might be right."

"How can you say that?" continued Poko. "Has fear made you go crazy? We can never lasso one of these animals. We would be killed straightaway."

"Maybe not" said Tork. "Can't you remember? We often managed to tame wild bigbugs and other ferocious animals. The technique must be the same."

"I know" said Poko. "I could see the technique you were using to tame that last animal which almost tore your head off."

"He could sniff our fear. If we show confidence when we get to the nest, that flying reptile could easily be ours."

"If you want to die, so go on" said Poko. "But as you know, it will be difficult for me to climb a mountain with my leg like this. I'll stay on the ground while you go up."

"We could guess that" said Aron.

"How is your finger?" Makuro asked.

"Still bleeding . . ."

Makuro picked up a piece of cloth and gave it to his brother.

"Tie this to stop the bleeding."

Aron tied a knot on what was left over of his finger and they got dressed again. They picked up the backpack and went in the river, going upstream toward the mountains.

The forest was dense and difficult to get through, even though they were in the river. There were a number of fallen trunks, entwined with lianas and broken branches everywhere, making it difficult for them to go on. Tork was at the front, opening up the path with his machete. The more they walked, the further the mountains appeared. During their journey, their only worry was the insects, in addition to Poko's constant complaints.

The sun was setting when they found the lake into which the river flowed, at the foot of the mountain to which the huge flying reptile had taken its prey. Its peak was covered in snow, which made Makuro think of how strange it was that ice should form in a place where the climate is so warm.

The mountain was high, but its ascent did not seem so difficult, as there was a spiral path around it, as if someone had leveled it for some reason. Poko once again felt that he was being observed, but this time he didn't manage to find anything near.

It was after four o' clock in the afternoon. With the exception of Poko, the boys rolled up their trousers and began to climb the mountain, following the spiral path. It was easy to climb, and they did not need to use rope, or even their hands. They just walked, and the further up they were from the ground, the more spectacular the view of the surrounding forest became.

Aron once again took out the binoculars. From up high, it was possible to see for some thirty miles beyond the valley. In every direction there was greenery, a number of tall coconut trees above the level of the other trees, the river running freely between them, and some giant cogus whose colored domes made them stand out.

The boys quenched their thirst and continued, trying to breathe regularly. In front of them, the path became more narrow, the air thinner, making them dizzy. Although their heads felt heavy, they seemed to be lighter.

"Don't look down" warned Makuro, who could see his brothers contradicting him by feel vertigo when they looked down.

They went on a few more paces; the wind was strong and tried to blow them down. At the end of the last bend, they found a mast attached to the ground with a flag waving on top. This territory did not seem to be as unexplored as they had thought.

On the flag, there was a simple figure of an unexpressive face with three eyes, the third on the forehead, on a red shield with a green background. In the lower part, there were a number of inscriptions, also in red, written with symbols which the boys were unable to identify.

Aron took down the flag from the mast and rolled it up, putting it in their backpack. If they managed to return to

Kafria, this would be the main proof against their grand-father's teaching.

"Let's go" said Aron. "The nest must be near. Something tells me we have little time."

At the end of their path, they finally saw the nest, which was large, made of clay and dry branches and twigs. It was not exactly on the top of the mountain, but a few yards from the mast, so that the ice and mist would not affect it.

Inside the nest the head of the huge flying reptile feeding its chicks could be seen. Makuro took the ropes out of the backpack and made a lasso, offering it to Aron, who immed-iately refused.

"This animal does not seem very tame" he said. "I don't know whether I'll be able to dominate it."

Makuro smiled.

"Didn't you always think that you handled the lasso better than anyone else in the tribe? Now it's your chance to show us."

"I've just lost a finger" said Aron, seriously. "I don't think I'll manage to control it if it becomes aggressive."

"It certainly is aggressive" said Makuro. "Didn't you see what it did to the other animal?"

"I'll go" volunteered Tork, taking the ropes. "Wait here for me to get the eggs."

Tork crouched and crept towards the nest. The reptile noticed his presence and stood up, opening its threatening wings. It was a real cold-blooded monster, measuring some twelve feet from its tail to its nose. It eyed Tork for a number of seconds, but then returned to look after its chicks.

Tork got nearer and nearer, lasso in one hand, and the other hand leaning on the stones, making sure he didn't make any noise. He lent over the nest and saw three recently hatched brown chicks, and four eggs ready to hatch. The adult reptile seemed not to be afraid of the boy or to have any intention of attacking him.

"It's tame" he shouted to his brothers, who were now curious.

Tork held out his arm to stroke the head of the huge reptile, feeling its wrinkled skin. The reptile's body shivered, and it closed its eyes, as if it were thanking Tork. Tork lifted the rope and put it around its neck. The animal was not angry, lowering its head and allowing itself to be captured.

Tork improvised a muzzle and some reins with the ropes. And, with little effort, he managed to pull it out of the nest.

"Strange" said Makuro. "This reptile seems to have been domesticated."

"It's docile" said Tork. "I think it's never seen human beings, and because of this, is not afraid."

"Either it's never seen human beings or sees them pretty often" added Makuro.

Tork got up onto the reptile, putting his legs around its neck.

"I'll have the honor of making the initial flight" he said.

"Wait" said Aron. "Let me go in your place. She's pretty tame. I won't need my injured hand if it's an easy flight. Give me the reins."

Tork got down and gave the ropes to Aron, who immediately got up onto of the upper vertebrae.

"Haaaa!" he shouted, excited.

The reptile opened its wings and took off from the cliff. Tork and Makuro took advantage of its absence by collecting the eggs.

Aron flew high around the surrounding areas, not distancing himself from the mountains. The reptile glided through the air, only flapping its wings occasionally to stabilize itself in the air currents, using the wind to circle around.

But when it noticed that the boys were collecting its eggs, it completely changed. It roared and brought in its wings, darting under the clouds. Aron held firmly onto its back, trying to signal to the boys to stop taking the eggs, but they couldn't hear him. They emptied the bag and were putting the eggs inside it, and did not notice how furious the reptile was.

It shook its body, freed itself from its reins, there was no alternative for Aron but to sink his nails into its neck, with the result that his finger began to bleed again. He was sweating and holding on firmly in order not to fall, but his muscles soon weakened. He could not control them, and his body stopped struggling, his pupils contracted, and his fingers slowly opened.

Aron groaned and finally let go, quickly falling. During the fall, memories of his childhood came back to him. Those seconds seemed to last for decades. He could see Miku smiling and Hanara angry. He saw his first ride on a bigbug and Daiara getting undressed.

Then came total darkness . . .

CHAPTER 8

THE EVOLVED ONE

A huge furry animal loped over the sands of the infinite desert, in boiling heat which evaporated all humidity out of the air. Its ears were pricked up, listening for the least noise, and its flat muzzle could sense any smell blown by the wind. The man riding on its back looked around for some shade where he could rest. He was wearing a long brown tunic with a hood covering his forehead. It was hot under the tunic, but he knew he could not take it off; and, if he did so, he would lose water and die of dehydration.

The man had not looked at the sand or the bright sunlight for a long time, and he was now tired after traveling non-stop for two days. The anesthesia in his veins reduced the pain in his back and feet but changed his mental faculties so that he felt as if he were drunk.

The shirt under his tunic was sticking to the skin on his back, but the man did not know whether it was because of the sweat or something else. He had not eaten since he began his journey, and it was difficult for him to coordinate his arms to get food or his canteen which was tied to the animal.

According to the nurses, the anesthesia could last a whole week, though, on the third day, its effects would begin to wear off. His pain was now returning, slowly increasing, and proving that the forecast was not so precise.

From time to time the animal stopped in order to rest or chew an occasional cactus or palm leaves, when they were found. At times, it twisted its neck around to look for the water canteen which was tied around its body. The man put up with its frequent attempts to steal water, not worried by the fact that the animal was drinking it. To the west, the Olin Rapids could be heard, so that the canteen could be refilled whenever necessary. Neither did the man get angry when the animal stopped to recover its energy or looked in the saddlebags for food, as he believed that the welfare of the animal was more important than his own. If the animal died in the heat of the desert, he would be lost, and he would have a slow painful end.

The pain in his back increased as the sun went down and the sky darkened. The anesthesia was quickly losing its effect and would not last the expected time. He felt the energy flowing in his arms, and he took advantage to exercise them, unscrewing the top of the water canteen. He tried to pour its contents into his throat but there was not a drop left. He checked the bottom of the canteen and saw that a piece had been bitten away.

"Damned bizort!" he cursed the animal, but did not get angry. He could easily ride to the banks of the Great River to get as much water as he wanted. He pulled the reins to the right and the animal went eastwards.

He rode for another two hours, but there was no sign of the Olin. Night was quickly falling, and the man was exhausted from riding so much. He finally realized that the river was not near and that he had confused the sound of the water with the strong wind. It was now late, and he was weak and hungry and thought he would soon lose his consciousness.

The man was grateful for the close atmosphere which could hardly be penetrated by the sun, with the result that it was never too hot during the day, and hotter weather would certainly have killed him. But he did not know how long he would last without food or water, or without the anesthesia which was quickly wearing off, leaving him with an intense pain which was difficult to bear.

He tried to put his hand in the saddlebags to find some left-overs. He could only find a number of cogtas, the only food he had brought which was not part of the diet of the animal.

He had never liked the taste of the cogtas, not even when they were diluted to make tea. But on this occasion he would even eat the prickles of a cactus.

The cogtas seemed to him to be small brown limes covered by fungi. And their taste was like a mixture of sweet potato and citric fruits. A strange combination. But when he now swallowed them, perhaps because of his hunger or because of his changed palate, their taste reminded him of wild strawberries covered in honey.

He swallowed the last four after hardly chewing them. He was still hungry, and when searching the bottom of the rucksacks once again, his hands came on a hard object. He took it out of the rucksack and looked at it, opening it. It was his old notebook. His own handwriting was difficult to read. He tried to read some of his old notes, and bouts of hatred came into his mind.

"Damned Hatis!" he said angrily, punching the back of the animal, whose body trembled and began to quicken pace, as if it had received an order to accelerate. "Damned, damned Hatis! I hope they all die and their mothers drown in their own blood!"

He found those words of repulsion appropriate and decided that he should note them down. He hadn't written anything for a long time. His hand holding the pen shook when it touched the last white pages. But he didn't write very much. Night soon came and prevented him from seeing anything. The man returned the notebook to the rucksack and carried on, wondering whether he should camp or not. He no longer had any strength to take the tent out of its bag and set it up, with the result that he preferred to sleep in the saddle, as he had done for the two previous nights. It would be better to continue traveling while he had strength and he could put up with the pain.

In the distance he could see the shadows of some date trees. Any food would now be good, but dates would be a treasure. The trees slowly approached and they were not a mirage. They were really there, solid, full of fruits, and their branches swayed in the wind.

The man took his crutches and dismounted, dragging himself to the trees. He picked a number of dates and filled his mouth, chewing them with pleasure. He also fed the animal, which devoured them rapidly, almost swallowing his hand together with them. He clenched his fist and gave a sharp punch on the muzzle of the beast so that it would behave itself, and took advantage to check the compass on his wrist.

He realized that he had not gone even a millimeter off his route northwards in all the time he had been riding. He then put his finger in his mouth, pressing his tooth to see that the micro-transmitter was still there. The time to swallow it would soon come.

The man put a number of dates in the rucksack and mounted onto the saddle again, continuing northwards. Shortly afterwards he fell asleep, which was an effective defense against the pain which was now coming back strongly in his back and feet.

Far away, due to the time difference, night had not yet appeared in the sky above the beach. The last beams of light coming from the clouds hurt the half-open eyes of the boy, who felt as if there was a power shortage. Whispers could be heard nearby, and he couldn't make out what they were saying.

"Get back. He is opening his eyes" he heard someone saying.

Aron did not know whether he was alive or dead, if he was in the beyond or if he was waking up from a strange nightmare. He dreamed that he had died and had been reincarnated in his own son. Daiara, his mother, had rejected him and left him in a basket which was floating downstream, just because he had not accepted the relationship when he was alive.

He woke with an enormous weight in his head, realizing that it would be difficult for Daiara to be a single mother. This must have been a dream, but the pain of rejection helped him to take a decision. He would talk to Daiara and accept their relationship.

His eyes took a long time to focus. He noticed that he was lying down on the white sand on the beach. He turned his head, saw a black boot and became alarmed. A man in shiny black clothing was staring at him. He was wearing a black helmet, which hid part of his face, revealing only the tip of his nose and his mouth. His eyes were protected by an opaque reflecting visor, which prevented them from being seen. The top of the helmet was almost twice as big as a normal helmet, though Aron had never seen anyone wearing one before.

"Are you okay?" asked the stranger, speaking with a strange accent of somebody who spoke the Myra language.

"Am I dead?"

"Not at all."

Looking around, Aron realized that the beach was the one near the forest on which the accident had taken place the previous morning. Behind him, the old Hati vehicle, totally repaired, was clean and working perfectly. His brothers and Poko were smiling beside a flying reptile, which was even bigger than the previous one they had seen.

"What happened?" he confusedly asked.

Before his friends could reply, the stranger took the initiative:

"You fell. I managed to hold on to you in the air before you reached the ground, using my mental faculties and, of course, the help of my animal" he said, stroking the wings of the huge reptile.

"I can't remember anything."

"Of course not. When someone falls from a height, they generally faint before they reach the ground. It's a natural instinct to turn your body off to avoid the vision of the end, which is coming" explained the man.

"I had a nightmare. I dreamed of strange things. My mind must be upset..."

"The subconscious is very powerful."

Aron had already heard this before, but he couldn't remember where.

"Who are you?" he asked.

"Oh, I'm sorry. Let me introduce myself: I am Judis, and I am a herberist knight. Herberism is a sect, which believes in the worship of nature. My people defend the few forests that still exist. I am Guardian of the Reforested Continent, Lord of the reptiles and protector of the living creatures of these lands. I'm a representative of the evolved people."

"Evolved people? Reptatiles?"

Judis took off his helmet and showed his face. He had a human face, but his chin was pointed and his head was almost twice as big as a normal head and was hairless. His nose was no more than two holes above his lips. There were two protruding bones on his forehead. Aron did not know whether it was a common characteristic or some kind of sign, or even a ritual scar to identify his tribe.

"Our brains are expanded," explained Judis, "as our minds are. We can do many things with our mental power, things which you could never understand."

"Like what?"

"Telepathy and telekinesis, moving small objects. Some of our wise people have reached an extremely high level of development and can even read the thoughts of those who are less evolved."

"Prove it" said Aron, in doubt.

"I haven't yet reached this level, but I'm studying my own self-knowledge. By the way . . ." Judis suddenly stopped speaking and stared into the eyes of Aron, who was unable to move and heard a deep voice echoing in his mind:

"Take care with negative thoughts. A dream is just a dream. Never forget this. Don't confuse marital love with maternal love. Remember that not everything is what it seems. Talk to the girl. Don't be so severe with what she has to tell you."

Judis blinked, and Aron came back to himself, frightened by what he had just experienced. He remained thoughtful for a number of minutes, eyeing the Guardian's smile.

"Was that it...?" he stammered.

"Yes. That is what we call telepathy. You must be feeling somewhat strange . . . That's quite normal, as you have a virgin mind, which has never received psychic messages."

"What are reptatiles?" asked Poko, interrupting the guardian.

"They are the animals which you tried to capture. They only live here in the Reforested Continent. We control them with our minds and we prevent them from turning against human beings. They are as docile as lambs, but you should not have touched their eggs . . ."

"We thought they were flying dinosaurs."

"No. They belong to a different line of evolution."

"Why are you helping us?" asked Aron.

"I wanted to meet the unusual group of young men who were invading my land. This is not something we see every day . . ."

Behind them, Makuro now asked:

"Sir, by any chance are there high levels of radiation in the atmosphere here?"

"We've been living here for a long time, boy. We are a peaceful people. The air here is as pure as anywhere. Besides, I can tell you that our atmosphere is even purer, as we have so many trees." This, therefore, proved Makuro's theories.

"Your clothing seems so closed and suffocating" remarked Aron. "How can you wear black in a place where the climate is so hot?"

"It is refrigerated inside . . ."

A green light began to blink on Judis's right arm. When he saw it, his expression completely changed.

"Sorry, boys. I have to go. And you too! I repaired your vehicle. Go back where you came from. My people don't like strangers. Go back or you'll have problems. Sorry . . ."

Judis mount on the saddle on the reptatile and held out his hand to Tork, saying:

"Give me back the eggs and the flag which you guys took from the mast."

Tork obeyed. He opened the bag, took out the rolled up flag and three of the four eggs which he had taken, giving them to Judis.

"Let us keep at least one" he asked. "This egg will soon hatch, and in our land we don't have flying animals to use for transport. It will help my people a lot."

Judis agreed, and gave him another egg.

"So in this case take also a male, so they can procreate in the future."

Tork agreed but said nothing. However much he tried to measure or weigh the eggs, he could find no difference between them. How Judis could know the sex of the animals which had not yet been hatched was impossible for him to understand.

"It's getting dark" said the guardian. "Get going before nightfall. Promise to say nothing about our existence and never, *never ever*, come back here. Don't try to look for us, as it's impossible to find us. My people will not put up with disobedience."

The boys promised.

"What do those inscriptions on the flag mean?" asked Makuro, shortly before Judis flew off.

"Victory and Evolution."

Then, the reptatile flapped its wings and flew out of sight in the violet sky. And the boys had nothing else to do other than agree with the stranger and leave.

They got back into their repaired vehicle and went away from the beach towards the sea . . .

CHAPTER 9

THE CALL

While they were returning, a strange thing happened: the further they got from the Continent, the stormier the atmosphere above became. The instruments of the vehicle went wild, as they detected a large radioactive mass nearby. The sky over the beach became overcast, and powerful electric charges hit the ground.

It was as if an electric storm was only taking place there, over the territory of the Continent. The boys became anxious, and Tork pulled the hand accelerator. When they reached the high sea, however, and the coast of the Continent could no longer be seen, everything became calm and the instruments returned to normal.

"There must be variations in the coastal climate" they said, trying to calm down.

After this episode, they continued their journey more anxiously, talking about the adventure which had finished. A number of questions came up, of which the most curious was: "How did Judis discover their presence so quickly? Was it really because of his telepathic powers? Or was it some kind of communication with the animals in the forest?"

According to Poko's deductions, the long object with the lens on the end which he had seen might be a camera with its own movements, used by the evolved people to spy on those who invaded their lands. This was a good explanation, which they all agreed with.

The journey home was quiet. The presence of the drophins and balerias swimming on the surface of the Tetis had lost its charm.

In order to share tasks when he slept, Tork taught the other boys how to pilot. They learned quickly, and Poko was the only one who did not need to take the controls: When it was his turn to work the directional levers, they were getting near home, and Aron, the pilot at that moment, refused to let down the control.

They traveled quickly, and at three in the morning they could see the ruins in the distance. The night was dark as always. They turned the headlights off in order not to be seen by the sentries in the towers and drove in the dark. When there were less than two miles left, they got out of the vehicle and walked the rest.

They went into the northern entrance and went over the hill. When they went through the pasture, they saw that the barn was not being observed. They were incredibly tired and were soon snoring on the hay . . .

The following day, they woke before sunrise.

"Irresponsible boys!" said Hanara, walking from side to side on the scaffold before the temple, once again in the presence of all the community in the square. "Just look at them! I bet Aron was the culprit! Tork and Makuro would not think of doing anything as stupid as escaping from the village. And look how bad he looks! A big cut on his forehead, and he's lost half his finger . . . Just look at poor Poko! How could he walk with his leg like that? You're lucky to be alive. It's as if we were living centuries ago, when it was common for young men to behave like this . . . But no. We are speaking about boys — *Men* - who had grown up in a native community, where good habits are still maintained. This behavior is unacceptable. They don't know how to follow rules, respect the authority of the elders, and to risk their lives for the least little thing.

I am not only the leader of this community. With the exception of Poko, I'm also your grandfather, and Tork's godfather. I have the duty to bring you up and look after you. In the good times I would even have expelled you from the village. I'd like to see how you'd survive. Don't you want to be independent? And I'm sure you'd crawl back, begging forgiveness.

I hope you have a good argument to reduce your punishment, or your bodies will know the meaning of deprivation. It is not only to me that you should explain things to, but also to your mother and the whole community. Poko's parents almost had a heart attack. How could you be so immature? And I still haven't mentioned the theft of the vehicle. Who gave you orders to enter my laboratory? You should take that smile off your face and try to explain." He wound up his speech, crossed his arms and tried to calm down.

Aron was struggling to keep calm too.

"Can I speak for the rest?" asked Tork.

"Go ahead" said Hanara. "Try. We're listening..."

"My dear Master, godfather and grandfather, and my dear Kuata-Noan neighbors..."

"Stop messing about and get on with it" said Aron.

Tork paused, looking at his brother. Aron winked, and then he continued:

"Your teaching does not coincide with a number of facts:

First, you always taught us that these ruins were the remains of an ancient civilization, which was destroyed, and that I and my brothers are the only ones who are different to the natives of this tribe."

"Yes, that's true" said Hanara.

"Secondly, you also told us that the Forbidden Continent is a dangerous lifeless place, whose atmosphere has been completely destroyed by a huge mass of radiation."

"Yes, that's what I said. What are you saying?"

"But, grandfather, we trod on the soil of the Forbidden Continent" Tork's voice began to change. "We breathed its air and talked with a member of the race who live there. There is a brave new world out there, a world which has always been hidden from us. We are not as immature as you think. It was not Aron's fault of disobeying you. I'm sorry to say this, granddad, but I believe that the only culprit was you yourself."

Hanara started.

"It is the last thing I'd expect. You, the person I most devote myself to, is now against me! How can you say this, boy?"

"We have proof, grandfather. We met a being called Judis, a representative of a more evolved human race, who disproved everything. There was never any radiation on the land of the Forbidden Continent. Its atmosphere is clean. Everything you taught us was a pack of lies."

Hanara was silent, thinking of something to say to defend himself, as Tork had now broken his defenses, and he knew that Tork was not lying. Hanara had always depended on the legends, and he had flown over the Reforested Continent many years before. It was a place he was afraid just to remember: its sky was always stormy, electric charges where continually hitting the ground, and the dark clouds produced frightening turbulences.

Perhaps the boys were confusing something. They might have trod on some paradise island, thinking it was the lands of the Forbidden Continent.

"We have proof on that, granddad." said Makuro. "We have brought two reptile eggs. They are large flying reptiles which only live in that continent. It's no good to go on hiding the truth from us. We found out about your farce! The best thing you can do is to reveal to us everything we have the right to know."

"And we don't only want to know the truth just about the Forbidden Continent" continued Aron. "We want to know the truth about everything, from what really happened to our father, to the meaning of the holes which our mother has at the back of her neck."

Hanara was once again surprised. Guessing lies and wanting to know the truth is one thing . . . but wanting to know about the plugs was too much.

"I'd also like to know where the books which disappeared from the library are" added Makuro.

Before Hanara turned to shout at Makuro, he felt a softly hand touching his shoulder, and Miku's sweet voice whispered:

"The time has come to tell them. They're old enough. They'll understand."

Hanara looked down, clenching the straw hat which he held in his hands.

"You are right" he said. "It's no good to continue hiding things".

The Noans were divided into two camps. The majority did not know that Hanara had been lying to the boys, and those who did know (the elders), had orders not to reveal the facts to the generation which was born after the last Hati invasion.

"Calm down!" shouted Hanara, trying to stop the tumult which was now increasing. "I guarantee that the boys did not reach dry land. There are no evolved human races or flying reptiles living in our world!"

"As Makuro said" began Aron, who was happy to see his grandfather being questioned by the tribe, "we have brought two eggs, which prove their existence. According to Judis, the herberist guardian, there is a male and a female."

"Ah!" said Hanara, sarcastically. "And where are these eggs now?"

"They're in the vehicle. We parked two miles west of the village."

Hanara turned to Poko.

"Get the bigbugs ready and bring the vehicle to me. I must have a talk with your friends alone."

"I still don't know how to pilot the vehicle . . ." said Poko. "Tork taught me what to do, but I didn't . . ."

"Don't be stupid. Put it on a cart. Get help and saddle the bigbugs. Hurry up."

Poko obeyed and ran towards the pasture while Aron, Makuro and Tork went together with Hanara and Miku into the house. Night was falling over the village, and the rest of the community remained in the square, waiting for Poko to return with the eggs.

Inside the house, the boys sat on the kitchen chairs, but Hanara offered them the armchairs in the living room, which were further from the noise the crowd was making.

Hanara sat down and remained silent, stooped over and leaned his chin on his hands, thinking of the best way to begin to speak.

"Be straightforward, grandfather" said Tork. "We'll understand."

"As long as it's the truth" reminded Makuro.

Aron seemed indifferent. He had not yet seen Daiara, and after hearing his grandfather, he would have to confront the pressures which came from an 'unwanted pregnancy'.

"Boys . . ." Hanara began to speak, without daring to face them. He took off his hat and put it on the floor. "It's now the moment to reply to your questions. What I have to say is very serious and delicate. I haven't told you before because it might have affected you growing up but now you're men."

He hesitated for a long time, staring at the melted wax on the candelabra.

"I would have liked to have never told you this, but . . ." he stammered. "I am not your real grandfather."

The boys did not seem to be very shocked, and so he continued:

"Miku is not Aron's real mother."

The silence confirmed that they were prepared for anything. Aron looked towards Miku's eyes, and she admitted this by nodding.

"Makuro and Tork are both Miku's sons" said Hanara, "though they have different fathers. Tork is a half-brother both to Aron and Makuro: Aron on his father's side, and Makuro on his mother's side. However, Aron does not have the same blood as Makuro. They are not brothers or even relations.

This last statement made the boys look at each other, frowning.

"You've already noticed that I've devoted myself to teaching Tork. That's because a war is coming, and I might be able to make a peace agreement between the two rival societies. I and Tork. Tork is a Myra-Hati, the hope of these peoples who do not want the war to begin. According to the prophecies, Tork will be thought of as "the Messiah of the New World", the being who have the mixture of blood of the two races, who represents their union. As was foreseen in the Sacred Scrolls, he was naturally conceived, without the intervention of geneticists.

They all looked towards Tork, but Hanara did not pause.

"Let me clear things up: There are two peoples living separately in our world, the Myras - the race to which Aron belongs — and the Hatis — the people of Makuro. They are different races, with different people, habits and language. And because of this I needed to teach you, in addition to Kuata-Noan, the other two languages, as you may need them in the future. Miku and I are Hatis. She fled from our society as she was illegally pregnant and I was expelled . . .

"What does 'Myra' mean?" asked Makuro.

"Myra means 'ant' in the language which the prophet of their religion spoke.

"Myras and Hatis!" exclaimed Makuro. "Ants and Bees! Why do they have these names?"

"The name is an allusion to the human-like behavior of the organization of these insects, which is clear in both societies. The Myras live underground, in the depths of their city-colony, like a colony of ants. And the Hatis possess a technology which enables them to fly individually. They live in a closed city known as the 'Hive'."

Miku interrupted:

"I think this is the moment to tell them why you were expelled." She had been waiting sixteen years for this explanation.

Hanara once again refused.

"Not for the moment" he said. "We are still not safe from the threat of war. This is a restricted piece of information, which is connected to the plans of the Emperor in relation to his real interests with the inter-plug. I'm sorry, Miku, but the most I can reveal for the moment is how I was expelled and not why."

Miku was satisfied with the little information she would receive. Maybe she would manage to assimilate the facts herself. However, before Hanara began to describe how a respected general had been taken prisoner and expelled from his society, a shrill noise came from inside his pouch and interrupted him.

He opened the pouch and took out a small device which was beeping. He looked worried, and his heart began to beat fast. It was the tracking device which he had been hoping to hear for the last sixteen years and which would announce Kliver's freedom. On its miniature screen there appeared the request for help showing the place where he would meet finally the old Myra. It had come at the right moment. Hanara had already lost hope, and the conflicts he was now having with the boys would be modified by their father's presence.

Hanara stood still for a long time, now looking at the device, now looking at Miku and the boys. Kliver must be camped somewhere in the desert. Hanara had to find him and unplug him, and then bring him to the ruins.

"Stay here" he said, calmly. "I must get ready for a journey. Your father is sending me his signals. He's asking me for help. I must find him. When I return, we shall continue our talk."

"Is our father alive?" Aron was the first to ask, though they had all often wondered whether he was alive.

"A long time ago," explained Hanara, "I put a micro-transmitter in your father's tooth, and I asked him to swallow it when he was released. At the time I didn't think it would take so long . . . During all this time, your mother and I thought it was better to lie to you and say that he had died. If we had told the truth it might have awakened a desire to rescue him, and you would have ended up being killed on the road . . ."

The boys looked away, feeling that they had been betrayed.

"Now I must hurry" continued Hanara, taking his hat. "I can't leave your father waiting . . . I need some tranquilizing darts and a dagger."

"Why do you need the darts?" asked Miku.

"The Hatis would only free Kliver after plugging him, making all his senses accessible to the inter-plug. I must make him sleep. If not, I shall be exposed to the Empire through his vision. And this is why I'm taking the darts. With Kliver unconscious, I will be safe from the inter-plug."

Miku was annoyed:

"The inter-plug is a ridiculous dream made by ambitious lunatics which will never become real!"

Hanara stood up.

"You are wrong, my dear" he said, convincingly. "The inter-plug exists. It's real. One of the reasons why I was imprisoned was my opposition to the new inter-plug project. If my calculations are right, its technology was released to civilians three years after you escaped, only during the hu-tae-mui championships... Don't you realize that our direct communication can only work through the inter-plug audio signals?"

This silenced Miku.

"What are plugs and the inter-plug?" asked the boys.

Hanara leaned against the door and crossed his arms.

"Don't worry about it, boys" he said. "You'll find out soon. I'll soon tell you everything you need to know. But now, if you allow me, I'm going to meet an old friend. I need the vehicle."

"Kliver was never your friend!" shouted Miku. "You only used him to escape from the Hati squad sixteen years ago." It seemed that these words had been engraved in her throat for a long time.

"I didn't use your husband to escape, but to help you and your sons to escape. If it had not been for Kliver, we would now probably be prisoners and have no hope for peace. The Banjins would be slaves, and the Myra-Hati would be dead!"

Aron jumped up.

"If you're going to meet our father, we'll go with you" he said with authority.

Miku wiped her tears.

"Take them" she pleaded. "That's the least you can do for them."

"There is no room in the vehicle for five people, including Kliver."

"We'll fit in" said Makuro and Tork together.

The sky was overcast. Hanara and the boys left the house and saw that the natives were still in the square, waiting for proof. Hanara went through the crowd up onto the scaffold, telling them that they should continue with their work while he was absent for a couple of days.

They refused to obey him. They wanted to wait for Poko to arrive with the eggs, so they could decide who was right.

"Do as I tell you" said Hanara, gesturing. "I promise that, when I get back, I shall tell you everything about the world in which we live."

Don't take so long to Poko to return with the eggs. He brought them together with the vehicle and was proud to have learned how to pilot the machine, followed by the bigbug, who was panting behind the machine, trying going along with it.

"I've brought the eggs, sir" he said after climbing up onto the scaffold, giving the bag to Hanara.

Hanara took the eggs out of the bag and held one up for everyone to see.

"Here it is" he told the crowd. "But a big egg does not mean that it was laid by a flying reptile. Wrap them up and wait for them to hatch. Then we will know whether the boys are telling the truth." He put the eggs back into the bag and handed them over to one of the nurses, who would carry out his orders.

"Reinforce the guard when I'm away" he ordered, and turning towards the boys, he said: "Let's go. The journey might be long."

Hanara came down from the scaffold and got into the machine, taking the driver's seat. The boys got into the other seats.

"Where are you going?" asked Poko, supposing that they would return to the Continent to bring back more proof.

"We're going to fetch our father" Aron replied.

One of the warriors went down to the laboratory and brought back one more uranium rock, in case they needed to extract energy, and unenthusiastically wished them a good journey.

Hanara turned on the engines.

"Where did you get the uranium?" asked Tork, from the back seat.

"Didn't you see the ultracentrifuge in my laboratory? I enrich uranium and keep it in the locker. One day I will show you how to split atoms. Hold on."

The turbines started up, and the vehicle went towards the desert, quickly passing out of the eastern gate of the village.

Poko stood watching them getting distance, wondering where they would be going. He thought he had heard Aron saying something about looking for their father, but he was not sure . . . no. This wasn't what he had heard. 'Aron's father is dead, and dead men cannot be rescued'. He shook his head and went to look for something to do.

Little by little, the vehicle was reaching its top speed. Trained in mechanical engineering, Hanara knew how to use the controls of the machine. He could pilot it even with his eyes closed.

This was the quickest the boys had ever traveled. Tears were coming out of their eyes because of the wind, their stomachs were turning right around, and it seemed as if their clothes wanted to fly off and their skin come away from their bones.

They traveled for a number of hours through similar landscape: dry sand, pebbles and some occasional cactus, separated one from another by great distances. They went toward the Southeast, following the pulses from the tracker that Hanara had brought. They flew over the greenery on the banks of the Olin and reached an immense plane, where herds of wild big-bugs and hard-shelled bizorts migrated to. They crossed the plain, turned toward the south, crossed three small savannahs, and then Hanara began to be worried.

They had already traveled a long way, and had almost reached the edge of the dark blot on the map on the screen that protects them from being exposed to the Hati satellites.

Nobody had yet discovered why this blot appeared on the electronic maps. It was a dark circular stain that covered almost all the planet, becoming invisible when seen through satellite images. The Loagy Oasis, the Reforested Continent, and the Ruakan installations remain inside the blot, and, therefore, could not be visualized from the Hati Empire. This was possibly the reason why the Myras had never been found during all these troubled years.

Inside the area covered by the blot satellites are useless, even for communication or weather forecasts. The signals from the Hati transmitters, however, use radio waves which are transmitted below the level of the clouds and therefore work perfectly.

To Hanara's relief, the tracker signals began to get stronger, and supposedly Kliver was near, inside the safe area. Hanara slowed the machine down and climbed a high hill, stopping at the top, where it was easier to check the territory and safe areas.

He turned the headlights and the turbines off. It was a cold windy night. Aron was dizzy after stopping so suddenly and could not prevent himself from vomiting. He turned around and threw up on the sand. Makuro and Tork also felt sick and threw up too.

"Softies" smiled Hanara. "At your age, I was already the leader of a reconnaissance squad. Your father must be near, behind those dunes" and he pointed towards the East.

"We would also be leading a squadron if we hadn't been imprisoned by so many lies." Aron could not resist returning his grandfather's comment.

They got out of the vehicle and began to walk, looking for tracks or footprints in the sand. The air was dry and windy. Hanara predicted that the weather could change and a sandstorm might begin at any moment, which was common at this time of the year.

He decided to hurry. If there was anyone else near besides Kliver, they would have to be careful not to be seen. In addition, there was not much time, and a sandstorm could be dangerous.

"Sit down over there" Hanara said, pointing to a mound of rocks on top of the hill. "I am going down to the fields alone. I have to reconnoiter the territory."

Hanara cautiously went down the hill towards the dunes, around the shadows. At every moment he checked the tracker in his hand, which was beeping frequently, as the signal was coming from nearby.

Hanara was sure there was no danger and returned to get the vehicle and the boys. They returned to their seats and drove slowly, trying to find Kliver. The tracker began to beep much stronger on top of a high sand dune. But there was no sign of the old Myra (Kliver must be fifty-two year-old right now), and Hanara began to get worried.

"Strange" he said, getting out of the machine.

"What's the problem, Granddad?" asked Tork.

"There is no one near. The tracker says that this is the place."

"Maybe my father spat the device onto the ground, instead of swallowing it." suggested Aron.

"Impossible" disagreed Hanara. "Covering it there was a layer of fibers, which had to be dissolved in his stomach before it began to work."

"Maybe he regurgitated the device after swallowing it" said Makuro.

"And where did it end up?" asked Tork.

"I don't know. It must be a small device, mustn't it?"

"It's very dark. It will be difficult to find it."

"Tork, turn on the headlights."

Tork returned to the vehicle and turned on the lights, but nothing could be seen, only sand, gravel and stones. The boys knelt down to look for the micro-transmitter on the ground, but found nothing.

"Boys" said Hanara "Spread out and look for clues around. Don't wander off and get lost. I'll stay here, checking on things. Come back in twenty minutes at most. I can smell a sandstorm coming in less than an hour."

The boys spread out, and each went into a different direction, disappearing in the darkness of the night. Hanara crouched down at the side of the dune and lit his pipe, waiting for them to return.

In less than fifteen minutes, Makuro came back, excited. He breathed deeply and stammered out to Hanara:

"I found something . . . An animal . . . I found an animal . . . a big animal! Like a bigbug, but bigger and much more hairy."

"Ah" said Hanara. "A bizort. It's also an animal that is used for carrying goods. At this time of the year it's common to find them around here, as they migrate to escape from the sandstorms which devastates their food source."

"But this one was unusual."

"What's wrong?"

"I found it watering at a spring nearby, over there" pointing to a row of rocks in the Northeast. "It is carrying some equipment on its back, and is saddled!"

"Saddled?" Hanara frowned.

"Yes, it has a saddle. It is also carrying a number of saddle bags. I was afraid to get near, as I thought it might be a dangerous animal . . ."

Hanara put out his pipe, and placed it in the pouch.

"Take me to it" he said.

Hanara followed Makuro, and they passed the row of rocks into an open area beyond, where they saw the back of an animal, which was as big and heavy as a buffalo, drinking water from a spring that came up from the ground.

"There it is" pointed Makuro.

Hanara asked him to keep quiet, and bent over, trying to get near, as he needed to check the saddle and the bags it was carrying. He crept near and the animal noticed his presence. Hanara stopped for a moment and kept absolutely still.

The huge bizort turned towards him, looking at him suspiciously. Hanara bent over a little more, and the animal lowered its head and took a step back.

Hanara kept still, as he could frighten the animal. If the bizort ran off, it would be difficult to reach it.

"Makuro" he murmured, "find your brothers and fetch me the vehicle. Quick!"

Makuro turned and ran back. The animal further lowered its head and took two more steps back, snorting and tapping its hooves on the sand.

Hanara held his breath and took another step forward. The bizort took a further step back. The old man could see the dust clouds forming in the distance and realized there was not much time left. The wind was getting stronger and stronger.

'Damned bizort' thought Hanara. 'Keep still and let me see the bags'.

Hanara continued to eye him. He wondered whether there was something in his appearance which could be frightening him, making it move back. It might be his old straw hat. He took it off and put it on the ground, and then slowly took a step nearer. The bizort did not move. Hanara took a further step forward and it kept still. Another step, and the animal began to snort and shake its ears.

"Shhhh, shhhh!" comforted Hanara. "I don't want to frighten you. Calm down."

The vehicle with the three boys inside suddenly appeared, with its lights on, behind Hanara. The bizort turned and stamped off into the desert, splashing the spring water and making the ground shake.

"You frightened him." shouted Hanara. "After him!"

Tork jumped into the back seat, and Hanara took over the controls. The turbines revved up, and the vehicle went faster, chasing the animal. They easily reached it, driving alongside it, as the bizort had changed direction and was going towards the east. Hanara turned the machine to follow it. The boys held on tightly in order not to be thrown out their seats.

Hanara accelerated, and the vehicle approached the animal, so that Makuro could stroke its hairy back, but the bizort turned to the right and began to trot backwards.

"We must do something" said Tork.

"We could lasso it" suggested Aron.

"Don't be stupid" groaned Makuro. "We aren't strong enough to pull it with a rope."

"But we could tie it to the end of the vehicle"

"Did we bring any rope?" asked Hanara.

"I don't think so" said Tork.

"So stop talking about it. We are wasting time."

The bizort still had the strength to run a long way, which made Hanara take a difficult decision. He tapped some commands into the panel, and the missile launcher was put into action.

"Are you going to explode it?" Tork was shocked when he realized what Hanara was going to do.

"Have you got a better idea?"

But before Tork could reply, the automatic sight focused the target, and the missile was launched. It went through the air with its wings of fire and exploded in the back of the bizort, just above its hind legs. The animal shrieked, but continued running ever faster. The hard shell protecting its body prevented the explosion from causing serious injuries.

Three more missiles hit it on the back and in its side, and a series of laser beams finally made it fall to the ground.

When the smoke went down, the vehicle approached the animal. Time was getting short. On the horizon it was possible to see three cyclones forming, devouring everything in front of them.

"Those were my last three missiles" lamented Hanara.

He got out of the machine and examined the shell of the bizort, picking up what was left of one of the saddlebags it had been carrying. Its lock had become twisted as a result of the explosions, and Hanara had to open it with his dagger. He emptied the contents of the bag onto the ground. Inside, there was a canteen of water with a hole in it, a map of the Kafrian continent, a digital compass, camping utensils, and a watch which had been smashed.

He crouched down and cut the strap of the other saddlebag, inside which there was a sleeping bag, a flashlight, a number of alkaline batteries, a telescope and a notebook with a black cover, tied by wire to a pen.

Hanara picked up the flashlight and lit up the notebook, opening it. The pages were old, and the writing confused, written in Myra. He read the first page to himself:

Today I discovered two new civilizations, but I lost everything which I have of value: my family and my freedom. But I'm still alive, and my thoughts and memories are still intact. Until when I don't know . . . Maybe until I'm obliged to use one of these plugs.

My diary. First day far from home. June 213 AE. Leo Kliver.

Hanara breathed deeply and looked at the boys.

"It is your father's notebook" he said. "The Hatis must have given him the bizort, so he could use it as transport when he was free."

"What happened to him?" asked Aron.

"There is no way of knowing. We would have to read the whole book first, but there is no time now, as the storm is getting near. It will be dangerous to stay here. It is best to leave now and return early tomorrow."

"No!" shouted Tork. "We can't stop! If we leave him in the desert, the storm will kill him!"

Hanara looked down.

"Look at the bizort" he said. "There is a bag stuck to its body. A tent bag. We can use the tent and camp tonight far away from danger. We'll sleep around here, and at dawn we'll continue the search."

Hanara turned towards Aron and gave him the dagger.

"Get the bag and bring the tent, son. There is nothing else we can do. I'm sorry . . ."

"Damn it!" said Aron, kicking the bag. He cut the strap which attached it and took it to Hanara. It was covered in the bizort's blood, but it was somewhat light.

Hanara opened it but was taken aback when he looked inside.

"The bag!" he said, surprised.

"What's about it?" asked Aron.

"It's empty!"

"What's the problem?"

"The tent is not here. And this means that your father must have camped somewhere near. I wonder . . ."

Hanara was almost seized with a fit before he finished the sentence.

"Damn it" he said. "Why didn't I think of this before?"

The boys looked at each other, but understood nothing.

"Quickly, boys!" he continued. "We have little time. Get into the vehicle."

Hanara gave the flashlight to Aron and the notebook to Tork, asking them to keep them safe. The turbines revved up, and the vehicle shot off like a rocket.

In less than three minutes they were back again in the spot which had been indicated by the tracker, on top of a high sand dune, near the entrance to the row of rocks. The wind was strong, blowing their hair around. Hanara checked the tracker in his hand, giving an order to the boys:

"Quick. Begin to take the sand away. Dig!"

"Why you . . ."

"Don't argue. Dig!"

The boys obeyed. They knelt on the dune and began to dig, using their own hands to remove the sand.

The storm was getting nearer and nearer, and they had to struggle against the wind in order to stay up. The hole in the dune was getting deeper. The boys were working hard and began to sweat.

The sand which had been removed began to form another mound half as high as the big dune, and when he put his hand in the hole, Tork felt his fingers touch something. He cleared the sand and noticed that it was flexible and had a moss-green coloring.

"I've found something!" he said.

Hanara checked.

"It is made of synthetic material" said Hanara. "You have found a part of the tent. Your father must be down there . . ."

The boys' eyes opened wide. They began to dig three times as fast.

"If we're lucky he'll still be alive."

They dug until they were covered in sweat, but there was still a long way to go. They had no more time, as the sandstorm was only half a mile away, furiously heading towards them. They couldn't keep their eyes open as the sand was blowing at them, and the wind was strong enough to knock them down.

Hanara took the dagger and cut the material, improvising an entrance in the top of the tent. Inside, it was dark. Aron turned on the flashlight and gave it to Hanara, who illuminated its interior. They could see a body lying on its stomach, clothed in a brown tunic, beside a pair of crutches. There was air inside the tent. The sands from the dune had not got inside, making it a good protection.

Hanara rolled up a leaf and put it between his lips. He put a dart inside it and blew it onto the man's body. The dart went through the tunic and hit his neck. The body trembled a little and then remained still.

"What are you doing, Granddad?" asked Tork, surprised.

"We need to protect ourselves . . . Don't worry. This is just a tranquilizer. Its effect will go away in eight to ten hours. Now hurry up. Get into the tent and lift him so we can pull him out."

Tork went in through the rip, handed the crutches to Hanara, turned the body over. Hanara pointing his flashlight on the man's face. It was the face of a man in late middle-age, with silver hair and smooth skin. He was unconscious but alive. There was a strip of cloth tied over his eyes. Hanara examined his features and immediately recognized him. There was no way to deny it.

"Yes!" he said. "It's your father. He is different, clean-shaven and has short hair . . . But it is Leo Kliver. Look that! After so long, he remembered to cover his eyes! A good memory! The wind must have buried the tent after he camped, forming the dune."

Tork lifted his body up and his brothers pulled it out. Hanara put the man onto his shoulders and dragged him to the vehicle, putting him into one of the seats. Aron, who was bigger, took the other seat. Tork and Makuro shared the back seat. Hanara accelerated and they escaped from the sandstorm by just a few seconds...

Some hours later, while they were returning home, Hanara pulled the brake lever. The boys were thrown forward and Tork needed to hold on to his brothers in order not to fall out.

"Damn it!" said Hanara, punching the control panel.

"What was it, Granddad? Why have we stopped?" they asked.

"I left my hat in the exit to the row of rocks!"

Tork looked at him, worried.

"But you're not thinking of going back to get it, are you? By now the sands must have buried it."

"Probably . . ."

'Damn it!' thought Hanara. His plug was hidden under the hat straw, and inside the device contained the images of the place where he had hidden the sword.

He thought of going back to find it when the storm was over, but it would be in vain. He would not find it. And even if somebody else found it, and checked the contents of the plug, the image of the sword was protected by the filthy cloth which was wrapped around it.

Hanara shrugged. His most valuable object was safe. If the worst came to the worst, he could hide it elsewhere . . .

He got out of the vehicle, pulled Kliver out of the seat and lay him on the ground. He took off his blind, and the boys wondered what he was going to do.

"What will you do with him, Granddad?" asked Makuro. "Aren't we leaving?"

"You don't intend to leave your father here, do you?"

"Don't be stupid, Aron. Get out and help me."

Hanara turned the body onto its stomach and took off its tunic, placing the flashlight beside him. He knelt down over the unconscious man and touched the back of his neck, feeling something small and protruding, almost like a tumor under his skin.

"Put your finger here on the spot" he asked Aron.

Aron obeyed.

"Not that hand, fool! Use your other hand!"

"Sorry. I forgot that I had lost my finger . . ."

Aron felt the protuberance on his father's nape.

"What is it?" he asked.

"It is a fixed internal plug. I must take it out before your father awakes" said Hanara, taking out of his pouch a piece of coal, a strip of gauze, a small bottle of alcohol and the dagger.

"Your bag is more cluttered than Poko's house!" joked Aron, smiling.

"Don't be ridiculous. I've only brought that which I knew I would need."

"Just kidding . . ."

With the coal, Hanara marked the place where the plug was and with the dagger cut into the skin around the device. Aron didn't like to see that, he turned his eyes away and went back to the vehicle.

This was a delicate operation, and Hanara did not have the right instruments. If he made a slight mistake and made a cut a millimeter the wrong way, he might condemn Kliver to spend the rest of his life in a wheelchair. The plug acted on the root of the spinal bone marrow, which is responsible for all the nervous stimuli that the brain receives.

'If I only had a scalpel' thought Hanara, seeing his glove-less hands becoming dirty with the blood running down the dagger.

After nearly two difficult hours, continually telling the boys off for making noise, Hanara finally managed to unplug the man and extract the small device from his vertebrae.

"Finished!" he said, enthusiastically.

He cleaned the cut with alcohol and sewed it with thread and an improvised needle, and then put the gauze over it. They all got back into the vehicle, and went on their way, leaving the device beeping on the ground, in a dark slop of coagulated blood near the tunic.

CHAPTER 10

During the second half of the journey Kliver woke up. Frothy white saliva was coming out of his mouth, and, still under the effect of the tranquilizer, he was trying to say something, but he did not manage to speak anything clearly. He turned his head and saw a strange looking boy, with long hair and suntanned skin beside him, asking him to keep calm. He heard someone telling that they would have to hold his tongue if he had another attack, but he was not able to understand what they were saying.

Kliver could not see who was driving him or where he was being taken, but this was hardly important. He was still alive, and, after having been through inhuman situations inside the enemy civilization, the fact he had now been kidnapped would hardly make any difference. He tried to relax and rest. Waiting for the effect of the tranquilizer to wear off would be the best thing he could do for now.

The vehicle entered the Eastern gate to Ruakan a little before dawn. Hanara stopped the vehicle near the scaffold, climbed out and asked the nurses to take Kliver to his wife.

The leader's return had been announced by the sentries in the towers, so that all the native people were waiting for him in the square. The previous night's protest was still fresh in their memories.

Hanara confidently stepped up to the scaffold. No one in the crowd dared to show him any lack of respect. The eggs had now been hatched and a lovely pair of reptatiles had been born. It could be seen that the boys were right and Hanara was not, and therefore support for Hanara had fallen, and the Noans were discussing whether they should change their leader.

But the great majority still supported him, regardless of the result of his explanations.

It began to drizzle. Hanara cleared his throat and faced the natives.

"Please do not interrupt me while I'm talking" he said, leaning on one of the stakes. "I realize I must clear up a number of facts that have not been explained. But I shall not give these replies right now. During the thirty-six years I have been leader of this tribe I have always wanted to transmit my knowledge to the young people. I have never intended to omit any facts. I'm asking you to keep your confidence in me.

After lunch, I shall give you all the replies I can. I will give you a lecture in which I shall tell you everything I know about the era in which we live. I want you to all come along, and the lecture will be given in the temple, not outside, as the rain is getting stronger, and I don't think it will stop . . .

But we need to prepare the room in the temple. Get blackboards and chairs, and repair the benches. Dismantle the scaffold and put it together again in front of the altar. Bring the books which are in the laboratory . . . Kliver will help me with the explanations."

The crowd and the boys, including Poko, were happy with Hanara's decision. The day had finally come when all the enigmas of the new world would be revealed. The natives decided to wait to hear the explanations. If Hanara didn't convince them, then they would gather together to renew their protest.

The drops of rain came in through the window of Miku's room, just like the tears which ran down her husband's eyes. She had never seen him cry before. Lying on the bed, Kliver wept like a baby held in her arms. Miku thought it better not to insist on asking what had happened to him in the Hive. It had probably been, as he had been prisoner for such a long time, a terrible experience.

Kliver wanted to hug Miku, kiss her, stay together with her, but something was preventing him. His memory had clearly been affected by some temporary effect of the tranquilizer. The memories were coming back little by little and were bringing worries and fits of desperation. When Miku turned around to get a scarf from the bedside table, she showed the back of her neck. When he could see the holes of her connector, Kliver began to groan and struggle with himself.

Hanara entered the room.

"Leave him" he said. "Don't put him under pressure. He will soon get better. The effect of the tranquilizer will only wear off in a number of hours."

"He looks good" said Miku, with a sincere smile. "Clean shaven, short hair . . . just like the day I met him."

Kliver was sweating, and his fever was burning. Hanara thought it was better to leave him to the care of his wife. So many risks to rescue him, and she hadn't given him a single 'thank you'.

"It's hot!" was all Kliver could say. "So hot! Painful . . . It's burning . . ."

"What is he saying?" asked Miku, getting another cloth to wipe his face, as the one she had been using was now soaking wet.

"The fever is making him delirious" said Hanara. "Take his clothes off and cover him with a blanket. Let him rest."

Miku began to unbutton his shirt.

"If there is any change, tell me" said Hanara. "I'm now going to get some books from the library. I have to prepare a lecture for this afternoon. I've decided to speak about everything the Banjins want to know about our Era."

"Will you tell the whole story?"

"I intend to. I owe it to them. I'll tell everything, from the appearance of the plugs to the beginning of the Great War of Extermination."

Miku hesitated for a moment.

"It is you who know . . ." she said. "Do what you think best."

"I would like Kliver to be my assistant."

"Ask him. You'll have your chance to ask him."

Hanara lifted his hand to adjust his hat. 'Damn it! Force of habit.' He then left to go to the library, if it was not raining too hard. He was going through the kitchen when Miku gave a shout which could have been heard in the barn.

"What happened?" Hanara asked when he returned.

Miku was scared, pale, holding Kliver's shoe in her fingers. However, everything apparently seemed normal.

"What's happened?" Hanara repeated.

Miku did not reply. She only held out her arm and lifted the shoe as if she wanted to show something.

Hanara approached her and took the shoe. It was an old worn out shoe, with a hole in the sole and untied laces. There was nothing special about it. Until he saw Kliver's foot.

His foot was swollen and dark, twisted and covered in blisters. The heel bone was visible and there was a bad wound on his shin. A third degree burn! Hanara then took his other shoe off, and saw that the other foot was the same, but not quite as bad.

"It's burning . . . Painful . . ." Kliver repeated, deliriously.

Hanara then began to take Kliver's clothes off himself and look for other injuries. He opened his shirt and could see that his chest and stomach were red and swollen, but only his feet were badly burned.

Kliver tried to sit up.

"It's hot . . . my back . . . it's burning . . ."

Hanara turned him onto his stomach and tried to take off his shirt, but it was stuck to his skin. When he cut the cloth with his dagger, Miku almost fainted. Kliver's back was red raw, covered in pus, and gave off a horrible rancid smell.

Hanara shivered.

"Quick, Miku, call the nurses. Bring them here. Tell them to bring thyme oil and antiseptic herbs."

"What is wrong with him?" she asked, anxious.

"He must have been given the ancient Hati tortures. Quick. His injuries have not yet formed into scars. We need to clean them before gangrene sets in!"

Miku became desperate. She ran out, and soon after three nurses were surrounding Kliver's bed. Hanara told her not to stay in the room. He said it might be unpleasant and that she would only get in the way. He threw her out and locked the door.

Miku sat down at the kitchen table for a long time, waiting for news of her husband. It was still raining when Tork came in, soaking wet and tired. His brothers had planned to sleep the rest of the morning in the barn, and he wanted to wrap himself up in a towel and drink a cup of hot tea before lying down in the hay. When he saw how depressed his mother looked, he immediately asked what was happening.

"Your father . . ." she said. "Your father is bad. Very bad! I must know what they did to him during all these years."

Tork understood his mother's pain. He looked down and whispered to her:

"If you really want to know, I have his notebook."

Miku looked up.

"Read it to me" she pleaded, "It must be written in Myra. I don't know Myra . . ."

Tork went into the square and shortly afterwards returned with the notebook with the black cover. He lit a candelabra with five candles to give some light. The sun had now appeared, but the dark clouds still prevented its light from entering the house. Tork had hardly managed to sleep during the journey, but sat down by his mother and browsed through the notebook:

> Today I personally met the Prime Minister. He seemed to me to be a good and just man, and he promised me to be tolerant if I collaborated with his demands. I kept quiet, trying to convince them that I could not communicate in their language.

> The Prime Minister said I was lying and that I was able to talk in Hati, and ordered the guards to be strict with me if I continued not to speak. As I kept silent, they took me to an interrogation room, where there was a strange morbid, bloody smell, disguised by cleaning chemicals. Inside, there was a long table with rests for the feet and hands, and also for the head. In one of the corners I saw a strange device. It seemed to be very old, and was connected to the table by wires, which had electrodes on their ends.

> The guards gave me a punch, trying to make me communicate in their language. As I remained silent,

they put me on the table and place the straps around my arms and legs.

They connected the electrodes to my fingers and turned on the machine. I felt a strong electric shock throughout my body. I managed to resist for a while, but they soon increased the strength and my body began to fry. I felt my skin burning, my muscles contract and my mouth froth. The pain was unbearable, and I ended up admitting that I knew the language.

My hand still trembles when I write.

My diary. Second day far from home. Leo Kliver.

Today is the fourth day. Yesterday I didn't write because I hadn't slept, and, when they freed me I could hardly hold the pen. However, it was a short day. They gave me a definite place to stay, in the solitary wing of the prison. It is a small place, but I have everything I need: a bathroom, a mattress, clean clothes and personal hygiene materials.

They give me two meals a day, and I'm already sick of the smell of fish. I have contact with no one, and they also refuse to let me go out into the sun. I'm locked in the whole time, except when they take me to the Ministry of Justice to be interrogated. It's not a far way from the prison to the Ministry, and until now I have only seen this part of the city. I would like to see more, as the Hive fascinates me.

On the way to the Ministry, I saw that the air-car which took me there was being observed by the press. Only then did I understand why they made me have a haircut and shave: I would have contact with the local media. I had already forgotten how good it was to get rid of my long hair.

In the Ministry, the Prime Minister asked me to collaborate. The press was there and would interrogate me, and if I accused him of any blasphemy, I would suffer a punishment I would never forget.

One of the reporters was in charge of asking the questions.

"A traitor" he said, checking his form. "A traitor abandoned our society nearly two years ago. Six days ago she was tracked to the top of a mountain chain. The Command sent a soldier on an individual mission to rescue her. The soldier failed and was assassinated. Hours after, the Army managed to track his vehicle, which was located near the ruins of an abandoned village. A platoon was sent to the location, and they found you with the vehicle. Were you, Leo Kliver, of the Myra race, responsible for the death of our soldier?"

I thought a little and realized it was best to tell the truth:

"Yes. I killed him with an arrow."

"That was what we thought" the reporter told me. "The tattoo you have demonstrates you belong to a military body. Was your action on the command of a superior?"

"No" I replied. "I abandoned Myra society nearly two years ago. I only killed the person who invaded my territory and killed my bigbugs. I was within my rights of protecting the territory."

"I understand . . . may we know why a soldier like you abandoned his society?"

"I am a deserter" I confessed. "I was in torment . . . Maybe it's better to say 'mad'. My wife died when giving birth to my first son, and I lost my mind. I couldn't stand collective living together, so I abandoned the Myras and tried to find peace in solitude."

"You said 'first son'. How many children do you have?"

"*Only one*" *I lied, and I began to sweat out of anxiety over this. I needed to gauge my words and I couldn't contradict myself. "Just my little Aron. I had said 'first', but maybe I should have said 'only'."*

"*And where is this child now?*"

"*I left him in an orphanage as Aron was very small, because it would have been cruel to take him with me to the desert.*"

"*I understand . . . Why were you in possession of the vehicle?*"

"*I was afraid that other Hatis might appear. I got my things and fled to the mountains. My bigbugs had been killed, and so I thought it was convenient to steal the vehicle in which the soldier had come. I wandered around with no fixed destination for many miles, and I finally found the ruins. I decided to hide there for a number of days.*"

It seemed that the reporter was very serious and professional.

"*We have concrete data to state that inside the ruins there was a chicken farm, a number of chained up hities, plantations, and a herd of bigbugs. Can you really state that, when you reached the ruins, the city was really abandoned?*"

"*I saw nothing. I was hungry and needed nourishment. I used the oven in one of the houses to cook a chicken.*"

"*Thank you, Mr. Kliver, for your help.*"

I was beginning to feel relieved when he continued.

"*There is another question I would like to ask, which I have left until last*" *he said, turning over the page of his form. "Can I ask you it?*"

"*Yes, sir, I'm ready.*"

"Before asking it, I need to clear up certain information about our individual transmitters. The transmitter of any Hati citizen is attached inside his personal
plug connector, which is permanently implanted in the
root of his spinal bone marrow. The surgery for the
implantation of the connectors is obligatory for all Hati
citizens, according to our laws for the prevention of
crime and escapes.

It must be clear to you that it is impossible to take
out the connector from the bone marrow of the user
while he is alive. And so, it is therefore impossible to
extract his internal transmitter. Being aware of this, I
can assure you that Miku, our fugitive traitor, was
always connected to her transmitter, though, for some
reason, our trackers could never locate her . . .

Six days ago, as I told you, the signals from her
transmitter were detected in the mountains. However,
the Command was not able to locate her, neither in the
mountains or in the ruins.

I would therefore like to ask you in all honesty: how
and when did you meet Miku, our traitor? What did you
do to her? And why have the signals from her transmitter been detected in your territory?"

Now I became anxious. The reporter was playing
the game well and had cornered me. I wasn't expecting
these questions. If I said that I had married Miku, this
would bring a series of other questions, which would
not be easy to reply to. They might even link our relationship with the birth of the Myra-Hati. If I said I
killed her, they would probably condemn me for the
death of another Hati . . .

However, this second option seemed more reason-
able to me. As she was considered a traitor, her death
would not be important to them. But what had I done
with her body? I had thrown it in the lake, of course. I
was just about to say this when another possibility

occurred to me: what if they looked the bottom of the lake and found nothing? What had I done with the body?

"Mr. Kliver" continued the reporter. "We are waiting for an answer."

Without thinking I said:

"I ate her . . ."

All the press was astonished, including the man who operated the cameras. Even the prime minister was surprised.

"So you ate Miku as if you were a cannibal?" verified the reporter.

"Yes. Weeks ago I found her near the banks of the Olin and I took her into the mountains. She was very weak and would end up dying anyway. I was hungry. I couldn't eat my bigbug as it was still nursing its young. I could no longer stand eating leaves and cogtas . . . so I killed her, on the grass near the cave. I found a device beeping in her nape and tried to get rid of it by throwing it into the lake. I roasted her body and ate the flesh from her thigh. Then I saw the Hati vehicle coming towards me . . ."

"And where did you deposit the mortal remains of Miku?" By now the reporter had lost a little of his professionalism.

"I took them with me in the vehicle. Some hours later, the sun spoiled her flesh. I abandoned the body and carried on traveling . . ."

The reporter breathed deeply.

"When you found her, did Miku have a son?" he asked. "Was there a child with her?"

"No. She was alone."

"Questions finished."

The reporters left, and I returned to prison after I was once again electrocuted.

My diary. Fourth day far from home. June 213 AE. Leo Kliver.

I haven't written for a long time. I haven't wanted to. After the interview with the reporters, the Empire never again asked about my past, though apparently I had not convinced them. They were much more interested in knowing about the weaknesses of the Myras and the exact place where our Colony had been built.

I never revealed anything and made up the lie that I had forgotten, but this lie had no effect, and from then on, I have to suffer two hours a day of electric shocks until I would reveal everything.

The pain didn't matter to me. The oath I had made to the Myra flag is more important to me than my own life. I am fulfilling the promise I made to the Regent, my society and the army to which I belonged. If I die, I hope that these words will prove my loyalty.

Nothing else to write.

My diary. I no longer count the days. Leo Kliver.

The days are all the same. I have no idea what year it is. So many problems about knowing the day while I lived in the cave, and now I feel that time is no longer important. The guards don't tell me, and neither do I bother to ask.

They used to hit me if I refused to speak. Now any word I say gets me a slap. I have to keep quiet the whole time, except when they ask me a question.

I have no idea why I have wanted to mark this page today. Perhaps in order not to become mad. My mind and this notebook are my only friends, but I don't know until when I can confide in them. My mind is already becoming a traitor.

My diary. I no longer count the days. Leo Kliver.

I am writing today because it was an unusual day. A number of hours ago I met Major Tadashi and his lovely daughter Yuka. I could clearly see Miku's features in the girl, and I felt an unbearable longing for her.

The girl is sensitive and delicate, very different to her father, who is rough and authoritarian. He is the favorite to become the future General of the Hive, and his age will help him get the job. He was still wearing his imperial uniform when he asked his daughter to leave us alone in my cell.

He approached me with short steps. He said nothing, and there was no torture greater than waiting to see what he would do. I realized he was there with the very intention of beating the man who had dishonored his marriage. He did not look at me, or maybe it was I who did not look at his eyes.

After a stifling silence, he finally spoke:

"You will pay dear for what you did to my ex-wife!"

That worried me. A threat was worse than an action. I defended myself by attempting to show that I did not fear him. This was my only defense.

"What I did to your wife was a favor to you. You should thank me. She dishonored her wedding vows and humiliated you before your superiors and subalterns."

He had a furious look in his eye.

"How dare you speak to me about dishonor? You know nothing about me . . ."

"The Hive is a small place. News spreads like electrons on a copper plate."

"This is old news. I married again and I'm now respected. Not even Yuka knows she is the daughter of a fugitive traitor. Leo Kliver, you are hiding something. It is not common for a man to suffer so much and not reveal what they are asked to."

"I have no choice" I said. "If I knew where the Colony was, I would have told you even before the first shock."

"I'm not talking about the Colony, Mr. Kliver, but about my ex-wife. I'm sure Miku is alive and that you are covering her up for some reason. It is a pity we haven't brought the vehicle you stole, as our experts could have discovered whether the remains of Miku had really been carried in it. We lost its signal a long time ago. Its power must have finished. Our satellites cannot locate the ruins, and because of this we haven't managed to find the vehicle . . ."

"I don't understand why you are so worried about" I said. "If a Myra woman did the same as Miku did, she would be burned alive!"

He lifted his hand and punched me in the face.

"We are not like your primitive people. Never again make such comparisons."

The Major began to sweat. He took a packet of tablets out of his pocket and swallowed one without water.

"I pity you, Mr. Kliver" he said, wiping his forehead with a handkerchief. "I've been requesting a personal meeting with you for years, and now that the Command has authorized me to visit you, the only feeling I have for you is that of pity. I'm not the same man I was years ago. Now I need to control my nerves" and he showed me the tablets. "In addition, I promised my daughter I would not be aggressive. Sixteen years ago I would have torn your liver out!"

"Sixteen years ago!" I repeated, incredulous.

"Yes, Mr. Kliver. You've been a prisoner for sixteen years. Almost a lifetime, isn't it? Your son must almost be a man. Difficult for you to put up with it, isn't it? Now, as far as prison is concerned, don't worry. I will make sure they free you soon."

When saying this, he gave a strange smile, and turned around to leave. While he was going out, I heard him chuckling in the corridor.

My diary. Leo Kliver.

Tork stopped reading. Miku asked him to carry on, as she had still not seen what had happened to the husband. Tork was silent for a moment, looked her in the eyes, and then asked:

"Is Yuka my sister?"

Miku wiped her face.

"Yes, Tork. You have a half-sister called Yuka. Major Tadashi is Makuro's real father. When I left him, he was still a recently promoted First-Lieutenant . . . Are you okay?"

Tork was thoughtful. He breathed deeply and looked at his mother.

"Yes. Shall I continue the reading?"

"Yes. But before this I want that you promise me you won't say anything to your brothers. Makuro cannot know his real father is alive. He should be happy that Kliver is his father."

"I'm sorry, Mother, but I think he should be told the truth. You promised us you would no longer hide that which we need to know."

"Yes, Tork. But this is a piece of information will not help. What you need to know will be revealed this afternoon, when Hanara calls the tribe to the lecture he will give. Makuro's father is a nasty man who will never accept him as a son."

"I agree with you, mother, but the problem is not Makuro's father, but our sister."

"She doesn't know about you two, and I don't think that she should know until it is necessary. When the time comes, I will tell my secrets to your brother, but now be a good boy and promise me you won't say anything to anyone."

"As you wish, mother. I give you my word" Tork lifted his hand and swore.

"Swear with your two hands".

Tork lifted his other hand.

"Now finish reading. When you finish, leave the notebook with me. I'll burn it. No one should have these papers."

"Aron will be furious with you" warned Tork.

"Tell him it was an accident. I will say that the notebook slipped out of my hands into the fire. And your father is now with us. He will tell the details of the experiences he went through."

Miku looked hard at her son and made him promise. Tork said nothing, just looked down and continued to read. The letters were big, the sheets were small, and most of them had been scribbled on. He thought that these might be his father's last notes:

> Damn Hatis! Let them all die and their mothers drown in their own blood! Thanks to them my worst memories had been engraved on my mind, and I will carry the consequences for the rest of my life! I will never be able to walk again without the help of damned crutches!

> I cannot think straight. I have come a long way from the Olin and I'm writing while I still have strength, as when the effect of the anesthetic wears off, the pain will be difficult to bear. Cretins!

I'm blindly riding through the desert on the saddle of the bizort, which they gave me to ride. The small transmitter is still in my tooth. Hanara was right. The device resisted the acid in my mouth and never fell out.

Tomorrow or the day after I will camp, and I will carry out the plan made by Hanara I don't know how many damned years ago! I hope the old man is still alive.

What did they do to my legs and feet?

Two weeks after meeting Miku's ex-husband, the Hatis took me to a torture chamber, the damned "gigantic frying pan". They fried me alive! After, they took me to the clinic where they gave me an anesthetic.

When I woke up, I was already riding the bizort, trotting through the sand. At least everything I have is still with me and they were not interested in this old notebook. Strange . . . I wonder what is going through their damned heads.

The wind is beginning to blow strong, and the pain is coming back. I think it is better to carry on and camp soon, before it becomes unbearable . . .

Leo Kliver.

Tork closed the notebook.

"Is that all?" asked Miku.

"Yes. It is finished . . ."

"Fine. Give me the notebook and go to bed. Remember what we agreed on."

"Don't worry. Although I don't agree, I won't say a word to my brothers."

Tork gave the notebook to his mother and went out into the rain. He was tired and wanted to check whether he could sleep in the house of Poko's parents, as he had no courage to face his brothers in the barn after reading the notebook, and the nurses were still busy and making noise in his own house.

Back at the kitchen table, Miku browsed through the notebook without understanding any of the words. She separated the last sheets, with her husband's last notes, and threw the rest on the fireplace. She waited until the pages were burning and went to the bedroom.

The door was still locked. Inside, a number of voices, mixed with other unidentifiable sounds could be heard. Miku knocked on the door, but no one came. Twice more, harder. But nobody opened the door, and the sounds continued. She was going to turn the knob, when she saw it was turning from the inside. The door opened suddenly.

"What do you want?" asked one of the nurses, staring at her.

'What a stupid question!' thought Miku, but she managed to keep calm.

"News of my husband. I want to know how Kliver is."

The nurse had hardly began to speak when Hanara approached and ordered her to go back to give Kliver an injecttion.

"How is he?" she asked Hanara.

"Kliver is fine. We cleaned his wounds, and he will survive." But there was something strange in his voice.

Miku showed the pages she had torn out of the book to Hanara.

"What kind of punishment is this?" she asked.

Hanara took them and looked through them.

"It's an ancient form of torture. The Empire had stopped using it . . . I didn't know you could read Myra."

"Tork read them to me. What are they doing to the prisoners?"

"The torture is called *Furaipan,* "frying pan", in the ancient Hati vocabulary . . . But it's not really a frying pan at all . . . It is used just to punish, without intending to kill.

The prisoner is taken to a room in the shape of a cube, but with an open roof. The cubicle is deep and each side measures exactly three meters. The prisoner is freed if he manages to get out of the room, and the only exit is through the roof.

The walls around of the cube are made of wood and do not absorb heat. But the floor is an iron plate connected to electrical resistances. The prisoner is covered in oil or lard, which makes him slip and slide when he attempts to escape. He is thrown naked into the cubical room, and the electricity is turned on.

The iron floor begins to heat up, and little by little the prisoner is fried alive! The oil on his body prevents his skin from sticking onto the floor, but this greatly increases his pain. Kliver must have resisted for a long time standing up, seriously injuring his feet, and when he could no longer put up with it, he probably fell on his back.

This torture lasts on average for two minutes after the iron plate is hot. While he was still conscious Kliver must have been taken to the clinic, where they gave him the anesthetic and implanted the plug under his skin. Then they finally gave him his freedom, survival tools, and a bizort to carry him.

As they left him with serious injuries, the Command was planning to give him no alternative of survival other than to return to the Colony, so they would discover the route he took to the Myras, through the signals emitted by the plug."

Miku was still shocked.

"I'm sorry, Miku" continued Hanara. "I didn't think the Command would do such a horrible thing. If I had known that they were going to reactivate the *Furaipan* on him, I would never have allowed Kliver to be captured . . ."

"I'm sure it was Tadashi who gave the order" she supposed, about to cry. "That inhuman son of a bitch! I can't forgive myself for having left Yuka with him."

"We can't blame a single man for everything. Tadashi is just a mere cog in the machine. The manipulation of the Hati Empire is the worst thing."

"Can I see him now?" she asked.

"Not for now . . ." replied Hanara, placing his hand on her shoulder. "There is something I must tell you, my dear . . . You'd better sit down."

Miku felt her heart miss a beat when he spoke. Hanara saw that she was ready to hear him and had no scruples in saying:

"Kliver's condition has got worse. We've tried everything possible, but he has not reacted to the medication. His body resisted until all the effect of the tranquilizer passed . . . Then the pain got worse and his body 'turned off'!"

"Turned off!" shouted Miku. "How come turned off? You said he would survive!"

"He is alive and will stay alive for a long time. But he's lost his senses. I'm sorry to tell you this, Miku, but your husband is now in a coma! He is vegetating . . . But unfortunately there is nothing more we can do. I'd like him to help me in the lecture I will give this afternoon, but I can see it will not be possible . . ."

Trying to calm down, Miku managed to whisper a question:

"How long will the coma last?"

"I don't know. You can't say. It could last a day, a month or a year. There is no way of knowing . . . I needed to put a tube into his throat so he can breathe, but I don't know how long he will be able to live like that . . . we have to make sure he doesn't get an infection."

"No, no, no! You must do something! Wake him up! Please! I want my husband back!"

"I've done everything I could. Now it's a question of time. We managed to save his feet, but he will never be able to walk again without help . . ."

Miku quieted down.

"Rest, my dear. Have some tea and try to sleep. You need to rest."

"No. I want to see him."

"Later. I'm now going to finish closing up his wounds, and then I'll select the books I will need for the lecture. The Banjins will not forgive me if I put it off. It's turning out to be a long day . . ."

Outside was still raining. Miku went out of the bedroom and returned to the kitchen. She opened the pantry, and for the first time in her life, she took out a bottle of babadune, a strong fermented drink, forbidden to the women of the tribe. She took out the cork, and poured its contents into her throat.

And then she took a second bottle . . .

CHAPTER 11

ORIGINS

Water began to drip from the roof of the barn. This made the boys, who were asleep, uncomfortable, and they returned home. Aron was fast asleep in bed when he was awoken at eleven o'clock by a noise at the window. His bed was by the wall, and he opened the window without getting up. He stuck his head out but did not see anyone nearby.

The window looked out on to the western side of the village. The rain had stopped, and the birds were singing on the neighboring rooftops. The weather was clear outside, but it was cold, and there was at least an hour before lunchtime. He decided to go back to sleep. He was closing the window when an object hit him in his face.

Aron heard somebody running away. He picked up the object and closed the window. It was a crumpled piece of paper. He got dressed and went to the corridor, taking care not to wake up Makuro, who was snoring in the other bed. He noticed that Miku had not yet slept, probably because she was looking after Kliver.

Aron went into the bathroom and unfolded the paper. It was a handwritten note in Kuata-Noan:

"Meet me by the waterwheel."

Aron began to get annoyed. This message could only be from Daiara. He remembered the dream he had had in the Forbidden Continent, and decided to be tolerant with her.

He went back to his room and put on some light clothes. He once again opened the window and climbed out, closing it from the outside. He went around the back of the village and took the northern road towards the waterwheel.

When he crossed the stream, he saw that a girl was waiting for him. She was wearing a white veil, and, even from far off, seemed tense and anxious.

"Daiara?" he asked when getting near.

"No. It's Jana . . . Daiara's sister" said the girl, as she took off her veil. She looked like Daiara but was a little younger. "Daiara asked me to meet you. She asked me to tell you that she is waiting for you in the cornfield."

"This is getting ridiculous" said Aron, annoyed. "Bring her here. I'm not at her beck and call."

"Please, do as she asks. The cornfield is safe. Nobody will bother you there."

"Look, Jana . . . I'm tired. I've hardly been able to sleep. I'm worried about my father and sorry for my mother. My life has become a mess. I need to sleep before I go to the lecture my grandfather is preparing. It's not the right moment to discuss the problems of a pregnancy that . . ."

Aron stopped speaking and looked at Jana, who had a similar expression to her sister when she wanted something from Aron, a look which made him vulnerable so that he simply agreed with everything.

"Where is she?" he asked.

Jana took him by the arm and led him to her sister, who was sitting in the middle of the cornfield. She left them alone.

Aron tried to avoid Daiara's eyes. He picked a cob of corn and began to peel it, just to give himself something to do.

"Look, Daiara," he finally said. "this is all very confusing at the moment. I don't think this is the right moment to discuss your pregnancy. How do you think my grandfather will react? And your parents? And I'm sure we will have some time before your belly begins to grow."

"You didn't look for me yesterday" she said, angry. "You spent the whole night without looking for me. We haven't seen each other since you fled with your brothers to the Forbidden Continent, and when you came back, you haven't been in contact . . ."

"Daiara, I didn't want to make people suspect anything . . ."

"Go to hell!"

Aron shut up. Daiara got up. She pursed her lips, and her eyes glistened. She sighed, hesitated a moment, and then told him:

"I was lying."

"What?" It seemed that Aron didn't understand.

"There is no child in my womb. I'm not pregnant. My sister and I invented everything to make you accept our relationship. But now I regret it, and I realize that this is not the best way to win a man's love . . ."

Aron frowned, surprised. He tossed the corn on to the floor and turned around.

"Not everything is what it seems". He remembered Judis's words.

"I love you very much, Aron. It's you who have to decide: accept our relationship, or everything is finished between us."

Aron looked at her in disdain, showing his decision. He promised to be patient and so did not get aggressive. Instead he turned around and left, without looking back a single time. He had to attend a lecture in a few hours' time, and what he least needed was a girl to tell him what to do.

At five o'clock, the Ruakan horns were blowing out once again. This time it was not a real or false alarm, or a speech, or a warning about an invasion, but a signal that the lecture would shortly begin, and that all those who wanted to attend should go to the temple hall.

The natives left their tasks, and the village stopped. Baskets of dirty clothes were left under the clothes lines. The older women in their aprons arrived in a happy mood, the hunters got off their bigbugs, the chicken farmer left his fowl, and the fruit pickers left their baskets in the plantations.

This was the perfect moment for an invasion to take place, as even the warriors and the sentries left their positions, leaving the village unprotected and with no lookout. Kliver and Miku were the only ones not to attend. Miku remained in her room, beside her husband, looking after his wounds. In addition, she also knew what he would say in the lecture.

There was a pleasant atmosphere inside the temple. There was plenty of water, which was served in jugs and bowls. The phosphorescent lamps substituted the candelabra. The history books were brought out and put on the stage in front of the altar, and from now on, all the meetings would take place there. If it were not for the plaster images and the strange architecture, no one would think that the temple was the same place as the previous day.

Hanara went in through the door (which had not yet been repaired from the damage that the boys had made when they went through it with the vehicle) and saw that there were not enough chairs for everyone. Many people would have to stand up. Hanara gave the instruction that latecomers should sit on the floor.

"Please, be silent" he said, when he climbed onto the stage. "I don't want to speak louder than necessary."

Everyone was silent.

"Good afternoon to you all" he said, as he looked down to the books. "What do you know about the facts which have taken place in the world which passed from the ancient Era to the New-World in which we live?"

No one replied, proving that they knew little.

"Don't worry. We have until nightfall to explain everything.

The story I will tell you begins a long time before any of you were born. A long time ago, when the sky was still blue, the world was overpopulated. Nine billion of people were piled up on top of each other, all over the planet, making the labor market extremely competitive. As a result, poverty and violence were widespread.

But it was not just overpopulation which caused conflicts in this period. In the second half of the 22nd century, in the ancient calendars, there was also a lack of drinking water, though this was a small problem, as, with the technology of the period, it was possible to desalinate ocean water. Oil reserves ran out, and this made countries search for new energy sources. In spite of the conflicts, humanity remained under control for many decades.

But the most important fact, which had no apparent solution, was the fact that the sun was getting hotter and hotter, melting the polar ice caps and increasing the level of the oceans. Various countries and islands were flooded over, and completely disappeared from the maps."

Hanara took a sip of water and continued:

"Let's now talk about an unexpected fact that took place. At the end of the 21st century, before the floods came, Japan joined South Korea and a number of Chinese states to form the so-called 'Great Oriental Alliance', becoming the most powerful and wealthy

Empire on the planet. This was because they invented,
developed and commercialized the 'plugs'.

I'll try to explain in simple terms how the plugs work. Their origin is very important for you to understand the facts which began the so-called 'War of Extermination'.

Hanara opened a book about the devices and read the following information:

"'Plugs: they were invented by chance, in an attempt
to fight obesity. From then on, they became the main
attraction of humanity, the most popular entertainment
men had been able to invent. This entertainment was
later transformed into a necessary device.

The plugs were interpreted by various religions as the worst drug ever invented — the so-called 'Technological Drug'. Everyone wanted to use them, from boys and girls to old people. At a certain time, it was so common to use them that more than ninety percent of the population had their own plug. They worked and still work in the following way:

Japanese scientists discovered a way to reduce obesity through the manipulation of the senses. In order to do this, it was necessary to control the function of the thalamus, the part of the brain which is responsible for distributing signals from the five senses to the various regions of the brain. The scientists registered these nerve signals and stored them so they could be reproduced later.

They managed to synthesize a biochip, which was able to detect the signals that the thalamus receives, and it was from these chips that the plugs were developed.

Before any nerve stimulus reaches the brain, they firstly reach the spinal marrow. The root of the marrow is situated at the back of the neck, in the nape. And it is there that the plug acts.

Using state-of-the-art nanotechnology, the Japanese developed an electronic memory with these biochips, which could store signals from the five senses which had been detected by the root of the spinal marrow. In other words, the chip, scientifically known as 'artificial thalamus', was able to register in its memory the nerve messages of the various senses.' "

Hanara closed the book and looked at the natives.

"I realize this is a bit confusing, but these details are really difficult to explain . . . I'll try to simplify things even more, and give you an example of the first human guinea pigs who volunteered to test the new invention. In order to do this, we should go back in time a long way:

We can return to the last years of the 21st century, or the first years of the 22nd century. The truth is that no one knows the exact year, but it is known that Catandism had already been founded. In this period, we find Mr. Jushu, a respected sumo wrestler who was overweight. Unless he lost some kilos he would lose his motor skills and might die.

The scientists led by the neuroscientist Dr. Morioshi, the inventor of the plugs, made a small cut Jushu's nape and implanted the first plug.

Jushu fasted for three days, and on the fourth day, while he was plugged in, lying on a laboratory bed, they allowed him to eat anything he wished. He could ask for everything he wanted, any dish, in any quantity.

Jushu asked for a meal with more than fifteen thousand calories, pasta and puddings, extremely fatty and full of sugar. While he was stuffing himself, his senses, when they passed through the root of his spinal marrow, were captured by the plug and stored in his memory.

The next day a light meal of vegetables and sea food was given to Jushu.

And now the magic began:

Using an advanced program, directly connected to Jushu's plug, the scientists were able to inhibit signals coming from his sight, smell, and taste. These signals reached the root of the marrow and were then deviated by the plug.

When turning on the plug to reproduce the senses which had been captured from the previous meal, Jushu was eating the vegetables and sea food, but the reproduction gave him the impression that he was once again eating the dishes from the previous day. That is, Jushu was eating vegetables, but his sight, smell and taste convinced his brain that he was eating exactly the same as on the previous day, when he had eaten more than fifteen thousand calories.

And this is how the plugs work. The device deceives the brain, inhibiting present senses, and replacing them by those which had been recorded previously.

Other experiments were then successfully carried out. A week after the tests on Jushu, it was the turn of Mazume, another overweight sumo wrestler.

After this week, Jushu lost a number of kilos, but, as could be seen on the recording, he took a dislike to eating the same food every day. He was then allowed to choose another menu, which also had no calorie or quantity limit. This time, Jushu did even better: in a single meal, he ask more than nineteen thousand calories. However, the meal chosen by Jushu had been given to the now plugged in Mazume.

The procedures were the same. While Mazume devoured the delicacies Jushu had asked for, his senses were captured by and recorded in the plug. This experiment now established an interesting progression:

The senses captured in Mazume's plug were faithfully reproduced in Jushu's plug. Or rather, while Jushu was routinely eating his vegetables, he was convinced that he was enjoying the meal being served to Mazume. Do you under-stand?

The plugs make it possible to record and relive one's own sensations, and share them with other people.

But there was a small problem in the second phase of the test: at the moment when Jushu was reproducing the sensual experiences of Mazume, all of Mazume's reactions and sen-sations, such as muscular reactions, pain and even blinking, were faithfully reproduced by Jushu. Everything was copied. If Mazume coughed during the recording, Jushu would also cough. If Mazume choked, Jushu would also have the feeling that he was choking.

When the plugs are being used, one relives exactly the same sensations as those who recorded their sensations had. There is no control of the body, the muscles or the senses dur-ing the reproduction, but thoughts come freely . . . It's com-plicated, isn't it? Let us examine another example:

Let us imagine that a user recorded in his plug a visual experience. At the moment when it is reproduced, only one's vision will be out of one's control. One's other senses will be normal, according to the environment, and the will of the user. One's touch, taste, hearing and smell will be sending present sensations, while one's vision will be sending those signals which were recorded in the past.

With this example, we can imagine the following situation:

If a user watched and recorded, only in terms of sight, a hu-tae-mui competition, and reproduces it, let's say, in a religious service, he will be hearing the sound of the present environment, he will be able to talk and pray, but what he will see will be that which a spectator of the hu-tae-mui com-petition would see. He will be blind to the present moment. He will be seeing the competition in front of his eyes, and will blink every time the spectator blinked when he saw it, or will look towards the sky every time the spectator had been looking up at the sky during the competition.

At no moment is one's thought recorded. Thoughts are chemical reactions from the neurons, not nerve messages coming from the senses. When the experiences of a plug are reproduced, the user is fully aware that that is a mere reproduction."

"So, when you use a plug recorded by someone else," asked one of the natives, "do you relive the same sensations he had, including coughs, sneezes, pains . . . but you won't have the same thoughts that person had when making the recording?"

"I can see you understand" praised Hanara.

"I would now like to go forward in time to the year when these devices were marketed commercially and became accessible to everybody. In short, they became a worldwide phenolmenon.

Let me give some examples of what you can do with the plugs:

Men and women recorded enjoyable sexual experiences and relived them whenever they wished. In order to do this, you just had to press a button on the device which was connected to your nape. The users could relive intense moments of their lives at any time, without needing to leave home: a pleasurable conversation in a restaurant, a visit to another country, a martial arts training session, a bigbug rodeo, or a jetpack trip."

Hanara paused before continuing.

"However, the main attraction of the plugs was always to share experiences with other people. By sharing recorded sensations, a user could have sexual intercourse with a friend's wife, without even touching her. Men could finally know the mysteries of female orgasm, and the emotions of giving birth."

"It must have been good to have used the plugs" said Aron in his corner.

"Everyone who lived at that time agreed with you" said Hanara.

"Years after, plugs with real or simulated experiences were sold on the market. If a user wanted to be in the skin of a soldier in the midst of battle, he just needed to buy a device with this content. Plugs with the experiences of celebrities brought in billions of dollars for the Oriental Alliance.

The most expensive experiences were those involving sexual experiences with famous people, murders or deaths. The plug which broke the record of being the most expensive of all times contained the death of a famous racing driver during a race. It was sold in auction for almost four and a half billion dollars.

Everyone, with very few exceptions, became blindly addicted to the plugs. Religious leaders, including the Pope, and the Catandist High Priest, protested time and time again in favor of prohibiting these devices. They used the argument that no one had the right to be, even for a few moments, another person. It was then that Catandism, the main religion to preach the non-use of the plugs, spread through the Old West, substituting many of the dominant religions of the time."

Hanara opened the book and continued to read:

"'Let us now describe the present uses of these devices:

Nowadays, the plugs are not only a sensational form of entertainment. They are also used to solve crimes. In the modern devices, there is a defense system which automatically records the senses of the user when he goes through a trauma, or experiences a chemical reaction, such as an excess of adrenalin or intense pain.

When a user is attacked, his device records what is happening, and this cannot be deleted, making it possible for the criminal to be easily identified. If the criminal tries to disconnect his victim, the plug will emit an electric charge, which will make him keep his distance.'"

Hanara turned over the page.

"'I shall now speak a little about the basic concepts of the 'inter-plug', the technology developed from the ordinary plugs, which was invented less than sixty years ago in the Hati city:

The inter-plug is a network which sends and receives the sensations of the plugs through electromagnetic waves sent through the air. The broadcast can be made live, from a single device to thousands of users. In the Hive, their use is forbidden to civilians except on the days of the official hu-tae-mui championship, using a closed network. The civilians have free access only to the audio network, which is used as a means of communication between users, and which substitutes previous direct communication technology, such as radios or telephones.' "

Hanara noticed that the natives did not understand this, as they had never heard about radios or telephones. After explaining what they were, he continued:

"The High Command officials have total control of the inter-plug, and they use it to monitor the whereabouts of their soldiers and all the Hati population. This is why I needed to unplug Kliver before bringing him, as otherwise his senses would be exposed to the inter-plug, and our people would soon be discovered."

Hanara took up another book and began to browse through it.

"Now we have finished this part of the lecture, I would like to explain why these devices had such an influence on the fate of the world."

Hanara could feel that the natives were feeling uneasy. He decided to have a half an hour break before continuing. Many had not been able to follow his explanations on the devices, and this was the theme of discussion during the break.

Outside, in the square, Makuro was talking about the fascinating possibilities of the devices, and he tried to share his enthusiasm with Tork:

"My brother, just think if we had one of these plugs . . . We could have recorded our trip to the Forbidden Continent and relive it at any time, or show it to the Noans."

"But we can relive it" stated Tork. "All you need is imagination . . ."

"But it is not the same thing. Our memory is faulty, and we forget things, but a recording is permanent."

"Mother has a plug connector" said Tork. "She might have a hidden apparatus."

"Granddad also has a connector. They are Hatis, but I don't think they will let us see the devices, if they hide anything . . ."

"Mak, you are also a Hati. You might have a plug one day."

"Who knows?"

After thirty minutes, Hanara went back onto the stage. Now it was getting difficult to keep the natives quiet, so Hanara decided to tell them a story about the plugs:

"Let's listen to an interesting story. I'll tell you about an unexpected event which happened to environmentalists in the Old-World, when they tried to carry out experiments with animals. The most important of them was the famous 'Day of the Taking'.

In short, it was an experiment carried out by a number of men who wanted to feel in their own skin what it was like to be a wild carnivore for a day. And the chosen animal for this was the lion.

Unfortunately today lions are extinct, but at that time they were considered the king of the beasts. Specialists suggested plugging in one of the lionesses of the pride, as it was the lionesses that did the hunting.

Using state-of-the-art technology for animal plugs, the environmentalists plugged in the lioness. They turned on the recording device and released her on the savannahs for her to do her hunting. The following day, the content of the recording was simultaneously reproduced in the environmentalists' plugs, who could now relive the sensations of a lioness while she was hunting.

The unexpected event took place late in the afternoon:

They were all concentrated on testing the event, and no one was worried about checking the level of the animal's hormones. In the afternoon, the lioness was on heat. The male lion approached her, and . . . 'took' her! Thus the name 'Day of the Taking'. The environmentalists went through the somewhat unpleasant sensation of being taken by an excited lion . . ."

Hanara tried to control the laughter of the natives. When they calmed down he continued:

"After this experience, we realized that the plugs cannot be disconnected when they reproduce a recording, as they may harm the mental health of the user. I could continue talking about plugs for the whole afternoon, without getting tired, but I need to continue the lecture" he said, picking up the book once again.

"Let us now examine the facts which brought about the beginning of the 'War of Extermination'. Listen carefully:

As has already been said, in the first decades of the 22nd century in the old system, the ocean water level increased, resulting in the formation of the Tetis, the only ocean which exists today in the New-World. The countries which made up the Great Oriental Alliance were completely flooded over, forcing their people to move to another continent.

The leader of the Alliance, the Emperor Yusi-Wan, made an appeal to the American countries, requesting the temporary use of their lands. The appeal was refused by the President of the World Peace Council (WPC), Ozack Pinnel, giving his reason as a lack of space to shelter three billion Orientals.

The Council insisted that the victims of the catastrophe would spread over the four other continents. But Emperor Yusi-Wan turned down this proposal, as he wanted all the citizens of the Alliance to be in the same place.

A number of European nations gave part of their territory to the Orientals, as long as they paid a tribute for the use of their land. Yusi-Wan accepted the conditions, and the Asians occupied a large part of Northern Europe.

But this peace did not last for long, as the continent did not have enough resources for everyone, and the unwanted guests suffered considerable prejudice from the original European inhabitants. There was a considerable difference between Western Europe, which followed Catandism, and the Asian occupiers, who did not accept the fact the Europeans were opposed to the use of plugs.

A decree to deport the Asians was then signed, and their future was indefinite. Realizing that a territorial war might begin, the WPC attempted to make a new agreement, this time with the North African-Arab countries, in order to find shelter for the Asians. Yusi-Wan refused to sign the new agreement, as he knew that the prejudice of the Europeans would be repeated by the Arabs, or by any other peoples on whose territory they might live.

The oriental diplomats attempted to demand the definitive expatriation of the Europeans, making them cede their territory, so that the part where the Oriental Alliance had settled would be a free independent nation.

However, this Asian supernation needed a very large territory for its inhabitants, and the Europeans would never accept such a large reduction of their lands. Diplomacy failed, and intolerance increased.

As a final measure, the Emperor was obliged to call up his armed forces to defend the new territory. So it was then, in Europe, on the ground and in the air that a territorial war began.

The Emperor's behavior was criticized by the World Peace Council, and those members of the Asian family, who were spread out over the world, were now constant victims of aggression and prejudice. The Europeans, believing that they would lose the struggle, joined the Americans, and what had been a simple territorial dispute became a Continental War.

During the next decades, the war spread over the whole planet. Ethnic groups isolated themselves, and relations between westerners and Orientals collapsed.

Ozack Pinnel attempted to unify the western weaponry against the Asians, but the WPC President did not realize that the Great Oriental Alliance had a powerful nuclear arsenal, hidden deep in the old Asian Sea, which had secretly been acquired through the years with the enormous profits coming in from the plugs.

Yusi-Wan used this arsenal, and bombed his enemies with heavy weaponry. The American and European continents were completely destroyed, and their population was decimated.

The fall of the West was inevitable, and the few remaining survivors tried to surrender to the Emperor, but Yusi-Wan never accepted the surrender of his enemies and killed them as he not only wanted to conquer the fertile lands where his Alliance could live but return the intolerant treatment his people had suffered throughout the years of the conflict.

The war received a number of names: 'The Great Racial War', 'The Conflict of the Worlds', 'The Ethnic War', 'The War of the Plugs' . . ., but none of these names was as well-known as 'The War of Extermination'. And it was so well-known that it marked the end of an Era, resulting in catastrophes with biblical proportions, and a new calendar was even started. The following years would be known as AE, which means 'After Extermination'.

The nuclear weaponry destroyed a large amount of the flora and fauna of the Old World, burning the gases in its atmosphere, which became the red color we see today.

Yusi-Wan's victorious Empire moved to the African continent. Although Africa also went through great changes after the world flood, forty percent of its territory remained dry. The surface of this new territory has the shape of a huge 'K', and thus became known as 'Kafria'. Although its cities had also been devastated by climate disasters, Kafria was the continent that least suffered bombings and became the only continent that was able to support life and remained stable in the next centuries.

In the south of Kafria, the Orientals of the old Alliance built a fortress-city call 'The Hive'. And because of the fact that their technology gave them the ability to fly individually, its descendants became known as 'Hatis', which in their language means 'bees'. And so Yusi-Wan became the first Hati Emperor.

The books do not say anything about it, but the Emperor never believed he had totally exterminated its enemies. If the westerners had survived the attacks, they would be hidden somewhere in Kafria.

We now know that the Emperor was right: the few westerners who remained had formed into a single race, and had built a small secret subterranean hiding place, which increased in size as the population increased, becoming a huge underground colony. They were given the name 'Myras', which in the language of the prophet of their religion means 'ants'.

Even two centuries after the War, the policy of the Empire has not changed, and the Hatis are still looking for the Myra Colony in order to exterminate or enslave their people. However, in these two hundred years, the Myras have been able to get stronger, and there are signs that the War might now start up again."

Hanara interrupted his reading and looked seriously at the Noans.

"The books say that due to climate changes and the War, the world population decreased and separated into just two groups. Anyone who did not belong to one of these groups was isolated and forgotten by history. If you ask me, I will not know to explain how you, native Indians, are alive here today.

You are the only descendants of the tribes that inhabited the Old World, and who History believes to have completely disappeared. I believe that you don't even know your own origin. Maybe your ancestors came to these ruins to flee from the storms which buried other cities."

"And what about the Evolved Beings?" asked Makuro. "How did they appear in the Forbidden Continent?"

"I really have no idea" said Hanara. "If they really exist, then the other continents are no longer affected by atmospheric radiation. But the Hati satellites still detect a large radioactive mass over those lands . . . I don't know what to think . . ."

Hanara closed the book.

"There are many facts which do not fit into this great historic jigsaw" he said. "I am sure that the present Emperor has knowledge of something which nobody else knows about."

He made a long pause.

"I have nothing else to tell you" he said, nervously. "The lecture is over. You may go home."

Hanara climbed down from the stage and left the temple. The natives looked at each other, puzzled.

CHAPTER 12

NEW DAWNS

Well over a year had passed since Hanara had revealed everything he knew about the New-World. Inside the walls of Ruakan, everything was harmonious. The task of the sentries had eased, and as the young people knew about the real risks of breaking the rules, it was no longer necessary for the warriors to keep a constant watch from the towers.

The year had been one of revelations, anxieties and decisions. Hanara had made the proposal that, when it was proven that the other continents might have life, they would abandon the land of Kafria and move elsewhere. Although the Noans needed a strong motive to leave the ruins, a galleon, which would be able to take all the natives and their belongings, was being built. Its route had already been decided, and everyone agreed that "The Islands of the Painted Balerias", a group of islands to the west of the Tetis, would be an excellent place for them to flee to. The various islands were protected by the dark blot on the electronic maps of the enemies, and Hanara flew over the surrounding areas with the vehicle to make sure they were safe.

It would still be a long time before the ship would be ready, and at the speed they were building it, it would be at least another two years before they left. This was a plan which needed to be approved by all. This time, the decision would be that of the Noans . . .

Aron had decided to put a stop to his relationship with Daiara and began to treat her indifferently. He had not got involved with anybody in the last year.

Makuro had taken charge of the disappeared books and began to study the Hati laws, and he also practiced hu-ta-mui twice a week. Aron had tried to train with him, but soon stopped, as he lacked balance and concentration, and as he was over-anxious to quickly reach the level Tork had reached, he made little progress.

Kliver was still weak. His toes were stuck together due to the burns, but he would be able to walk with crutches if he were not in a coma. Miku fed him through a tube which went up his nostrils to his stomach. She rubbed coconut oil over his body to prevent rashes, she trimmed his beard once a week and read to him every night, as if he could hear and understand.

Although her feelings had been covered by many layers of bitterness, they still existed, and now he was in a coma, she realized how much she loved him. Hanara tried to reduce her pain, and always said that Kliver had needed to be very strong to put up with the torture which had left him like this, and that he had loved her and her children very much, as he had not given in at the first difficulty.

Miku tried to accept the situation, always hoping that Kliver would wake up some day. This was a possibility, and Hanara knew about it. When he had been in a coma for two weeks, Kliver could breathe without the tube in his throat, and he showed signs of life such as movements in his muscles and eyebrows. This comforted her and gave her faith.

However, his physical condition was getting worse: he had lost twenty kilos in a year, defecated in his clothes, vomited the mush which was put into his stomach through the tube, and, from time to time, had strong convulsions, so it was necessary to tie him down so he would not hurt himself.

Miku tried to put up with the situation, but it was difficult . . . she often thought about suffocating him with the pillow. This would mean neither of them would continue suffering. But whenever she found courage to put the pillow on his face, she had no strength to press it down, and she thought about her sons, the men who saw her as a heroine able to put up with everything, whose only consolation was hope, that damned hope which made her able to embrace her husband and one day, perhaps, to be embraced herself. This was her fate, as she could not bring up her sons, for she had given this task to an old, long-haired stranger . . .

The sun appeared on the horizon, announcing a Thursday. Due to disagreement with the hunters, the hu-tae-mui training days were changed to Thursdays, and Tork and Makuro were now ready.

Aron had not spent the previous night in his room.

"Do you think he slept in the barn?" asked Makuro, tying up his belt and looking at Tork in the mirror.

"I don't know. It's been a long time since he spent a night out."

"Do you think he is dating another Noan?"

"I don't think so. After our father returned, Aron has seemed calmer and more obedient."

They finished getting ready, left through the kitchen door and walked towards the hill. On the way, they met Poko's mother, who was hanging out clothes. After they said hello to her, she asked if they knew where her son was.

"Didn't Poko sleep at home?" asked Tork.

"No. Do you think he is going to start giving me problems again?"

"Aron also spent the night out." said Makuro. "They must have been together . . ."

"That is what I'm afraid of. When they get together it means they are going to bring a heavy rainstorm!"

Tork and Makuro laughed and told her not to be worried. Aron had changed, and they must have both slept in the barn.

They said goodbye and continued to walk. On the road to the pasture, they admired the frame of the galleon which rose up from the wheat fields as if it was floating on a straw-colored ocean. No work was being done on it, but the frame of the boat was now upright, and it was so huge that it looked like a diluvial Ark.

Makuro realized that something was happening in the village. It was harvest time, but the fields were deserted; they didn't see a single worker in the fields.

When they got to the pasture, they saw a crowd of natives inside the fence, near the barn, and even Hanara was there.

"Aron and Poko must have got up to something" deduced Makuro. "What could it be this time?"

"Let's ask." said Tork.

They went up to a young Noan girl, who was carrying a baby playing with a rattle, and asked her what was going on.

"Aron and Poko have a new plan" she said enthusiastically. "I think they'll be successful this time."

"They never stop!" sighed Makuro. "I should have realized . . . I wonder what they are going to do this time."

"No one knows for sure" she said. "But a lot of people had got together to see. I heard that they have built a square object made of straw, tied with string."

"A square object?" asked Makuro. "Made of straw?"

"Yes. They say it is light enough to float. I think that this time Buba will make it."

"Buba already knows" Makuro contradicted. "She learned by herself. It is Bubu who still can't do it."

"Sorry. I always confuse their names." And she continued to rock the baby she was carrying.

The boys went into the crowd to look for Hanara, who was waiting with his arms crossed in front of the barn door.

"We are ready for the class, Granddad. Today we are going to learn how to press the points to make our opponent faint, aren't we?" asked Makuro.

Hanara took his pipe, emptied the bowl and filled it up with fresh weeds.

"Wait" he said, as he lit his pipe. "For the time being, the class is postponed. Poko and Aron think that this time Bubu will manage. We are all waiting . . ."

Makuro was disappointed.

"These attempts are becoming an obsession" he said. "He will never learn."

"Believe in your brother. Aron is doing his best."

Tork and Makuro turned around and left the crowd. They leant on the fence and looked on from a distance, complaining about the fact their class had been postponed.

A few minutes later, the doors of the barn opened. The natives stood back, and Aron ran out, holding a thread in the wind. He was barefoot and his trousers were turned up to help him run. At the end of the line, there was a kite, made of straw and pieces of cloth, which was light enough to fly.

Aron ran through the Noans and went up the hill, coming down on the other side. The kite began to fly, and Aron started shouting: "Come on, Bubu, come on . . . get the kite. Come on, boy, come on. Get the kite. Show you can do it."

Out of the barn doors came Poko, holding the reins of Bubu, the reptatile, now aged one year and several months, and which was trying to lift itself off the ground. The animal was now adult, its body was big and strong, but it had not yet learned to fly.

Bubu flapped its wings, was in the air for several meters, but soon got tired and fell to the ground.

"Come on, Bubu, don't stop!" shouted Poko, getting into the saddle. He was the only one who dared to ride a reptatile which couldn't fly. "Come on, get the kite."

The reptatile opened its winds and glided for a number of seconds, looking at the kite which was far away in the sky. It retracted its claws and gained speed, trying to gain height.

"Come on, my boy! You are learning!" said Poko.

Over the other side of the hill, Aron was panting. He sat on the sand, and let go of the piece of bone he was using as a spool, allowing the kite to be blown away by the wind. He had already run two kilometers away from the pasture and was now in the open desert. Far away he could see the shape of a number of curious Noans, who were running towards him.

The wind was strong. The thread was unrolling quickly, and the kite was getting higher and higher. The reptatile was only a few meters off the ground. It stuck out its neck and threw its wings back, as if this would help it to fly.

Bubu was a docile animal, who had grown up with the care of the children in the tribe. However, without its mother to stimulate its instincts, it had never had courage enough to attempt to fly, however much the boys tried to help it. Hanara and the Noans had already lost hope.

On the other hand, Buba, the female, learned to fly alone. The women in the village boasted about her, saying that females were superior to males, and this offended those men who had no sense of humor.

Hanara was one of the few to remain in the pasture. When he saw the difficulty Bubu had to stay in the air, he went into the barn and released Buba from her chains. If she tried to fly after the kite, this would be a great incentive for Bubu.

In fact, Bubu tried much harder when he saw Buba was coming up behind him. He roared, as if he wanted to intimidate her, rose a few more meters, and finally gained confidence in his wings. He flew for fifteen minutes behind the kite, and at the moment when he would take it in his mouth, Buba flew past him and almost swallowed it. Bubu got furious, and began to chase Buba. Poko held on tight.

On the ground, the natives were enjoying the dispute, looking at the two dark shapes in the sky, whose outline could only be seen because of the position of the sun between the clouds. The thread broke away from the reel. Aron was not bothered. His plan was now successful, and he was happy to see the animals fighting over the kite.

A hundred meters in the sky, Bubu got nearer Buba, and was now roaring loud. He twisted his neck and tore the kite out of her mouth, breaking it into pieces. The pieces of straw were blown away by the wind. Poko managed to control Bubu's reins and returned to the pasture, landing on the roof of the barn, with its wings open and the remnants of the kite between its teeth. Buba also came down and threatened to attack Bubu, circling quickly overhead.

"We beat her" said Poko, stroking Bubu's neck.

From this day on, every morning Poko and Aron went for a flight around Ruakan. Poko riding Buba, and Aron getting the reins of Bubu.

A week after, Aron went to the barn at 8 a.m., putting the reptatiles into big steel cages. He bolted and locked the cages, and returned to the pasture. Makuro came to compliment him:

"You've done well, Aron. I have to admit it. I never thought Bubu would beat Buba in a race . . ."

"Thanks" said Aron, still with a victory smile in his face. "Even Granddad has complimented me. Something he's not done in years."

"The animals have grown quickly. We'll soon have to find bigger cages for them."

Aron began to walk, looking down.

"I don't like to see them locked up" he said. "I hate the fact that Granddad makes us lock them up."

"He is afraid they'll fly away from the village, and if they get lost, they won't be able to adapt to the desert and will probably die of hunger."

"You're wrong, Mak" said Aron. "Buba has been flying around since she was a chick and has never got lost. Granddad must be worrying about something else. I'm very close to them, and I don't like to see them in cages. I can feel them blaming me with their eyes. It makes me feel like a jailor."

"You shouldn't be so close to the animals, Aron" advised Makuro. "They won't live forever. Their lives are short."

"I've discovered that in the books I found, reptatiles reach adulthood when they are two, but can keep reproducing for almost fifty years."

Makuro was surprised.

"And where did you find books which speak about reptatiles?"

"Well . . . I've just found some articles and stories about pterosaurs. Reptatiles can't be so different from pterodactyls . . ."

Makuro tried not to laugh out loud.

"Aron, these books are not accurate. They are just based on the imagination . . . how can they know how long animals which died out millions of years ago lived?"

Aron got angry.

"I don't know why we are having this conversation" he said. "I'm not interested in how long they could live. I'm happy to follow their lives, and soon it will be time for them to mate, and we'll have a lot of eggs to look after."

"They are brother and sister" said Makuro. "Do you think they will mate? Bubu doesn't seem very happy in Buba's company . . ."

"We'll know when it's time. Now excuse me. I'm in a hurry. I have to feed them."

Makuro walked onto the hill, where Tork and Hanara were waiting to begin the training, and Aron returned to the village. He reached the chicken farm and picked up a huge sack, filled it with cackling chickens. The chicken farmer, a well-built man covered in feathers, complained:

"If your animals continue to eat up my chickens at this speed, there will soon be no chicken to eat for the tribe." he said, in a bad mood. "I can't allow this to happen. Your dinosaurs are eating more than sixty kilos of my chicken a day."

"Firstly," said Aron, "Buba and Bubu are not dinosaurs. And secondly, these chickens are not yours. They belong to the village. You just have the job to look after them, and our leader has authorized me to take as many as necessary."

This was not the first time that Aron had heard the chicken farmer's complaints.

"I work hard to look after them so you can give your animals a banquet. I must talk to Hanara . . . tonight" he said, crossing his arms, and looking angrily at Aron.

"Well" replied Aron, "you never complained when we used them to feed the hities . . ."

"That's different. We only have five hities, and they don't eat more than four kilos every three days . . ."

Aron tied up the sack and put it on his back.

"You let the hities go hungry, something I won't do with Buba and Bubu" he said as he left the chicken farm with his sack full of chickens, sure that he would need to return to get more and hear more complaints. Each sack weighed some fifteen kilos.

"If we fed the hities everyday, they wouldn't be so aggressive" he heard before he crossed the street.

The bad-tempered chicken farmer was partly right. If the hities were fed daily, they would lose a lot of their aggression, which the tribe needed, so they would keep people and animals who dared to invade the ruins away. Aron disagreed. As for the invasion of animals, the hities were certainly useful, as at night there were a large number of carnivorous animals around the ruins, which tormented the bigbugs and the chickens, and there were also the herbivores which could ruin the plantations in a matter of seconds. But Aron had never seen any person near, other than a member of the tribe.

Still angry after hearing all the insults, Aron returned to the barn. He was sweating after carrying the heavy sack two kilometers from the village to the pasture. He fed the two reptatiles three or four times a day. And carrying fifteen kilos on his back for two kilometers several times a day had given him muscles.

He opened the barn doors and entered the part reserved for the reptatiles, avoiding the bigbugs, who slept in the store.

In the last year, the Noans had needed to build a wall at the back of the main stable, on the first floor of the barn. The reptatiles began to grow, and every day was common to appear bite marks at the bigbugs members. Now they had been put in cages and did not share the same space as the bigbugs, but were at the back, and the hay which had been stored there was now kept on the floor above.

In the last few weeks they had noticed a change of mood in Buba: she was more aggressive, snarled when they locked her up, bit Bubu's neck and furiously attacked the chickens when it was time to feed. Bubu did not attack her, and defended himself by making a strange sound of a chick, making it clear that he had not yet become completely mature . . .

Aron placed the sack on the ground and untied it. In order to prevent fights at meal times he had developed the following strategy: He let Buba eat first, then tied her up again and released Bubu, who finished off the rest of the chickens. However, as there were not many chickens left over, he always had to return to the village to get more. But as today he had heard so many complaints from the farmer, he decided to give Buba only half of the chickens, so that Bubu could have the other half.

The chickens desperately ran around the area, trying to hide wherever they could, while the cages were unlocked. When he opened Buba's cage, Aron had to hold on so as not to fall. She violently rushed out to chase the chickens, gobbling them up one by one as if she were taking part in an eating competition.

The scene of the cackling chickens being torn into pieces no longer shocked Aron. At the end, only the feathers were left, and Aron gathered them together to give to the craft workers, who would use them in earrings, bracelets and head-dresses.

At night, Poko came to tell Aron that Hanara wanted to see him. Hanara had a delicate topic to discuss, and Aron thought he knew what it was about: the chicken farmer had been complaining about him.

Hanara's house was set apart from the village, a few meters along the road behind the temple. It was a shady place surrounded by trees. The river was near, and there was a bridge to cross to reach it. Aron called out Hanara's name. After taking off his shoes, he asked if he could come in.

In the main room, the air was full of the strong smell of incense, which was burning in beautifully carved censers. There were a number of Buddha sculptures around the room, which were lit up by lamps made of tattooed human skin. On the wall, there was a picture with yin-yang, balancing strengths of dualities, and a strange statue, which had come from the Old World, in a reliquary near the cushions. That sculpture represented a white being, half man half elephant.

When he entered, Aron realized that Hanara was not alone, as the chicken farmer, as expected, was also there.

"Sit down" Hanara said, taking his pipe from his pouch. "I called you here to settle the problem with the pterodactyls."

"They are reptatiles, Granddad" corrected Aron.

"It doesn't matter . . . I called you here because I have received various complaints about them, not just from the chicken farmer, but also from the hunters and the bigbug farmers."

Hanara looked at the chicken farmer, who was still dirty from the chicken feed and feathers, and asked him:

"Tell him about the situation, calmly and without getting angry."

The chicken farmer sat down with his legs crossed.

"The chicken farm is very important for the village" he said. "It feeds our children with eggs and white meat. We can't only live from hunting and plantations. A year ago, when the reptatiles were chicks, they only ate four or five chickens a day

. . . now they are adults they are eating an average of sixty chickens a day. If they carry on like this, we can foresee that there will be no white meat to eat in the next three months."

Hanara sucked on his pipe and looked at Aron:

"Can you see how serious the situation is?"

"Yes, sir. I can understand . . ." replied Aron. "What do you want me to do?"

"Solve the problem. You are clever and will know what to do . . . If you don't manage to do so, I'm afraid we will have to sacrifice them."

"No, Granddad!" pleaded Aron. "You can't kill them. Buba and Bubu are the only reptatiles we have. They are so useful for . . ."

"For what?" interrupted Hanara. "What do we need them for? All they do is eat and sleep. They are no use to us."

"That's because you keep them caged up. In the Reforested Continent, among the Evolved Beings, reptatiles are considered sacred animals."

"We are not on the Reforested Continent, and I don't know any Evolved Being" said Hanara, with irony.

"Listen, Granddad . . . if you don't let me look after them, then release them."

"Never. It's out of the question to release them. I'd rather see them dead. They don't know how to hunt to survive, and they would end up by dying . . ."

"That's it!" said Aron, as if the solution had suddenly come. "I can teach them to hunt. If I manage to teach Bubu to fly, hunting won't be difficult. And if they share their prey with us, they could even bring food to us."

"Impossible" disagreed Hanara. "I won't allow them to fly alone."

Aron became furious.

"What's the problem, Granddad?" he shouted. The chicken farmer was smiling, apparently enjoying their argument. "Why are you so afraid of them flying alone? We've allowed Buba to fly on many occasions, and she's always returned to the village."

"That's my fear" confessed Hanara. "They are adults and will follow their instincts. Flying animals seasonally migrate and always return to the place where they were born. If they fly off and are seen by one of our enemies, they will want to capture them, as they are rare animals on the continent. And when they fly back here, they will bring our enemies to the village. We have not been invaded for almost eighteen years, and I want it to continue like this."

Aron realized that his grandfather was really thinking ahead.

"So let's lock them up for the time being. Let me feed them until we leave for the Islands of the Painted Balerias. The islands are isolated from the continent, and they won't be able to fly far. There they will learn to hunt alone."

"It will take a long time for us to finish building the boat" said Hanara. "If they don't learn to hunt now, while they are young, they will never learn. So, we will have to feed them for the rest of their lives, which should not be necessary."

Aron got up.

"In this case, Granddad, you don't leave me another choice. I will take full responsibility for the animals and will teach them to hunt, with or without your permission. Tomorrow Poko and I will fly to look for hunting . . ."

Hanara thought a while and filled up his pipe once again.

"Okay. You win. I see I can't prevent you. I agree that you teach them, as long as you don't let them fly alone. I think you are capable of this."

Aron thanked his grandfather for understanding and asked permission to leave. But Hanara gave him a warning:

"You can teach them, I shall allow it. But I don't want you to go beyond the area which can be seen from the towers. Don't go far off. Teach them to hunt within the observation area. If you disobey, I shall order them to be sacrificed."

Aron agreed, bowed to his grandfather and went to the door. While he was leaving, he could hear the chicken farmer muttering to him:

"You'd better take the smile off your face. The leader won't allow you to go beyond the fields which are within the observation area, and there's not much to hunt there."

Hanara looked at him.

"How dare you?" he angrily asked. "Leave. Your problem has been solved. I don't give you the right to criticize my grandson's actions."

"Y-yes sir . . . But he is not your grandson . . ."

"Do you want to be whipped?" Smoke came out of Hanara's nostrils. "Leave. I don't want to see you here any longer."

"Y-yes s-sir. I'm sorry" pleaded the chicken farmer, standing up.

"And clean yourself up. You need a bath . . ."

The farmer left and shouldered Aron as he went out of the door. Aron frowned at him, but kept calm. After he had left, Aron returned to the room to try to make a new agreement with his grandfather.

"He is right, Granddad. In the fields that can be seen from the observation towers there is not much to hunt. It's a very small area."

Hanara looked down.

"There is a lot of prey around; you just need to look for it . . ."

"But it's just small animals, which come to the village walls at night. If we have to hunt at night, it will be difficult to see anything in the dark. I'm asking for permission to hunt in the same places where the hunters go with the bigbugs."

"You are trying to take advantage of my generosity" replied Hanara, who had not yet got over the anger he had felt towards the chicken farmer.

"Think about it, Granddad. The areas the hunters go to are still safe."

Hanara looked up.

"If you fly outside the observation areas, what will prevent you from flying beyond the safe areas?"

Aron looked down at his bare feet.

"Nothing" he whispered. "But this will not happen. You have my word."

"Your word?" said Hanara with surprise. "I'm sorry, my boy, but you have still not managed to win back my confidence. You caused me so many problems in the past . . ."

"If you don't give me another chance, Granddad, I'll never be able to get your confidence back. And you have to agree that the only culprits for everything that happened in the past are you and my mother, as you hid those important secrets from us . . ."

Hanara breathed deeply.

"Okay, son. I have to agree with you. You have my permission to fly over the hunting fields, beyond the observation limits of the towers."

"Thank you, Granddad. You've understood."

"I agree with this on one condition" warned Hanara.

"What condition?"

"That the rider of the other animal is one of your brothers. I don't want you to go flying around with Poko. He was always your accomplice. I have confidence in Tork and Makuro, who won't hesitate to tell me about anything you get up to. And if by chance something happens, you can say goodbye to your pets!"

"As you wish, Granddad. Tomorrow I shall ask Makuro to go with me."

"Are you still having problems with Tork?"

"No sir. It's just a question of affinity . . ."

It was dinner time. Aron thanked his grandfather once again and left the house, returning to the village to get another sack of chickens . . .

CHAPTER 13

OPPOSITE PATHS

The next day, Makuro was thrown out of his bed in the early morning. Aron pulled off his blanket and opened the window, through which the first light of dawn could be seen.

"What do you want?" asked Makuro, covering his face with his pillow. "It's early."

"Close the window, and let us sleep" grumbled Tork from the other bed.

"I need Makuro" explained Aron. "We have to teach Bubu and Buba to hunt. They've already been saddled, and they are waiting for us in the pasture road. Hurry up, Mak. Get dressed and have a breakfast."

Makuro had not yet been told.

"Why do we need to teach them how to hunt? You feed them every day . . ."

"Granddad doesn't want us to give them so many chickens. Come on. Hurry up."

"Ask Poko. He likes to ride Buba."

"I can't. Granddad will only let me fly if one of you comes with me."

"Take Tork."

"Don't even think about that" said Tork, rolling up in his blanket. "I've got a lot to do, and it's two hours before my time to get up."

"Come on, Mak, get ready" asked Aron, shoving the bed.

"Ahh, okay . . ." Makuro agreed, sitting up on the mattress and stretching. "Wait in the kitchen while I get ready."

Makuro got up and stumbled into the bathroom. He pumped up water and wet his face, brushed his teeth, using home-made toothpaste made of mint and tobacco.

He went to the kitchen and sat down at the table, scratching his groin, still wearing his pajamas. He spread butter over a corn cake and put it into his mouth, chewing it as if he were ruminating, looking into the distance.

"Hurry up" said Aron.

"Calm down. I still have to get dressed."

"You only have ten minutes. Granddad is waiting on the road."

"What does he intend to do?"

"Probably make you swear to tell him everything I do. We don't have permission to go beyond the hunting fields."

"It won't be easy to teach Bubu to hunt . . ."

"He will copy everything Buba does. Let's go."

"Take it easy . . . go ahead, and I'll catch you up."

Minutes later, dressed and walking along the road, Makuro questioned Aron:

"Do we have to go hunting every day?"

"Yes" replied Aron. "I can't use the village's chickens any longer. We'll go hunting in the morning and afternoon unless we get enough food just in the morning . . ."

Makuro thought.

"I can't come with you every day. I have classes I don't want to miss."

"You have to settle that with Granddad."

"Why doesn't he ask Poko, who doesn't have anything to do all day?"

"As I told you, Granddad can't rely on him. And Poko has problems with his parents. They don't want us to spend so much time together."

"I understand."

Hanara was waiting for them near the pasture, leaning against a tree. Bubu was tied to one of the branches and roared with happiness when he saw Aron, as he probably connected the young Myra with food. Buba gave him a bite on his wing so he would shut up.

"You're late" said Hanara, with a vacant look in his eye, his white toga blowing in the wind.

"It was difficult to get Makuro out of bed" accused Aron.

"It's because was a bit early. I spent last night studying the elections system of the new Hati Emperor . . ."

"That is no excuse" said Hanara. "I also went to bed late. But I'm here, strong as a rock. And I'm much older than you."

Makuro shut up, with a grin on his face, looking at the sky which was becoming red as the sun got higher.

"Okay" continued Hanara. "According to the discussion we had last night, you are both in charge of teaching the repta-tiles to hunt. Don't go beyond the limits of the hunting fields" he said, looking into Makuro's eyes. "I rely on you to tell me if your brother fails to obey."

"I have things to do" complained Makuro. "I won't be able to accompany Aron every day. Why don't you send Poko?"

"Obey me. The decisions have been taken. I have changed times to help everybody. It's either this, or the animals will be killed."

Makuro breathed deeply, and his breath could be seen in the cold air.

"Okay" he agreed. "But I'm sure it will be a complete failure. I've never hunted before, not even with the bigbugs . . ."

"Let their instincts guide them. They will know what to do."

"Makuro is afraid of flying," joked Aron.

"It wasn't me who was scared stiff, shouting like a little girl, when their mother saw us taking the eggs."

"That was almost two years ago" said Aron. "And you were too far off to have heard anything."

"Spare me your argument" said Hanara. "You're wasting time. Get the reins and hurry up."

Aron smiled to challenge his brother and got onto Bubu's saddle. Makuro tied up the protective equipment and reluctantly got onto Buba's back. Hanara released them and waited at a distance, as their take-off might be dangerous.

Buba flapped her wings and rose smoothly into the air. Bubu needed to run a lot and jump off a ledge to maintain stability and gain height. From the sky, Hanara became smaller and smaller.

Aron found it difficult to pilot Bubu. The problem was not that the animal had only begun to fly a week before, but rather the fact that he continually disobeyed commands. His competitive spirit to outdo Buba made Buba's pilot decide the direction both of them would take. If Buba turned to the right, Bubu followed her, even though his pilot ordered him to turn left.

There was no such problem with Buba. Although she was ferocious and more violent, she would always be guided. Perhaps because she had been trained from the time she was a chick . . .

The shadow of her wings could be seen on the ground below. Looking behind, the ruins got smaller and more distant, and they became almost invisible because of the planet's natural curve. The flight was calm and peaceful, and they could hardly notice the change of pressure when they were high up.

The hunting fields were getting near. The countryside, which had been a desert of dry and burned vegetation, gave way to small savannahs full of trees.

"Hey, Mak, we are now flying over the hunting fields" said Aron.

"I can't see any hunting from up here" said Makuro.

"It's too soon. The animals must be asleep. Let's fly around the fields."

Clouds were slowly rising in the sky, and Makuro suggested they flew lower. He loosened the reins, and Buba went under the clouds, gliding down with her wings open. Bubu clumsily followed her. Aron loosened his reins and let him fly freely in a straight line, turning just a little to the East. They were no longer over the hunting fields, and in the distance, the beginning of the vegetation near the River Regit, one of the tributaries of the Olin, could be seen.

"Hey, Aron" said Makuro, shouting so his brother could hear him. "I think we've already gone beyond the hunting fields."

"I know" shouted Aron back. "But we still haven't seen any animal to hunt."

"That's because we're too high. Let's return and land in the hunting grounds. On the ground it will be easier to locate the animals."

"I think we'd better wait for the hunters to come to the fields so we can see what they do."

"It must be seven o'clock. The hunters only leave the village at eight. And, riding the bigbugs, they will only reach the fields around midday. I suggest we do something now or return later."

"We can't return later. Granddad has decided on this time so we don't get in the way of the hunters."

"This is already becoming a nightmare. We have no idea of how to hunt, so how can we get sixty kilos of meat for them to eat?"

"If we attack a big animal, we'll get enough for the whole day."

"It's difficult enough for us to capture a chicken when it escapes from the coop . . ."

"If I had known you would only moan, I would have asked Tork to come."

"Let's land and decide what to do."

The animals spiraled down and landed near an area full of mushrooms. Makuro dismounted and tied Buba to the trunk of a big cogus tree, which had bluish pulp. Aron told him off:

"We've come here to teach them to hunt, not to tie them up while we do all the work."

"I know, but before teaching them we have to find the hunting, don't we? And we have to do that."

Aron stretched his back, rubbing his eyes and looking around, getting used to the territory. He then suddenly pointed to something above.

"What are you trying to show me?" asked Makuro.

"Shut up" he whispered, continuing to point. "Look up."

Makuro walked away and looked up above the cogus. On top of it, a strange bird was looking at them. It must have measured a meter and a half long from tail to beak. It jowl was yellow, its feathers were red, and it had a plume.

"Keep still" said Aron out of the corner of his mouth. "This is our first catch."

"And how are we going to get it?"

"I'll get up onto Bubu and you throw a stone at it. I'll try to catch it in the air. It will be like catching a kite in his first fly."

"I don't think it's a good idea," disagreed Makuro. "Until Bubu takes off, the bird will have flown away . . ."

"So you go with Buba and I'll throw the stone."

"I'd rather throw the stone, and you can ride Buba . . ."

"What's the problem, Mak?"

"I don't think I'll be able to control her when she's chasing the bird. She might get out of control."

Aron looked at Makuro in disdain and took Buba's reins. While he was mounting her, Bubu, maybe feeling rejected, began to roar. The bird was frightened and flew off.

"Haaaa!" shouted Aron, hitting his heels into Buba's neck. "After it!"

Buba flapped her wings and took off, chasing the bird. Makuro jumped onto Bubu and also took off, managing to reach them in a short time.

The bird was small, and most of it was made up of tail feathers, but it was very fast. It got further and further from its pursuers and was almost reaching the banks of the Great River.

Aron and Makuro were now way beyond the boundary of the hunting fields, and they might get lost. They crossed the bed of the river and were now near the mountains in the East. The reptatiles were beginning to get tired.

A flash of light suddenly broke the sky and threw a huge ball of white light above them. This frightened the bird, which flew away into the clouds. They then heard the powerful sound which accompanied the flash. It was like thunder but much more intense, and made the air shake.

Although it was similar to the natural phenomenon which brings rain, this flash of light could not have been lightning. It was like a field of energy spreading, something caused by a strong explosion. It came from behind the mountains in the East, less than fifty kilometers beyond the banks of the Olin.

Full of curiosity, the boys stopped pursuing the bird and flew towards the mountains, landing on top of one of the lower rocky peaks. They dismounted and climbed a high pile of stones on the other side of the cliff, looking at what was taking place.

The explosion was not repeated. However, down at the bottom of the mountain, they could see an open plain where thousands of red rays where sparkling on the desert sands.

One of the rays changed its angle and bounced upwards, reaching the mound of rocks where the boys were, almost hitting Makuro's leg. Buba was frightened, opened her wings and began to fly away on the River's direction. As always, Bubu began to chase Buba and also flew off, leaving Aron and Makuro alone on the mountains, lost and without any way of returning home.

"They've abandoned us!" shouted Makuro. "We're lost!"

"Don't worry" said Aron. "We're near the banks of the Olin. The river cannot be far from the hunting fields. We just need to return to the fields and wait for the hunters."

"You're wrong. We are very far from the hunting fields. We flew for more than half an hour beyond their limits. We must be more than a hundred kilometers away."

"There will always be a way to return" continued Aron. "If the worst comes to the worst, the reptatiles will fly back to the ruins, and Granddad will send a rescue team."

"I hope you are right . . ."

"The most important thing now is to find out what those rays are. Let's check."

Aron climbed down the mound and went down the curving path around the mountain, waving Makuro to accompany him. The path was at times difficult as there were many steep narrow parts, which made them hold on to the rocks and get down onto the backsides in order not to roll down.

The path widened as they got lower, and the sound of the rays became louder. It was as if a battle was taking place down below. Explosions could be heard among the noises, followed by the sound of arrows whistling through the air.

"What are those noises?" asked Aron. "A natural phenolmenon? Electric discharge?"

"Yes. It is electrical discharge," said Makuro, "But they are not a natural phenomenon. It seems as if the Myra-Hati war has finally begun."

"Are you sure?" said Aron, not as shocked as his brother.

"It seems to be the case. Let's look from near."

Makuro went on ahead, and they went to the bottom. At the foot of the mountain they found a deep fissure in the rocks which went down to the plain where bursts of fire and lasers hit the blowing sand. They lay on the ground and crawled to the fissure where they could see everything.

"My God!" shouted Makuro.

"What the hell!" said Aron.

On the horizon beyond them, three hundred meters away, thousands of men in black were defending themselves from the attacks of heavy war airships. Many of them were dying, though they counter-attacked with machine guns, crossbows and grenades. Iron balls were fired out of cannons on the backs of war bigbugs, which were equipped with infrared visors and anti-radiation armor.

The bigbugs furiously galloped over the machines, and many fell to the ground when receiving the impact of the energy bombs. Some had automatic artillery on the side of their saddles, and others had catapults and spear launchers. There were also a number of bizorts, which pulled large lead carts, where infantry soldiers were hiding from the airborne attacks.

The strategy of the men in black was simple and easily understood by Makuro: as they had no chance of challenging the strength of the enemy, their intention was to capture the enemy commander. They tried to reach him or kill him, take him out of the battle, but capture was their clear priority.

Archers, spear-throwers, shield-bearers and marksmen were strategically positioned to capture him. The commander of the opposing battalion was easily identified, as his armor was red while that of the rest was golden, and they had wings with turbines on their backs.

When realizing what the enemy was intent to do, the commander in red turned on his jetpack and took refuge in his airship, flying at a height which could not be reached from the battlefield.

The men in gold were also suffering losses. Although their power of attack was much greater, they had no more than a few hundred men, while there were thousands of men in black. From time to time their airships were hit by the fire coming from the catapults and the cannons, which shot them down. Some were hit, and then plunged into the sand. They knew they could easily win the battle if they attacked with heavy weaponry, but keeping the Kafria territory was more important than victory. They could not destroy what, according to their belief, was the only inhabitable continent in the world.

"What's happening?" asked Aron, who could not understand what he was seeing.

"The war has begun." said Makuro, without looking away. "We must tell Granddad. The men in black uniforms are Myras. And those in golden armor belong to the Hati race."

"So what we are seeing is a Myra-Hati battle? Really?" Aron could not believe it.

"That's what it seems to be. When Granddad told us about the threats of war, it seemed to be a long way off. However . . ."

A short distance away, the battle was spreading, and the ground was full of Myra bodies. Contradicting what many believed, they also had machines. Automatic cars, anti-bomb armored vehicles, and drilling wagons were slowly advancing on the Hati defense.

On both sides, a number of troops were led by women, which went against what Makuro had learned and made him wonder:

'Has the oppression of women in the Hive finished? Did his mother's escape bring about changes in the general opinion of the people, resulting in demands for places for females in the command? Or had the Hati Emperor been changed, and maybe the new Emperor had more open and fair ideas, which included women leading battle troops?'

The new Emperor might even be a woman. This was a possibility, and Makuro knew about it. He had recently been studying Hati laws and discovered that any citizen could become the new Emperor. All that was needed was to have the pure blood of the race. Even Hanara or his mother, who were considered traitors, or even he, who had never had contact with the Empire, might one day take the throne (if they fulfilled the requirements of).

He stopped thinking about this when he started admiring the strategic ability of the Myras: With their cannons and harpoon-launchers they managed to hit three enemy airships, making them fall to the ground without damaging them. Drilling wagons destroyed their protective covering, and the marksmen went in and killed all their crew.

The battle carried on for more than an hour. When the Hatis had forgotten about the captured airships, a mechanical digger came out of the ground. Three Myra soldiers wearing silver vests got out, climbed into the airships and took their controls. These were three combat engineers, able to pilot airships.

They took off and opened fire on the leading enemy airship. The Hatis were not expecting this: three airships, which were apparently theirs, were attacking them. The proton cannons were turned on, and the leading ship was finally shot down. Myra soldiers surrounded it when it reached the ground. Under the aim of the machine guns, the Hati commander got out of his cabin and surrendered.

The battle was now interrupted. The men in black commemorated their capture and proudly waved the red flag of their clan.

"My God!" said the boys, protected between the rocks.

On the plain in front of them all the soldiers put down their weapons, waiting for orders. The Hati commander was handcuffed, taken prisoner by the Myras, and guarded by a large number of soldiers. If the Hatis attacked, their commanding officer would be killed, and an attack could only be ordered by the officer who had given himself up. Peace was temporarily established.

"What shall we do now?" asked Makuro. "Shall we carry on looking or go away?"

"We can't go" whispered Aron. "There are lots of soldiers looking this way. We'll have to wait for the troops to disperse, and then we can return to the Olin, so that the Noans can find us."

"Are you sure Granddad will send a search team?"

"If the reptatiles find their way back . . ."

The situation on the battlefield was delicate. The Hatis did not move, and the Myras did not lower their defenses.

Aron began to stare at a lovely Myra girl who was looking after the supply wagons. She was wearing a shiny black uniform which showed off the curves of her body, emphasizing her breasts and her hips. She was carrying a huge machine gun, and, because of the hot sun, took off her helmet, showing her long honey-colored hair. Aron was enchanted. He had never seen such a lovely girl and was sorry he had not brought the binoculars.

At the moment she turned around, Aron lost concentration and only then realized that some stones were falling from the slope behind, hitting his hand. He turned his head and shuddered with shock. His breathing became heavy. Makuro noticed he was behaving strangely and also looked behind, reacting in the same way.

Behind them there was a soldier holding a crossbow, ready to shoot, aiming directly at their heads. Aron and Makuro shrank against the stones and remained still, their hearts beating quickly, and their knees began to knock.

The soldier was tall and wore a tight black uniform with green stripes on his chest. His arms were bare, showing the tattoo of a number on his left arm. He had a helmet with two lights at the side and an aerial in the shape of a "V" in the middle.

"Who are you?" he asked.

Makuro didn't say anything, and Aron stuttered:

"W-we are h-hunters of a tribe . . ."

"How do you know Myra language?" but he didn't wait for an answer. "Get up" he said, pointing the crossbow at them. "Walk."

They immediately obeyed, getting up and beginning to walk. The soldier made them put their hands on the back of their necks and follows then, and his crossbow was always pointing at their backs.

All the interest of the battalion was now directed to an un-usual scene as two young men, one apparently a Myra, and the other a Hati, were walking together. It was difficult to say what races they were from, as their sunburned skins and long tangled hair made them look alike.

Although they seemed somewhat primitive air, the boys were not savages. Their posture eliminated this possibility. They had certainly grown up together in some isolated place, and seeing them together surprised even the most experien-ced of the officers.

Few of them remembered the story of Kliver and Miku. Al-though they were well-known in their societies, nobody rem-embered these facts. How could they know that their paths had crossed? How could they know that Kliver's son had grown up with Miku's son? The probability of the Myra deserter meeting the Hati fugitive was small. But it happened. And the result of this was a boy of mixed-race who the world did not yet know.

Taking advantage of the fact that the Myra troops were so distracted, the Hati commander managed to escape. Nobody noticed him, a man in red armor desperately running away, pulling chains attached to his handcuffs.

"Who are you?" asked the Myra Major, a bald man with a grey moustache.

"We are hunters." Makuro tried to explain, tense.

"Where did you learn to speak Myra?"

"We don't know, sir. We were abandoned when we were very small, and we have always spoken this language." Makuro lied in order not to harm the Noans.

The Major called the soldier who had brought them.

"Where did you find them?" he asked.

The soldier clicked his heels and stood to attention.

"Sir, I found them spying on the sides of the mountain" he said out loud, speaking fast.

"At ease. You will earn a medal because of this." And he turned to the young men once again. "Where do you live and with whom?"

"We live in a native village, upstream" said Aron, and Makuro began to worry about the information Aron was giving away.

"Natives?" asked the Major, trying to hide his surprise. "What do you know about the Myras, in addition to the language?"

"We don't know very much, sir. We were just hunting in the region when we heard the sound of explosions."

"I understand . . . There is no time for explanations. We must leave. Be aware that we will take you with us . . . Captain" called the Major.

A man in the black officer's uniform appeared from among the rest of the soldiers. He marched towards the Major and saluted him.

"Yes sir?"

"The battle is over for the time being" said the Major. "Apparently the Hatis are not planning to reopen fire. However, the enemy commander managed to escape. We will take these two young men with us as trophies of victory. Handcuff them."

Differently to the Myras, who understood every word of the enemy language, the Hatis understood nothing about what was said between the Major and the boys. However it was not necessary to understand the language to decipher their intention. The fact they had been handcuffed showed that they had been taken prisoner and would be taken to the Colony.

The Hati commander could not allow this to take place. He also had to win his trophy. He opened his helmet communicator and called for one of his negotiators, ordering him to make his demands from the loudspeaker of the airship, which hovered over the Myra troops, announcing:

"The negotiator of the Hati command is speaking to you. If you wish to take the young Myra prisoner, do so. But we will not allow you to take the Hati. If you do so, we will open fire. Do not do anything stupid. Hand over the Hati, and you will live."

It was necessary for the Myras to know the language of their enemies, and therefore, like good soldiers, they quickly raised their weapons to get ready for the fresh attack.

"Put down your weapons" shouted the Major, confirming his order with his hand. "Captain, give the other boy to the Hati command. It will be enough just to take the young Myra with us. So we can go back to our people in peace" he said out loud, speaking Hati, so his enemies could also understand.

So Makuro was handed over to the Hati troops. The leaders of the battalions agreed to a truce and went off in opposite directions.

Aron and Makuro looked at each other for the last time, their hearts heavy, and waved a painful goodbye. They would probably not see each other or their family and friends for a long time

The noise which the heavy warships made as they left was excruciating. Makuro was taken to the Hive in the South while Aron went to the North, in a caravan consisting of lines of thousands of men and women, and carts and carriages pulled by draft animals.

Shortly afterwards the battlefield was abandoned. In holes in the sand, there were now only the mutilated corpses of

Myra and Hati soldiers, the only signs that the first Myra-Hati battle had taken place.

CHAPTER 14

CHANGES

The Myra caravan, which was slowly crossing the desert, was being observed through the polished lenses of a telescope. Hidden at the top of a mountain pass, Poko, together with his father and dozens of other hunters, could not see the boys among the wagons. Hanara's intuition told him that they had been captured.

"A Myra caravan crossing the deserts" said Hanara. "I'm sure there was a battle. From here I can see the injured being treated. There are war bigbugs and men in uniforms. I'm sure my grandsons are with them."

"The reptatiles would not have returned without them" said Tork, looking through the binoculars.

"What should we do?" asked one of the hunters. "Should we leave or continue the search?"

"We must first be sure about what happened. Let's follow the caravan trail in the opposite direction" ordered Hanara, sitting on his bigbug. "If we can't find the boys, we will be sure they have been captured. And if either of them mentions our existence, and I think they will, we must immediately abandon Ruakan. We are running a serious risk by continue living there."

"How can you be sure they haven't been killed?" asked another hunter.

"It is not in the interest of the troops to kill them . . . They will be interrogated. Let's go before it's too late."

"Can't we go up to the troops and try to negotiate their freedom?" asked Poko.

"Don't be silly, boy. We don't know how the Myras will react. Do you also want to be taken prisoner?"

"Granddad is right" said Tork, on the back of the bigbug. "Let's follow the caravan trail. This is not a search team anymore, but an investigation team."

The Noans waited until the caravan was in the distance and began to follow the trail it had taken, going down the mountain. There were nine people on five bigbugs: Tork was on the back of Hanara's bigbug, and Poko was together with his father. One of the hunters rode alone, carrying the baggage in case they needed to camp.

The trail left by the caravan could hardly be seen, although it was very recent. Although the dry arid ground was hardly marked they did not lose the trail, and in less than an hour they reached the open plain between the mountains, where they found hundreds of bomb craters, and corpses on the ground.

"I was right" said Hanara. "Look. Myra and Hati bodies. The war's begun, and if we want to keep our tribe out of trouble, I suggest we speed up the construction of the boat and leave the ruins as soon as possible."

They dismounted and began to look for the boys. One of the natives remained on the outer edge of the plain, watching the surroundings and making sure that the bigbugs did not run off. He tied their reins together in a big knot.

Tork felt bad when walking near so many corpses. The smell of blood was so strong that he had to pinch his nostrils. Vultures hovered over the fields and tore holes in the corpses when they landed, regardless of the people looking on.

Some of the corpses were so maimed that, if it had not been for the remains of their uniforms, it would be impossible to tell which race they belonged to. Others were not yet completely dead. A Hati soldier, whose legs had been crushed, grasped on to Tork's foot, trying to move his lips to ask for help. Tork turned away and felt his stomach turn over. Hanara stroked his hair, and, shortly before the soldier lost consciousness, said:

"Don't be shocked. They have died doing their duty. For a soldier there is no honor greater than giving his life for something he believes in. This is the result of human ignorance and will never change."

After the search, Hanara concluded that Aron and Makuro had really been captured by the Myras, or by the Hatis. That night, he would need to organize the natives to immediately leave the ruins.

Not far off, traveling handcuffed in one of the first wagons in the caravan, Aron could hear the happy Myras getting drunk and singing the victory song of the clan. They were traveling slowly and making a loud noise wherever they went. He could not concentrate on anything that went through his mind while he was looking at the monotonous landscape as they slowly passed slowly through it. Aron was sorry that his Hati brother had been taken by the opponents.

It passed through his mind that he would never again see Makuro, Poko, and Hanara, the native community or the ruins again. However, he was not afraid and tried to believe that Makuro would be okay wherever he was.

"Do we have far to go?" he asked the wagoner.

The man turned to him and smiled.

"A month or two" he replied.

"Months?" said Aron, surprised.

"It is a long way to Loagy. But don't worry, son. While you're with us, nothing will happen to you. Have a bit of our liquor. We've brought a number of barrels. It will help you to relax."

Aron got a cup, coordinating his handcuffed hands with great difficulty to take it to his mouth. He sat down on the floor of the wagon and tried to forget his worries.

In a short time he felt his muscles relax and the tension disappear. He then felt happy and began to accompany the rhythm of the Myra songs. More barrels were opened. The soldiers, including the women and some of the officers, began to dance and jump on the wagons. His handcuffs were soon taken off, and he was now free, but nothing in the world would make him run away . . .

In the afternoon, the Ruakan horns were blown once again. Perhaps for the last time. Hanara had called everyone for a meeting in front of the scaffold, which was now inside the temple.

"I've called you here so we can organize our departure" he said. "The war has begun, and we are at risk if we continue living here. We must finish constructing the boat and leave as soon as possible for the Islands of the Painted Balerias. Unfortunately, Aron and Makuro have been captured by the troops. I believe they will undergo severe interrogation, possible being tortured, and I doubt whether they will keep their mouths shut to protect us . . ."

Tork, Poko and the hunters gave further details, telling what they had seen on the battlefield: hundreds of mutilated corpses, which were a banquet for the vultures.

The people were frightened. However, a few of the Noans refused to leave. They said that their beliefs forbade them to abandon their birthplace, and they decided they would defend their territory at all costs. They also said that there was the possibility that the Islands were covered by atmospheric radiation, and this would also kill them.

"There is no time for discussions" continued Hanara. "We have to act as quickly as possible. I will not impose my authority on those who decide to stay. I will just warn them about the risks. The plan is to get everything we need, and, in the early morning, to take it to the shore on the western coast of Kafria. There we will finish building the boat, as, in addition to gaining time, it will be easier than dragging it over the many kilometers which separate us from the ocean. However, as its structure is now ready, we'll have to drag it anyway. But the structure is light when we compare it to the completed boat.

We need all the available raw material: cloth for sails, wood for the hull and the masts, and a lot of ropes. The scaffold, the barn and the towers will be dismantled, so we can use their wood. The bigbugs, the old vehicle and the reptatiles will help us with the transport.

We have to build wagons which can carry big loads. We'll need tents so we can camp during the days we will spend on the beach, building the boat.

But, first of all, I need to know who will come with me. Those who are not against leaving, take a step forward."

The women were the first to take a step forward. Then the men. The majority thought that leaving would be the best decision to take. After all, Hanara would not abandon his grandchildren in the middle of the desert, merely to give credibility to his intentions.

However, a number of Noans continued to go against the majority. If dying was the question, then they would die with honor, and they would not run away from a threat which might be false. In addition, they still had the old hiding place in the catacombs they could escape to in case of invasion.

It quickly got darker. Tasks were given, and they began to make the move. There was no time for idleness. Some of the Noans packed the library books, and others gathered the big-bugs together. Some looked after the water and food, and others collected the necessary material to build the boat.

The work needed to be done quickly, as they were afraid of a possible invasion. There was no time for perfection. Babies cried, women shrieked, and men shouted at each other.

Hanara, impatient with all the complaints, studied the electronic map in the vehicle, trying to find the best way to reach the coast. But, because of the black blot, which was always on the monitor screen, he gave up and used one of the printed maps in the library.

His greatest doubt was whether to take his sword on the journey. He thought it over and decided not to take it, as it would be open to the Noans' curiosity, and it would be diffi-cult to hide it. In addition, the sword was now safe between the cracks in the uranium mine walls, under the laboratory. Its entrance was protected by a steel door, and a six-figure password was necessary to open it.

Not even Hanara remembered the code. It was recorded in the plug which had been lost in the desert, in his old straw hat. It was now buried deep down in the sand, and it would be very difficult for anyone to find it.

While Hanara decided on the route they would take and the natives were working, Kliver continued weak in his bed. He was very thin and debilitated, and Miku thought he wouldn't survive the journey.

They needed to work for three long days for everything to be ready for them to leave. The bigbugs, loaded with all the Noans' baggage, were waiting at the western gate of the village. The frame of the galleon had been placed on huge logs, used as rollers, and its beams were roped to the harnesses of the animals and the axle of the old Hati vehicle.

In the square, Hanara tried for a last time to persuade the Noans who had decided to stay to come with them, but it was in vain – they would not listen to him. They said that, as the Hati airships were so fast, if they didn't invade the village in three days, they would never do so.

Hanara respected their decision and ordered that one of the towers should be left standing. He told them to hide in case there was a threat, and they should continue to live as they always had done. From that moment, he was no longer their leader, and they needed to elect a new representative. This should be simple to do if they found two or three candidates. This group consisted of only sixteen natives, the majority old, of whom only four were women.

Hanara gave them his blessing, telling them to go to the west coast of the continent in case they changed their minds, but he didn't leave them a map as if an invasion took place in the next few days, it would show their location to the troops, and this would be dangerous for the Noans who would go on the journey. But Hanara was not worried about their being interrogated as they could neither speak Myra or Hati, and the troops could not speak Kuata-Noan. An interrogation would thus be useless.

And so, on a warm Tuesday morning, the natives began to move. There were few bigbugs to carry so many people, and the carts which they pulled were being used to carry the baggage and the elderly. The majority had to walk. The stronger warriors were pulling the heavy frame of the boat along the ground, with the help of the bigbugs and the traction of the vehicle.

Tork and Poko flew over the surrounding areas on the reptatiles, looking out for danger. From the sky, they nostalgically looked back and said their last goodbyes to the ruins which were becoming smaller and smaller. Their memories were there, and they were slowly leaving them behind. A tear ran down Poko's cheek. He was missing the brothers, especially Aron. Although they belonged to different races, Aron had always been the elder brother he had wanted.

Time went by, and the day got hotter. The air was dry, and the wind blew up the sand. The slowness of the journey made the exhausted Noans go delirious, and many swore they saw a Hati squadron drawing near, but it was only a collective mirage.

The vehicle used all of its power to pull the boat, and a dark liquid spilt out of its turbines. From up on high, mounted on Bubu, Tork was getting worried. The fuel of the vehicle made it a dangerous bomb in case the engine exploded, but Hanara knew that the risk of this happening was small.

At night, the warriors took turns to take watch while the others rested. The Noans rarely camped. When they slept, they lay in the open air or sheltered under the carts, and in order to prevent the animals from escaping, the bigbugs were tied by the legs, and the reptatiles were locked in their cages.

Kliver remained under a sunshade made of palm leaves. He had lost the use of his arms through lack of movement, and his fingers were twisted as a result of a lack of calcium in the bones, but at least he was alive, and there were even times when Miku could swear that he could understand what was taking place around him.

With great effort, the natives reached the West coast a little before they thought they would, after no more than a three week journey. Throughout this time they prayed for it not to rain, or for there not to be a sandstorm, which was very common at this time of the year.

Hanara leant on a coconut tree trunk and filled his lungs with the fresh sea air, the strong wind blowing his toga. He got out his pipe and lit it, looking on at the warriors who were dragging the frame of the boat to the shore.

"I thought we would never arrive" he said. "This beach is so pleasant, with coconuts and banana trees everywhere. There is enough food for us to spend a year here, if the construction of the boat is delayed."

"There is also sea food" said a native, as he took out of the water a small crab on the end of his spear.

The Masters of the Harvest finally set up camp on the beach, and they had permission to sleep and eat properly. At dawn the next day they would begin to work on the boat, which might take weeks or even months to be ready to be launched.

Poko was happy to see the sea again, and his joy was greater than his hunger or tiredness, so he took off his clothes and dived into the sea. His body was covered in sand. The sea water refreshed him, particularly as he had not bathed for days.

A kilometer away from the beach, the natives dug a well to obtain fresh water for as long as they needed, until the boat was completed.

While the women picked fruits, the men dismantled the carts and piled up their wood. As there was no pasture, the big-bugs could only eat coconut straw, and a meter and a half high fence had to be built to enclose them.

In the afternoons, the children bathed in the waters of the Tetis while the hunters took their recently built rafts onto the high sea, where they could fish. When they returned, the children were amazed by the amount of fish they brought. And the cooks made a tasty fish stew.

But more than half of the fish were needed to feed the reptatiles, and the hunters thought this was outrageous. Hanara tried to calm them down saying that this was only temporary and on the Islands, unless the animals learned to hunt for themselves, they would be sacrificed.

And as for Kliver, Miku mashed up bananas, diluted them in a bowl, and put this liquid into his tube in order to feed him.

The days went by and the boat took shape on the construction site. With the exception of the hunters, who were working more for the reptatiles than for the tribe, the majority of the Noans were happy with the changes. The time to launch the boat would soon arrive.

CHAPTER 15

MEETING WITH THE REGENT

Far away, Aron was looking at the landscape, which now began to change. The dry and hot ground, with small patches of rough grass, gave way to scattered bushes and trees. The Myra territory was near, and they would arrive in Loagy after another fifty kilometers.

They had marched slowly for the last four weeks, and in the middle of their journey, the liquor in the barrels had finished, so the soldiers spent most of their time playing cards.

During the journey, Aron wondered what had happened to Makuro. He had probably reached the Hive a long time before, maybe the same day he had left.

Aron had made friends with various members of the Myra battalion. The soldiers loved to hear his stories about disrespecting the rules of his old Hati grandfather. They could not believe how sociable he was, especially as he had been brought up so far from civilization. But the best friend he made was Irvine, a young man who had only been a soldier for few months. They were the same age, which helped them to become close friends and share experiences.

Night was coming on quickly. The soldiers were exhausted, but apparently they would not pitch camp. When Aron asked why, the wagoner pointed ahead.

"There's no reason for us to camp today" he said. "We've arrived. Can't you see?"

Aron looked up and saw a large group of trees some distance away, in the middle of the endless desert.

"Loagy?" he asked.

"Yes, Loagy Oasis. The largest in the world. The entrance to the Colony is in the middle, camouflaged by the trees."

The nearer the caravan got, the bigger the Oasis seemed to be. Bugles were blown from various places to announce the return of the troops. The soldiers also blew their own bugles in response, and various lights came on when the carts entered the wooded area.

Animals were jumping from one tree to another, curiously looking on as the caravan arrived. Well-built men came out of the dark to carry the equipment and the weapons to the arsenal. Women and children approached, hoping to see fathers, husbands and sons. A number of Catandist priests, in their white cassocks, also came up to them to bless the troops and pray for the souls of those who had died in combat.

There were various women whose only intention was to give themselves to the unmarried soldiers as a sign of welcome. Thinking that Aron was one of the soldiers, though she had never seen a soldier with such long unkempt hair before, a girl in a short skirt with golden hair and fair skin threw herself into Aron's arms, kissing him on the lips.

"Leave him" shouted an officer. "He is being escorted as a prisoner. You have no right to embrace him."

Aron swore at the officer but did not get angry. He was enthralled by the way in which the Myra women behaved, and this seemed just to be the beginning. He had not even reached the Colony and he had been kissed by a gorgeous green-eyed blond.

When they were a hundred meters away from the entrance, the Major ordered the prisoner to be handcuffed once again. Irvine carried out the order and tried to calm Aron down.

"Don't worry. The handcuffs are necessary to take you to the Regent's Palace. They represent safety and respect for the Regent. After he gives his consent, you will be freed."

"I'm not worried" he replied, holding out his hands to help Irvine to handcuff him. "Getting to know your people has been the best thing that has happened to me."

"Don't be so hurry. Did you like Clea?"

"Who?"

"The green-eyed blond. It seemed a sincere kiss . . . When all this is over, I can put you in touch with her."

"What are they going to do with me?" asked Aron.

"They will probably put you in the army. Your father had an important career in our society. He was a respected sergeant, who was a shooting instructor. It will be an honor for you to follow his footsteps."

Aron looked surprised.

"Did you know my father?"

"Everybody knows your father, but they haven't noticed any similarity between you and him. A young Myra with the exact age of Kliver's son would not have come out of nothing. But don't worry. I'll keep your secret."

Aron was now very sorry about what had happened to his father, and he began to think of how much Miku must be worried, and there was also the possibility that Makuro had revealed the location of Ruakan to the Hatis. This would mean that the Noans were in danger, but his grandfather was not stupid. Hanara must at this moment be carrying out a plan to prevent anything from happening to the Noans.

Thinking about this, Aron tried to relax. Nothing could prevent him from following his new path. The beginning of the war was of little importance to him, as it had nothing to do with him. If he was really called up for the Myra army, he could just refuse. One less recruit wouldn't make any difference.

The first wagons reached a clearing in the middle of the Oasis. The crowns of the trees hid the springs, the sources of the Olin, which ran into the Oasis. In the center of the clearing, the bushes opened out, and Aron saw a large concrete circle, about eight meters in diameter, on which there was a huge yellow "X", and around it there were six smaller circles positioned at regular intervals.

There were surveillance cameras on the branches of the trees and an interphone on the top of a stake; Myra technology did not seem so old-fashioned, after all.

The Major typed a code on the panel. The huge concrete circle began to vibrate, and the "X" opened up in the middle of the concrete circle. Aron stretched his neck and saw an immense illuminated hole, so deep that it seemed to have no bottom.

"This is the main entrance" explained the Major. "The other entrances are used for emergencies or for small groups of people. Once you enter, you will never leave the Colony without permission. Your freedom will depend on this. The cameras are always on. They were installed after a sergeant disappeared with his son to go God knows where . . . wait a bit . . . what's your name, son?"

"Aron K-Kliver, sir."

'Kliver! So he's Leo's lost son.' thought the major. 'It's good the Regent knows about this.'

While they were talking, a platform came out of the depths. All the battalion pushed each other to get in, almost resulting in an accident."

"Line up!" shouted the Major. "Officers first, then privates, and civilians last."

The Major pushed Aron to one of the smaller entrances and called one officer.

"You're responsible to make sure everyone enters in order" he said. "I will go in first, as I need to escort the prisoner to the Palace. Private Irvine will go with me as my auxiliary." After having said this, the Major got on the platform, and in a few seconds they were deep underground.

As the platform descended, Aron was able to see a large part of the Colony, which was a fabulous city, built kilometers underground. It must have had fifteen to twenty floors, each of them big enough to house thousands of people. There were thick colored pipes everywhere, which brought water from the Olin and took out sewerage. There were large filters and numerous air purifiers which were connected to the engines of the vents.

On each floor, there was a dense cloud of steam, which covered the streets with a low mist. There were a large number of signs, which gave information about each section and warnings about common risks. While he was descending, Aron caught a glimpse of the following warning on the pillar of one of the engines: *Vent 4A. Section 1, Level 2. Do not go beyond the safety line. Danger of suction.* It said in the Myra alphabet.

The sections were subdivided into floors, known as "levels". The first section was strategically designated for the military barracks: If there was an invasion, the soldiers would be nearer the exit to counterattack.

Below them came the civilian sections, with crowds of people and bigbugs wandering around the streets, performing their needs without any control. There were floors for commerce and business, where there were markets which sold all types of goods.

The high birth rate was a problem. Places designated for ten thousand people housed more than forty thousand. Scantily clad women came to the elevator cage to offer their services. It was impossible to tell which ones were the prostitutes, as, with few exceptions, they all wore short provocative skirts.

The further the platform went down, the more Aron believed that this was not an underground city, but an underworld. The Colony was dirty and smoky, with a precarious, badly designed structure, which seemed to have been built much too quickly and unplanned. The walls were of rough rock, full of bits of wire which connected the roof lights.

Further down, there were the housing districts and the coal mines. In all, there were six levels for the housing and another for the mine, the main Myra energy source. Every minute one heard the wagons rattling along the tracks, bringing and taking the filthy miners in and out of its dark throats. The air was full of sulfur, which made those who were not used to it feel sick.

Minutes later, the platform finally reached its destination, on the lowest level of the city, the eighteenth floor. The Regent's Palace, however, was some more meters below, which made them enter the cage of another elevator, which required passwords and an access card.

The Major swiped his card in the machine, and the cage opened. Aron and Irvine went in and descended further, finally reaching the area which was out of bounds, the Regent's Level.

The Major had not slept for a long time. He was the highest ranking officer in his battalion and was responsible for the lives of his men. It would be he who would notify families of soldiers who had died in battle, and this was on his mind more than the fact that he had to escort Kliver's son to the Regent. Informing the family of the dead soldiers was never easy. He felt as if he were the father, the brother or the mother and feared their reactions.

Sometime before, the Major had been shot in the left shoulder by a father who was disconsolate after his son had been killed in training. And one day the brother of a recruit, who had been accidentally crippled, scalded his back with boiling water. The burns got better, but the memory and fear was still there . . .

When the cage opened, Aron stepped on to a red carpet, which rolled out along a corridor shaped like an arch, covered in pink marble and decorated with statues and flower arrangements.

This small space between the elevator and the entrance to the Palace was very different from the rest of the Colony. It was clean, perfumed, and the walls, which were so polished, reflected the shape of his body.

The gates of the Palace were high and thick, with the sculpted figure of two bigbugs facing each other, reared up in position of combat, with their Myra riders crossing the ends of their spears. Below them there was an inscription with symbols that Aron could not identify.

"What are those marks?" was the first question Aron asked when he entered the Colony.

"They are Catandist runes" replied the Major. "Don't ask questions. Wait in that room," and he pointed to a passage in the middle of the corridor. "I will go into the Palace alone first, as I shall have to ask permission to accompany you in."

Aron and Irvine entered the room and sat down in the arm-chairs. Aron suddenly felt tense. The moment he would come before the Regent was arriving, and he had no idea of how to behave.

The room they were in was small and high, with walls full of old portraits of Myra heroes. On a counter near the entrance there were hundreds of piled up old newspapers. Irvine began to browse through them looking for news of Kliver. He found the following headline from July 211 AE:

Disappeared soldier returns to the Colony for a single motive: to kidnap his own son.

The columns referred to Kliver as a deserter, a traitor of the Myras, and mentioned the bad behavior of a Catandist priest at that time, who had helped him to escape. Irvine decided that he should not show the newspaper to Aron, as he did not want to make him feel even more uncomfortable with these past events.

The Major came back some minutes later, looked at Aron, and gestured for him to get up.

"The Regent is waiting for you" he said. "When you are in his company, only speak when you are asked something. Don't say too much, and take care what you say. Come with me."

Aron got up from the chair and followed the Major. Irvine whispered to him:

"I've never been introduced to the Regent. For a private in the beginning of his career, it is almost impossible to meet him. I only know him what he looks like through posters and television. Remember that, from now on, our Regent will be Your Majesty. He will be your king. Take advantage of this moment as this will probably be your only chance to meet him personally. I cannot cross this line and go with you."

"Our sovereign is good and fair, but don't provoke him" warned the Major. "Obey all his orders, agree with all his opinions, and always address him as 'Your Majesty'. These are the age-old forms of politeness. I will only accompany you to offer protection, as I am an officer who is respected by the court. During the introduction you will remain handcuffed, and at the end you must thank His Majesty for his attention and patience and apologize for disturbing him."

"Don't worry". And "Good luck" were Irvine's final words before Aron entered the Palace.

When the doors opened, Aron could see the beauty and luxury of the Palace. The walls were painted by famous local artists, the roof was held up by huge solid gold pillars, and the floor was covered by fine silken carpets.

A carved pool occupied almost all the center of the Palace, and its warm waters were burbling. Stuffed animals looked on the artificial waterfall, in positions which showed their habit when alive: the carnivores looked threatening and ferocious, and the herbivores were peaceful and quiet. Before approaching the throne, Aron was distracted by a glass container which occupied the space between the two columns. It was filled half-way up with fine white sand and was surrounded by clear water on all sides, as if it were a miniature island. In the center of the island there were daisies, plum leaves, and fruit and vegetable skins covered in mildew, where there were a number of larvae and minuscule bigbug insects.

At one of the ends of the container there was a wooden tree trunk with a curved end where a swarm of tiny black bees flew around a nest. On the opposite side, ants crawled between the anthill and the place they would collect from in the middle of the room.

Aron noticed that something strange was happening to the bees. They were anxious, flew around in small circles, and violently beat their heads against the glass. He was fascinated by this, firstly because he had never seen the details of a bee hive so clearly before, and secondly because he was trying to find a good reason for a respected monarch to keep in his palace something so large and as useless as a container full of insects.

"It's natural for them to leave their nest" anticipated the Regent, sitting in his distant throne.

Aron turned his head.

"Sorry?" he asked, automatically.

"The bees. They are abandoning their nest. That's why they are so anxious" he said, loudly.

"Go up to His Majesty and bow" ordered the Major.

Aron arrived near the throne and stood still, not knowing what to do.

"Bow!" repeated the Major, strictly.

The Regent smiled.

"There is no need for these formalities" he said. "After all, this is the first day the boy is here to live with us. It is quite normal that he feels lost and does not know how to behave. He is a rough diamond, who must be polished."

The Regent paused and looked at the boy's face.

"Tell me, young man, you seem to be fascinated by the insect farm. Do you like my insects?"

"Yes, very much. What is this aquarium used for?"

The Major frowned in annoyance, and the Regent continued to smile.

"This 'aquarium', as you call it, is in reality a replica of the continent in which we live. It's incredible how a society of such small beings, especially ants, is so similar to the organization of human beings. No other animal acts in such a similar way to ourselves.

Did you know that the interior of a colony of ants is divided into various chambers? The queen is kept in the royal chamber, the eggs are taken to the nurseries, and the dead are taken to the mortuary. They are very organized.

The ants 'milk' the aphid bugs, taking from their bodies a thick liquid which is rich in glucose, which they love, in the same way as we milk the bigbugs, in order to use their milk, which many believe to be sacred. This is why the 'Equus evolutus' were known as 'bigbugs'."

"Equus evolutus?" asked Aron, impressed.

"Equus evolutus is the scientific name of our bigbugs. It means "developed equine" in an extinct language. But there are disagreements among our scientists whom refuse to believe that the bigbug derived from the equines. . . But let's talk again about our allies, the ants" continued the Regent. "What fascinates me in these little beings is their peculiar hostile behavior, which is found in no other animal, except man: they go to war. Ants go to war. They make war on other insects and even on other ants. They fight for sovereignty over the area they food from, for the use of a source of water, or even to protect the queen. Moreover, there are some kinds of ants that steal the eggs from their beaten rivals, making their descendants slaves, forcing them to serve their colony.

Because of these behaviors, ants have always shown us to best strategy to fight against the Hatis. As faithful believers in Catandism, we believe in the knowledge which Nature tries to give us. Aware we could win, we went into battle with confidence . . . and we won."

Aron seemed somewhat confused.

"Let me explain" continued the Regent. "According to our customs, days before we enter a battle against the Hatis, we put the ants to attack the bees in the insect farm. Depending on the result in the replica, we know whether we shall win or lose. There are many more ants, but the bees are able to fly, and their poison is much stronger, which makes their stings deadly. And just like us: We Myras have a larger army, but the Hatis have much more advanced technology.

Strategically the ants in the insect farm attacked the enemy queen and killed her. This is why the bees are so restless. It is like chess: The king is captured and the game is over. A lot have died, don't you see?" he pointed to the swarm in the container. "They've lost their sense of direction. In the last four weeks they have had no idea where to go. In a few days, a new swarm will be placed inside, and the present one will be taken out.

Our troops learned these tactics, attacked the enemy battalion, and tried to capture the Hati commander. When they managed to, we had completed the expected victory."

Aron prevented himself from making a skeptical comment. This tradition did not seem very serious. How could they have so much confidence in insects?

"Mr. Regent," he said. "What is the motive behind the battle I've just seen?"

The Regent tried to find a comfortable position on his throne and gave an explanation:

"The truth is that there is just one motive: we have been fighting against annihilation. The Hati Empire follows the ideals of the ancient dynasty of Yusi-Wan, the Emperor who led the Oriental Alliance during the War of Extermination. Even today, two centuries after the war, the Hatis still believe they are a superior race to the Myras and the Wild Savages they thought were extinct. In order to be the only remaining race, they need to make us totally extinct, and it is against this that we are fighting.

Some weeks ago, a number of our sentries, around the continent, saw a Hati squad coming towards the Colony. The army was radioed by the sentries, and the command sent an attack battalion to prevent our enemies reaching us.

The Hatis were still a long way off, but we could not take risks. With more than three thousand men, our troops attacked the enemy squadron and easily defeated it, making them surrender more than four thousand miles from here. But the Hatis had asked for reinforcements shortly before their defeat, and when the Myra caravan was returning to the Colony, it was surprised by the airships, which retaliated, thereby beginning the battle which you witnessed.

But as you could see, we were victorious, and we almost made the Hati commander a valuable prisoner. Everything came out perfectly well, within our expectations, until you were found on the slopes around the plain . . ."

Aron looked down.

"Don't worry. We would have freed the commander or killed him anyway . . . bringing a Hati to our society could be risky, as he would see the route we would take. We need to take pre-cautions against the transmitter in his plug connector . . ."

Aron seemed to be relieved.

"Let's now talk about you, young man. Tell me: where have you been all these years, and who was the Hati who was with you when you were found?"

Aron tried not to reveal too much.

"We lived together. My brother Makuro and myself . . ."

"'Makuro is a Hati name" said the Regent. "Was this boy your brother?"

"Yes, he has Hati blood, but is not one of them. We grew up together, in a small ruined village."

"Can you tell me how it is possible for a Myra to be the brother of a Hati?" asked the Regent, leaning his chin on his hands.

"We are not blood brothers." explained Aron. "My father had married his mother and . . ."

"Leo Kliver married a Hati?"

Aron frowned.

"Do you know the name of my father?"

"We know many things, my son. Your father was an honorable man, who for many years faithfully served in my army. He was a respected sergeant, who was a shooting instructor, the best crossbow archer we had. However, after the death of his wife, Jill, your real mother, Kliver became depressed and was dismissed. He volunteered to go on a secret mission and abandon our society, leaving you, his only child, in our orphanage. Your father then disappeared and was never seen again. And you, Aron, when you were only two months old, also disappeared from the Colony, only weeks after his departure. Some days later, a Catandist priest confessed that he had helped your father to escape with you in his arms and was defrocked . . ."

Aron felt that he had been betrayed. His whole life was no more than a lie. Hanara had told him some things, but he had never known his real story.

The Regent saw how surprised he was, but didn't prevent himself from asking:

"Do you have any idea where your father is?"

Aron did not hesitate.

"He is in the Ruakan ruins, in a coma, as he was tortured when the Hatis captured him."

"Your registration as Kliver's son has been lost" said the Regent. "Your reappearance is a shock for all of us. Tomorrow I shall make sure that you are officially recognized as a Myra by the people. Don't worry. Your Myra citizenship will be returned to you."

Aron said nothing. He neither disagreed nor thanked or showed any joy.

"Tell me the truth, my boy. Did you grow up in a savage tribe? That was what you said, wasn't it, Major?"

"Yes, Your Majesty" the Major bowed, showing his bald head. This was the first time he had spoken.

"Yes, that's true" said Aron. "I spent my whole life in Rua-kan with my stepmother, my brothers and my Noans neighbors."

"Noans?"

"Yes, that is the name of our tribe: 'Kuata-Noan'. In Myra it means 'Masters of the Harvest'."

"Very interesting . . ."

Aron felt unsure of himself. Telling the truth might be dangerous for his people, but the Regent noticed his worry and once again tried to calm him down:

"Don't worry, my son. I won't order an attack on the savages. They've never been a threat to us. Our fight is against the Hatis and their intolerance of the races they believe to be inferior . . . their ideals must be defeated . . . they must be abolished!" he stressed. "But calm down. Your Noans will be welcome to live with us. Tomorrow I will designate a search squadron to go to the ruins to propose an agreement of union between the Myras and the Wild Savages, so they can take refuge here in the Colony. With this agreement, the natives will become our allies."

A sincere smile of gratitude appeared on Aron's lips.

"Would Your Majesty do this?" and Aron began to treat the Regent with the expected formality.

"Why not? We could learn a lot from each other."

"I think it will be easy to seal this agreement" underlined Aron. "The Noans are a peaceful people. There will be advantages on both sides. The only problem will be to convince my grandfather and my mixed-race brother to join . . ."

"A mixed-race boy!" said the Regent in amazement. "A Myra-Hati?"

"Yes, he is a mixed-race Myra-Hati, the result of the relationship between my father and my Hati stepmother."

The Regent leant back in the throne, intertwining the fingers of both hands.

"That's astonishing nowadays. I'm afraid he might be rejected by the conservatives amongst us . . . However, I'm still the leader. Don't worry, young man. Your brother will be welcome. You can rely on me."

"This is why they elected you to be Regent" said Aron, with great admiration.

The Regent felt really noble before Aron's enthusiasm.

"When they seal this agreement," continued Aron "be careful with my grandfather, who is a really old man, but he is very wise and unpredictable, and might not agree with this union."

"Tell this to the commander of the search party" said the Regent. "You'll go together."

"Me?" asked Aron.

"Of course. There is no one better than you to persuade the savages to join us. You know well their territory and also their language. The squadron will leave tomorrow after you're evaluated by our army and you are re-baptized into Catandism."

The Regent interrupted his own speech. He lifted the scepter up high and placed it delicately on Aron's forehead, over the scar from his old wound. Aron interpreted this as a sacred act and bowed. The sovereign pronounced a number of words in a strange language, perhaps Catandist, and once again lifted up the scepter, saying:

"From now on, as the official leader of the Myra Colony, I decide your destiny: Like your father, you will follow a military career and will join my army."

The Regent lowered his arm.

"Early tomorrow you will be evaluated by the recruitment section of our army. The Major will be in charge of instructing you and acquiring the necessary documents. Now it's time to rest. Clean yourself up, cut your hair and put on suitable clothes."

"Major" ordered the Regent. "Show the young man out. Make sure he has everything he needs so he is comfortable in the next few days."

Aron thanked him as arranged and apologized for disturbing him, as was also arranged. He turned around and accompanied the Major to the Palace exit. He now felt incredibly hungry.

The Major found Irvine in the waiting room, and they went along the corridor to the elevator. Before they went up, however, the Major took a bunch of keys out of his pocket and gave them to Irvine, ordering him to take Aron's handcuffs off.

"Private Irvine" he said. "You'll be responsible for Aron. Take him to the barracks for new recruits. Make sure he is cleaned up, has clean clothes, has a haircut and is fed."

Irvine accepted the order, bent down and opened Aron's handcuffs.

"You've taken a long time!" he said. "I've been waiting for ages. How was there?"

"I won't just be your new friend" said Aron, enthuseiastically. "I'll also be your fellow soldier."

"Great! What did the Regent say?"

"I'll tell you after. What's there to eat?" he asked, shortly before the cage closed, and the elevator began to go up.

After the Major left, the Regent received a call on his private videophone, a device which was hidden in the palace. In order to receive it, it was necessary to type a pass code on buttons which were hidden in the eyes of the stuffed animals. The Regent pressed a panel on the arm of the throne and the doors of the Palace locked on the inside. The lights went off. The Regent got up and walked towards the stuffed animals and typed the numbers: the left eye of the hitie, the left eye of the drophin, the right eye of the bizort, the left eye of the crane.

In the center of the circle of the animals, the floor now became a clear and crystalline screen to receive signals. On it there was the shape of a man in shadows with narrow anxious eyes.

"*Good evening*" said the image, speaking in a strange language, which was neither Myra, Hati, Catandist nor Kuata-Noan.

"We haven't spoken for a long time" said the Regent in the same language.

"I heard the boy, and this is why I called you. A nice speech! You impressed me! So why do you have to be the pious one, and me the tyrant?"

"Don't do any spying without my permission" said the Regent. "How do you want the dispute to be fair in this way?"

"I'll make a truce for a number of years" said the shape. "I want to see what Hanara is preparing for the Myra-Hati."

"Did you meet the Myra-Hati?"

"I was just told about him. Kliver confessed when he was drugged . . . But I didn't personally meet the father of the 'Messiah'."

"Did you enter me?" asked the Regent.

"Yes, I did. My plug has been linked to yours for three weeks, ever since Tadashi's son arrived here. Makuro is a clever boy for his age. Hanara must have brought him up well."

"Do you think Hanara will do anything?"

"Not for now. He has his principles . . . how could we imagine he would win the Battle of the Convicts?"

"He will try to prevent the war" said the Regent. "In order to do this, he will use the Myra-Hati."

"I don't know whether he is able to do this. People really believe in prophecies . . . but if anything drastic happens, we can once again change the world . . . we are gods, we are eternal, and we are omnipresent!"

"I don't feel like a god at the moment" said the Regent. "The boy managed to awaken old emotions in me. I feel that a revolution is ready to take place. There are conspiracies in the streets. People are looking for the truth."

"They are just anxious after the first battle. Let them wonder about what is going on. The truth will never be discovered. People are foolish, my friend. They can easily be manipulated. The only one to hear us talking was Hanara, but not even he can decipher the 'Language of the Gods'. Everything is under control."

The Regent was quiet for a while, looking at the image on the floor.

"I need to turn it off" he said, soon after. "And please do not enter in my plug again. Not without my permission . . ."

"When will you change the law so that your people can also use them?"

"So that you can dominate us? Don't you realize that I know what you intend to do with the inter-plug? Do you think that I believe that only Hanara knows how to use the 'WCP'? I'm sure that your officers also know the results of the project . . . and in addition, the law is open to changes. It's my people who won't accept it. Almost ninety percent of the Myras follow Catandism. It will be difficult to convince them to use plugs."

"Bullshit" said the shape. "Begin with the young people, and in less than fifty years everyone will be using them . . ."

"It will take too long for the changes to have any effect. I need immediate plans. Investing in plugs would be a waste of money."

"I don't know what's happened to you . . ."

"We are no longer the same person. I like to be good and fair, and I enjoy being the leader of the Myras. Stop calling me."

"Very well, if that's what you want, I won't disturb you anymore."

"Turn it off, and don't enter in my plug anymore" said the Regent. "If you do, I'll reveal everything to my people."

"You wouldn't do that, as I wouldn't do it. In addition, your people can't do anything to me."

"If Aron takes me to Hanara, you're finished! The Myra-Hati will unite our races, and not even you will be able to prevent the beginning of a new era."

"Don't depend on this" said the shape. "Hanara will not be found."

"We shall see . . . Now excuse me. I need to turn off."

"As you wish. I'll close the transmission . . . But as for the treaty? Are we still in agreement?"

"You know we are. But I'm not as keen as I was two hundred years ago. I've accomplished a lot of things, and I don't want to run the risk of losing them."

"I will therefore advise you to unplug yourself or to install a firewall against the inter-plug."

"I'll do so. My plug is no longer any use."

"I can install new programs in yours. We have new forms of enjoyment today."

"New programs will not entertain me. For now, I just want to rest. Call me in five or six years, or when you have some really worthwhile information."

The image on the screen began to fade.

"Wait" said the Regent. "Before closing I'd like to know something . . . What's the Myra-Hati's name?"

"'Tork'. As the prophecy requires."

"Ah, yes . . . I'd forgotten your prophecy."

"Not mine, but 'ours'" corrected the shape.

The Regent seemed to be insulted by this correction.

The shape continued:

"People are naïve, mere children. Catandism, Christianity, Buddhism . . . religions are fairy tales, and God is the 'Santa' of adults."

The monarch said nothing, absorbed by these words. However much he tried not to, something inside him made him agree.

"Look. I must really turn it off" he said.

"So, until next time, Mr. Regent. And don't worry about the plug. I won't enter it again."

"See you, Mr. Emperor."

The call finished, and the shape disappeared from the screen. The lights came on, and the Regent returned to his throne, not having decided whether he would get rid of his plug or not. He was not using it any longer, and it was an open window for the Emperor to enter whenever he wished.

He thought it better to leave the decision to the following days. He sat back on the throne and unlocked the Palace doors, interphoning his private harem. He asked for fruits and three nice young girls to give him a relaxing bubble bath.

CHAPTER 16

SHORTCUT

That night Aron had a terrible nightmare. He dreamt that the Noans had been killed at the moment when the agreement of union with the Myras had been seal. And he, unable to do anything, looked on in horror at the massacre with his hands tied to the stakes of the scaffold. Fire was everywhere, destroying the houses and the temple. The woman he had always thought was his mother sobbed at his feet while Daiara was being raped by the soldiers.

He woke up startled, his heart beating quickly, and his face wet with sweat. He found himself in the lower part of a bunk bed, in a dormitory full of unknown people.

"Come on, get up" said Irvine, holding out his hand. "It is already dawn."

Aron sat up on the mattress, bending his body in order not to hit his head on the bunk above, wearing only a loose pair of shorts.

"My God!" Irvine was surprised. "Just look at you! You're covered in sweat! Are you okay?"

"I had a nightmare" said Aron. "I dreamt that the Regent had ordered my people to be assassinated."

"It's just a dream . . . the Regent would not do that."

"Yes . . ." he said, looking around. "I hope not. What place is this? A dormitory?"

"Did the dream affect your memory?" joked Irvine. "Almost. It is the dormitory for male recruits. Remember the number of your bed, which is yours until further orders. Your uniform was brought last night, and it is in the locker. Here is the key."

Aron got up, and, with the key, opened the doors of his locker, which was beside a window which looked on the laundry. He remembered nothing about the previous night. He must have gone directly to bed as he now felt twice as much hunger as he had the previous night.

"Here in the locker there is everything you'll need" said Irvine. "Toothbrush, towels, razor blade, and toiletries. They're your only belongings. Keep them safe. The entrance to the bathroom is in the middle of the corridor. There are twenty showers and thirty lavatories. Even so, in the morning, you have to line up to use them. Don't spend more than five minutes in the shower. Get ready and go to the refectory."

At this moment, a totally naked recruit came up to them. He opened his locker, took out a towel, and wiped himself.

"This is Giamo" said Irvine. "He'll share the bunk bed with you."

"Pleased to meet you" said Aron, holding out his hand.

Giamo did not shake his hand. He blew his nose with the towel and threw it onto the top bunk.

"I sleep on the top" he said more as a warning than a piece of information. "I sleep lightly. If you want to avoid problems, try not to fidget or snore during the night."

Aron looked at him for a moment, then looked away. He took his toothbrush and went to the bathroom line. A group of recruits wearing just underpants were talking. No one said hello to him, but one of them commented:

"His skin is darker than ours."

Aron looked at him.

"That's because I was brought up in the open air, and not in a city where there is no sun." The recruit did not like the remark.

Aron had a shower and went to the refectory, sitting down in one of the few free places. Differently from his welcome by the soldiers in the caravan, in the barracks he was treated as if he had no right to be there.

At the end of the day, Aron was tired. He'd slept a lot the previous night, but it had been a long day. All his attention had been required, and Irvine accompanied him everywhere he needed to go. Firstly he had to go to the civil register office, where he managed to get back his Myra citizenship. He gave a press conference, in which he spoke about his father and his life in the savage tribe, and he also took a written exam which was necessary to enter the Army.

The result of the exam would only be published in a few days. If he were lucky and got ninety percent right, he would enter the Officers' Academy, where he would become a lieutenant after three years training. If he didn't get ninety percent, which was probable, he would go to the School for Privates, where he would be called a "private", and his training would be no longer than eight months.

In no way would he be failed, as he had the support of the Regent, and this was important. The Regent was in a hurry to announce that he had passed, as it was in his interest to put Aron in an important position in the Army. Aron had a personal connection with Hanara and the Myra-Hati, and it wouldn't be a bad idea for these two to join the Myras.

With the help of Aron, it would be easy to convince them to join. Aron only had to take the exams for bureaucratic reasons, just for the media not to be given a chance to print the fact that he was receiving privileges. If this didn't happen, there would be a rebellion amongst the candidates who had tried and not managed to get a place in the training camps.

In a sanctuary on the Level of Faith, during his re-baptism ceremony, Aron learned a number of the basic elements about the Catadism religion. He learned that its prophet and founder had been called Solveig Ca-Tand, a man who had lived in the Old-World and considered himself to be the reincarnation of Jesus Christ. Solveig had been born wealthy and had an easy life, and in addition, was extremely good-looking.

When he was unable to win the love of a woman called Erika with his looks and fortune, Ca-Tand sold his soul to get her. The Devil carried out his promise. Erika married Ca-Tand, but his soul was already condemned.

Years after, his wife fell ill, and Solveig joined the faith in order to cure her. God had appeared to him in a dream and revealed the secrets which could not be found in the old Bible. He had revealed that Solveig was the new Messiah, and that his privileged birth had been a test to see whether he would fall into temptation.

As he did fall, God gave him two difficult choices: either to save human kind, and for this he would need to recover his lost soul, or to save Erika, the person who he most loved. Ca-Tand decided to save his wife, and humanity fell into wars and misfortune. This was when he founded Catadism with the principles he had learned in subsequent dreams.

At a certain moment, Ca-Tand was considered to be a mad-man when he preached his faith, and spent the rest of his life in an asylum. Shortly before dying, Solveig predicted that soon plugs would be created, and these devices would be one of the main causes of the war that would almost exterminate human kind from the planet.

At the time, no one gave him credit, but when the devices appeared, and History began to follow Ca-Tand's previsions, his teachings began to gain followers, and Ca-tandism spread through the Old West as the main Christian religion on the planet. It became established, and today it is the main religion of the Myras. It forbids the use of plugs, it teaches the faithful to control their libido, and preaches the non-consumption of meat, which is a voluntary choice of the follower, and not obligatory.

In the afternoon, the new recruit tried to relax in his bed. Aron was now wearing the uniform for internal use, which was beige, different and with less equipment than that which was used in combat. He did not have the official black uniform yet, as he still did not belong to the Army, but his measurements had already been taken.

Lying down on the bed, Aron thought about his Hati brother. What had happened to Makuro? Had the Hatis treated him as well as the Myras had treated him? Had Makuro entered the armed forces of the Empire? It didn't matter. Both had crossed a boundary beyond which there was no return.

As far as Aron was concerned, at least he had an advantage over Makuro, who was alone in the Hive, and soon, with the agreement of union between the Myras and the Noans, he would soon be together with Poko, Tork, Hanara and his parents. This was what he believed. Then he remembered that he would go together to help seal the agreement, as the Regent counted on his knowledge to guide the search squadron to the ruins. Then he realized he wouldn't be able to do this.

Then his head began to spin around. He didn't know the Kafria geography very well, and he wouldn't know how to guide the squadron. The only thing he was sure of was that he was in the underground part of a gigantic oasis, which was located somewhere in the north of the continent

When he finally decided that this should not worry him, he heard in the distance the sound of the bugles calling the recruits. He had to get up and go to the auditorium. But rather than going of his own free will, he preferred to wait for someone to come and call him.

This did not take long, and a recruit came into the dormitory, went to his bed.

"Come on, Kliver's son. Duty is calling us!" said the recruit in a hoarse voice. The recruit was short and thin, but had a big belly, and had a severe myopia, which made him wear a thick pair of glasses, and everyone wondered how this awkward young man had passed the physical recruitment tests.

"Your name is Mentare?" asked Aron when he read the badge on the recruit's chest.

"My name is Bob Mentare, second class soldier at your service" he said, proudly.

"Whatever" said Aron with disdains, tightening his belt and standing up.

"Come on, Kliver's son. All the squadron is ready in the auditorium. The commander is waiting for us . . . ."

"My name is Aron. Stop calling me 'Kliver's son'."

Aron followed Mentare, and crossed the patio. They went around the back of the refectories and entered the auditorium, which was beside the infirmary. The room was full of new and older soldiers, who were sitting down.

When he entered, everyone began to laugh at him: His beret was crooked, and it was almost twice as big as his head. His uniform had been borrowed and still didn't have any identification. It was loose and baggy, and even the commander smiled.

"Silence!" shouted the commander, the Major who was already known to Aron, trying not to laugh. "Anyone who makes a comment will be punished. There are a lot of toilets to clean." He then turned to the new recruits. "Aron, Mentare, sit down."

The new recruit sat down on the first row, and everyone continued to look at him.

"I've called this meeting" continued the Major "so everybody will know about the recruitment of Aron Kliver into our Army. Today he took the written exam, and after taking the physical tests, he will begin his career in one of our Schools. He will be known as 'Kliver', just like his father. Get used to the idea and treat him as one of you."

He went to the table and picked up a number of forms.

"We won't speak about this anymore" he continued. "I have more important things to deal with. I have called you here as I need ten volunteers to take part in a mission. We need to form a search platoon, which will leave tonight for the southwest of the continent, in order to make an agreement of union with the people of Ruakan, so they can live here in the Colony. Aron will go with us still as a civilian. Who would like to go?"

Many were delighted with the possibility of adventure and raised their hands.

"I must remind you that those who we will rescue are the people Aron grew up with. They are primitive, and the majority are savages."

When he said the word "savage", the recruits were no longer euphoric. Their hands went down and they were silent. Only Irvine and three other soldiers kept their hands up.

The Major was disappointed with the lack of motivation, and once again tried to convince them:

"I was also surprised when I was told about the existence of the savages. But it is my duty as a soldier to follow the orders of my superior. This task will be on your military reports. They are direct orders from the Regent. Who will go with me?"

The silence was broken, and everyone began to speak at the same time:

"Savages?"

"Wild savages?"

"Aren't they extinct?"

"No. You are wrong."

"Haven't you read the newspapers? All the Colony is talking about this."

"They still exist. And there are lots of them!"

"What do they say?"

"I don't want to share the dormitory with primitive people!"

"If they come, I'll ask to be dismissed and leave the army."

"Bringing them to the Colony might not be a good idea . . ."

"In fact, it is a *terrible* idea!"

"The Regent must be crazy!"

"There's not enough space."

"We'll have to build more levels."

"We can force them to do the building."

"We can make them into slaves to serve us."

"But that's ridiculous!"

"I'd like to have a slave . . . ."

"I'd like to have a *female* slave!"

"Are wild girls going to come?"

"They would be interesting . . ."

"If I go on this mission, it will be just to finish exterminating them!"

"Me too!"

"My father told me that this would happen someday . . ."

"Order!" shouted the commander. "Remember that we are at war only with the Hatis. If I hear the word 'savage' again, everyone will go to the tear gas chamber, understand? Who volunteers? Even under these conditions?"

Only Irvine and the three other soldiers kept their hands up.

"We have four" said the commander. "We need another six. I must remind you that if no one else volunteers, I'll choose. Or rather, I'll give this honor to Kliver."

"I'll go" said a mature soldier, who was well-built, with the name 'Barbarez' on his badge.

The commander looked up.

"If you're volunteering in order to avoid going to prison, forget it! Whether you go or not, your sentence will not be pardoned." the Major told the soldier.

"No problem, 'boss'. I admit my mistakes and I'm ready for the mission" said Barbarez, convincingly.

"So be it. Anyone else? No? Kliver, pick another five."

Aron got up and looked around the soldiers' faces. He wanted to choose those with whom he had had some contact. Irvine had already volunteered, and so only Mentare was missing. The other four would be chosen at random.

"I've picked Mentare and those four who are sitting at the back, laughing." This choice made those sitting at the back angry.

"Volunteers, stand up" shouted the Major. "Our search platoon is formed. Everyone else may go. Return to the dormitory and wait for the call to go to the parade ground."

The soldiers quickly left the auditorium and it was soon empty. Aron went to the commander and told him that he would not know how to guide the squadron to the ruins. The

Major reassured him that his function in the platoon would only be to talk to the savages. The directions would be decided by Hugo, an old civilian professor who was a cartography expert. Nothing could go wrong.

Aron now began to feel happy. He would continue to live in the Colony, and he would soon be in the company of Poko and all his fellow people. This was at least what he believed. The only problem would be the prejudice that the Noans would feel from the Myras, but this was something that would be solved with time. But he did not know that, at this exact moment, his family was far from Ruakan, on the western coast of the continent, ready to sail to the Islands of the Painted Balerias.

When the meeting had finished, the soldiers went to get their bigbugs ready. Aron still didn't have one to ride, and he only had the choice of four in the stables. He chose the biggest one, which had large round eyes and thick shells on its legs. He gave him the name of Buddy — he always wanted to have a bigbug with that name.

He took about an hour to saddle Buddy and put on the metal armor and the helmet with the infrared visor, which would increase the limited vision of the bigbug. The platoon was waiting for him at the exit to the Colony, which was near the main elevator.

The Regent wanted to send them quickly, so that they could arrive at the ruins before the Hatis. And so, before the sun went down, the search platoon left the Loagy oasis. With the exception of Aron, they were all carrying their crossbows and their automatic pistols, even Professor Hugo, who was a civilian.

After some time, they once again began to cross the arid desert, riding three times more quickly than normal. This was because of a product they were carrying called glicorjiu, an injectable liquid which increased the production of adrenalin in the bigbugs, but it might also affect their health, making them unable to carry out certain tasks. Because of this, and also because it was an expensive product, which was difficult to obtain, it was not advisable to use more than half a dosage for each animal every three days.

In the darkness, only the thirteen pairs of eyes lit up in red, running in double line through the moonless night, could be seen. After they had ridden for three days, taking stimulants to control their sleep, the soldiers injected some more glicorjiu into the bigbugs, so they could travel in a quarter of the time. In other circumstances, the Major would never have allowed the excessive use of that product, but they needed to reach the ruins as quickly as possible, and the search platoon had few animals, which made it cheaper.

Because of the lack of time, Hugo, the cartographer who had established the route, decided to take a shortcut which passed through an unknown region, which they had never seen before: white sands were moving like water, changing position in a huge sandy sea. There was no vegetation nearby, and neither were there any hills or valleys. It was an immense flat moving extension of sand which form waves even without any wind.

It was day time, around two o'clock, and they felt the heat in the sky, which was a little less red than usual. There was no other route to follow unless they went back where they had come from, and the area was so big that it would take too long to go around it. So the only solution would be to cross it.

The Major pulled the reins to stop.

"This area seems strange to me" he said, looking at the cartographer. "I've never seen so much movement on arid land. Should we carry on or go back?"

"If we return," replied Hugo, "we will have wasted three days journey."

"Is it safe to cross?" asked one of the soldiers.

"The land seems unstable. It must be dangerous."

"With your permission, boss, I volunteer to go on ahead" said Barbarez, somewhat excited.

"Permission granted" said the Major. "Go ahead and be careful."

Barbarez's bigbug foresaw the danger and refused to obey him. He turned off the bigbug's visor in order to reduce its vision, and whipped it. The animal was surprised and ran off across the sand.

"Firm land, sir", he shouted from far off.

With the Major at the front, the platoon began to cross the area, traveling as quickly as their bigbugs could run. As they were riding, they could hardly notice the movement of the ground, and if they kept up a steady speed, they would be able to cross all of the area without any risk of being buried.

To the front, the back and the sides, the horizon was the same: sand and more sand, which formed waves of different sizes, but which were not too high to they jump. The air was still, showing that the movement was not caused by the wind. Hugo thought that they were over a field of lava, which was continually moving, and deep enough to not consume all the sand which was on top of it, producing these waves.

The strong heat made the metallic protection of the bigbugs and their helmets burn like pans on a stove. The Major thought that they would not be able to run for much longer in such a high temperature, and that the men would not put up with such heat.

They had been riding for more than two hours when Mentare and Barbarez saw some objects coming up out of the ground. They rode towards them, and when they got near, they pulled the bigbugs' reins so they would trot more slowly and not sink their hooves into the sand.

The soldiers then checked the objects. There were eight ivory stakes, which formed a circle with a diameter of three meters. Only the tops of the stakes could be seen. The sand seemed to be moving much more inside the circle, closing up into a single point, rather than expanding outwards.

"Quicksand?" asked Mentare, cautiously.

"All the area is a huge concentration of quicksand" replied Barbarez. "But it seems that the sand is moving much more here. What are those stakes for?"

"Someone might have put them there on purpose, to warn travelers not to pass through the circle" deduced Mentare.

"And who would have come here before?"

"Perhaps the Hatis, or the savages, or even Kliver."

"I'm not sure I agree with you. Why should they warn somebody about the danger?"

"Maybe in order to . . ."

Mentare was interrupted as his bigbug began to appear strange and skittish. It reared up on its back legs and shook its body, trying to throw Mentare out of its saddle. It released a loud roar and went inside the circle, as if the movements there were attracting it.

"What's wrong with your bigbug, soldier?" asked the Major.

"I don't know, sir . . . I can't prevent it" he said, panicking, trying to pull the reins backward. "It seems to be magnetized, sir. It'll be swallowed up by the sand."

"Jump off!" ordered the Major.

"I can't, sir. A good soldier never abandons his bigbug."

"Jump now, soldier!" shouted the Major. "It's an order!"

Mentare released the reins and jumped off. His bigbug was being sucked up by the sands inside the circle. One of his boots had been caught in the stirrup, and so Mentare was also being pulled down. The more the bigbug sank, the further more Mentare was being pulled into the circle. The bigbug had now sunk up to its neck. Mentare was holding on to one of the stakes. The bigbug's head disappeared under the sand. Mentare was sweating all over, trying not to let go.

Barbarez dismounted and held out his hand. Mentare hold on, and Barbarez tried to pull him to safety while Mentare's leg was being pulled under the sand. Aron, Irvine and two other recruits joined Barbarez, holding on to each other as if they were in a tug-of-war, helping him to pull. The chain of the stirrup finally broke, and the soldiers fell back onto each other, and so Mentare was saved.

His boot was still in the stirrup when he sat down on the sand.

"You can ride in my saddle, if you want" offered Barbarez, mounting his bigbug.

Mentare continued sitting on the ground, swaying with the movement of the ground.

"Okay, okay" he panted. "Let me rest here for a moment... I need to breathe." And he felt his eyes. "My glasses! Where are my glasses? I can't continue the journey without them. I can't see anything without them."

"Forget your glasses, soldier" said the Major. "Your bigbug is dead. You won't need to control its reins. Concentrate on the mission."

While the Major spoke there was a cracking noise coming from the middle of the circle. It was a brief noise, just like a dry branch breaking.

"Did you hear it?" asked Professor Hugo.

"It seemed that something was breaking."

"Maybe the bones of Mentare's bigbug."

"Impossible" said Barbarez. "Quicksand swallows up any-one who treads on it, but they don't break their bones."

"The sound must be coming from the stakes" deduced Aron.

"Things are getting strange" said the Professor. "We'd better leave."

"Mentare, get up and get onto the back of Barbarez' big-bug" ordered the Major, seeing that his own bigbug was beginning to show the same symptoms are those of that which had disappeared.

Mentare got up, still with his heart beating fast, when the noise was repeated. This time it was not a simple crack, but a series of them, like the crackling of wood burning.

Before Mentare made his first step, the ground began to shake. Mentare lost his balance and once again fell onto his bottom. There was suddenly a strong eruption inside the circle, making the sand fly out. The metal pieces and the helmet of Mentare's bigbug were violently thrown out, making an arch in the air and falling some meters away.

The soldiers initially thought that this was a landmine or a geyser, but they soon changed their mind. In the place where the circle had been, an immense creature came out of the ground. It could now be seen that the stakes were the fangs, in between smaller teeth, in a huge black oval gum.

It was a desert worm, approximately twenty meters long. Its body was soft and yellowish, with some thick hairs on its back. Its eyes were small, at the sides of its enormous mouth cavity. Although it had four pairs of legs, it began to slide on its back and didn't seem to use its legs.

Mentare got up and began to run. The monster bent down and easily seized him with his mouth, swallowing him and then spitting up his clothes and equipment.

The worm turned towards the platoon and began to chase it, leaving a slimy track wherever it went.

"Run!" shouted the commander. "Don't look back! Just run! Put an extra injection of glicorjiu into the thighs of your big-bugs" he recommended, giving a syringe to each of the men.

No one had ever been authorized before to give such a high dosage of the product to a bigbug. This might overheat their muscles and destroy their nervous system, irreversibly altering their small brains. It might make them useless, or even kill them, but there was no other choice. The lives of his men were at risk, and this was more important than the loss of a few big-bugs.

The effect was immediate as the bigbugs began to run as if they were taking part in an Olympic sprint. Aron, who was not used to riding a bigbug at that speed, fell off when his animal jumped over a small sand wave.

When he saw Aron rolling over the hot sand, Barbarez pulled at his reins and immediately returned.

"Come back, Barbarez" shouted the commander. "Come back now. It's an order."

"It's always an order, sir" said Barbarez. "But it's also a duty to have confidence in my skill. I think I can rescue the boy."

Aron was just about to be devoured as the worm was quickly reaching him, releasing spit and other sticky fluids. Barbarez rode to get him. His bigbug left the others, and when the beast saw that he was approaching, it lost interest in Aron and faced Barbarez, who was a greater threat.

The forty year-old soldier adjusted the visor of his helmet at the same time as he took his crossbow from his saddle. The enormous mouth of the beast opened wide, showing innumerous rows of teeth, and it attacked. With a quick movement that almost made his bigbug fall, Barbarez dodged the attack, and the worm ate sand.

This movement gave him the perfect aim to fire into the left eye of the monster. This is what he did, as the well-targeted arrow exploded when it reached its eyeball, blinding it. The monster raised itself with a strong roar. Barbarez held Aron by the arm and lifted him on to the back of his saddle, returning to the platoon. Looking back, Aron could still see the tail of the worm burying itself in the sand.

"The danger's passed, men" said the commander. "Rest your bigbugs" and turning to Barbarez, he said, "Congratulations. You did very well. You've earned my respect."

"Very kind of you to say that, boss. I was just carrying out my duty."

"I'll try to do something for you, but don't be very hopeful. It will be difficult for the courts to annul your sentence . . ."

"I'm not worried about that, boss. I took a risk to save a life, and not for my mistakes to be forgotten. I accept going to prison."

The Major dismounted and opened the canteen which he was carrying, watering his bigbug. The barbells of the animal trembled when they sucked the water, and its armor sounded out like cymbals vibrating.

"They are hyperactive" noticed Hugo. "We can't stop now. We have to continue until all the effect of the glicorjiu has finished. They need to run to free their extra adrenaline. If we stay here, they won't be able to bear it."

"Where's Buddy?" Aron wanted to know.

"He's over there" Barbarez pointed to the East.

"Bring him and let's go" said the Major. "We can't lose another bigbug."

Aron jumped out of Barbarez's saddle and ran towards his bigbug. When he made his first steps, the ground began to shake again. The sand spread out to the side, forming a high hill which began to pass over the ground, as if something below was dragging it.

When he got near Buddy, the hill fell apart and the big worm came out of the ground, rising up with an even greater fury. Lumps of earth were stuck to the mucus which ran out of its left eye. The beast quickly seized Aron's defenseless big-bug, and huge sharp teeth chewed its armor, grinding it up and then swallowing it, regurgitating the equipment and the metal helmet. Still hungry, the monster released a roar and started pursuing the group once again

Aron quickly mounted the back of Barbarez's bigbug and galloped away. During the escape, Barbarez made a risky move: He stood up in the stirrups and ordered Aron to take the reins.

While Aron stretched out to reach the reins, Barbarez moved back. Aron passed under his legs, and they changed positions. Barbarez then turned his body around and sat on the back of the bigbug, leaning his back against Aron's back. He took his quiver out of his backpack and fed arrows into his cross-bow, which buzzed then they were shot at the worm.

But none of them hit it. The monster managed to avoid them all. Barbarez breathed deeply and took the aim up to eye level. When he once again pressed the trigger, an arrow finally hit the monster, exploding into the side of its body. The worm gave a shrill roar, but did not stop, instead of backing up, it increased its speed.

And with its greater speed, the monster reached the back of the platoon, seizing the two soldiers at the rear in its mouth, spitting out their uniforms and the bigbugs' equip-ment. Its hunger had not yet been satisfied.

Barbarez had only three arrows left. One of them would have to stop it.

He took aim with the first and shot. The worm dodged to the left. Barbarez took aim again. He waited until it opened its mouth and shot it inside there, but this was just an ordinary arrow, which merely stuck into its gum. Barbarez had only one arrow left and hoped this would be an exploding arrow.

His bigbug stumbled at exactly the moment when he had the perfect aim. Barbarez fired once more and missed. The arrow exploded on the ground near the worm, but did not wound it.

It now seemed to be the end. He had no arrows left, and the monster was getting nearer and nearer to his bigbug.

In such desperation it was difficult to think. It didn't occur to any of the recruits that they could share out their arrows, and Barbarez didn't think about borrowing any.

Fortunately they were now reaching the end of that damned sea of moving sand. To the southeast there was a stone path extending over a vast rocky landscape. The soldiers immediately rode towards it, and after the last of them had crossed the boundary which separated the sand from the stone, the worm stopped pursuing them.

In the distance the disconsolate roars of the monster, which had lost its feast, could be heard. The bigbugs and their riders were now safe, but they didn't stop running. They still had a lot of energy to spend, and the effect of the extra dosage of the glicorjiu would not pass until the end of the next day.

Professor Hugo took a map out of his saddle and checked their location. According to his calculations, by following the stone path and deviating to the west, they would arrive in Ruakan in just another day.

"Damn it!" said the commander, punching the back of his bigbug. "I'll have three more dead soldiers to tell their families about when we return. I hate it when they make me hand over a stupid medal to their families."

During the journey, they made Hugo swear that they would return by the longest and least dangerous route. Aron and Barbarez followed together behind the professor. The young man was now beginning to get used to scenes of death, and this was not easy. Death is never pretty . . .

CHAPTER 17

FIRST LOVE

Memories. Memory is the most natural and ancient way of temporarily using something which has passed. An experience, a traumatic event, or seeing people who are no longer with us. Things that have passed are files in our memory, the main fuel of our imagination.

There are both simple ways and sophisticated tools which have been created to help and bring to life the fascinating interior world of our memories. Firstly came hieroglyphs; then, written documents, paintings; and lastly, photographs and films, curious methods and inventions, created by man to register and document facts. However, none of these methods was able to sub-stitute the personal memory of someone who had lived through an event. None of them! Until plugs were invented.

Text published at the end of the Old-World by Dr. Yakun Morioshi, neuralscientist and inventor of the plugs.

Everything in the Hive was different. It was a much more reserved environment, and people were colder. On the 68th floor of the clinical sector, Makuro was waiting in a clean cor-ridor. He was about to undergo a small surgical operation, and he would shortly be called to the operating theater. It was a simple operation in which three holes would be made in his neck to connect him definitively to the incredible world of the plugs.

The corridor was so clean that it reflected images. On the wall, there was the silhouette of a serious young man, who was holding the bonsai that had been given to him as present. Remembering the first weeks that he had spent inside the technological city, the young man felt a happiness he did not want to show.

After the first Myra-Hati battle, Makuro was taken directly to the Hive. He was required to remain under observation while a Hati squadron went to search for the ruins in order to rescue Hanara and the Banjin Indian tribe.

According to the local news, the route memory which was registered by the vehicles of the platoon that was after Kliver eighteen years ago was recovered and, in this way, the squadron managed to locate Ruakan. Makuro did not know what could happen to the Noans if they resisted and there was a battle, but he was sure that Hanara had taken pre-cautions in order to secure the safety of his people.

Meanwhile, Makuro underwent various blood tests in order to prove that his blood was compatible with that of the race, and if it was not, he would be considered a Banjin. The test was successful, and the biomedical officers were surprised by its results. The discovery was kept secret. Only the medical authorities and the Emperor were aware that Makuro was son of the recently promoted Lieutenant-Colonel Tadashi, the result of the illegal pregnancy of Miku.

The local media merely said that Makuro's blood was that of the pure Hati race and that he would soon be plugged.

During his first weeks in the Hive, Makuro learned a lot about the Hatis' customs and politics. He also discovered more about the strange way a new Emperor is chosen and crowned. This imperial tradition takes place in the following way:

Anyone may become the new Hati Emperor as long as he or she has pure Hati blood.

When they are crowned, the Emperor places a secret password in a letter, which is sealed and kept in a safe, and whose code to open it is only known to him. According to the beliefs of the civilization, the spirit of Sakyamuni reveals in a dream the password of the letter to the chosen one. When someone says that he or she has received the dream, the stands of the official hu-tae-mui stadium are full at an enormous celebration, so the population may pay homage to the new Emperor.

The supposed chosen one says the password into a microphone before the press and the awaiting crowd. The safe is open personally by the Emperor who is still on the throne, and the letter is solemnly unsealed.

If the spoken password is correct, then the chosen one will carry out the will of Sakyamuni and becomes the new Emperor, while the previous Emperor is exiled in the luxury 'Chamber of the Exiled', where he will spend the rest of his days in the company of the ex-Emperors who are still alive.

However, if the spoken password is not that which has been written down, the present Emperor remains on the throne, with the obligation to write a new secret password, which is also sealed and returned to the safe. The false Chosen One is then executed in the most painful way possible, together with all the members of his family, including all of his descendants.

This barbarous law was passed merely to prevent a waste of time and resources. The possible Chosen One should only manifest himself when he is certain, as if the password is wrong, he will pay dearly and will sacrifice the lives of all his innocent family, according to the ancient Hati saying: 'When a citizen makes a mistake, all must pay for it'.

So, almost no one ever tries to guess the password. The majority of those who tried were killed, with the result that there appear a number of openings for couples who were waiting in the line to become parents.

Anyway, before an Emperor dies through natural causes, a substitute will always appear with the correct password. A number of years ago, the press published a story about this, saying that the Emperors should reveal the correct password to someone they have chosen. But nothing was proved, and the people were disgusted by the lack of faith of the journalists, accusing them of defaming their beliefs. A number of them are still in prison.

After this, the press shut up and never again raised suspicions about the traditional methods of this choice.

Makuro stood up and went to one of the windows in the corridor, looking at the gray edge of the building on the horizon. He was on the 68th floor of the clinic, where neural surgery took place, and because it was so high, it was possible to see almost all the inside of the Hive:

There were thousands of shelters on the inside walls, as if they were part of the walls, but the center of the city was a huge open space. Under the huge dome there were just three buildings, the highest of which had a cylindrical shape, and around it there was an intense traffic of air vehicles going in all directions. This was the heart of the city. The building housed the nuclear reactor, the vehicle and the electronic factories, the textile industry, and the refineries. Near the ground there were water filters, reservoirs and food stores.

The smaller buildings were the headquarters and the Imperial Palace. The headquarters housed the military shelters, training schools, the prison and the press offices, and the hu-tae-mui stadium was positioned on its roof. The ministries, the Chamber of Exiles and the research laboratories were situated in the Palace.

Three elevated ring roads, one above the other, went around the internal circumference of the city, connecting the sectors. Each of them had eight bridges which were directly connected to the main building in the center.

Although it was day, the lights of the shelters were on, illuminating the city from the roof to the ground. The solar rays which the dome received were not able to reach the distant sectors and were concentrated only around the center.

Seen from the inside, the dome was concave. Although it was made up of innumerous hexagonal plates, it was very similar to the blue sky of the ancient world.

Despite the fact he was happy to be experiencing new things, Makuro found it difficult to put up with the fact that he was away from his family. He liked changes, but he discovered that he didn't like to live them. While he was looking at the cars flying through the sectors, Makuro wondered where Hanara, Aron, Poko, and his mother, his stepfather, and especially Tork, were. How could someone who was as fragile as his brother be able to change the destiny of thousands of Hatis and millions of Myras?

Myras and Hatis. In spite of their differences, they were people just like him, made up of dreams and the same material of all human beings. How could one race want to exterminate another? Have they developed so much that they had now become machines? Robots programmed to kill?

Makuro would not find answers to these questions, but maybe Tork one day would.

Wondering about all this, he looked down and saw a tiny green point, which must be a public garden. He pressed the bonsai he was holding. His heart beat quickly. That must be the same garden where he had met the beautiful girl who had given him the midget tree. He began to smile to himself. Just the fact he knew about the existence of this beautiful girl made it worthwhile for him to exchange the free world in order to become a Hati citizen:

In a green garden surrounded by bushes and rare flowers, the sounds of a sad melody could be heard. A girl, sitting on a carved bench, played a sad song while she watched the birds jumping from one branch to another. They were playing, bathing in the fountain, and whistling to the sound of her flute. Up above, higher than the buildings, the top of the central dome could hardly be seen.

The girl was alone, accompanied only by her feathered companions, and her clothes were the colors of nature. She wore a silk moss-green kimono, embroidered with cherry blossoms. Her smartly cut hair, expensive necklaces and earrings, made her appear to be a noble.

Above, the huge ring around the base of the dome opened at various points. From the outside dozens of war airships came in, slowly moving inside the Hive. The girl looked at everything. The ships were coming in, and the buildings were shaking. The birds were fleeing the din, the girl stopped playing and left, leaving her flute on the garden bench.

This was the day when the Hatis had taken part in the battle against the Myras, and she was anxiously waiting for news. She was praying for her father, one of the commanders of the battalion, to return home alive.

The first contact of Makuro with the Hati civilization was to be taken to the Army laboratory, inside the headquarters, where a sample of his blood was taken to check whether it was compatible with that of the Hati race. In the reception room, one of the first floors of the headquarters, from the window which looked out onto the garden, he could hear the sound of the flute which once again took up its melody.

Attracted by the sound, Makuro disobeyed orders, went through the door to the garden as if he were enchanted by the music of a mermaid. And then he found her. Without even exchanging a word, Makuro's mermaid smiled to him. She delicately picked up a bonsai from the ground and gave it to him, as if it was a symbolic present. Then his absence was noticed, and when he heard his name called he turned and went back to the headquarters.

Makuro felt in his skin the language of love that needs no words. He had never seen such a gorgeous girl. She seemed to be the same age as he. She must be noble and skillful. He longed to see her again.

This was almost a month ago and, since then, the bonsai which had been given by those so delicate little hands have never left him. It was now withered. The acid from the sweat of his hand had destroyed it, but the feeling he felt had blossomed more and more, just like the garden where he had found her.

He returned to the garden whenever he could. He watched the birds bathing and the flowers opening out, but he never again saw his mermaid, or heard the sad tune of her flute. And he had no proof of her existence. He had found the girl of his dreams and had not dared to even ask her name. He had let her escape from between his fingers, just like the fisherman who allows his greatest ever catch to escape. A noble girl. The one and only girl, in amidst of so many others . . .

The internal sound system finally told him to go to the psychologist's office. Before undergoing the surgery, Makuro would have to complete a number of tests, and he felt somewhat nervous. He left the window of dreams and went along the clean corridor towards the office.

The door lost its opacity and opened automatically. A loud 'Come in', coming from inside, invited him to step in. He entered the room and saw a middle-aged woman leaning over a number of forms. She had curly hair and wide eyes, and a mouth which smiled when she welcomed him:

"Good afternoon" she said in Hati. "I am Dr. Meling. Come away from the scanner and fill out these forms, please."

Makuro took the papers and sat in the armchair.

"Now, now, look who is here! The young man who grew up with the Banjins!" said the doctor, recognizing the face she had seen on the news. "You seem to be a bit tense. Have this" and she offered a sweet biscuit while she dipped another in a cup of hot tea.

"No, thanks . . . I'm just a bit scared about the operation."

"Don't worry. These operations for the connectors are quite simple. They are usually carried out on children when they are twelve. A strong young man like you won't even feel the anesthetic needle."

Dr. Meling took about ten minutes to make the psychological evaluation of Makuro. Although he was tense, he seemed immune to the risks.

After the tests, he was taken to the theater, which was a small room with a large number of electronic devices and no other patient. The nurses told him to lie down on his stomach on a bed and strapped him down, and then gave him a local anesthetic. He shivered when he felt the thin needle entering his skin, but then his neck went numb, and the surgeon put him on an artificial respirator, as the anesthetic might block his glottis.

The surgeon made three small holes in Makuro's nape with a pointed instrument. A wire was placed in each of them, and the other ends of the wire were connected to a computer. Strong electric currents went through the wires, and Makuro twisted when he received the shock.

"Calm down, my boy. I'm sending the data from the program to your marrow and connecting with some cells which belong to the main nerve" explained the surgeon.

A bio-chip was delicately implanted into the root of the marrow, and the external connector was attached.

"It's ready" said the doctor. "The effect of the anesthetic will wear off in fifteen minutes. For now all we need to do is to wait for the program to download into the chip, and from tomorrow you'll be ready to become a new user of the plugs."

"Why just tomorrow?" asked Makuro, disappointed.

"It's a security norm. Your body needs to adapt to the chip and the connector, so that it will not reject it. The plugs can only make contact with the connector twenty hours after the operation. Inside the connector there is an electronic lock, which will prevent you from connecting in case you get a borrowed device. Tomorrow, when you return, the lock will be taken off, and you will receive a personal plug as a gift from the Empire. Be ready. Tomorrow you will experience the 'initial sensation', your first experience as a user.

"What happens in this first experience?" Makuro wanted to know.

"That's the usual question of those who have their first plugs. You're a very curious boy for someone who has growing up by Banjins" joked the doctor. "Tomorrow you will know."

The surgeon taped the wound and made an appointment for Makuro to come at four o'clock the following day. Still under the effect of the anesthetic, he went along the corridor and waited for Corporal Mazada, who was temporarily responsible for him, to return from his errands. He had arranged to leave him in the clinic to undergo his tests and operation, and then pick him up afterwards. So he would not take long to return.

Makuro looked out through the window once again and saw that it was getting dark. The sunbeams coming from the red sky through the blue dome became purple rays shining on the buildings. The air traffic was increasing at the end of the afternoon. People wanted to get home quickly, and this was maybe why Mazada was late.

"At the beginning you think everything is marvelous, but then you get used to it, and you begin to feel an unbearable loneliness" spoke a voice from behind the boy. "Are you ready?"

Makuro nodded. He pressed his neck to see if he could feel it because of the anesthetic, and then accompanied Mazada to the exit of the clinic.

It was not necessary to go to the ground floor as Mazada's taxi was waiting at the exit to the 68th floor of the clinic, floating by the landing platform. The vehicle made very light movements up and down while it hovered in the air.

The taxi door opened, and a kind of metal belt projected out. Mazada and Makuro got in and sat down. An electronic voice asked them if they were ready.

"Yes, we are" said the corporal.

"Where are you going?" asked the machine.

"Military shelter 13, central sector" said Mazada.

"User name and number"

"Corporal Mazada, B-210."

"Confirm the number of passengers."

"Two."

"Destination and information accepted. Bon voyage." said the machine just before they took off and increased its speed. The automatic pilot, or the 'chauffeur-robot', as the Hatis called it, faithfully followed the air traffic code. At exactly fifty knots, the taxi zigzagged between the vehicles in front of it.

People were everywhere, walking over the bridges connecting the sectors, or flying with their titanium wings. Makuro followed a girl who was flying some meters above them, but soon lost sight of her when the taxi went behind the headquarters building, slowing down and stopping on a landing platform. It had been a quick journey. A round door opened below a bright number thirteen.

"Military shelter thirteen, central sector." Informed the robot. "Journey completed. Have a good evening."

"Thank you" said Mazada, walking onto the platform.

"Permission to leave until the next call."

"Given. You may return to the garage."

The taxi took off again and Mazada went through the door. Makuro accompanied him. They went along a long crescent-shaped corridor, where there were three more safety doors, which were controlled by a retinal scanner in the first door, a weapon metal detector in the second one, and an x-ray scanner which checked unauthorized objects in the third. Then they were finally inside the structure.

Makuro was now free to do what he wanted inside the limits of his space. But as there was no one in the refectory or the recreation room to talk to, and the television rooms had the same dull programs as ever, he decided to return to his cell. With the shy steps of someone who is still not used to his environment, Makuro went to the dormitories.

The Hati military dormitories were the same as any other dormitory in the Hive, a long and narrow corridor in which both walls were full of hexagonal cells.

The cells were small dwelling spaces with just one room, set in the walls of the dormitories, connected to each other from below, above and the sides, looking like huge honeycombs. They might house a single person, or married couples.

There were no kitchens in the cells, as all meals were taken in the refectories. The Empire distributed clothes and food free of charge to the population, in exchange for the services they gave to the Empire. The fringe benefits were gained according to the importance which each individual had in this society.

The use of the cells was a measure taken by the first Emperor who studied a practical way of housing the population. If each family had its private home, there would not be enough space in the Hive for everyone, and the Empire would have to extend its birth control schemes.

According to an Imperial law, while the problems of the atmospheric radioactivity, the shortage of uranium and food, the lack of raw materials, and the threat of the Myra-Hati war remained unsolved, a second Hive could not be built.

Still holding on to his bonsai, Makuro walked slowly into the dormitory, where everything was silent, scanning looking at the high walls on either side for his cell. The outside of a number of them was mirrored, preventing him from seeing what was happening inside.

Inside the cells he could see into, Makuro noticed that the occupants were sitting still in their chairs, being entertained by their plugs. Nobody was discussing anything, nobody was talking, and nobody was playing cards, chess or draughts. All they were doing was to use their plugs.

A brief dialogue in Hati broke the silence. Two young men, each in his cell, were talking:

"Tikawa" shouted the first.

"What do you want?" shouted back the other.

"Did you have sex with that girl who helps to deliver the clothing?"

"Which one?"

"You know . . . that one with the double piercing in her eyebrow and dyed red hair. Did you have sex with her?"

"Yes, I did."

"Did you record it?"

"Yes."

"Can you lend me your plug?"

"Later. Mazaki is using it. And there are another two in the line, waiting to use it . . ."

That was the only thing he heard that night.

CHAPTER 18
A TRIP OF THE SENSES

That night Makuro was suffering from terrible insomnia. Anxiety was preventing him from sleeping. He was worried. He opened his sleeping capsule and felt around on the metal wall for the switch. He turned on the lights and saw that there were more than two hours left for day to arrive. There was not much he could do. The occupants of the other cells were all asleep, and it would be a long time before the day's routine to begin.

It was no use to put his head on the pillow and try to sleep. His capsule was small, and he couldn't stretch his legs to relax. He had been used to sleeping almost naked from the time he was young, but was afraid that if he took off his clothes, he might be breaking a rule, or someone might see him.

It was difficult to have privacy in the cells. His only private space had a transparent facade where he could hardly take off his clothes without someone seeing him. He looked at the control panel and read the following instruction on one of the buttons: 'External Mirrored Cover' written in Hati.

Makuro pressed the button and saw that the glass in the facade lost its transparency and slowly became opaque. He was pleased to discover this and now had the courage to take off his clothes, only keeping on his underpants.

He picked up a book which described the plugs and began to browse through it. He read one, two, three pages, and looked at his watch. Only fifteen minutes had passed, and he couldn't concentrate on the book. He decided to have a shower. He hid the book under the pillow and went to the nearby bathroom, turning on the water heater. He got into the ofuro bath and felt his muscles relax, dozing and thinking about the girl who had given him the bonsai.

After the siren sounded at the beginning of the day, Makuro went into the refectory and felt his stomach turn when he found out that chowder would be served for breakfast. Since he had arrived in the Hive he had only eaten fish and seafood, and his stomach felt bad. Just the smell coming from the tables made him feel sick.

He sat down and just ate the rice balls which came with the soup. His look was distant and vacant. Not even the din that the recruits made when they woke up could distract him. When one of the other recruits tried to attract his attention, he had to poke him three times.

"Yes?" said Makuro, overcome by sleep.

"What's your problem? You seem to be 'doped'" asked a wide awake recruit.

"I couldn't sleep last night" he said after a huge yawn.

"Why not? Are you ill?"

"I'm worried about the experience with the plug I'll use this afternoon. I'm very worried. This will be my first experience as a user . . ."

"I realized it when I saw the tape on your neck" said the recruit. "But if this is the case, I suggest you sleep for the rest of the day. Before they connect you, the doctors will test your motor coordination. If they discover you didn't sleep, they'll put it off."

"I can't sleep. I've tried everything . . . what do you do when you have insomnia?"

"Well, we program our plugs for involuntary sleep. It wakes us up whenever we want, and we can still choose whether we want to dream" he explained.

"But I don't have a plug yet" said Makuro. "I don't know what to do."

The recruit thought a little.

"I can help, but you have to swear you won't tell anyone."

"I swear" he said, impulsively. "I'll do anything. I really must sleep."

"But you'll have to pay."

Makuro looked up in surprise.

"I thought that there was no money in the Hive" he said.

"Don't be stupid. Our payment is made through favors."

"Favors?"

"Yes, favors. You know . . . I do something for you, and you do something for me . . ."

"What type of favor?" asked Makuro suspiciously.

"Hmmm . . . let me see . . . do you know Dr. Meling?"

"Who?"

"Meling, the doctor responsible for the psychological tests for people who undergo plug surgery . . ."

"Oh, yes. I met her. She seemed to be a very pleasant and devoted woman."

"Yes, well. Did you know she's married?"

"No, I didn't" said Makuro. "So what?"

"Simple. I want you to get me the plug belonging to Lieutenant Iagushi, who is her husband. I want you to get me a plug with recordings of their wedding night. One which has a recording of them both . . . well, you know . . ."

"Sex?"

"That's right!" said the recruit, immediately.

"Are you attracted to her?" asked Makuro.

"From the day I had my first plug connected!"

Makuro thought this was strange, taking into account the fact that Meling, though very attractive, was a little old for him.

"She's different from the others . . ." the recruit explained. "She is the only woman I know who has curly hair . . . You must have seen her in their wedding. Lovely, happy, perfect! Try to locate the plug of their wedding night, when she was still young . . . And so? Deal?"

Makuro was shocked.

"How do I manage to have access to such a plug?"

"Easy. You'll have to fly to the sector where she lives, enter her shelter, and get into her cell!"

"And do you think this is easy?"

"Well, it is not as complicated as it seems . . . the only thing we need is a good plan."

Makuro was quiet for a long time. The recruit was losing his patience.

"Don't you want me to help you?" he asked, getting annoyed. "Would you rather wait another day to get connected?"

"And in which sector is the doctor's shelter?" Makuro wanted to know.

"I don't know. It must be number five, which is where the doctors live. But, in order to be certain, ask her this afternoon, when you go back to the clinic. You have to get this information today. Be discreet. Start talking, and when you have a chance . . ."

"Okay, I'll do it!" In his desperation, Makuro thought that there was no choice and gave in. "And for my problem?" he asked. "Can you help me with my insomnia?"

The recruit brought his chair near.

"Do the following" he said secretly. "Go to the infirmary and say that you're not feeling well. Ask permission to spend the rest of the day in bed and put me as a witness on the forms. Then return to your cell, lie down in your capsule, and take one of these" he held out his hand and offered him a big red tablet. "This will make you sleep like a stone."

"What's this?"

"Alpazin-10. A tranquilizer for war wounds! Just half a tablet is enough."

Makuro frowned.

"How did you get it?"

"Well, I'm a soldier . . . in addition, there are various people who owe me favors . . . what do you say? Is it a deal?"

Makuro threw his chopsticks onto the plate and got up, discreetly taking the tablet from the recruit's hand.

"Okay" he replied. "If I have to put you as a witness of my illness, what's your name?"

"Mujiro" said the recruit, also getting up. "Don't forget our deal, new boy. If you refuse to get the plug for me, I'll accuse you to the authorities of having made use of illegal toxic substances! And you will not like spending a few days in our prison."

Makuro turned to him.

"Are these tablets illegal?" he asked.

"Well . . . their use is controlled by the Empire. But you won't need to show it to anyone."

Makuro thought for a moment.

"Okay. Don't worry" he finally said. "I'll carry out the deal", and then he went into the infirmary.

"I'll wake you up at half past three" said Mujiro disdainfully. "Sleep well!"

Makuro turned around and went out into the corridor. Before he entered the infirmary, a man who was passing warned him:

> "I saw you two talking. You're new here, my boy, and somebody must tell you something. Take care with Mujiro. He's not to be trusted. He's always looking for people to owe him favors."

'Yes, but what can I do?' Makuro was now in Mujiro's hands, but he couldn't bear the idea of his first experience with the plugs being postponed. He shrugged and went into the infirmary.

In his cell, after swallowing one of the halves of the tablet, Makuro slept deeply for almost eight hours. But because of the effect of the tranquilizer, he thought he had slept much longer. He woke up refreshed and eager, and it was not necessary for Mujiro to wake him up. As there was another half hour before he would be taken to the clinical sector, he had another shower and got ready. This would be a magical day, the day when he would finally get to know how the marvelous entertainment of the whole Hive actually worked.

"Hey, Makuro!" shouted a voice from the neighboring cell.

"Yes?" he replied, still in the shower.

"Mazada has asked me to tell you that the taxi has arrived and is waiting for you at the exit of the shelter."

"I'll be down in a minute" he said while he was wiping himself.

Back in the clinic, the young man with Hati blood but of Banjin origin entered and was soon invited to present himself to Dr. Meling. He was a bit worried, especially about how he could obtain the information he needed to carry out the favor he now owed Mujiro. He had no idea of how he could ask for her address, and, if he asked for it, it would seem strange that he noted it down.

"Good afternoon, Makuro. Did you sleep well?" she made a sign for him to sit down.

"Yes, I did. In fact, I'd never slept so much" he added, with a shy smile.

"Good . . . let's look at the results" she said, putting a number of brochures on the table. "I should tell you that we have a wide range of experiences for beginning users, which are chosen according to the results of the psychological tests of each individual. In case you've obtained information from a friend about this initial experience, you should know that this varies from person to person, okay?"

"Don't worry . . . I haven't tried to get any information."

"Fine! The initial experiences are chosen according to the personality of each user. Take maximum advantage of these sensations, as, once you relive them, the file will be deleted from the plug. The first experience can only be lived once. Do you understand?"

"Yes, doctor."

"The content of each experience lasts about half an hour. Although they are real, you must remember that it is a recording. The user who recorded it will become incarnated in you. He was chosen as a result of the test you took yesterday. Are you ready?" asked the doctor, putting on her glasses.

"Yes."

"So, let's go to the room next door to carry out the motor coordination tests, measure your blood pressure, and check your reflexes."

Makuro got up.

"Doctor . . ." he said, shyly.

"Yes?" replied Meling, leaning on the table.

"I'd like to know something . . . are you married?"

"Yes. Why do you ask?"

"Nothing. I just wondered about the lives of married people here in the Hive . . ."

"Perhaps one day you'll have the chance to find out" she said dryly. "Can we continue?"

"My mother was married. Did you know?" he insisted. "Did you know Miku?"

"What's this leading to?" asked Meling, wondering what his reaction would be if she told him that it was she who had helped Miku escape from the Hive. And that if it had not been for her, Makuro would certainly have been killed when he was born, or would have been used as a guinea pig in the Palace laboratories.

"Nowhere" he replied. "I just want to talk. I'm very lonely here, and I still haven't had the chance to meet anyone . . . Anyone of the opposite sex, you know?" Makuro sweated and stammered.

"Don't you think I'm the least appropriate person to tell this to?"

"No, no . . . I mean, you're pretty and you must have had a lot of men interested in you . . . maybe you could help me . . ."

"My advice is: learn alone. Life and nature will teach you. Let's begin?"

"Thank you" Makuro didn't manage to express himself. He was very tense. "Just one more thing . . ." he said, almost giving up. "Where are the female shelters?"

"Why do you want to know?"

"So I can have contact with . . . girls!"

"Boys are forbidden to enter the female shelters. I can't give you this type of information."

"And the shelters of married couples? They are in Sector Five, aren't they?"

"No, Sector Five is for the exclusive use of military doctors"

"Do you live in Sector Five? Do you belong to the army?"

"Young man, let's stop this conversation here and now!" she began to get annoyed. 'The results of the tests gave a very different impression of him,' she thought.

Makuro shut up. He would have to find another way to get the information. Dr. Meling got up and asked him to follow her, taking him to the testing room, where an elderly man waited for him with a pressure gauge.

"Mr. Jung, this is Makuro, the new boy" said the doctor. "He needs to take the routine tests to use his first plug. I'll leave him in your hands."

Makuro entered, and Meling left. When he noticed the tension that was between them, Jung immediately asked him:

"The doctor seemed irritated. Was it something you did or said, young man?"

Makuro had an idea.

"No, sir. I just tried to discover her address so I could give her a surprise . . . but I couldn't find out."

"A surprise?" asked the old man, curiosity appearing between the wrinkles of his face. "What kind of surprise?"

"I wanted to give her . . . a bonsai! I wanted to give her a bonsai as a present, as a symbol of my gratitude to her for having been so attentive to me in these last days."

"A bonsai is not the best present to show your gratitude" said the old man. "Here in the Hive they symbolize the fact you want to date the other person."

"Really?" once again the image of the girl came back to him.

"Give her a bunch of takaras" suggested Jung. "They are rare flowers which only grow in magical regions. Takaras can represent gratitude."

"That's it. I'll give her some 'takarias'! Thanks for the suggestion."

"Takaras!" corrected the old man. "It won't be easy to find some. But, if you want, I can give her one in your name."

The chance was now escaping him.

"It's not necessary . . . I'd prefer to give it to her."

"In this case, I'll try to get you some."

"Thank you . . . But I don't yet know the doctor's address."

"No?" asked Jung.

The old man thought, scratched his bald head, and then said:

"If it's to give her a present, I'll tell you her address. But it will have to remain between us two. If they discover that I gave you her address without her authorization, in addition to losing my job, I'll also run the risk of going to jail. And I would not like to spend some days in our prison, especially at my age . . ."

'So what's the problem of the Hati jails?' Makuro wondered.

"Don't worry" he said. "I'm not the kind of person to accuse those who helped me."

Jung went to the counter and came back with a card he took out of his drawers and a piece of white paper on which he wrote something. He gave both to Makuro.

"On the card you'll find the address where you'll be able to get the takaras" he said. "And on the paper there's the doctor's address. Do you know where the post office is?"

"Yes, I do. Thank you." lied Makuro when he picked them up, trying to close the conversation.

"So, let's get to work" said the old man, telling Makuro to sit on a chair with armrests.

Jung measured his blood pressure, tested his reflexes, and then sent him to a room called the 'Initiation Room', a small dark room in which it was only possible to see the red exit sign over the door.

The lamps were turned on, and Makuro found himself in an empty room with soundproof walls, which contained only a machine to measure brainwaves next to a computer, and a reclining metal seat, which was similar to the old electric chairs.

"Good afternoon. Are you fine?" asked the surgeon on entering. This was the same surgeon who had carried out the operation the previous day.

"Yes, sir, but I'm a bit anxious."

"So take off your T-shirt, and sit on the 'magic chair'."

Makuro checked to see whether the addresses were still in his pockets and took off his T-shirt, sitting down in the chair. The doctor pressed his stethoscope against Makuro's chest.

"I can see that you're really worried. Your heart sounds like the regimental band in the hu-tae-mui championships!" joked the doctor.

"Is there any problem?"

"No, none . . . everything is normal. Bend your head, please."

Makuro did so.

"Bend over a bit more, so I can reach the connector."

Makuro bent over a little more, showing the holes of the connector in his neck. The doctor took off the tape and connected the wave measuring device on to his forehead, taking out of his coat a completely new plug. He unscrewed the bottom of the device and opened it, showing three threatening pins which would be connected to Makuro's nape.

"This is a standard civic plug" explained the doctor, turning it in his fingers. "With it you will be able to record and share experiences with friends. But you will not be able to access the inter-plug, unless through its audio network, which will only allow you to communicate with other users. The plugs with complete access to the inter-plug can only be used by soldiers on a mission or by civilians with certain benefits which have been awarded by the Empire. In the military plugs there is an identifier to recognize the DNA of its user, which prevents unauthorized personnel from connecting . . . but don't worry. If one day you enter the Hati army, you'll get one. In the meantime use this. It's an excellent toy!"

Makuro held out his hand to take it, but the doctor didn't give it to him.

"After the first experience is finished" continued the doctor, "I'll show you how to record and reproduce experiences, and also how to use internal programs. Among them you have the sleep programmer, pre-programmed games, and other types of entertainment. There are also simulators which will teach you how to pilot vehicles, such as aircars and jetpacks. With these programs you'll be able to become legally qualified as a pilot . . . take care of your plug, my boy. Together with the connector, it is your main identity as a Hati citizen. Only lend it to those you trust. Are you ready?"

"Yes, sir" said Makuro, fascinated by the possibilities of the plug.

The surgeon transferred the data of the computer to a memory chip and inserted it into the new device. The content of the experiment would be deleted after it had been reproduced. He attached a number of electrodes to Makuro's nerve points and pressed the pins of the apparatus into the holes in his neck to connect him. On the screen the lines representing Makuro's heartbeat and brainwaves showed a considerable change.

"Relax, Makuro!" advised the doctor. "If you don't, I'll have to put it off until next week. Try to breathe deeply."

Makuro breathed deeply and panted, like someone who was going to be tattooed for the first time.

"Something else" remembered the doctor. "Once the plug connector is grafted onto your vertebrae, you're registered on the inter-plug, even if you don't access it, and your movements are monitored by the Empire. Inside the connector there's a transmitter which is always on, and which informs your position in the Hive. The transmitter uses the bodily heat of its own user in order to work. It was placed there against your will according to Article 5 of Law no. 3.607 for the prevention of crime and escapes from the Hive. You'll carry the connector in your nape for the rest of your life. Once it is there, it's impossible to take out. Am I clear?"

'Hell!' thought Makuro. That information told him that it would be difficult to get into Meling's cell without being tracked by the Empire. He began to feel very anxious, and the screen began to show that his brain was very tense.

"What's the problem, my boy? Has this worried you?" the doctor was suspicious of something. "Shall we wait until another day?"

"No!" Makuro swallowed and tried to calm down, drops of sweat appearing on his forehead. "The waiting is making me tense, doctor. Can we get it over with quickly?"

"As you wish. Chew these herbs while I finish programming the device. They will help you to relax . . ."

Makuro chewed the leaves for another three minutes, and the doctor finally turned on the plug. At the beginning, Makuro felt his feet were slightly numb, and this sensation spread up his legs, his thighs and further upwards. Although he was sitting down, he felt as if he was standing up in the room. When the numbness reached his neck, there was a shock which twisted his neck muscles, he then felt drunk, and his sight darkened.

Anxious, he now tried to rub his eyes with his hands, but his muscles failed to obey him. Makuro was no longer in the room with the doctor, but in another world. A dark, silent world.

"Plin", "plin", "plin" . . . Makuro heard a dripping noise in the distance. He tried to locate the origin of the noise. When he walked, he felt lighter, thinner, and shorter. His body was not the same as it had been a few minutes before. But his mind was the same; it was he who was there, walking in the dark as if he were not going anywhere. He wanted to feel his new body, touch it, feel it, but he couldn't control his hands, which acted on their own free will, as did his arms and legs.

In the darkness, the sound of the dripping directed him. When the sound became more distant, his legs stopped, his eyes looked around, and he soon began to walk again.

When he found the dripping, which was coming out of nowhere, his arm stretched out, and the drops fell on his palms. He felt them on his fingers and realized that the liquid was somewhat thicker than water. He lifted his hand up to his eyes and tried to look at them. Then he became frightened on seeing that his fingers were covered in blood!

'My God!' he thought, as he incarnated the experience. Everything was too real. The air could be breathed; the blood in contact with his skin, and he even had the sensation of walking.

"Help!" a voice came from above. A weak, dying voice.

Suddenly it became light. Makuro lifted his head and stepped back. The blood was dripping from a body which was still alive, and tied by its feet to the dry branches of a tree.

"Help me!" pleaded the voice.

"M-Mo . . . Mother!" shouted Makuro, desperate when realizing that the body was that of Miku.

The woman said nothing else but looked to her son with deep eyes and slowly closed her eyelids.

Makuro was desperate, and this time his body obeyed him. He threw himself into his mother's arms and tried to revive her, leaning her head on his shoulders and pulling at the rope. His palms were hurt, and he was unable to release Miku.

Then the ground began to tremble. A crack opened up at his feet, and with his hands covered in his own blood, Makuro fell into an abyss.

Then the horizon opened up, and Makuro saw himself falling down the sides of a cliff. When he reached the ground, his fall was softened by bushes. He got up, wiped the leaves off his clothes, and was once again there, alone, walking over green grass surrounded by hills.

He looked all around, as if his eyes wanted to show him the beauty of the place, but Makuro paid no attention as his mind was still troubled by the image of his dying mother pleading for help. Then he remembered that the scene might be false, and he tried to remain calm.

"Hey, stranger!" sounded a voice coming from behind.

Makuro automatically turned around and saw a thin man with sunburned fair skin. He was limping and wore a black uniform with green stripes, which was very similar to those of the Myras who had been fighting in the battle he had seen with Aron. The man was wearing a helmet, which hid most of his face, preventing him from being identified. In his hands he was holding an arc-shaped weapon, which Makuro realized was a crossbow.

"Who are you?" asked Makuro, aware that his voice was not the same.

"Don't ask questions" ordered the stranger in Myra. "Let's go, come on!" and he pressed his crossbow against Makuro's chest.

"I refuse!" challenged Makuro. "I'm not going anywhere unless you identify yourself."

"How dare you disobey my order?" shouted the man.

"This is a dream. It can only be. I don't think anything here is real."

The man unclenched his fist and gave Makuro a heavy slap in the face.

"Feel the weight of my hand" he said. "Does it seem to be unreal to you?"

No, it didn't. Makuro felt the slap. And it was real! As real as real could be.

The stranger clicked his fingers, and the hills around the grass filled up with men dressed like him, with weapons directly pointing at Makuro's head.

"Do you want to feel what it's like to be shot by perforating arrows?" he asked. "Do you still believe that all this is unreal? Come on, walk!"

This time Makuro obeyed, or rather, the user who had recorded the experience obeyed, but, if it had been him, he would have done the same thing.

One of the men dared to say:

"Hey, Kliver, your son is not as stupid as he seems."

"He's not my son" the man replied. "I have no mixed-race children. I used his mother just to reach the Hatis. And this aberration is the result. Ah, but it was enjoyable . . . and it was successful! Miku must now be at the top of the cliff. She was tied to a tree after being raped by the Regent's soldiers!"

'Now, you . . .' said Makuro in his real self. That man could not be his stepfather, as Kliver had disappeared from Ruakan together with Hanara and the natives. He was in a coma and very ill. But he couldn't be sure. The black helmet covered almost all his face, making it impossible to identify him.

The boy said nothing. He went on faster, with the cross-bow pointing at his back. Further on, far from the grass and the hills, he saw an iron wagon in the desert, ready to leave. Two Myra soldiers were guarding it.

The man who was escorting him gestured with his weapon for him to get into the wagon, inside which there were a large number of Hati prisoners piled on top of each other. They were of all ages, from five to seventy, and were filthy with blood and feces. Scars could be seen from whippings, and other bodies were full of bruises left by heavy blows. Some had fainted, and others were lying in their own vomit.

"Oh, my son!" said an elderly woman, one of whose eyes was missing. "Were you captured? I'm so sorry!"

"The prophecy was wrong!" said an old man shrunk up in one of the corners, who lowered his head when looking at Makuro.

"I'm sorry you're here!" said a boy whose nose was bleeding, and who appeared to be his own age. "The Myras have won for the time being. I hope the Emperor's troops can take revenge."

"Who are you?" asked Makuro.

"Don't you remember? You tried to rescue us from the Myra prison after the first battle. But you couldn't . . . now we're all on our way to the execution camps in the Colony."

"Who do you think you're talking to?" Everything was so confusing for Makuro.

"It is normal that your memory is affected after that blow . . . you are the mixed-race son of Miku. You are a Myra-Hati mixture, the chosen one who has come to the world to save us. Your name is Tork!"

"What?" shouted Makuro, wondering how it would be possible to be in the skin of his younger brother, as Tork had never had access to a plug.

Shortly afterwards, the thin man in the black uniform appeared again to check whether the prisoners were tied up well. He took off his helmet and winked at his son. Makuro felt a lump in his throat and could not prevent himself from shouting. The man was really his stepfather, who a few weeks before in Ruakan had been so weak and close to death.

The man closed the metal door and left. The wagon, pulled by four bigbugs with strong legs, began moving away with a jerk that made everyone lose their balance and fall over. The prisoners were taken to a camp on the banks of a gigantic oasis, where Makuro, now incarnated in his own younger brother, looked on in amazement at the captured Hatis, including women and children, being executed one by one.

He began to feel an enormous hatred for the Myras, especially for his stepfather Kliver. Now he was able to think more clearly, he understood that the experience might not be false. Since he had arrived in the Hive, Makuro had never mentioned his brother. If it were a simulated recording, how could they know about Tork? How could they know his name?

"Bring my son here" ordered Kliver. "I want to personally execute him."

Makuro was tied to the trunk of a date tree. His eyes had not been covered. Kliver took aim with his crossbow.

"I'm very sorry about this, my son" he said without appearing to be worried. "You represent peace and the union of the races. And peace is something that cannot exist. Not while the last Hati is still breathing." And when he was going to press the trigger, someone held him by his arm, preventing him from shooting.

"Give me the honor of killing him, father."

"As you wish, my only son."

Makuro immediately recognized the voice. It was Aron! He was smiling, proud to be wearing the uniform of the Myra Army. He took the weapon from his father, and, taking aim, said something before shooting the arrow:

"A Myra can never be the brother of a Hati, or even of a stupid mixed-race mongrel like you" he said, and finally pressed the trigger.

When he felt the arrow in his forehead, he once again blacked out, and the message in Hati appeared in front of his eyes:

"End of recording. Device turning off . . ."

He was disconnected. Makuro opened his eyes and saw that he was sitting in the chair in the small soundproof room. The surgeon was still there, measuring his brainwaves. Makuro anxiously got up. He took the wires off and tore the plug out of the connector. He lifted the device and hurled it onto the floor, breaking it in a thousand pieces.

"You're all crazy!" he shouted in a fit of anger, feeling an uncontrollable hatred.

"I'm sorry you've made the discovery in this way, my boy" said the doctor. "We found this plug in Myra territory. Its content was recorded by your younger brother moments before dying."

"No, it can't be! It can't be! Tork is alive! And even if he were dead, he would never have access to a plug. He could not have recorded his own death." Makuro wanted to believe this, but the recording was proving the opposite.

"Hanara connected him one day after you came to the Hive" the doctor explained. "I'm sorry that your stepfather has been a traitor. The Myras hate us. Kliver would never have married your mother if it had not been for a strategic army plan."

Makuro tried not to vomit. He looked around, and the walls began to turn. He covered his mouth with his hands and ran along the corridors of the clinic, totally disoriented and tormented.

Doctor Meling got out of his way and approached to the surgeon.

"Did we need to do this?" she asked. "Did we need to show his mother's death from the point of view of his own younger brother?"

"These were orders which came directly from the Emperor" explained the surgeon. "Give him some time to think. While Kliver was here as our prisoner he was very useful to us. Makuro doesn't understand how we discovered the name of his mixed-race brother. With Kliver's help, and also the plugs which the soldiers recorded on the battlefield, capturing the voice and face of Aron, we have managed to simulate this experience. It took almost a month to finish, but it was worth it."

"So this is why you took so long to plug him in? You spent all this time making this cheap simulation?"

"Yes. But from what we saw, everything came out perfectly according to plan. The important thing is that Makuro believes the great Myra-Hati to be dead, and that Aron and his step-father are betrayers."

"We should not have lied to the boy. He might well lose his mind."

"He grew up with Banjins and a Myra he considers his brother. It would be difficult to persuade him to feel hatred for the Myras. And you know the philosophy of the Empire: 'All Hatis must hate them', without exception. Without Kliver, it would have been impossible to simulate this experience. And without this experience, Makuro would never feel hatred for our enemies." concluded the surgeon.

Doctor Meling thought for a while.

"And how did you discover the mixed-race boy's name?" she then asked. "When Kliver was our prisoner, he confessed under the effect of drugs that the baby still didn't have a name, didn't he?"

"Yes, he did" agreed the surgeon. "But he also said that Hanara probably had become his protector. We were sure he would give the name of 'Tork' to the boy, as this is what the prophecy required. Have you never read the Sakyamuni scrolls?"

"Yes, I have. But what if Hanara had given another name to the baby?"

"This was the risk we took".

Doctor Meling continued to think.

"Kliver lied, that is something we both know," she said after a brief silence. "He had not eaten Miku, as he told to the reporters, but married her. The plug we obtained from the soldier who went out to look for Miku and was killed eighteen years ago shows this. It was not Kliver who killed the soldier that tried to rescue Miku from the mountains. There was a second person who hit him on the head, and everything indicates that this person must have been Miku. Not even the Command knows this, only the Emperor and the medical authorities that examined the contents of the plug . . ."

"That's true" confirmed the surgeon. "The Imperial Counsel didn't allow us to reveal the news even to our own military superiors. What are you saying?"

"I wonder . . ." said Meling. "If the Emperor knew from the beginning that Hanara and Miku were alive together with the Myra-Hati baby in Ruakan, why didn't he order an invasion of the ruins a long time before the beginning of the war?"

"The Emperor is a cautious man" said the surgeon. "He preferred to wait for the news to reach the people before taking measures. I don't know his methods very well, but I believe he is a wise man, who is fully aware of what he does. After all, don't forget that he was chosen by Sakyamuni to be our leader".

"If you say so . . ." Meling looked down. "But when Makuro discovers the farce, he will be furious with us."

"That's why he can't discover it." He looked confidently at Meling. "Don't worry, my dear. Everything came out well, according to the Emperor's plans. The Myras and the Banjins will soon be ours. Makuro is the key. He will take us to Hanara, Miku and the Myra-Hati."

"Haven't they been found yet?"

"All the Ruakan population is disappeared somewhere under the blot on our maps. The Banjins must be hidden somewhere inside the Continent . . . or maybe on some paradise island which is un-affected by the radiation . . ."

CHAPTER 19

RUIN OF THE RUINS

After another day's ride, the search platoon which had left the Colony finally reached Ruakan. Aron now recognized the region, and he guided the group to the pass which gave access to the eastern side of the village. They could see the higher buildings of the ruins. Now Aron led the group; if the Wild Savages were hostile, at least he would be someone they recognize.

"Don't worry if you hear the horns" he said.

But this time, the horns did not sound out. He thought it was strange, as there was a strict order to make a call them every time strangers approached.

They reached the eastern gate and saw that it was blocked by a high pile of stones, which may have rolled down from the tops. The soldiers then went to the southern gate and saw that it was also blocked. They walked around the walls and only found the northern entrance open.

The squadron cautiously made its way along the road, looking out for an ambush. There was no sign of life any-where. Apparently the village was empty, and Aron began to worry. The entrances to Ruakan had never been blocked before, especially in this very unusual way.

They noticed that the northern observation tower was lying dismantled on the dirty ground, and they could see that the ruins of the village had been completely destroyed and burned. There only remained the charred ruins of the houses, the temple, the chicken farm and the library, and a few unrecognizable carbonized bodies lay in the street.

Aron dismounted Barbarez's bigbug and went to the square. Tears came to his eyes when he saw his old house had been razed and was now no more than a pile of rubble. Maimed bodies, spears, and bomb craters showed a battle had taken place.

"We're too late" said the commander. "The Hatis arrived first. Look," he said as he pointed to a corpse which had a spear stuck into its gold-plated chest armor and another into its throat, making it clear that the natives had not died without fight.

"So many savage bodies and just one dead Hati" commented Professor Hugo in surprise.

"The Hatis did not perform the official rites for their dead soldier" said one of the recruits. "They left the corpse here to rot with those of the savages."

"They didn't want to waste time on just one soldier" said Barbarez. "The Hatis are inhuman, they're animals! They must have taken a lot of savage prisoner."

"If the savages were taken prisoner," said Irvine, "then they will become slaves."

"Stop calling them 'savages'" cried Aron, weeping. "They were civilized. They had their own language and knew how to farm the land. These bodies are those of my people and friends. Have a bit more respect."

"It's just an expression" said Irvine. "Don't get angry . . ."

They left the bodies and looked around the ruins, searching for survivors, but found nothing, and the journey seemed to have been in vain. A number of corpses were those of women, with rotting torn dresses and breasts as black as coal, showing that the Hatis showed no mercy to the weaker sex.

Five members of the platoon took off their vests and began to search through the huge pile of stones which had been part of the temple. Aron thought that if there were any survivors, they would be in the hiding place.

Before the sun went down, they found the iron trap-door which covered the entrance to the underground chambers. The soldiers broke the bolt and opened the trap-door, which led down into the darkness below. The commander ordered his men to turn on the light of their helmets and go down the steps.

There was no one in the dark tunnels. The Hatis had not thought about taking anything out of the laboratory, not even the ultracentrifugal device used to enrich uranium, which was a very expensive piece of equipment.

"We're too late" said the Major. "The savages are nowhere to be found. Either they managed to escape, or they were taken by the Hatis. Let's leave. There's nothing else we can do here." Then he turned to Aron. "Kliver, what is there in the lockers?"

"Er . . . I don't know for sure . . ."

"Barbarez, open the lockers".

"Yes, sir."

Barbarez took an explosive arrow from one of the recruits and aimed his crossbow.

"Move away" he said with a smile which always appeared when he was about to explode something.

He pressed the trigger, and the arrow exploded on the lockers, making its doors leap up to the roof as it caught fire and filled the room with smoke. Aron tried to turn on the suction fans, but the generator was taken away. The coughing soldiers went back into the tunnels and waited for the smoke to disappear. When they returned, they found a big hole in the lockers with piled up uranium rocks and burned sheets of paper on the floor.

"Did you see what you did, *bizort*?" shouted the commander.

"Too bad" said Barbarez. "Should I pick up the papers?"

"Leave them there. Who is going to want a pile of burned paper? Let's go, men. There is nothing else we can do here."

"We can take some uranium rocks with us" suggested one of the recruits. "They must be valuable."

"In the Colony they're useless . . . leave them where they are."

They left the hiding place and searched the village for a last time. They failed to find, or perhaps Hanara had the luck that they didn't find, the secret entrance to the uranium mines, the place where the *Sword of the Jade Dragon* was hidden.

Aron left them and went out of the village along the road to the north. He noticed that the plantations were all dried-up and scorched, and when he reached the pasture, he found just a pile of red earth in the place where the barn had previously been, with bits of hay being blown around by the wind.

It seemed that the barn had not been destroyed, because none of the planks with which it had been built were there. Neither had it been burned down, as there were no ashes or cinder. It had probably been dismantled to use its wood.

Aron left the pasture and went into the plantations. In the corn and wheat fields there were just ashes, and the reddened leaves which had not yet completely stopped burning gave off a wisp of gray smoke. Only the cogus plantation had not been greatly affected. Although their trunks were darkened, their pulp was several meters from the ground, and the organic material of the cogus would not easily burn.

Aron walked around the rows of cogus and stopped for a moment before returning to the platoon. He thought he had seen a fleeting movement in shadows, at the base of two twin cogus which shared the same trunk.

"Come on, Kliver" shouted one of the recruits. "The commander is in a hurry. We have to move if we want to camp before nightfall."

"Tell him to wait" said Aron with authority. "I think I saw something."

Aron began to sweat. His legs trembled, and he cautiously approached the twin cogus tree. The soldiers came to check what was happening, but from the anxiety on Aron's face, they realized that they should keep quiet. They followed him slowly, holding their weapons in case of danger.

When Aron passed the trunk of the twin cogus tree, someone caught hold of his feet. Aron instinctively kicked the hand which has holding him. But then he relaxed when he saw the face of an elderly Noan, lying beside the roots of the cogus.

"Old Father Zugu!" he said in surprise.

Aron bent down and held his hands.

Old Father Zugu was the elder of the tribe. All the natives respected him, and, because of his great affection for the village children, everyone found him a very kind old man. He was Hanara's main advisor, and when Hanara took the Noans to the Islands, Zugu was chosen as leader of those who wished to stay.

"Oh, thank Heaven! You're here, Aron. You're alive" said Old Father Zugu in joy. "Many people thought you and your brother had been killed. But I knew that you would both return to our humble people."

"What's he saying?" asked Irvine, who didn't understand the language of the tribe.

"He's saying that he's happy to see me" replied Aron, annoyed to be interrupted. He turned again to Old Father Zugu, "What happened to our village?"

"They came from far and set fire to everything. They are devils, young Aron, yellow devils" he said, after an attack of coughing. "How is your finger?"

"Better . . ." replied Aron, holding back his tears. How could a man just about to die be worried about his old wound? Aron thought of Zugu as the father whose company he had never been able to enjoy, or as a grandfather, if Hanara had not taken on that job.

"Where is your brother?" asked Zugu, beginning to cough again.

"He was taken by the Hatis."

"Oh, that's bad. So bad!"

"Don't worry. Makuro is also a Hati and will be treated as an equal."

"Those devils won't treat anyone as an equal" he said seriously. "It's in their blood that they think they are superior".

"Where are the others?" Aron asked.

Zugu breathed with difficulty.

"They're all dead, my boy. All of those who refused to leave in the boat are dead! I was born here, and I want to die here. But if we'd listened to your grandfather's advice . . ."

"The boat?" he asked with surprise. "Did they finish the boat? Where's my grandfather?"

"The Hatis . . ." continued Zugu, without replying to the questions. "They blocked the gates with stones, and no one could escape. They didn't take prisoners, Aron, they just killed people" he said, and this contradicted the guesses the platoon had made. "I was the only one who managed to escape. I am too old to fight, and so I hid here in the fields. When they noticed I was missing, the Hatis set fire to the plantations. The fire burned for many hours, but I managed to protect myself behind the twin cogus trees. The smoke . . ." he began to feel dizzy. "The smoke was my killer, not the fire. So I'm here, having put off death for a couple more days. But now we've talked, and I see that my task is complete and can finally rest in peace . . ." He held Aron's hand for a few seconds, then his fingers let go, his head fell to one side, and his eyes closed.

"Wake up, Father Zugu!" Aron shook him. "You can't leave us! Where's my grandfather? Where are my mother and Tork? I must know!"

Zugu whispered, still with his eyes closed, before he finally gave in:

"They are . . . they're safe. A safe place. They're on the sea, Aron . . . the Sea is safe", and he breathed for the last time.

Aron noticed that the old man's trousers were burned, as were his legs from the thigh down.

"What did he say?" insisted Irvine. "What did he say?"

Barbarez told Irvine.

"This is not the time to ask him" he said. "The boy's been through a lot of suffering. Put yourself in your place, soldier."

The nightmare which Aron had had days before now became reality. But differently to the dream, the massacre had not been ordered by the Regent. He let out a yell, clenched his fists, and punched the ground. He frowned and shouted, his lips trembling in a mixture of pain and hatred:

"The Hatis will pay for this! I'm going to the Hive right now. I'll kill them and rescue my brother."

Barbarez put a hand on his shoulder.

"Once a friend told me that the difference between an ordinary man and a wise man is that the wise man knows how to wait for the best moment . . . let's go. Alone you will only find death. Wait until you have joined our army and are strong, and together we will finish with the Hatis."

Aron wiped his tears.

"My grandfather was always telling us this. Did you know Hanara?"

"No . . . this friend of mine was your father, Leo Kliver. He was my instructor in the Sergeants' Academy."

Aron stood up.

"Were you a sergeant?"

"One day I'll tell you my story . . ."

It was getting dark. They got onto their bigbugs and left for the Colony. Along the way, they ignored the shortcuts that went through unknown territory. Aron felt that he would have to get used to the Myra city, as he would be spending a long time in Loagy's underground.

CHAPTER 20

RISKY MISSION

Disturbed. This was an understatement to describe how Makuro felt after his first contact with the plugs. If it had not been for the other half of the tranquilizer Alpazin-10 which Mujiro had given him, Makuro would never have slept that night.

The previous day, Mujiro had reminded him that he would have to get the honeymoon plug belonging to the husband of Dr. Meling, and if he didn't, he would tell the authorities that Makuro had been using illegal substances.

The tranquilizer took a time to work. It was a powerful drug which could sedate a strong man in less than ten minutes, but Makuro needed an hour, and during this time, he did not stop wondering whether Tork and his mother had really been assassinated on the orders of the Myra Regent or whether Aron and his father had been accomplices in treason. From time to time, the image of the girl who had given him the bonsai came back to him. But finally, he gave in and was soon snoring away inside his cell. Despite all the problems, he slept well and had no nightmares.

He woke at seven o'clock, and Mujiro was there outside his cell to invite him to have breakfast in the refectory. They went along the corridor together and entered.

The previous night Makuro told him that he had obtained the doctor's address, and even before touching the chowder Mujiro began to ask:

"And so? How do you intend to get Lieutenant Iagushi's plug?"

"Who?"

"Have you already forgotten his name?"

"Oh yes . . . I was thinking of taking a bunch of takaras to Sector Five to show my gratitude to the doctor, and when I have the chance . . ."

"Brilliant!" praised Mujiro. "In case you make a mistake, the flowers can be a good excuse for the authorities. And how are you going to get to Sector Five?"

"I'll call one of these air-taxis, I think."

"No. There are a lot of hidden cameras in the taxis. And don't forget that your movements are being monitored by the Empire. The safest way is to use a jetpack."

"I still don't have one" said Makuro. "And I've no idea of how to pilot a . . ."

"I'll lend you mine. And I'll also lend you my plug so you can learn to pilot it from the simulation programs. It's quite simple. It will take you less than an hour."

Mujiro disconnected himself and gave the plug to Makuro. This was a simple civilian device, which didn't require user identification.

"Finish your breakfast, go back to your cell, and simulate a jetpack journey in the plug. Meet me at the exit to the shelter at ten o'clock."

"I was thinking of doing it at night . . ."

"No. The risks of doing something at night are much greater. People are sleeping, and there's a good chance that your movements will be detected. In addition, you won't be noticed during the day, and Dr. Meling and her husband are at work. Their cell is empty."

"If her husband is working, then he must be using his plug now" supposed Makuro. "How can I get a plug whose owner is using it?"

"Meling's husband is a soldier, and soldiers have at least two plugs: an ordinary one for personal use, and a military one for restricted use, which has access to the inter-plug. Now he must be using the professional plug, and he will have left his personal plug in his cell. All you need to do is to go to Sector Five, enter the shelter, get into his cell, and locate the plug and . . ."

"And bring it to you?"

"Don't be stupid" said Mujiro. "Nobody can get a personal plug without the authorization of the owner. This will bring problems to us both, and we will be arrested. And you wouldn't want to . . ."

"'Be locked in the prison of the Hive'" completed Makuro. "I know. After all, what is so frightening about the Hati prisons?"

"Haven't they told you?"

"If they had told me, I wouldn't be asking you."

Mujiro drew his chair up to Makuro.

"The problem of the Hati prison is that there is just one" he said.

Makuro didn't get what he was saying.

Mujiro continued:

"The Hive is very big, but it has limited space. It was only possible to build one prison, to house exactly five hundred people . . . according to an Imperial law, if the number of prisoners passes the maximum capacity, an event called 'Battle of the Convicts' takes place. It's an event in which all the prisoners are released in the main stadium of the Hive and they fight to death with each other until there is only one survivor, who is freed and expelled from the Hive.

The people always believed that this law was a trick of the Empire to prevent crime . . . but it happened once. As there were five hundred and one prisoners in the jail, the Battle took place. Even those prisoners who would be freed in a few weeks had to take part . . .

The winner of the Battle was an ex-general called Yoshi Hanara, whose identity was taken away, and he was expelled from the Hive. No one knows what happened to him as the chances of his surviving in the desert are very small. And this is why no one wants to go to jail. Every prisoner increases the chance a little bit more that the Battle will be held, and today, almost forty years after, the number of prisoners is more than four hundred and fifty . . ."

"Wait a bit" interrupted Makuro. "What did you say the name of the winner of the first battle was?"

"Yoshi Hanara... Why?"

"Hanara was my master when I lived in Ruakan, and I always considered him to be my grandfather."

"Oh, really? So Hanara managed to survive" said Mujiro with great admiration. "I suggest this information is passed on to the authorities."

"It's not necessary. Haven't you seen the news? Hanara and the natives have disappeared." 'Might this have something to do with the death of Tork and my mother?' Makuro wondered.

"Anyway, this is why we can't make a mistake with the plan" concluded Mujiro. "A mistake will not only put our lives at risk, but also those of hundreds of prisoners."

At this moment Makuro thought about giving up. It was too risky. But then he remembered the threat that Mujiro had made, saying that he would accuse him to the authorities if he gave up, and this would also send him to prison. His ignorance of Hati laws didn't distinguish the difference between stealing someone's personal plug and taking illegal substances. And agreeing that he would be arrested in either case, he uttered the words that Mujiro was waiting for:

"Let's get on with it."

"Great!" said Mujiro, smiling. "As I was saying, you don't need to bring me the Lieutenant's plug. You'll just copy its data into the memory of the plug that I just lent you. Any problem?"

"No problem" agreed Makuro.

However, there was a problem. Makuro didn't understand how to work the device which was now in his hands. He didn't know how to record, reproduce or copy an experience. And as it was now eight-twenty in the morning, he would have less than two hours to learn.

"Simulate a jetpack journey in the plug" said Mujiro. "I'll be waiting for you at ten o'clock at the exit to the shelter. Don't be late."

Lying down again in his capsule, Makuro was struggling to get courage to connect himself once again. His first experience with the plug had been traumatic, and he was afraid to experience all that again.

In the plug there were the three pins which had to be inserted in the connector, and a button at the other end. Makuro pressed it and a small red light turned on, showing that the device was now on.

He was not sure what he needed to do to reproduce the jetpack simulation. Makuro sat up still in the capsule, stroking the metal of the pins, and feeling the holes in his neck, which were still painful after his recent operation. He got up and went to the bathroom, looking for the reflection of the connector in the mirror, but it was impossible to see the back of his neck without a second mirror.

Actually, Makuro was terrified of using Mujiro's plug. If the doctors in the clinic had made him experience such traumas, what could he expect from someone who helped him just to get something in exchange?

Furthermore, Makuro might also have a serious accident if he tried to pilot a jetpack without knowing how to do it.

Time was now passing, and he needed to decide. He lay down in the capsule, breathed deeply, and immediately plugged himself in, without fear of the consequences. Once again his feet became numb, but this time he did not suffer a blackout.

A ghost-like being appeared before his eyes, on the floor of the cell, as if it were a holograph. With no clear expression on its face, it said:

"Welcome to the fantastic world of the plugs. I can see that you are a new user, and I therefore advise you to follow my instructions. Are you ready?"

Makuro nodded, unsure of whether he should interact with the strange being.

"Let me introduce myself. I am the guide for the plug. I'm a ghost, and if you want to substitute me, just go to the commands 'Special Functions', 'Substitute Guide'."

At that moment, various command options appeared: Reproduction, Recording, Internal Programs, Special Functions, Database, and User Protection.

The list of commands and the guide were always visible, regardless of whether he closed his eyes or turned away. Makuro tried to touch the letters which were hovering in front of him, but his hands went through them as if they were not there - which was in fact true.

"Which of these options have you chosen?" asked the ghost.

"I want to go to 'Special Functions'." said Makuro. "Fine" And a new list of commands in Hati appeared before his eyes. "We are now on the 'Special Functions' page. Here we have the options 'Internal Alarm'; 'Sleep Programmer'; ' Update Date and Time'; 'Search Hive Map'; 'Personalize the Plug'; 'Substitute Guide'; 'Change Real Vision'; 'Hide List and Guide'; and 'Return to Previous Page'. Which of these options have you chosen?" asked the guide.

"I've chosen 'Substitute Guide'" selected Makuro.

"Aren't you happy with me?" said the ghost in a sad voice. "Let's go to the list of characters available. We have a wise master, a winged dragon, a ninja, a samurai, and an animated bigbug. Which of these would you like to substitute me?"

"I want a . . . I want the dragon."

"Very well. It's been a pleasure to meet you. See you next time."

The ghost disappeared in a cloud of smoke. The word 'Ghost' then appeared on the list of options, substituting the word 'Dragon', which disappeared. Then, a furious red dragon rose from the ground, crossed its arms, let out smoke of its nostrils, and seemed to be threatening the viewer.

"Who dares to awake me from my sleep?" it exhaled small flames from its mouth, which, though unreal, gave off a pleasant warmth. "Ah, was it you? What do you want from me?"

Makuro was impressed by the possibilities of the plug. He wanted to see and hear each of the guides, but as he didn't have time, he decided to continue with the dragon and learn how to use a jetpack.

"I want to learn how to pilot a jetpack" he said to the new guide.

"This choice is not on the list" said the dragon. "You must choose from the commands available".

"Then I choose 'Return to the Previous Page'." And the previous page returned. "I want to use the internal programs".

On this last command, the following options appeared: 'Games'; 'Simulators'; 'Sensorial Distractions' and 'Useful Tools'.

"What is there on the list of games?" asked Makuro out of curiosity, and the character gave him all the information contained in his guide program:

"In the 'Games' option, you'll have the chance of incarnating the protagonist of a fully sensitive game. But don't worry, they are not violent games. We have 'Chess', in which you can play this ancient game with your virtual guide at different levels of difficulty; we have 'Find Nanco', a game in which you will enter a complex maze where you must find the beautiful young girl, Nanco; there is 'Cluedo', in which you are transported to a somber mansion where you will have to solve a mystery; there is 'Spider', where you will incorporate a spider and have to make a web according to the required format; and there is also 'Dance', where you must dance to the sound of music. Do you wish to try any of them?"

"No, thank you . . ." said Makuro, with an enormous desire to do the opposite. "Not today. Thank you. What time is it, please?"

"It is exactly nine-three in the morning." said the dragon.

Makuro came back to his senses. He had less than an hour to learn how to pilot a jetpack. The dragon noticed this tension and said:

"I can see an enormous amount of tension in your spinal marrow. Do you wish to close the program?"

"No. Show me the list of simulators, please."

"As you wish" said the dragon. "On the page of the simulators we have the following options: 'Simulation of Vehicles'; 'Simulation of Bodily Combat'; 'Simulation of . . .'" the guide had not finished giving the following options when Makuro interrupted him, telling him to quickly show the list of vehicle simulators.

"On the page 'Simulation of Vehicles', we have: Combat Vehicles, Transport Vehicles, Load Vehicles, and Individual Vehicles."

"'Combat Vehicles', I think . . ."

"Refused!" said the dragon. "The registration of your connector indicates that you're a civilian and do not have access to combat vehicle simulators."

"In this case, 'Individual Vehicles'" said Makuro.

"On the page 'Individual Vehicles' we have jetpacks and flyboards."

"Jetpacks, please."

"Good. Do you wish to begin the program?"

"Yes" said Makuro, anxiously.

"I must remind you that once it has begun you'll have no more access to your guide until the end of the simulation," warned the dragon. "I must also tell you that it is impossible to turn off the device while it is simulating. The average time of the simulation is an hour. Make sure that you will not need to do anything important in the real world during this time. Make sure that you do not need to go to the toilet or anything else . . . can we begin?"

"Yes"

Once again the guide disappeared in a cloud of smoke. But this time, it was not just the dragon that disappeared. The entire cell disappeared, and Makuro now found himself on the top of a virtual mountain. Everything seemed to be real: the strong wind blowing his hair, the sun burning his skin, and the change of pressure due to the high altitude. When he tried to move his arm, he realized that he was paralyzed, and before he had a chance to worry about this, a female voice whispered:

"Welcome to the jetpack simulator. I can see that this is the first time you've tested the program . . . so let's begin with the 'Beginner's Level', where you will learn the basic commands to maneuver a jetpack without needing to make a score. When you are sure of your skill, we will move you to 'Advanced Level', where you will take a pilot's test. Are you ready?"

"Yes" said Makuro.

"Select the jetpack model you wish to use." There were three types: AZ13, AZ204, and D5A.

"What's the difference between them?" asked Makuro.

The models appeared before him, in three dimensional pictures. The voice described the differences:

"The AZ13 is an old model, which is no longer manu-factured. It has just one turbine and uses atomic combustion to work; the AZ204 is the most popular and stable. It has two symmetric turbines which expel air jets; the D5A model has no system of manual control. It is the smallest and lightest and is therefore recommended just for children. Which one would you like to try?"

Without thinking much, Makuro selected the AZ204.

At this moment, on top of the virtual mountain, Makuro felt the weight of the equipment on his back. The movements of his limbs returned, and he was now free to do what he wanted (even jump off the cliff if he wished to).

The voice continued to instruct him:

"Notice that there is a belt around your waist. This is directly connected to the jetpack and the connector in your neck. They will all work together to ensure the smooth functioning of the equipment. The warning systems are always on, and they depend on the plugs in order to work. The jetpack will switch on to automatic pilot if the user faints or loses control during the flight and is therefore totally safe. Look at the buckle on your belt."

Makuro looked down at the silver buckle on his belt.

"*Open it*" asked the voice.

Under the buckle he found various command buttons.

"Press the command 'Open Turbines'."

Makuro pressed it, and two titanium wings with flat connected turbines opened at the back of his shoulders.

"Now press the command 'Calibrate Collision Sensors'", said the voice, "and then the command 'Show Directions'."

When he had done what the voice asked, a transparent map appeared high up before him so it would not obstruct his vision, and two directional levers appeared at both sides of his waist.

"At the top of each lever you'll find a button" continued the voice. "These buttons connect and control the power of the turbines. Try pressing them."

Makuro pressed them. The turbines were turned on and began to blow a light stream of air downwards.

The voice continued:

"The levers determine the height and direction of the flight. With practice you will see that it is necessary to maneuver them in different ways in order to gain greater control of direction. Try lightly pulling them back."

Makuro pulled the levers. But the 'lightness' of the inexperienced hand pulled them a little too heavily. The turbines blew out powerful jets of air, and Makuro was launched like a rocket into the sky. Now desperate, Makuro immed-iately pressed the button on the right-hand lever. One of the turbines had been turned off, and Makuro began to spin around like a propeller. When he turned off the other turbine, the stored energy made him rise another eight meters straight up in a perfect physics, but he soon stopped and began to fall.

Makuro did not know what to do. He expected instruct-tions from the voice which had now abandoned him, and only when there were no more than four meters left before he would crash into the rocks did the automatic system come on and turn the turbines on again, landing him delicately on the top of the mountain.

"You pressed too heavily" said the voice. "Do you want to try again?"

Makuro felt he was sweating, but his face was dry. Still trembling, he decided to make another attempt, thinking that if everything had been for real, he could have had a bad acci-dent.

At the second attempt, Makuro pulled the lever as deli-cately as he could. The turbines on his back puffed just enough to raise him from the ground.

The voice then gave him the remaining instructions:

"By moving the levers to the sides, you will move yourself horizontally through the air. Try the different directions, with both levers."

Makuro took half an hour to get to know the commands. When he felt confident, he decided to go to the 'Advanced Level'.

"At the advanced level" instructed the voice "you'll be able to legally qualify as a pilot. In order to do this, you must obtain at least ninety points in the test, and then register them in the internal memory of your connector. Can we begin?"

"What time is it?" he asked, remembering his meeting with Mujiro.

"It's exactly nine-forty-two" replied the voice. "Is there any problem? Should I close the program?"

"Continue" he said.

Makuro knew that there was little time left, but he also knew that the more practice he had with the jetpack, the fewer risks he would have in the real world.

"*Very good*" said the voice, loading the advanced program.

On the horizon beyond the virtual mountain, innumerable blue hoops, each some two and a half meters in diameter, appeared. The nearest hoop to the mountain was green.

"In order to complete the test" continued the voice, "you must pass through all the hoops while flying, without touching them. The first hoop you will pass through is green. When you pass through it, the next hoop will also turn green, and your aim is to transform all the blue ones into green by passing through them all. If your body touches any of them, it will become red, which means that you have lost the point. You'll also lose points if you pass through a blue hoop, as the correct route is marked by the green ones. There are a total of a hundred hoops, and you must pass correctly through ninety of them in order to pass the test.

The test will finish when you complete them all or when you are eliminated. That is to say, when you have more than ten negative points, or when time runs out. You have a maximum of thirty seconds to go from one hoop to another, and half an hour to pass through them all. Are you ready?"

"Yes" confirmed Makuro.

At this very moment, two stopwatches, which showed the number thirty, appeared in front of him.

"The stopwatch above shows the number of minutes, the time-limit for the test, and the one below shows seconds, the time between one hoop and another. The countdown will begin from the moment you rise from the ground and go through the first hoop. Good luck" wished the voice.

When he was ready, Makuro opened the buckle on the belt and pressed all the commands he had learned in the previous level. He rose from the ground, and two zeros, his score, appeared in the center of his sight.

Makuro accelerated the turbines and went ahead, passing through the first hoop. The stopwatch began its countdown, and a number one appeared on his score. He shot off towards the nearest hoop, but this was still blue, differently to one above, which was green, and so was the next.

He realized that the route was not going to be obvious as the hoops were lit in green at random, which made the test difficult. When he saw this, it was already too late to avoid going through the nearest hoop, which became red, and so he lost his point.

He now saw that there were only nine seconds to reach the second hoop. He bent back and pulled the levers, accelerating the turbines. The speed he was traveling at made control more difficult, and his shoulders touched the hoop, which took another point away. But at least he now had thirty seconds to go through the next one.

There was no problem with the third hoop. Neither was the fourth difficult, and Makuro now had one point. The next was easy, and so were the next ones. Makuro was getting through the test. In less than twenty minutes, many hoops had turned green, and he had scored seventy points. He needed another twenty to pass the test, but it was then that the problems appeared.

The distance between the hoops now slowly increased. Makuro managed to pass through one of them with only seven tenths of a second left. If he didn't increase his speed, he would not have time to go through the rest. So he decided to accelerate his turbines.

However, he was not used to maneuvering the jetpack at a greater speed, and he touched the three next hoops, losing points. He passed the next one without any problem, but the fifth, sixth and seventh became red. Five minutes after he increased the speed, he reached the maximum number of negative points and was eliminated.

The simulation finished. His sight went dark and he was now at the starting point once again.

"I'm sorry" said the voice, communicating once again. "Your score is seventy-seven points, which means you have failed. Would you like to try again?"

"No, I can't. I need to hurry. Close the program."

"Do you want to save your score in the plug memory?"

"No, thank you. Take me back, please."

"With pleasure" said the voice. "See you soon and thank you for simulating."

The next moment, Makuro was back in his cell with the red dragon in front of him and Mujiro outside his cell, impatient with the delay. Makuro turned off the plug, and the dragon and the messages disappeared from in front of him.

"It's almost ten-thirty in the morning, new boy" said Mujiro. "What kind of joke is this? Do you think it's easy to wait at the exit of the shelter without being noticed?"

"I'm sorry. I had some problems in learning how to use the jetpack."

"Don't fool me. The simulations only take an hour, and you've had two. In addition, by using the automatic pilot system you won't need to do any piloting. In it there is a complete map of the Hive. Just give a voice command, and the program will safely take you wherever you want to go."

"It would have been very useful if I'd known this *before* I connected up" said Makuro. "Now it's too late . . ."

"Well, I couldn't imagine that you would be stupid enough to use the manual simulator."

"So, what shall we do? Shall we put it off, or is there still time to get the plug you want?"

"Yes, there's time. But you'll have to act quickly. The doctor will finish her morning shift in the clinic around midday. Her cell will be free for just ninety minutes."

"So we'd better get going."

"Come with me" said Mujiro, going towards the elevation platform at the exit of the cell. "By the way, I took advantage of the delay to get a bunch of takaras. This will save you some time."

"Don't you have anything else to do?" said Makuro, and seeing that the question might offend him, added, "You're a soldier. Don't you have work to do? Since I've known you, you've always been hanging around and . . ."

"Yes, I've been an official soldier for more than four years" explained Mujiro, annoyed. "This gives me the right to ask for leave as long as I carry out combat simulation at least three times a week. However, with the beginning of the war, I'm on emergency duty and could be called up at any time . . ."

They stopped talking and went to the shelter exit, stopping only for Mujiro to get the jetpack in his cell and give it to Makuro to use.

On the external platform of the shelter, Makuro tightened the belt and put on the equipment. Before him there was a deep drop, full of vehicles which were flying like projectiles in the huge air traffic space. From time to time a group of teenagers passed by on their flyboards, with dark jackets and their hair dyed red or purple.

"What was the model of the jetpack you used in the simulation?" asked Mujiro.

"It was . . . hmm . . . I can't remember . . ."

"Was it similar to the one you're using now?"

"No. The one I was using opened like wings on my back."

"So it was the AZ204 double turbine. Mine is the old model, the AZ13 simple turbine. It belonged to my father when he was alive, and I wouldn't exchange this for any other, as it has great sentimental value. Its stability is a bit different to that which you simulated. It's bigger and a bit heavier. But don't worry, as its commands are identical, and we'll put it on automatic pilot, which means you'll not need to operate the lever. If I find a single scratch on its body, you'll pay with your life."

Makuro followed Mujiro's instructions and programmed the automatic pilot to make a short journey to Sector Five. He held on to the levers and pressed the buttons, trying to turn on the turbine. Nothing happened.

"What's the problem?" asked Mujiro.

"I don't know. I can't turn on the turbine."

"Has the power gone? Let me see."

Makuro turned around, and Mujiro opened one of the compartments of the equipment. He saw that the energy capsule was charged.

"Strange. Try it again."

Makuro pressed the button again, but the turbine was not working.

Mujiro held out his hand.

"Give me the plug" he said, puzzled. "I must check something."

Makuro took the device out of his nape and gave it to Mujiro, who immediately plugged in.

"Research internal memory" he said to himself, and then added, "Recover files from the last registration. Show data from the recently used programs."

Makuro said nothing and failed to understand why Mujiro was speaking to himself and looking up.

"Seventy-seven points?" asked Mujiro, looking furiously at Makuro.

"What's up?" asked Makuro.

Mujiro threw the bunch of takaras onto the ground.

"Why didn't you tell you had failed the pilot's test?" he shouted.

"I didn't think it was important . . . ."

"Now you're not qualified to pilot the jetpack. This is why you haven't been able to turn on the turbine."

"So what can we do?"

Mujiro walked from one side of the platform to the other, thinking.

"My God, I can't believe I'll have to do this"

"What are you going to do?" asked Makuro.

"Shut up for a minute. I need to concentrate."

Mujiro began to talk to himself again:

"Activate the audio network . . . access plug 13.225C..."

He waited a moment and then spoke again, as if he was speaking to someone who was far off:

"Hello, partner. Are you working now? Great! Can you do me a favor? After you tell me what I can do for you . . . okay . . . enter the database and enable the use of jetpack for the number, let me see, F855 . . . That's right, Makuro . . . I know he's not qualified. Give him a temporary license . . . I'll be responsible for it . . . two hours is enough . . . that's right, I won't forget . . . thank you."

After saying this, Mujiro turned off the plug and disconnected it, giving it back to Makuro.

"Ready" he said. "Now you're authorized to use the jetpack under my responsibility. Your license will only last for two hours, so get a move on."

"How did you do this?" asked Makuro, impressed.

"I have important friends . . . your authorization will only allow you to use automatic pilot. We don't have much time, so get going."

Makuro once again pressed the button on the lever, and this time the turbine obeyed his command. When the automatic pilot came on, and he was getting ready to take off, Mujiro held out his hand and reminded him:

"Don't forget the takaras. The flowers are important for you to avoid any misunderstandings."

"What should I do when I get to Sector Five?"

"Everything depends on what you do and a little luck. Be careful and try not to get into trouble." he said, with a false smile. "Don't come back without copying the data from Lieutenant Iagushi's plug."

Makuro looked at him for a moment and then took off, letting himself be transported by the automatic pilot.

"Try not to mix up the plugs" shouted Mujiro, who was now getting smaller and smaller on the platform. "I'll go mad if you bring me the copy of Dr. Meling's plug. I don't fancy the Lieutenant . . ."

Makuro continued to gain height until the turbine became stable. Then it turned and continued straight ahead. Although the automatic pilot efficiently avoided the vehicles which were coming towards him, Makuro closed his eyes whenever a sharp maneuver was made.

When he flew under the great central dome, he noticed that outside it was raining. The water which was falling on the transparent covering of the dome was pleasant to see, and not a drop dared come in.

Further on, he went around the Imperial Palace and continued toward the eastern perimeter, flying near the metal
wall full of illuminated shelters, and then the jetpack began to
slow down.

Makuro was now in the most sought after suburb of the
Hive, and a huge number high up on the wall indicated that
this was Sector Five. The entrance to the shelter, a little beyond the platform where Makuro would land, soon became
visible. The turbine jet was slowly running down, comfortably
taking Makuro inside the landing area. The descent was soft,
the turbine turned off and automatically slid into the jetpack.

Makuro took off the equipment and quickly went into the
entrance of the shelter, which was closed by electronic locks.
There was an optic reader on one side, and an interphone
monitored by video cameras underneath.

The security system of this sector was one of the most
complex in the Hive. Sector Five was an area for doctors and
scientists, and those with degrees who were also officers in
the armed forces, and so these shelters were also considered
to be the headquarters of the superior militaries. It would be
difficult for Makuro to get in without authorization from those
inside.

After thinking for a long time, he decided to try his luck.
He pressed the interphone button and waited for a reply.
There was a brief noise of interference and it went dead.
Makuro pressed again, this time harder, and continued
waiting. When he pressed it for the third time, a female voice
asked him.

"Who are you and who would you like to speak to?"

"Er . . . this is . . . Makuro, the new boy. I'd like to speak to
Dr. Meling, please."

"She's not in at the moment. She's not yet returned from
the clinic. Would you like to speak with anyone else?"

"Er . . . is her husband there?"

"Lieutenant Iagushi is ill and does not want to be disturbed. Would you like to leave a message?"

"No, erm . . . I would like to give a present to the doctor. Can I leave it in her cell?"

"Impossible. Nobody enters the dormitories without permission. You can leave the present with the porter or return some other time."

"I'd rather give it to her in person".

"So you'll have to come back later." "Erm . . . look . . . it will be a bit difficult to return later. Can I wait in the reception?"

"Unfortunately, without the permission of somebody who lives here, I cannot authorize entry. I'm sorry. Please don't insist."

"I understand . . . I'll wait outside. Thank you". And the interphone made a noise and went dead, without even giving a 'Don't mention it'.

Makuro, standing on the platform of the shelter, thought about the situation. At a certain moment, he thought that he might be able to talk to the porter and gain his trust. But then he stopped when he discovered that the porter was a big square robot.

He tried to turn on the jetpack and fly over the surrounding area to find an open window or a gap through which he might pass, but then he remembered that he did not have access to the manual system of the jetpack.

Losing heart, he leant on the wall of the shelter and sat down. He was there for almost half an hour, thinking of a good excuse he could give to Mujiro when he returned.

When he finally decided to program the jetpack and return to his sector, an air-taxi came out of the nearby air traffic. It slowed down and came towards the shelter, stopping near the platform where Makuro was.

An elderly man, wearing white clothes, thanked the chauffeur robot for his good driving. He put his cane on the platform and awkwardly got out of the vehicle.

The old man looked at the boy, who was sitting down in a corner, with his head down and his arms around his knees.

"What are you doing here, young man?" he asked. "Are you lost?"

When he lifted his eyes, Makuro was surprised to see Jung, the man who had taken his blood pressure before he first had been connected. The same man who had recommended he give takaras and trusted him with Dr. Meling's address.

"Mr. Jung! How pleased I am to see you!" said Makuro as he got up. "Do you live here in this sector?"

"No, I don't . . . it's my day off, and I've decided to visit my daughter and son-in-law" he explained. "And you? What are you doing here?"

"I've come to give the present you recommended to Dr. Meling." And he showed him the bunch of flowers. "I'd like to give them to her personally, but she's not in, and they won't allow me in."

"The flowers are a bit scruffy and withered," remarked Mr. Jung, "But no problem . . . as they say, it's the thought that counts."

"Yes, it's the thought that counts." repeated Makuro with a smile.

"The rules of this sector are very strict" said Jung. "You'll have to come back later."

"Maybe you can make it possible for me to at least wait in the reception."

"Maybe . . . I can try."

Mr. Jung leant on his cane and pressed the interphone button.

"Who?" asked the interphone voice once again? "Er . . . hello, Mr. Jung. Are you here to see your daughter?"

"Yes, Miss. And something else: I'd like this young man to accompany me if possible," and he took Makuro by the shoulders, showing his face to the cameras.

"As long as your daughter is responsible for him, there is no problem."

"Thank you," he said, and the door began to vibrate, opening from the middle.

Makuro followed Jung and went along the security corridor to the reception. But before this, he had to hand over his titanium equipment and was only able to keep the bunch of takaras and Mujiro's plug in his neck.

CHAPTER 21

RE-ENCOUNTER

Mr. Jung asked permission to go into the luxurious hall for visitors where his daughter and son-in-law were waiting for him, leaving Makuro alone in the reception, waiting for Dr. Meling. Jung could not go to his daughter's cell as there was little space, and the visit of strangers was forbidden in the dormitories, even though they were family members. Makuro received instructions to remain sitting until the doctor arrived.

A few minutes later, Jung returned to the entrance to the hall, asking Makuro if he would like to meet his daughter. Makuro accepted, got up, and went with the man along the corridor. He asked whether Jung's daughter was a doctor.

"Yes, she is" he replied. "She's a pediatrician. And she's on maternity leave" he said, proudly. "Finally, after a wait of almost twenty-two years, my grandchild is about to arrive."

Jung pressed the end of his cane on a panel to open the first security gate.

"My son-in-law is not a doctor" he continued, "but gained the right to live in this sector through his marriage. This was unusual and resulted in my daughter losing certain benefits. My son-in-law belongs to the working class. He is a humble man but has strong principles. I'm very happy she married such a man. It's his day off today, and I've come to see them today because it would be impossible to find them together at any other time" he said, just before reaching the last entrance in the hall.

There was not much space in the visitors' hall, but it was clean and pleasant. There were a large number of tables, around each of which there were four or five people. The ceiling was transparent and concave, reflecting one side of the central dome, and it was possible to see that it was still raining. The lamps were of a special type, a mixture of the modern and the oriental past. An artificial stream ran around the floor, under transparent glass which covered the floor. There were also plants and exotic flowers.

All the social events between the inhabitants of the sector and their visitors took place there. It was a quiet place to talk and eat the delicacies which had been given by the Empire, something which did not take place in the sectors which were considered less important. But Sector Five was considered an area of great luxury, whose inhabitants had lots of benefits. However, they were forbidden to marry civilians or soldiers without a degree. This is why Jung said that his daughter's marriage to a worker was 'unusual'.

Although the room was full, it was very quiet. People whispered to each other. If they didn't, it would be too noisy, and nobody would be able to hear their own voice. There was pleasant background music, and children ran around, some already with connectors in their necks.

When they got to the table, the couple stood up. The man's face was already marked by time, and the woman seemed to be much younger than him. They were introduced to Makuro.

"This is my daughter Emi," said Jung, "and this is my son-in-law, Miazatsu."

Makuro bowed before the couple.

"Makuro is new here" said Jung. "I helped him use his first plug yesterday."

"And how was it?" asked Miazatsu.

Makuro kept quiet and looked at the empty plate.

"I hope it wasn't too traumatic" said Miazatsu. "My first experience was horrible! I was thirteen at the time, and they made me incarnate a soldier who had lost his arm in an explosion. What a terrible pain! After this, I gave up wanting to be a soldier and accepted the position the Empire gave me in the factory. I think that is how they condition the workers to accept their fate."

Makuro remained quiet, and Miazatsu decided to talk about something else.

"How do you like the Hive?" he asked. "A bit of a change for you, isn't it?"

"Yes, a big change . . ." said Makuro.

"Hey, Dad . . . isn't this the boy who grew up with the enemy?" asked Emi.

"No, they're not our enemies . . ." said Jung. "They're just Banjins, human beings like you and me. The only difference is that they are savages."

"Hush, Dad . . . you know the law. If the authorities hear you defending them . . ."

"I have no problem with the authorities. I'm just giving my opinion."

"Which is forbidden. Just think what will happen if they hear you comparing us to the Banjins."

Makuro asked for permission to leave.

"Excuse me" he said. "I need to return to the reception."

Jung looked harshly at his daughter, and she immediately tried to repair the situation:

"Don't listen to me" she said. "I should apologize to you. I've been a bit tense recently . . . I'm pregnant, and it won't be easy to have a child in these times of war. I lost a friend in the last battle, and he left a small child for his wife to bring up alone. I'm afraid that the same will happen with me . . ."

"The same thing won't happen to us, my dear" guaranteed Miazatsu. "You're a member of the military, but a pregnant woman, and also a doctor. They're not going to send you to the battlefront. And I'm a civilian. We won't have any problems."

"Who can guarantee that? Although you're a civilian, you're also in the reserve, and have basic military training. If the Myras attack with all their army, the Empire will need our help . . ."

"If this happens, we'll run away, just like Miku."

Emi smiled.

"Miku was a heroine for our generation" she said. "Just think, fleeing because of the love for the child she was carrying. If one day we follow her, I hope our cause will be as noble. I would do the same for Yoko."

"Our child will not be called Yoko" said Miazatsu. "We'd agreed on 'Yumi' . . ."

"But 'Yumi' is such a common name."

"My mother was also called Yumi, don't you remember?" said Miazatsu. "Don't forget that it was because she died you got permission to get pregnant."

Makuro kept quiet. If he revealed the fact that he was Miku's son, this would result in a series of questions which would delay his mission. He got up.

"Where are you going?" asked Jung.

"I'm late. I need to return to my sector. It's been a pleasure to meet you" he said, looking at Emi and her husband.

"The pleasure was ours, although we didn't talk very much . . . who are the flowers for?" asked Emi, looking at the bunch of takaras which he was holding.

"They're for Dr. Meling, to show my gratitude for being so attentive to me."

"Meling is a marvelous woman!" said Emi. "We went to the Military Medical Academy together. We grew up in the same sector. She and her husband have been our neighbors for many years. They live three cells above mine."

Makuro now realized he had the chance to get near her cell and needed to act quickly. Meling must now have finished her first shift at the clinic and would be on her way home.

"Can you tell me the number of her cell so I can leave the flowers for her in the reception?"

"Number 292, in the second dormitory. But if you wish, you can leave them with me, and I'll give them to her."

"Thank you. I'll do this myself."

Makuro left the hall and went towards the reception, where the receptionist was leaning over the counter, reading an article in an electronic magazine and did not notice him. He thought about stealing the access card to Meling's cell, but they were kept on the shelves behind the counter, and it would be impossible to get it without the receptionist noticing.

He looked at the wall clock: exactly midday. Lunch would be served shortly, and Meling would be back soon. What should he do? His feeling of gratitude towards her was false, and Meling would realize this. Why should he be so grateful to someone who showed him the death of his mother and brother?

Since he had been a boy, Makuro had believed that some-thing risky like this needed months of planning. He had only agreed to Mujiro's plan because he was anxious and drugged by insomnia. Only out of desperation did he agree to this stupid idea of copying the intimate data of a plug without the owner's permission. He knew little about the Hati laws but realized the seriousness of making such a mistake.

Sitting in the armchair, Makuro began to think. He remembered the number of the cell he must enter: 292. The best thing was to wait for the receptionist to be distracted, go to the toilet or something, and then to steal the card to the room.

But then he saw that there were a number of security cameras around the room, and this would prevent him from stealing the card.

While he was waiting, Makuro thought about how the plugs were both marvelous and terrible. If on one hand recording and sharing experiences was something quite incredible, on the other hand, it resulted in various forbidden desires. Mujiro was a small example of this. He was physically attracted to Dr. Meling, and stealing the wedding night plug of her husband was the only way of satisfying his desire. Perhaps the experience was not so good, and maybe the sexual relations of the couple were not as intense as Mujiro's own sexual desire. But the only thing worse than the plugs is the human mind.

"Hasn't Dr. Meling arrived yet?" he asked the receptionist.

"Not yet" she replied, without taking her eyes away from the magazine. "But she won't be long. Lunch has already been served, and she always eats here in the shelter."

Time was his enemy and he was hopeless to accomplish his mission. He didn't know what to do. Perhaps returning to his sector and trying to make a new agreement with Mujiro would be the best thing.

After thinking a lot, he took his decision. He would talk to Mujiro and return to Sector Five another day, when he had a good plan. Mujiro would not accuse him of having used forbidden substances as, although this was a crime, encouraging somebody to take them must also be illegal.

Makuro got up and went to the counter, and when he was about to ask for permission to get his equipment and leave, he heard a sound coming from the device next to the receptionist. She looked away from her magazine and up at the screen connected to the external camera of the shelter, on which it was possible to see Meling pressing the interphone button.

She automatically welcomed Dr. Meling and opened the door by pressing the panel.

Makuro was distressed. This was not the right moment to meet Dr. Meling again. He held out his arm and gave the flowers to the receptionist.

"Look, Ijira . . ." he saw her name on her badge. "I'm desperate to go to the toilet. Can't you give this bunch of flowers to Dr. Meling in my name?"

"She's just arrived. Wouldn't you like to give them to her yourself?"

"No!" said Makuro, a bit too shrill, thereby showing his desperation. Behind he could hear the final doors being opened by Meling.

His time was up. Either he faced Dr. Meling, giving a good excuse to give her the flowers, or he went to the toilet.

Without thinking, he picked up the flowers, and asked Ijira not to say anything about his visit, under the pretext of wanting to surprise her. She agreed, and he ran towards the toilet, just before Meling came through the door.

Before entering the toilet, however, Makuro bent down behind the wall of the corridor, where he could hear whether Ijira would break her promise and say something about him to the doctor.

"Hello, Ijira" said Meling, looking tired. "Sorry I'm late. I was held up with a patient . . ."

"Don't worry, doctor. Lunch is still warm."

"Marvelous! Is my husband any better?"

"He's still asleep . . . I've never seen him miss going to the army headquarters before . . . is he bad?"

"No, it's just flu. He must have been training too much in the sun."

"You're the doctor . . ."

"Well, I'm going to change and go down to the refectory. Give me my card, please."

"Oh, sorry, doctor . . . the card is with your husband. But don't worry. He said that he would not lock the cell."

"Did he say how long he would program his sleep for?"

"He told me to take his messages and not let him be disturbed before five in the afternoon."

"My God! Yesterday he slept almost twelve hours without waking up. He got up for a while today, before I left, and went back to sleep . . ."

"Well . . . you know what they say: 'sleep is the best of medicines'."

"I hope so . . . so long, Ijira. Today my second shift will begin at two."

"We'll see each other later, doctor. I'll be in the reception until six-thirty. I'm doing a favor for the new receptionist. I'll work her shift so she can get to the dentist."

"I hope you're not asking for very much in exchange . . . so we'll see each other later, in an hour and a half."

"See you later, and I hope Lieutenant Iagushi gets better soon and can go back to work."

Meling went towards the dormitories. Makuro went into one of the male toilet cubicles and was glad to have heard this conversation as now he knew that Meling's cell was open. The doctor's husband was inside, sleeping, but under the effect of the sleep programmer he would not be a threat to Makuro.

But what if the plug which Makuro was looking for was the same one as that which was controlling Iagushi's sleep? How could he make a copy of the data of a plug whose owner was using it? Well, before jumping to conclusions, the best thing would be to check. And Makuro only had the time which Meling would have for lunch. Differently to Lieutenant Iagushi, Makuro was hard at work.

The cells of the married couples, although they were somewhat larger, were not so different from those of single people. However, in Sector Five, there was a certain luxury in these small dwellings. In the bathrooms there were ofuro baths in which they could bathe in wine and refreshing aromas and herbs. Bed-sofas which obeyed signals and voices were placed in the rooms. Thick bizort leather carpets lined the living room. There were sensors in case of fire, the malfunctioning of the intelligent furniture, and even for stains and dirt on the walls.

Meling entered her cell and took some clothes out of her closet. She climbed over the capsule where her husband was asleep and typed a command on the control panel, making the outside screen opaque. She took off her doctor's clothes and put on a casual green dress. She called the elevator platform and left the cell. On the ground floor, she walk calmly to the refectory, without noticing the shape of a young man holding a bunch of flowers, who was hidden in the shadows of the dormitory.

Makuro waited for Dr. Meling to disappear from his view before acting. He looked around the entrance, making sure that she would not return quickly, and went along the corridor.

He kept his head down, avoiding showing his face. The cells seemed to be empty, but the outside of many of them was opaque, making it impossible to know what was taking place inside. Anyone who saw him and didn't recognize him might think he was illegally there and send a silent alarm call to security.

He reached the elevator platform and typed on the panel the number of Meling's cell. Warning lights came on, and the platform began to go up. The movement was almost imperceptible as the sensation of lightness gave him the impression that he was not moving, watching the cells going down, when in reality it was he who was going up.

The platform left him in front of the entrance to cell 292. The cage opened, and the ramp of the Meling dwelling extended outwards. When he was in front of the door, Makuro looked at himself in the opaque mirror-like outside of the cell and saw a frightened young man, who was afraid to be doing something he knew was wrong.

He stroked his recently cut hair, trying to disguise the fact he was looking for hidden cameras in the ceiling, and pressed the button on the console, trying to open the door. The device did not ask for the access card, as the doctor's husband had left the door open. However, it did ask for the passcode, another security requirement in the sector.

Obviously Makuro did not have the passcode, but he was not worried about this. He ignored the request and once again pressed the button. A red light blinked, showing the words 'Access Denied', and once again requested the passcode. Makuro once again ignored it and the device once again denied him access. On the fourth attempt, the console said that if he continued trying, the alarm would be set off in the security wing of the shelter.

He gave up. This was not going to be the day that he did the favor he owed to Mujiro. Even if he returned to the sector on another occasion, even if he managed to get into the shelter again without being seen, even if he could obtain Meling's access card, how would he discover the passcode?

However, this was really not important. It was Mujiro's problem. His part was done. If one day Mujiro managed to obtain the passcode, which was going to be difficult, then Makuro would return.

Without looking away from the mirror-like outside of the cell, Makuro sighed, feeling relieved that he did not have to break into a private residence. As for his obligation to return the favor, Mujiro had to understand that the security system had prevented him. The fact that Lieutenant Iagushi was inside the cell would be a good argue to explain the reason why he did not bring the copy of the plug.

Makuro returned to the elevator platform and went to the ground floor. He walked quickly to the exit of the dormitory, with the intention of getting his equipment and returning to his sector. When he went around the bend which gave access to the reception, he bumped into somebody who made him fall, dropping the bunch of takaras onto the ground.

"Are you okay?" asked a soft feminine voice.

"Yes . . . I'm sorry. It was my fault," apologized Makuro.

When he lifted his eyes, he felt his legs give way, and his hands began to sweat. His heartbeat quickened. In front of him, there she was: the only girl who had made him happy for having become a Hati citizen. The girl of his dreams. The girl who had given him the bonsai.

From the expression on her face, it was clear that she didn't recognize him. Makuro nervously slipped his hands into his trouser pocket, took out the midget tree, which was dry and wilting through lack of care, and showed it to her. She smiled. The same enchanting smile which he had seen a month before. She was now wearing a dress which was similar to the one she had worn on the day she met him, embroildered with lotus flower. Her flute was tied to her by a red ribbon around her waist. Makuro was unable to look away from her smile.

She delicately took the small tree from his hand and began to caress it. She looked at Makuro for a moment and gave it back to him.

"Take it. It's yours" she said. "When I gave it to you I wanted to show a little of my happiness on a sad day. I remember you. You're different from the day I met you. I have an image of you as a scruffy good-looking young man, with long ragged hair.

"Have I lost my good looks?" risked Makuro, stroking his now short hair. He had had the obligatory haircut.

"That's not what I meant" said the girl, shyly. "When I met you, I saw in your eyes that I no longer needed to fear the war. At that moment it seemed that everything would turn out fine. The serenity in your face made me feel secure. No one who had grown up in a free tribe, who had suddenly lost everything and had seen the horrors of war, could ever be so serene..."

"I see you know my past."

"Everybody does. In addition, it was my father who brought you. He is the commander of the air squadron, the highest rank soldier to take part in the battles . . . you must be special. What are you doing here in Sector Five?"

Makuro improvised an answer:

"I came to see you! I've been looking for you everywhere in the Hive. And my search has finally come to an end. I've brought you a present." And he held out the flowers. "I've brought you a bunch of takaras, a symbol of my gratitude for the fact that you have made it possible for me to put up with life here."

"And how could I have done this?" she asked, smelling the perfume of the flowers and not questioning the fact they were a bit crushed and had lost a few petals.

"Your smile answers the question."

The girl sighed.

"Let me help you get up" she said, holding out her hand.

Makuro covered her hand in his sweaty palm. His sun-burned skin made a perfect contrast with her delicate little white hand. He got up on his own and didn't take advantage of her offer to pull him up.

"Now it's my turn to ask" he said. "What brings you here to Sector Five? Are you by chance a doctor? I didn't realize doctors could be so young . . ."

"No, I'm not. My father has been living here for a long time, since before I was born. I've grown up with doctors. I live in cell 293, next door to Dr. Meling, who you already must have met."

"Yes, I have . . . it was she who gave me the psychological tests before the implant of my connector. Are your father and mother doctors? In addition to belonging to the military?"

"My father studied Medicine, but he gave up and graduated in Optic Physics. As he is now an important officer, and as there were not enough doctors to fill up our sector at the time, the Empire gave us the right to live here. And, as for my mother, she died when I was born."

"I'm sorry to hear that" said Makuro.

"Don't worry. I never met her, so I never had a mother. We don't miss what we never have."

"I thought that in the Hive no women ever died at child-birth. I thought that there were no longer any risks".

"It was a serious problem with a Caesarian birth" she explained. "A medical error. It was premature, and if the doctors had not carried out the operation, both of us would have died."

"Don't say that" said Makuro, seriously. "It's horrible to think that I might never have met you."

The girl gave a shy smile.

"You're nice . . ." and she stroked his face. "What is it like there?"

"Where?"

"Ruakan. What is it like to live in a tribe?"

"Well, it's not as simple as people think. Living in a poor community is hard work. However, people help each other and are much happier than those I see here. In spite of being a Hati in a place where the majority were natives, I didn't feel as different as I feel here. We lived like a big family. My grand-father was the leader of the tribe, and he taught us everything we know today. The majority of the tribe worked on the plant-ations, but there were also hunters, warriors, traders and merchants. I lived in a small house where it was possible to see the sky through the tiles of the roof, and the breeze that came in through the cracks made me aware of the need for a simple blanket. We spoke our own language and . . ."

"Say something in the Banjin language" she asked, inter-ested.

"Er . . . Let me see . . . *Cyut'o caiangne.*"

"What does that mean?"

"'You're lovely'."

She looked down and her cheeks turned as red as her lips.

"I'm jealous of you" she said. "You lived with free people. Not like here: etiquette classes, following orders, and obeying my father and the Empire. I haven't been out of the Hive for ten years. I've only ever been in the open air once, when my father took me on a picnic on the banks of the Olin. I was very young and didn't yet have a plug. I remember it was very hot, and it was my birthday . . . it was when he gave me this shino-bue", she said as she held up her flute.

"You play it very well" said Makuro.

"Thank you . . . it brings me comfort, and I only play when I go down to the gardens. It's only there, surrounded by trees and birds, that I remember the day when I really felt free . . ."

A tear ran down her cheek. Makuro held her in his arms and wiped her face. They remained a time in silence. He bent his head, his heart beating fast, and felt the warmth of her body. Their lips came together.

"Please, don't" she pleaded. "I don't have permission . . . and, neither do you."

"I'm not worried about the rules. We don't need permission."

"You're speaking spontaneously. Oh, how I'd like to be like you. I'm so sorry that fate has brought you here."

"I'm not. Meeting you was the best thing that could ever have happened to me."

She closed her eyes, and Makuro held her waist and kissed her strongly on the lips, wrapping his tongue around hers. The kiss was full of feeling, but unpracticed.

When they finished, she confessed:

"It was my first kiss. I've never had permission to meet boys."

"It was also mine. The girls in my tribe were considered sacred, and it was forbidden for my brothers and I to go near them."

"So you were not as free as I thought you were . . ." she said, smiling.

"I'm afraid not . . . our leader was a Hati."

They both started laughing.

"Tell me more about yourself," she asked. "Tell me about your family."

"You must have heard a number of things about my family already. My mother fled from the Hive . . ."

"Oh my God, are you the son of Miku?" she interrupted him, amazed. "Now everything started making sense. Please continue."

"Well, my stepfather is a Myra deserter; my grandfather is an ex-general who was expelled from the Hive; my elder brother was taken by the Myras; and my younger brother is a mixed-race Myra-Hati."

"So the Myra-Hati really exists?" asked the girl in admiration.

"I'm not sure . . ." said Makuro. "I saw my younger brother's death on the recordings in my first plug. I don't know whether that experience was real or false . . ."

"Oh, it's horrible!"

"Yes, but it's . . . it's already passed. And something tells me that Tork is still alive. I feel that he is alive somewhere, and this was just a trick of the doctors."

"I don't think the doctors would be so cruel. But I hope you're right . . ." she reassured. "I'm not sure if anybody else knows that, but you're the son and grandson of very well-known people to the Hatis. Your mother was the subject of great debate when she abandoned our society. After she left, there were many changes in the laws for women, and today women can lead battle troops and even gain important posts in the Empire . . . and your grandfather became a hero when he won the 'Battle of the Convicts'. Both of them are much admired by the people, but hated by the Empire. What I didn't know is that Miku was Hanara's daughter . . ."

"Actually, Hanara is not my mother's father. My brothers and I grew up thinking that he was our real grandfather, and this is the way I see him."

"I understand . . ." she now seemed worried, as if she wanted to finish the conversation.

"Any problem?" asked Makuro, noticing how tense she had become.

"I'm sorry. I must go now" she said. "My father must be returning from his meeting with the Command. He wouldn't like to see us talking . . . he and my stepmother are forcing me to marry the general's son."

Makuro looked at her with surprise.

"Are you engaged?"

"Not officially . . . but I think I will soon be. My father is planning to announce our engagement at the end of the next hu-tae-mui championship, when the general's son wins the last bout."

"And if he doesn't?"

"My father guarantee that he will."

"Do you love him?" asked Makuro.

"I haven't even met him" she said with sincerity. "It's a marriage of interests. My father wants to be the future General of the Hive, and marrying me to the son of the present General will help him be nominated. As his daughter, I'm obliged to accept his decisions, and disobeying him would be a great dishonor."

"Don't worry. Your father must be an understanding man. Talk it over with him and everything will be okay . . ."

"It's not that simple . . . but, thank you for thinking about me and the flowers. I must go before he arrives."

She turned around and began to walk away, but Makuro held her back.

"Wait" he said. "I must see you again. Can we arrange a meeting?"

"It's better not to. I'd really like to, but I can't . . ."

"We can meet in some secret place" he suggested. "My brother secretly met one of the native girls. We can do the same."

"I don't know whether there are any places where we can hide . . . the entire Hive is under surveillance, and we are monitored by the Empire at every single moment. They must already know that we are together."

"They know we are together, but they don't know what we are doing."

"If we are connected to the inter-plug, then they will know that we kissed" warned the girl.

"The doctor who implanted my connector told me that my plug could not access the inter-plug" said Makuro, as if the device in his neck was his own. "So we'll be safe."

"Your plug is a simple civilian device. It can't access any other though the inter-plug, but the military plugs can access yours at any moment. Almost no one knows this, or they forget, but it's law."

"In this case, we won't take our plugs."

"You don't understand . . . we can get rid of the plugs, but we can't get rid of the connectors. Inside the connectors there is a transmitter which is always on. There is no way which we can turn it off, as it uses the calories of our own body as fuel . . . so we can be located wherever we are."

Makuro looked down, thinking.

"So let me see you just to talk, in some public place" he said, taking her hands. "We won't be noticed."

She thought.

"Okay" she said. "Do you remember the garden where we met?"

Makuro nodded.

"Meet me there after it gets dark. I'll be there with my flute, in the company of my feathered friends. I can wait for you. I haven't been to the gardens for a long time, but today I have a special reason. Try to give the impression that we are meeting by chance."

"I'll be there" assured Makuro, and they sealed the agreement with another kiss.

"Now go", and she pushed him. "We can't take any more risks."

Makuro smiled and turned, going towards the reception.

"Wait!" she shouted. Makuro returned. "I still don't know your name. My father didn't tell me, and I don't watch the news."

"My name is Makuro . . . Makuro Kliver."

"Kliver? The same as the Myra who was our prisoner for almost seventeen years?"

"Yes, he was my father . . . I mean, my stepfather. I never met my real father. I don't know what happened to him. My mother never told me, and I never had the courage to ask."

"I might be able to help you find out. I think we have a lot to talk about . . . you're incredible! You've lived with the most famous people of our time."

She thought for a moment, taking in what had happened.

"Wait a bit" she said. "If Kliver is your stepfather, then he lied in the interview. He had not eaten Miku, as he told the reporters, but married her! Oh, what a beautiful love story, to risk his own life to hide the beloved! I knew that he would never have eaten her. My father took me to the prison to meet him, two weeks before he was freed . . . when I saw him in the cell, Kliver's eyes were sad, but full of goodness . . ."

"What are you talking about?" Makuro was confused.

"Don't you know the story that your stepfather told in his interview? There is even a song about it."

"What story?"

"I'll tell it to you tonight. Now I really must go."

Makuro held on to her, preventing her from leaving.

"Don't go yet. You also haven't told me your name."

"My name is Yuka Ozarra. I'm the daughter of Lieutenant-Colonel Tadashi Ozarra," she said and left, after their final drawn-out kiss.

CHAPTER 22

LUI'S TAVERN

In the Loagy territory, the Myra platoon that had returned from Ruakan was finally reaching the Colony, bringing the news that the mission had failed. All the soldiers were all dirty and exhausted and had not bathed in the last week, during which Aron heard continual complaints from the soldier whose saddle he shared about his bad smell.

Barbarez and Irvine sometimes allowed Aron to ride alone on their bigbugs while they shared a single saddle. The platoon had started out with thirteen men, each with his own big-bug, and they had lost three soldiers and four animals in the struggle against the gigantic worm.

The Major had radioed the Myras the time he would arrive without telling them the mission had failed, so that when they reached Loagy, a huge party was organized to welcome the Noans.

There was great disappointment when they saw the platoon returning alone, but an idea of the Major managed to save the ceremony: the nine brave bigbugs, which had survived the extra dosage of glicorjiu, were released into the wild in an improvised event which replaced the party.

The bigbugs did not initially understand what their owners were doing, but they soon galloped off into the Oasis, fleeing from the crowd who were warmly applauding them as they now became the focus of the regency press.

The platoon then broke up, and everyone returned to their duties. Aron went back to the barracks for new recruits, Irvine and the soldiers went to their squadrons, Professor Hugo went back to the Myra University where he taught Geography, and Barbarez had to carry out his prison sentence for his past misdeeds. The Major tried to do something to help him, but in vain. The ex-Sergeant would have to spend the next months incarcerated in one of the prisons on the Corrective Level.

The following day, Aron was called to the Military Junta Headquarters to discover the results of his recruitment exam. His score was thirteen, and so he now had a place in the Privates' Academy, where he was called 'Private Kliver Second-Class'. He would take only eight months to graduate and might be called up at any moment to take part in a possible Myra-Hati battle.

When this was published, Aron went to a smithy, where a well-built man heated an iron with a number, tattooing it on his left arm, in the same way that cattle are branded. Aron received the Myra coat-of-arms on his arm, with the Register Number 107.700-7 underneath.

"Memorize these numbers" said the man. "They belong to you and only you forever. Even though you may retire or die in battle, your number won't be used by any other soldier. Be proud of this."

Aron was given his uniform for use inside the barracks. It was beige (the official black uniform would only be given to him after he graduated in eight months' time), and he learned the Myra Army hymn.

On Wednesday afternoon, on his first day as a recruit, something unusual happened when the Commander officially announced Aron's new position.

"From now on," he said to the troops, "I declare that Private Kliver, RN 107.700-7, is officially a recruit of our glorious Myra Army, which in turn . . ."

"Big deal!" came from somebody's mouth.

The commander looked around to find who was speaking.

"Who made that comment?" he said, irritated.

Silence.

"I'm not playing games. I'll ask once again . . . who made that comment?"

Silence.

"If the culprit does not admit it, all the battalion will suffer the consequences."

Silence.

"If that's what you want, then you'll spend the rest of the day running around the parade ground until someone admits it."

"It was him!" a young corporal pointed to the culprit, a thin soldier who immediately stopped smiling.

The Major looked furiously at the accused.

"As a punishment," he said, "you'll run ten times around the parade ground for your insult, and the corporal will run twenty for having accused him . . ."

"But . . ." said the corporal.

"Capitan" ordered the commander. "Follow them with your whip!"

The captain took out his whistle and ran behind the punished soldiers, shouting, whistling and cracking his whip in the air on every lap. No one dared to smile.

"This is the philosophy of the Myra Army" continued the Major. "Admit your mistakes, or the entire troop will suffer the consequences. As soldiers, we should look after each other. Both men and women" he said, looking at the female squadrons. "The treatment is the same for everyone. There are no exceptions."

The Major looked at Aron.

"Kliver, turn around and march toward the flag" he ordered, and everyone looked at Aron, holding out their right arms as a sign of respect to the red flag of the clan, which because of the lack of wind, was hanging limply from the mast.

"Private Kliver, do you swear before these witnesses to use the authority which has been given to you only for the good of our society and your army companions?" asked the Major, beginning the Myra oath of loyalty.

"I do" replied Aron.

"Do you swear to obey your superiors and, if you are promoted, to treat your subalterns with respect?"

"I do."

"Do you swear to raise your weapon only to protect and defend our Colony against our enemies?"

"I do."

"Do you swear to reject the temptations of the outside world, such as lust, excessive use of alcohol, and the evil plugs, accepting Catandism as your only belief and religion? Look to the flag and swear!"

"I d-do."

"Do you swear to accept our traditions and conquests?"

"Yes . . . I mean, I do!"

"Do you swear not to humiliate or mistreat possible prisoners of war?"

"I do."

"Do you swear to follow the patriotism of your mother land, accepting the Myras as equals, respecting their laws and regulations, and consider Our Majesty the Regent as the highest authority?"

"I do."

"It is now finished. You may return to your place. You will have until Monday to adapt to our rules. Get your fellow members of the platoon to help you. They are here to teach you how to march and everything else you need to know. Get fit, private."

At the beginning it was very difficult for Aron to get used to the discipline of army life. He was not used to following any orders other than brushing his teeth every day. His entering the army was a headline in the main newspapers of the Colony, and the interview he had given weeks before was frequently broadcast on the radio and television.

Many people disapproved of the fact that the Regent had allowed the son of the deserter into the Army. They tried to find a way of making Aron pay for his father's mistakes. And immediately Aron began to suffer considerable prejudice from the older soldiers.

But Capitan Maximilian was by far his worst problem. He was an authoritarian and rough man, and was well-known as the 'terror of the new recruits', as Aron discovered.

From the end of the ceremony on Wednesday to the next evening, Aron was given various reprimands by the captain, who criticized him for not marching correctly, incorrectly saluting, having left a few hairs on his chin at inspection time, having dirt on his boot, having left a few crumbs on his table in the refectory, and even having used the drinking fountain incorrectly.

At the end of the day, Aron was ready to quarrel with the captain. He wanted to yell, swear, but he tried to put up with it. There were rumors that Maximilian had put a soldier into confinement for the whole weekend just because his opinions were different in a certain aspect of Catandism. And there was one recruit who had been imprisoned for insubordination, for having insulted the captain when refusing to clean the toilets in the barracks. Thus, Aron tried to keep quiet and to go unnoticed by the captain.

The following day, Aron was woken up by the sound of bugles. He had had a number of nightmares about the captain and the death of Old Father Zugu, but he became happy when he realized that this was not any old day, but a Friday morning, which was the day the soldiers looked forward to. With the exception of those who were being punished, or those who were on duty, the soldiers could spend the weekend at home, with their families.

At one-fifteen in the afternoon, almost an hour before scheduled, the recruits joyfully returned to their dormitories to change clothes, pack their bags, and half an hour later, the barracks were empty.

Without thinking twice, Aron accepted the invitation to stay at the house of Irvine's parents. Their bags were ready, and Irvine came back from the ATM with a small number of tokens.

"Saddle your bigbug" he said, putting the tokens into his wallet. "I want to get home for lunch."

"Shouldn't we leave them in the barracks?" asked Aron.

"It doesn't matter. The bigbugs are our property. I'd rather let them graze in my condominium. My father will look after them."

Aron agreed and went to saddle his new bigbug.

Mounted on their bigbugs, Irvine and Aron rode down a dark street towards the main elevator, where they will descend to the residential levels. In addition to the elevators, there was another type of public transport in the Colony. Each level had its sphereline unit, which every hour passed by on its winding tracks.

Spherelines could be thought of as a type of fast train, with rounded carriages and flexible movements. They were fueled by coal and complemented the elevators, as they traveled around the various levels.

A sign which said 'Sphereline Stop. Priority for Military Personnel.' caught Aron's interest.

"Can we catch one of these spherelines?" he wondered.

"And abandon our bigbugs?" asked Irvine.

"We can leave them in the stables in the barracks."

"Better not to . . . I don't like the way they treat the animals in the stables" said Irvine. "But don't worry. At night we'll go out for a drink with my cousin, as I do every weekend. We can go by sphereline, okay?"

"A drink?"

"Yes, a drink. Haven't you ever drunk alcohol?"

"When I made my oath, I swore I would never drink excessively. Don't you remember? At other times I would never have said that, but I don't want to break the rules . . ."

"Don't worry about the things you say in public. Don't practice what you preach. Tonight we're going out to drink, get drunk, and meet some nice girls. What do you think?"

"It seems that today will be the first really interesting day in the Colony" said Aron with enthusiasm.

Curious looks, especially from the children, followed his bigbug, as if he were a celebrity. Some people greeted and welcomed him, but others stretched to swear out at the boy who had grown up with the Wild Savages:

"Go back to where you came from" they shouted. "You don't belong here."

"Look over there, son, it's the boy we saw on television".

"Isn't he the son of the deserter?"

"Yes, it's the lad who was baptized last week."

"How could the Regent have accepted a savage into the Army?"

Indifferent to their comments, Aron waved to them all, while Irvine showed the coat-of-arms in his shoulder, trying to impose his authority.

After going down the main elevator, they finally arrived at the residential levels. The buildings rose on both sides of the streets in between abandoned scrapyards. Every tiny space was used in some way, and the open spaces between the buildings were filled in by stores of wood, quarries, and coal depots.

The underground spring of the Olin went from one end of the level to the other in the form of a narrow stream, which was greatly polluted by sewerage.

A number of blocks further on, the bigbugs turned a corner and stopped in front of a high gate, which was near the rocky boundaries of the Level.

'Restricted area, Markson Family Condominium' said a sign on the gate, at the bottom of which there was a drawing representing an electric shock, a warning that trespassers would be electrocuted.

"We've arrived" said Irvine with a smile. "Home at last!"

"Is your name Markson?" asked Aron.

"Irvine Markson, that's my name" he said while he typed the passcode on the electronic panel to open the gate.

In the condominium gardens, Aron could see that the Myra houses were built in openings which had been dug in enormous concrete steps, one on top of the other, and which rose like a step pyramid. In each pyramid there were dozens of rooms, all of which were inhabited by members of the same family. In the rooms, the lights were always on, as in the underground there was no difference between day and night.

When they went into the residence of Irvine's parents, Aron was introduced and they put away their bags and sat down on the living room couch, waiting for lunch to be served. Irvine's mother was a quick cook, and in a few minutes the kitchen bell rang to announce that the food was served.

Aron remained quiet during the meal, just replying to a number of questions which Irvine's parents asked him about Kliver and his past in the tribe.

After lunch, Irvine and Aron washed the dishes and went back to the living room. They watched television for a while, but all they saw was the repeated news about the threats of war.

Getting bored, Irvine got up and picked up the interphone, calling Donus, his elder cousin who lived with his uncle and aunt four floors above. Aron was impressed by how practical the phone, which allowed him to communicate at a distance, was. Although it had been in use for more than five hundred years, it was new to Aron.

A few minutes later, they heard heavy steps coming down the stairs, and Donus came in. He was tall, stout, limped, and had a metal plate which covered a large part of his head.

"This is my cousin Donus, ex-soldier" said Irvine. "He retired early after losing a leg and getting shot in his skull, which put him into a coma for six months. Am I right?" he asked, giving his cousin a punch on the shoulder.

Donus shielded off the punch and held out his hand to Aron, who was unsure about what to do.

"Aron is new here" explained Irvine. "He doesn't know how we greet each other."

"Aron with two 'a's?" asked Donus.

"No, just one" replied Irvine. "Tell him how you got shot."

"Hu, it was an antique that my friends had bought from an officer. An old revolver, 38 caliber. Lead bullet. Stupid game. Russian roulette" said Donus, confusedly.

"What shall we do, cousin?" Irvine asked.

They spent the rest of the day and some of the evening in the Markson's gardens, shooting arrows with crossbows at paper targets.

Inside the Colony, only the clock could tell whether it was day or night. At ten o'clock, Aron was in the bathroom in Irvine's room, looking at himself in the mirror while he put on a shirt which he had borrowed from Irvine. He wanted to look good for their night of adventures. He looked at his reflection and was pleased, concentrating on that which he thought positive, and trying to hide his defects.

"I've never seen anyone take such a long time in the bathroom" said Irvine at the door. "You seem like my sister!"

Aron looked at Irvine in the mirror.

"Have you got a sister?" he asked.

"Yes, but she's of no interest to you. She's married and has a good life with her hubby. She and my brother-in-law live a floor below, and I'll soon have a nephew" he said, proudly. "It's strange to think that I'll soon be an uncle. It makes me feel old."

"As my grandfather always said: 'Time is like a river. If you try to stop it, it will flood the valleys and change its course, but it will always continue to run'."

"Yes . . . there is no way you can stop time. And that's why we shouldn't be wasting it" he said, looking at the clock. "Hurry up. The next sphereline will leave in twenty minutes. If we miss it, we'll have to wait another hour."

"I'm ready" he said, adjusting shirt's collar. "How do I look?"

"If you want some advice, it's much too hot to wear long sleeves. I wore that shirt at my sister's wedding, and I've never worn it again. Come with me. Come to the bedroom, and I'll lend you some clothes which will be suitable for tonight."

Irvine gave Aron some scruffy looking jeans, a black T-shirt, old tennis shoes and a red bandanna.

"What do you think?"

"I don't know. I look like a bad boy" said Aron, looking himself up and down.

"Nowadays, the girls like a slightly more aggressive style . . ."

Donus came into the room.

"You're like two girls . . . Hu, one dressing the other," he joked. "Let's go, 'ladies'. It's a long way to the sphereline stop, and I haven't yet got used to my new leg. The joint is loose and creaks."

They left the room, said goodbye to Irvine's parents, went down the condominium steps, crossed the gardens, and arrived at the gate. Aron and Irvine walked slowly because of the difficulty Donus had to walk with his artificial leg.

The subterranean tunnels smelled of sulfur, which discomforted even those who were used to it. The respirators were unable to filter all the poisonous gases, and you could always smell the residues of monoxide and carbonic gas.

In addition to the gases, there was another problem of living in the underground: the lack of sun. The Myras had breathing problems and almost no pigmentation of the skin. They were as white as ghosts, and the artificial illumination gave them certain visual defects.

When they approached the sphereline stop, they could see a small group of people gathered around, waiting for the train which would shortly arrive. Two men got up and offered Donus their seats. The veteran soldier thanked them, but refused to sit down as he didn't like to be given special treatment.

A girl recognized Aron, opened her bag, took out a pen and a piece of paper, and asked for his autograph.

"Dressed like that you don't look like the person who was on television" she said. "I like your clothes."

"Can't you see?" said Irvine. "These clothes make men today."

"Don't be deceived" warned Donus. "These girls don't want you, but they want what you represent: a new attraction. In a week nobody will remember your face."

On the roof of the level, the track began to shake. There was a distant noise of brakes screeching, and the noise became nearer and got stronger. A strong light came from the tunnel with the luminous sign saying: 'To Commercial Level. Rings 1 to 8 full'.

Those who were standing up got into a line, and those who were sitting got up at the same time. The long train made up of round rings stopped a distance away, and the passengers had to get into the rings from number nine to eleven.

The rings are compartments of the spherelines, somewhat like carriages. They are large spherical cabins, connected to each other by flexible cables, allowing the train to freely move around the bends of the track. The tracks are fixed on the roof, rather than being riveted to the ground. This is how the train can reach the higher levels without going too slow when going up.

When everyone had got in, a loudspeaker told them to put on their seatbelts. Aron needed to be helped. He felt tense and at the same time excited that he was there, as anyone would be on their first sphereline journey.

The train jerked away and soon reached its speed limit. The seats vibrated and swayed at each curve, and when the compartment suddenly bent to follow the vertical tracks, Aron began to feel sick.

His stomach was turning over. He breathed deeply and tried to think about simple things, but he couldn't get rid of the present situation — the worst was going to happen. He wiped his forehead and felt the scar of his old wound. He pressed and scratched it with his fingernails, trying to forget his dizziness, but it was useless. Even with his scar bleeding again, Aron bent over and threw up his dinner.

A great embarrassment. The girls swore at him while he apologized for having thrown up over three men in front of him. The stink of vomit mixed with the stuffy air inside the ring. Many people got out at the first stop, and the cabin emptied. Those who were going to get in stopped when they saw the vomit, and only Aron, Irvine and Donus remained.

"Don't worry. Clean yourself up as soon as you can" consoled Irvine, who was now used to comforting Aron.

"Hu, I can see you're still popular with the girls" joked Donus. "Such a good impression you gave!"

After five bends, steep climbs and frequent changes of speed, the train finally reached their destination. The stain which Aron had made on his trousers was now dry and crusty, and would hardly come out with just water. They went to the entrance and showed their tattoos to the optic reader and then went down to the sidewalks.

The Commercial Level was a dark cave full of rubbish. Cockroaches and other insects crawled around the rubbish which was piled up on the sidewalks. Packages of paper and boxes filled the alleys. Small animals with smooth pink skin crawled up the wet walls. An old drunk snored out loud on the ground, rolled up in a filthy blanket.

When the sphereline left, and their view opened out, Aron saw that on the other side of the street there was a busy market, crowded with people walking around the shops and the stalls.

Various types of steam vehicles clogged up the streets, filling the air with smoke, which appeared to be colored through the neon advertising signs. Other types of fuel were banned in the Colony, as they would pollute the closed atmosphere. Drops of water dripped on their heads. Aron thought this was strange.

"Can it rain in here?" he asked.

"That's not rain" explained Irvine. "The steam which rises from the vehicles reaches the roof of the level, condenses, and drips down."

Buskers performed, pimps, beggars, whores, demonstrators, dancers, fanatics, wounded soldiers, musicians and thousands of people crowded onto the sidewalks.

The three crossed the road, dived into the crowd, and found their way into a bar whose outside was covered in obscene graffiti. The inside of the bar was dark, lit up only by a row of black lamps. Scantily dressed girls were dancing in cages hanging from the roof, and bearded men played snooker on chalk-covered tables.

Donus told them to turn down their shirt sleeves to hide their tattoos.

"It's better not to show that we are soldiers" he said. "We are here to enjoy ourselves, not to attract attention."

"Are you sure you want to stay here?" asked Aron, feeling somewhat uncomfortable.

"We've come here just to drink" said Irvine. "Then we'll go to one of the pubs, okay?"

"So, I'll go to the bathroom to try to clean the stain on my trousers . . ."

Donus asked for a table with three chairs and six shots of cheap brandy. He lit a cigarette and toasted to the evening with his cousin, downing his brandy in one. When Aron got back they were already on their third shot and were clearly more relaxed.

"Hu, you've wet your trousers!" joked Donus.

"It's better to wet your trousers with water than with vomit" said Aron, sitting down. It was now Irvine's round.

"Another six shots, please" he made a sign to the barman.

With their six full glasses, they made a toast. When he felt the brandy burning his throat, Aron turned his face and shut his eyes tight. His stomach had not yet recovered from the shameful sphereline journey.

"Hu, you kids! Here. Have a smoke" Donus offered Aron a puff of his cigarette. "This will help the brandy to go down."

Aron puffed the cigarette and the impact of the smoke as it hit his virgin lungs made him feel dizzy, and then he began to cough.

"Take it easy, new boy. Have a whole cigarette."

"Yes, please."

Aron began to feel his muscles relax and now he was enjoying himself more and more. He completely forgot that he had duties, that there was a war on, and that he was worrying about the members of his family who had disappeared. After the fourth round, they began to tell Donus about the adventure they had had with the search platoon, when they had fought off the desert worm.

"I owe my life to Barbarez" said Aron, as he remembered the moment when he was almost eaten up by the worm. "He could be with us here now . . . it's a shame he's in prison . . ."

Half an hour later, Irvine got up, now quite drunk, and leant on a chair in order not to fall over.

"This bar is too empty" he said. "I think it's time to go to the pubs. What do you say?"

"Hu, you're right" said Donus. "Let's have another drink and go."

They downed another double brandy and staggered out of the bar, joining the crowds on the pavement. They walked two blocks, and Aron pointed to a building with neon lights on the opposite corner from which loud electronic music was coming.

"That place could be cool" he said, after hiccupping. "Can we go in?"

"You won't like it" said Irvine. "Well, I hope you won't. That's a GLBT club."

"GLBT?"

"Yes, forget it . . . maybe one day you'll find out . . ."

Girls in miniskirts and transvestites balanced on their stiletto heels, attracting attention wherever they went. Men in colorful suits were inviting the single men to enter their nightclubs.

"This Level really changes at weekends" said Irvine. "If we came here on a Monday, the streets would be quiet and empty. You wouldn't believe you were in the same place . . ."

"All the women seem the same," remarked Aron.

"Here in the Colony we're all indirectly relations or descendants of our common ancestors" explained Irvine. "In ethnic groups who have been living in isolation, everyone tends to look like everyone else after some time. That's how different races appear."

They turned a corner and followed a sidewalk full of people wearing Catandist habits, preaching teetotalism and warning of the evils of prostitution, which was very common on this Level.

Further on, they had fun with a group of girls who stared at them.

"Wow! Did you see them?" asked Irvine.

"Hu, how could I have missed them?" said Donus.

"Let's go back and talk to them" suggested Irvine. "Let's go and invite them to sit down and . . . have a drink."

"More drinking!" said Aron. "I don't think I can take any more . . ."

"But you have to be polite to them."

"And what are we going to say to them?"

"Leave it to me" guaranteed Irvine.

They turned around and walked quickly back to the corner, Donus limping behind them.

"Evening, ladies . . ." said Irvine with all his charm. "Would you like to 'join the ants in the anthill'?"

The girls smiled cynically, and Donus put his hand to his forehead. He hated the expressions his cousin used.

"May we have the pleasure of knowing your names?" insisted Irvine.

Without taking the smile off her face, one of them replied:

"I'm Pamela, this is Tycia, and that 'big butt ant' in red is Claudia."

"'Bug' off, blondie . . ." and Claudia hit Pamela with her handbag.

"Would you care for a drink?" invited Irvine.

"What do you think, girls?" asked Pamela, apparently the friendliest of the three.

They talked to each other and accepted.

"We're on. But in Lui's Tavern, okay?"

"No problem. We were on our way there" and they took the girls to the bar.

Lui's Tavern was the most popular civilian place visited by soldiers of all levels. They would certainly meet old acquaintances there, and, in the company of these good-looking girls, they would impress their fellow soldiers.

Now drunk, Aron could no longer feel the tips of his fingers, and the prospect of drinking even more was enough to make him feel sick again. He looked at Claudia and saw three female triplets moving identically.

"Your friend doesn't seem to be very well" noticed Tycia.

Pamela picked up a paper bag from the gutter and gave it to him.

"Here, put your head between your knees and breathe deeply into the bag. This will help the oxygen to circulate more quickly."

"Hey!" said Claudia. "Isn't this the guy who was in the news?"

"Who?" it seemed Tycia didn't follow the news.

"You know . . . the one who grew up with the savages. Didn't you see the interview?"

"Yes, that's him" whispered Irvine. "But don't spread it around. I don't want them to see him like this . . . the poor guy is finding it difficult to adapt to things in the barracks, and it would be embarrassing for him if the press found out he got drunk. We might also be blamed . . ."

"Ten tokens" said Claudia.

"What?"

"Well, if you want us to keep a secret, you'll have to pay" said Pamela, stuffing a tobacco chewing gum into her mouth which was covered in sticky lipstick.

Irvine got angry.

"Now I realize" he said, furiously. "You're no more than cheap whores! We won't give you a single cent's credit and you'll keep your mouth shut. I'm a respected soldier and an important person on this level" he showed his tattoo. "If you say anything, you'll be in trouble."

Donus and Irvine carried Aron on their shoulders and went alone into the tavern. The girls stared at them with disdain.

"What shall we do?" asked Tycia.

"Wait" replied Pamela, chewing her gum. "Lui will know what to do . . ."

When they were in the tavern, Donus asked for a table and two mugs of beer while Irvine took Aron to the toilet, splashed water on to his neck, and made him vomit once again. He immediately improved, and they went back to the room and sat down. Irvine picked up his mug and asked for a fruit juice for Aron.

The place was full. The tables filled up all the space in the room, and on the stage a band played background music. Aron was the only one who was sorry the girls had not come, and to get over his loss, he stared at all the women around.

"Why didn't we come here first?" he asked, still feeling somewhat sick.

"The drinks are dearer here" explained Donus.

"We would come here anyway" added Irvine. "It's a good place for soldiers and we don't need to hide our tattoos."

"I'm no longer in the Army, but my coat-of-arms and my RN are still there" said Donus, counter-proudly.

"This tavern is much more pleasant than the other bar, and the people seem more friendly, don't they?" asked Irvine.

"Yes, everything seems better, especially the music" said Aron, admiring the saxophonist's skill. "What type of music is that?"

"It's derived from jazz, an inheritance of black culture" said Irvine.

"The black people in my tribe didn't have these rhythms."

"I'm sure the black people in your tribe used primitive instruments, didn't they?"

The conversation was interrupted when Donus' intuition warned him about the danger. Without any apparent reason, a number of men at the next table were looking at them with disapproval. The veteran soldier warned his friends, and below of the table he put his fingers on the grip of his gun.

"Hu, there are five fools staring at us at the next table" he said. "If you don't want to get into a scrap, don't look at them."

Aron ignored this advice and turned to look at them. They talked, laughed and stared at them once again, as if they were looking for trouble.

"Let's go somewhere else" Aron suggested, feeling uncomfortable.

"Don't worry. The bar is full of people we know" said Irvine. "Sergeant Tolkias is at the counter, celebrating with his soldiers. We're safe."

Time passed and the stares didn't develop into anything more serious. Apparently the supposed trouble-makers were not going to do anything. But a little later, after the band stopped playing, and Sergeant Tolkias had left with his men, the three girls, Pamela, Tycia, and Claudia, entered the bar and went to the counter, whispering something into the ears of Lui, who appeared to get angry.

Lui, the owner of the place, was actually their pimp and had made a lot of profit from them. His tavern, which was full of soldiers, was the perfect place for him to do his dirty work without arousing the suspicion of the Catandist demonstrators who patrolled the Level to look for unfaithful activities.

A few minutes later, a well-built man came to their table, wiping the inside of a glass.

"Do you know those girls?" he asked, nodding at them.

"Maybe . . ." said Irvine. "Why?"

Lui said that you owe them credits.

"How many, exactly?"

"A hundred."

"Ah?"

"Ten for a favor they did you and another thirty for each of you for you know what."

"Ridiculous!" shouted Irvine. "Tell Lui that they are lying."

He banged the glass down on the table, threatening them with his finger:

"It's better to pay up, or there will be trouble."

Everyone in the room began to look at them, and it was the ideal moment for the group at the next table to speak out.

"What's going on here?" asked one of them, a middle-aged man whose muscles were visible under his shirt.

"These worms owe credits to those young ladies at the counter and refuse to pay."

"If I may add something, they were also giving my daughter dirty looks. Especially that suntanned one in the middle" he said, pointing to Aron.

"He's new here in the Colony" Irvine once again tried to defend him. "He doesn't know how to behave in public."

"Ah, so that's the son of the deserter! I thought I'd recognized him . . . it's another good reason to smash his face in!"

The man showed his palms.

"Can you see these corns?" he asked. "I've been working on the farms for more than twenty years. It was your father's fault for having failed me in the crossbow examination when I was dismissed from the Army."

"It must have been your fault . . ."

Aron's comment was enough to provoke a punch which hit him on the forehead.

The recruits put up their fists, the fight began, and things became mayhem. Chairs were thrown, women shouted, and other men joined in. Irvine and Donus took out their pistols.

Captain Maximilian, "the terror of the new recruits", was on the sidewalk when he saw people rushing out of the tavern, shouting.

Inside, Donus shot into the air. Their adversaries hid under the tables and also took out their guns, and when one of them finally pulled the trigger, a bomb was thrown from some-where and exploded near the counter. There was a strong flash, then darkness, and nothing else could be remembered .
. .

CHAPTER 23

CONSEQUENCES

Saturday afternoon, a man riding a bigbug greeted the soldier on guard at the entrance to the desert barracks on the Second Level of the city.

"Good afternoon. Is there any officer in the barracks?" he asked.

The soldier lowered the volume on his radio and got up.

"No" he said. "Just the recruits on sentry and patrol duty. You know . . . weekends are slow. You can only find officers on the Third Level."

"Can you tell me the name of the sentry who is guarding the arsenal?"

The soldier checked the duty roster and replied:

"Private Roger. He will be on duty until three o'clock and will be substituted by Private Went."

"Can I speak to him?"

"Yes, I can give you permission, but you must register your name, and I need to see your papers."

"Why do you need to see my papers?"

"I can't allow anyone into the barracks without being identified. I need to register your visit and give the information to the next guard. It's part of my job. If I allow you in, and anything happens, it will be my fault. Do you understand?"

"If I give you . . . let's see . . . a hundred tokens. Will you let me in without being registered?"

"Are you trying to bribe me?"

"Of course not. I'm just trying to do something that the authorities should have done a long time ago. I just need your help. And you, my friend, need a pair of new boots."

"You seem to be getting up to something suspicious. Leave. Go away, before I tell my superior . . ."

"You don't need to tell anyone. I'm not plotting anything. I just want to show a certain boy that our barracks is not a holiday camp, and that is necessary respect and discipline to live with the Myras."

"Are you speaking about the new recruit?"

"Yes. There was a big fight last night. Because of him, my uncle and two cousins are in hospital. I need to teach him a lesson."

"I didn't hear anything in the news."

"Captain Maximilian had to bend over backwards to prevent the news from getting to the press. Let me in, please. I'm also a soldier. As the commander says, 'as soldiers we need to help each other.' If anything wrong happens, you have my word that I won't put you in a difficult situation. But I need your help. I must get into the barracks without my name being registered."

The soldier felt his pride was hurt.

"Ok, you win" he said after thinking a little. "I'll let you in. I won't register you, but I need to know your name and the squadron you belong to."

"Okay. As long as you don't write my name down, I'll show you my papers."

"Thank you . . . now, as for the hundred tokens . . . I need two hundred to pay a debt."

"What?"

"What you're asking for has a price, partner. It's my neck that is at risk, so it's up to me to make a price . . . I want two hundred tokens in advance."

"So, if I give you two hundred tokens, then you'll have to do me an extra favor. It's my condition."

"What type of favor?"

"First, let me ask you some questions: what was your schedule yesterday?"

"The same as today. I was on sentry duty from one to four in the afternoon and from seven to ten at night."

"On Friday things stop at two o'clock in the afternoon, don't they?"

"Normally they do, but yesterday there was no ceremony, and the commander decided to close things down early. At one in the afternoon, all the battalion was free to spend the weekend in their condominiums."

"That is what I wanted to hear . . . has yesterday's report already been handed in?"

"Not yet. All the weekend reports are only sent in on Monday morning, when our activities begin again . . . what do you want to know?"

"You'll have your two hundred tokens. Now, what I want you to do is to alter the reports from Friday. Don't let anyone see until they are sent in on Monday morning. Write the following: that during your shift, Kliver was the last private to leave the barracks. Write down that he left at about two-thirty."

The sentry was taken aback, surprised.

"What! I can't do that. No really! It's too risky! I can't alter the registers. I could be imprisoned or even dismissed from the Army."

"Think, my friend. The risk of our being discovered is small. Leave the rest to me. Kliver is not one of us. Don't forget that he is the son of a deserter. He's only here because the Regent is protecting him. My uncle was thrown out of the Army because of the deserter, and now he's in hospital because of his son. I have to take revenge for the honor of my family."

The soldier thought for a while. He took the two hundred tokens, and, after altering the Friday report, opened the gates. The stranger left his bigbug at the entrance and went to the arsenal, speaking to Private Roger, the sentry on guard.

He tried to make a new agreement with Roger, unpocketing more tokens. He asked the report in the arsenal to also be changed, telling him that the soldier at the gate also knew about the change and would cover him up if anything went wrong.

Roger agreed and gave him the key to the arsenal. However, the stranger did not take it. He broke the lock with a pair of pliers, entered the store, and left with a heavy case under his arm. He then went to the barracks for new recruits.

After the explosion, all that Aron could see when he opened his eyes were a number of flower arrangements hanging from a white roof. He woke up in a bed in a clean room, feeling muddled and with no idea of where he might be. He turned his head with difficulty and saw Irvine lying in another bed, apparently awake, but not moving.

"Where are we?" he said. "Are we dead?"

There was no reply. Irvine seemed to be paralyzed, sleeping with his eyes open as if he were vegetating. Aron had no way of helping him, or helping himself, as he could not move his body. His arms were tied by strips of Velcro, and his neck was in a stiff plastic brace. Tubes connected his nostrils to a breathing apparatus above the bed.

He waited for a long time, wondering what had happened. He began to feel pins and needles in his feet when a woman in white came into the room with a board under her arm.

"Aron Kliver?" she asked.

"Yes, that's me."

She picked up a pen and began to study the form on the board.

"Let me see . . ." she said. "You were in a big mess on Friday night, weren't you?"

"Who are you? Where am I?"

"I am Sister Sergeant Myrian. You are in the infirmary in the barracks. You were brought early on Saturday morning by Captain Maximilian."

"Maximilian!" said Aron, scared, as he was already familiar with the severity of the captain. "What day is it today?"

"Monday. Day is almost breaking . . ."

"Have I slept for all this time?"

"Yes. It's a natural reaction of the soporific effect of the grenade to sleep at least forty-five hours . . . in your case, you slept exactly fifty. Irvine has not yet recovered" she said, pointing to the other bed. "He seems to be awake, but in fact he's sleeping like a baby."

"A soporific grenade?" asked Aron, once again confused.

"The captain threw the grenade in order to stop the hullabaloo on Friday night . . ." she bent her wrist and looked at her watch. "It's getting late. I need to clean you. During your sleep you dirtied yourself twice."

Aron continued:

"Was he there? Was Maximilian there in the tavern?"

"He was called in by one of the customers in the bar, who said that you were drunk and were using your guns. Lui filled in the papers and blamed you for the tumult. You will have to write a statement to defend yourself. Captain Maximilian did his best to prevent the mayhem from reaching the press. He asked me to tell you that your bad behavior will give you six negative points in your record and that you have lost the right to leave the barracks at weekends, and also to carry a weapon."

Aron now began to think.

"It was not my fault . . . I wasn't even carrying a weapon . . ."

"Whether you are to blame or not, you were wrong. I'll now untie you and clean you. After this, you'll be free to take part in today's schedule. This is your first shooting class, isn't it?"

"Yes."

"I'm sorry to inform you that your shooting classes have been canceled until you are allowed to carry a weapon."

"Ah, that's not fair!" answered Aron. "And what about Donus and Irvine? Will they also be punished?"

"Donus is no longer part of the Army, and so it is not for us to judge him. At this moment he is recovering in a civilian hospital and will be punished according to civil law. And as for Irvine . . . he'll receive two negative points on his record."

Aron felt that he had been unfairly treated.

"Why is my punishment greater?"

"According to Lui and the witnesses in the bar, the fight started because of you . . . it's also a norm in our Academy that the new recruits are given greater punishments than the older soldiers . . ."

Sergeant Myrian untied his wrists, freeing his arms. He could now take the tubes out of his nostrils, and he felt his breathing return to normal.

"You have permission to leave the infirmary. But I'll have to test your reflexes. You must now go to the barracks for new recruits and wait for the dawn call. Get your uniform on. You will parade as on a normal day. Your bad behavior will not exclude you from routine activities . . ."

"And what about Irvine?"

"He will be under observation until he wakes up."

After having a shower and getting dressed inside the infirmary, Aron went down the steps into the street behind the refectories. He walked around the walls, and on the way to the barracks, greeted the man who was sweeping the classrooms, asking him the time.

"Ten to seven" he said, interrupting his sweeping.

Aron thanked him and continued. He could smell the freshly brewed coffee coming from the refectory. If the sweeper's watch was right, he would now have forty minutes to shave and get ready, before the day's routine began.

The majority of the recruits had still not reached the barracks, and those who had arrived were probably getting ready. Aron had the unpleasant feeling that he would suffer a severe punishment from Captain Maximilian for what had happened on Friday. He needed to control his anxiety and decided to go to the refectory to have a couple of cups of coffee.

When he turned into the street which led to the refectory, he had to change plans. All of the squadron was lined up on the parade ground in their platoons, wearing only their underwear.

This seemed somewhat unusual, to be lined up there before the obligatory time, just wearing their underwear.

Something must be happening. The commander and his officers were facing the troops, shouting to the platoons.

Aron left the refectory and immediately located his own platoon. The soldiers who were now returning from their weekend furlough were also surprised. Thinking it might be because of some Hati invasion, they put down their bags and joined the platoons.

Aron whispered to the recruit in front of him, asking him what had happened.

"The officer of the day got us out of bed in the middle of the night" he whispered, without looking behind. "We all had to come to the parade ground. We didn't even have time to put on our trousers. Something serious happened, it seems. As far as I know, it seems that something has been stolen from the arsenal. No one saw anything. The soldiers on patrol in the night said that they didn't see anything suspicious."

"It wasn't last night" a soldier to the right said, without turning his head. "It was during the weekend. I was on guard duty during the day, when I saw someone going around the walls of the arsenal."

"Are you sure?" asked the first soldier. "When was this?"

"Saturday afternoon, about three o'clock, when the barracks were empty . . . but don't tell the commander. I don't have any proof, and you know how he treats stool pigeons . . . he could even accuse me of being an accomplice because I didn't tell the patrol . . ."

The two recruits interrupted the conversation when the Major began to speak to the troops:

"It would be good for the person responsible to admit his guilt, and if he doesn't, everyone will be punished. The weapons which disappeared have still not been found. If they don't appear within an hour, you'll spend the whole day running around the parade ground. And when you are sweating, you'll be 'invited' to enter the tear gas chamber. You all know what happens when the gas acts on skin which is wet from sweat. It'll not be very pleasant . . . but don't worry. There will be doctors on duty."

An officer marched towards the Major and gave him an envelope, inside which there was a letter with the Commander's seal. The Major read it quickly and then announced the following to the privates:

"I have direct orders from the Colonel. I'm obliged to search your lockers." Then he turned to the officers. "I need ten sergeants to search the barracks and the bags of the privates who have just arrived. Everyone's belongings will be searched. Confiscate the keys belonging to all the battalion. Break open the lockers of those who have not arrived and put the repair bill on their accounts."

He once again looked at the soldiers, giving the following order:

"Return to the barracks and remain beside your beds. Wait for your lockers to be searched. When you go through the door, hand your keys over to the inspection sergeants.

The privates left the parade ground and returned to their dormitories. Aron looked for his key in his trouser pocket and was worried when he couldn't find it. He'd probably left it somewhere in the infirmary or in the condominium of Irvine's parents."

He went to the inspection sergeant and told him that he could not find his key.

"No problem, private. We have some good crowbars" the sergeant replied.

Aron went into the dormitory and waited by his bunk. Giamo, the soldier who slept in the top bunk was also there, apprehensive and silent.

As the keys were now in the possession of the sergeants, the recruits were still wearing their underpants or shorts when the search of their lockers began. After ten minutes it was the turn of Aron and Giamo.

Inspection Sergeant Huigas opened Giamo's locker and looked inside for something suspicious. Inside there were just clothes, three uniforms, toiletries, tins of food, and plastic knives and forks. He then opened Aron's locker with the crowbar and found piles of clothes given by Irvine, his well-ironed uniform, toiletries, and an old case, which had also been given him. Huigas picked up the case and as it was light he realized that it must be empty. He was going to close the door when, suddenly, Giamo gave an insinuating cough as if he wanted to tell him something.

Huigas looked at Giamo, who said nothing, just looking at something at the bottom of Aron's locker.

The sergeant once again searched the belongings of Aron, who was surprised to notice that, under his towels, there was something long, with a sharp metal point. Huigas picked it up and looked at it. It was an arrow.

Then, under a pile of cloths at the bottom of the locker, he found a long black heavy case, which he could only lift with both hands. And when the case was opened before the recruits, Aron went pale as he stared at what was found inside it.

He didn't know what to say to the sergeant, as, inside the case, there were two automatic submachine guns, a dismantled crossbow, three rounds of bullets, a quiver of arrows, a number of hand grenades, and a telescopic precision lens.

Huigas closed the case once again, giving an order to Giamo:

"Call the commander. Tell him that the weapons have been found."

Then he turned to Aron, without altering the tone of his voice:

"You have a serious problem now, private!"

"It wasn't me that took them" said Aron, trembling. "I spent the weekend in the infirmary. Ask Nurse Myrian. She will confirm it."

"Come with me" said the Sergeant, leading Aron by the arm to the exit of the dormitory.

The Commander was livid and put the case under the responsibility of Captain Maximilian, who had asked to examine it. Maximilian invited witnesses, reported to the High Command, filled in the papers, and Aron was taken to the military tribunal, where a judge, under direct orders from the Regent which prevented him from exonerating Aron, decided to send him to a medium-level prison, where he would spend the next months.

In order to defend himself, Aron appealed to the High Command and to the media. He looked for the private who had told him that he had seen something suspicious on Saturday, asking him to make a statement in his favor. But the private had no proof and decided not to involve himself.

He also asked for help from Sergeant Myrian, who was a witness in his favor at the trial, confirming the alibi that Aron had been asleep during the whole weekend in the infirmary. But this didn't help. Private Roger, the sentry that day on duty at the arsenal, showed his register to the jury, proving that the weapons had been stolen on Friday afternoon, several hours before Aron was under the effect of the soporific bomb.

Roger was punished for not having prevented the robbery, but he said that he had left his post just for a few minutes because of a stomach ache, and when he returned he found that the lock to the store had been broken.

When the guard who was on duty at the gate said in his statement that Aron had been the last soldier to leave the barracks on Friday, Aron's guilt could not now be questioned, and Aron had no one else to appeal to. The gate register proved that Aron had left the barracks at about half past two in the afternoon, and activities had finished at about one o'clock.

No one, not even Irvine and his cousin Donus, could help him. The military tribunal gave the verdict that Aron was guilty, and his crime was made worse by his poor disciplinary behavior and for having started the fight in the tavern.

His picture appeared once again in the main newspapers of the Colony. The Regent was very disappointed by Aron's behavior and agreed that a number of months in prison would help his image, which was negative until now.

Aron lost his right to wear his uniform and was given prison clothing. On the Corrective Level, accompanied by one of the prison warders, Aron looked for his cell. With his hands handcuffed in front of him, he carried folded towels, pillows, and bed clothes.

He heard repeated comments from the prisoners, who were not even told off by the warder. He glanced at the cells, and he noticed that they were cubicles made of concrete blocks, with a single toilet in a corner and a bunk bed in another, which hung from chains connected to hooks. He knew that he would have a cellmate, and he was afraid that, with the bad luck he had had, his cellmate would be a troublemaker.

The warder went around a bend and pointed to the walls at the end of the corridor, which were spotted with blood turned yellow through time.

"Your cell is the third at the back and on the left" he said. "At the moment it's open. Ask permission from your cellmate and get in before it's locked. Be careful with what you do. Your behavior will be monitored twenty-four hours a day. It's impossible to escape, and any attempt will be punished by death."

The warder turned around and Aron went towards the bars of his cell, saying, without daring to look at his new cell mate:

"I'll be your fellow cell mate. Can I come in?"

"Kliver?" came the voice from inside.

That voice seemed familiar to him, and when Aron looked up, who should he see but Barbarez sitting on the bunk, playing cards with another prisoner.

"You can go, Nyetto. My new cellmate has arrived" said Barbarez, smiling.

"I'm off, but don't forget I won" said Nyetto, a man with a thick beard, which would be difficult to shave because of the various scars on his face.

"In your dreams, my friend . . ."

Nyetto left and Aron went in. But, before leaving, Nyetto warned Aron to take care with Barbarez as he usually cheated when playing poker.

Barbarez swore at him, Aron and Nyetto smiled at each other and Nyetto left.

"Nice guy Nyetto" said Aron as he put his belongings on the empty bed.

"Yes, nice . . . but he has no sense of honor."

"What do you mean?"

"Nyetto speaks too much, he's a misfit. He'll never be successful in the army."

"What did he do?"

"Insubordination. Something pretty stupid. Just look: Captain Maximilian caught him running around the parade ground during the interval between classes. It's forbidden to run around the barracks, except during training. But what annoyed the captain was that Nyetto didn't salute when he met him. As a punishment, Maximilian made him clean the toilets. And while he was about to do this, guess what Nyetto said to the captain."

"I have no idea" said Aron.

"He said that he wouldn't clean any toilet and told Maximilian to go and milk the bigbugs. Can you imagine that?"

Aron smiled.

"Nyetto is a big mouth" continued Barbarez. "He could have kept quiet. To tell anybody to go and milk a bigbug is a serious insult here in the Colony, and an enormous disrespect to an officer, and disrespecting an officer is a serious military crime. He got the maximum punishment. He has been sentenced to two years in prison."

"I think I've already heard this . . ." said Aron.

"And what about you? What have you done to be here?"

"I was set up" replied Aron. "Some weapons were stolen and hidden in my locker. I'm innocent. I'd spent the weekend in the barracks' infirmary, unconscious as a result of a soporific grenade . . ."

"Soporific grenade?"

"Captain Maximilian let one off in order to stop a fight on Friday night. There was a disagreement between me and some guys who were in Lui's Tavern. They accused me of eyeing up an ex-soldier's daughter."

"And were you eyeing her up?"

"Maybe, I don't know . . . I'm not sure. I'd drunk a lot and I can't remember everything."

"The impression I get, some of these guys who you got into the scrap with must have had something against you and managed to incriminate you."

"I don't think so . . . the fight was Friday night. And according to the proof, the weapons were stolen on Friday afternoon, a long time before I went to the tavern."

"What type of proof was used to show that the theft took place on Friday, and not during the weekend?"

"The reports from the guards at the gate and the arsenal."

"So everything incriminated you."

"What do you mean?"

"The reports are generally handed in to the Military Department the next day, after the end of the shifts. But, on Fridays, the Department is closed, and all the weekend reports are only sent in on Monday morning, when it is open again. It's quite possible that during the weekend somebody had changed the reports in order to invent proof against you . . ."

"Are you telling me that the theft did not take place on Friday?"

"If the reports were altered, then the weapons could have been stolen on Saturday or even Sunday."

"Now you're telling me, certain things are beginning to make sense. A private told me that he saw something suspicious on Saturday. He said he had seen somebody going around the walls of the arsenal . . . I tried to get him to help me, but he didn't have any proof and preferred to keep quiet."

"It's probable that the person he saw was one of the guys you quarreled with in the tavern . . ."

"But when the grenade exploded in the pub, the guys I'd argued with were all together. So weren't they also under the effect of the soporific gas during the weekend, as I was?"

"Yes, they must have been asleep . . . but the person who arranged everything might have been one of their relations, a son or a friend who also wanted to take revenge. I think that the criminal might be a soldier, as it seems that he knows the daily routine of the barracks. He knew that the Friday register would not be given in until Monday morning . . ."

"I think you must be right. The sentry at the gate said that he had registered my name on Friday afternoon, stating that I had been the last soldier to leave the barracks, and this is not true as, on Friday, I left with Irvine and stayed at his parents' condominium . . ."

"You should have asked Irvine to make a statement in your favor."

"I asked him, but he couldn't help. We had no proof of the time we left . . ."

Aron thought a little.

"Do you think the gate registers were also altered?" he asked.

"Probably. Somebody must have got the sentry to change them. As the weapons were found in your locker and the Friday register said that you were the last soldier to leave the barracks, your weekend alibi became invalid. Whoever acted against you, planned things well."

"But how did they manage to hide the weapons in my locker?" asked Aron. "Nobody has ever had access to the key to my locker."

Barbarez thought a little.

"During the inspection, did your key open the locker correctly?" he asked.

"I don't know" said Aron, now understanding the question. "I lost my key . . . during the search, Sergeant Huigas opened my locker with a crowbar."

"I bet your lock was changed" said Barbarez. "Someone must have broken it, hidden the weapons inside and put another lock on. It's a pity you lost the key, as you could have checked to see whether the lock was the same."

"What should I do?" asked Aron, shaking. "Should I call the warder and demand a retrial?"

"If you want my advice, leave things as they are" said Barbarez, sitting on the bunk bed. "You are under a dangerous surveillance. Every single soldier is angry or jealous by you. Let the time pass and soon you will be forgotten. Your punishment was not so great. While you're here, try to chill out. Being in prison is sometimes better than having to follow orders every day. At least here inside it's peaceful."

"If I had known that crimes like this existed in the Army, I would never have agreed to become a soldier" said Aron, angrily. "It's completely unfair. I don't want to stay in the Army. Soldiers have to live by rules and duty, while civilians have complete freedom."

"I agree" said Barbarez, patiently. "You might think that military discipline is pretty bad, but I've seen it put young man worse than criminals on the straight and narrow. Now the world is under threat, and being a soldier, even a simple private, is the greatest honor in our society; and it's the best way to get girls."

"Why?" doubted Aron. "The majority of Myra men is or has been soldiers. What makes them so special?"

"The fact that civilians lock up to you, in addition to belonging to an organization which gives you access to information. The top people like to marry their daughters to soldiers. It's the best way to get status for your family."

Aron calmed down.

"Are you married?" he then asked.

"Yes. I have two sons and a daughter."

Barbarez held out a photo which he kept under his pillow and showed it to Aron.

"Here they are" he said. "My wife is in the middle, beside her sister."

"Nice family" commented Aron. "What's that horrible smell?" he said, changing the subject.

"So you've only smelled it now? Carcasses. There is a meat storage plant behind the walls. The minister decided to move it to this Level, as it would be more isolated. Its smell upset those living near its former location. They tried to sterilize the stink, but there are always some parts of the animals that become rotten . . . not very pleasant, is it?"

"No. It's pretty bad."

"You'll get used to it in a couple of days."

"It's going to be difficult to get used to it . . . what is a meat storage plant?"

"You don't know? A meat storage plant is a freezer where fresh meat is kept. But there is also a slaughterhouse, and the smell comes from there. That's where they slaughter the bizorts and the bigbugs which are farmed for their meat."

"Bizorts?"

"A bizort is a large animal with hard leather skin, but its meat is tender and very tasty."

Aron remembered the day when he was looking for his father in distant deserts, when Hanara killed a large hairy animal which was carrying the bag in which his father had kept his diary. Aron didn't tell Barbarez.

"Haven't you ever tried bizort meat?" continued Barbarez.

Aron shook his head.

"You should. It's very popular here in the Colony. It costs ten tokens a kilo, but it's worth it . . ."

The cell fell into an uncomfortable silence. Aron, now lying on his new bunk bed which was less comfortable and dirtier than his previous one, tried to relax. He looked down and found some written papers on the mattress.

"What are these papers?" he asked, as he picked them up.

"They're my memoirs" said Barbarez. "I'm writing my auto-biography on what it's like to be a soldier who has lost his rank, but who has not lost his honor."

"What will it be called?"

"The Barbarities of Barbarez".

Aron frowned in surprise.

"A good title, I think" he then said.

"Thank you . . . if you don't mind, I would like to use you as a character in the last chapter. I'm going to describe our journey with the search platoon, when we fought the desert worm."

"Of course I don't mind" said Aron.

"Good. I'm going to dedicate the chapter to you: 'To my friend Kliver, the new soldier who was free for less than a week'. What do you think?"

Aron looked up at the roof.

"What about dedicating it to your friend 'Kliver, the ex-soldier who asked to be dismissed for having been treated unfairly?'"

"I can see it's difficult for you to understand how mar-velous it is to live in a disciplined hierarchy. Even more for someone who has grown up in a free village . . . but, anyway, time will show you . . . how long is your sentence?"

"Seven months."

"I hope it's enough for you to get a bit more mature. While you're here, try to relax. Seven months will go by quickly. We've got a lot of time to talk about how you should or should not behave, and I'll try to help you as much as I can."

"Thanks, it'll be a great help . . . but, what about you? How long will you be in prison for?"

"Eight months."

"If I'm right, we will get out almost at the same time. By the way, why were you in prison?

Barbarez got up and went to Aron as if he were going to tell him a secret.

"I'm in prison because I have an uncontrollable addiction in an activity which is considered illegal. This is the same addiction through which I was demoted from sergeant to corporal and from corporal to private. And, as I can't be demoted anymore, they put me here in this cell. It's not the first time I've been in prison, and it won't be the last. I'm sure that I will commit the same mistakes when I get out. I have to be careful . . ."

"What type of addiction?"

"I'm addicted to gambling. When we get out, I'll take you to a gambling den, in an old refinery, on the abandoned level. I can guarantee that you'll never feel as alive as when you're betting. If we take care, no one will find out."

"I'd love to" said Aron. "But if it's illegal, I'll be afraid of being discovered and sent to prison again."

"I'm man enough to take the blame for what I do and my mistakes. If anything happens, and we are discovered, I'll take all the blame. You won't be accused, I can assure you. I give you my word. And my word is the most valuable thing I possess."

"What kind of gambling is it?" asked Aron.

"I can't tell you now. You'll find out in seven or eight months, when we get out. I want it to be a surprise. Get ready for the greatest attraction that this city has to offer you!"

"But at least give me a clue" insisted Aron.

"I'm sorry. I can't. Let's stop talking about this for now."

Before the cell was locked, the warder came to undo Aron's handcuffs, tell him about the times for lunch and dinner, the forced labor he would have to carry out, and left.

Aron and Barbarez got to know each other better. Barbarez taught him how to become an exemplary soldier, and Aron told Barbarez about the Wild Savages. They didn't talk about the setup, demotions or gambling for a long time.

CHAPTER 24

PLANS FOR THE FUTURE

"

A respected general, the commander of the armed forces and the right-hand of the Emperor. When I was a sixteen year-old cadet in the Academy, I was in first place in all the tests and established a record which has still not been broken.

My graduation ceremony was unforgettable, with hundreds of men marching and swearing their oaths to the Empire. The ground shook to each step, followed by the tunes of the regimental band. A jetpack fly-past opened the ceremony. The soldiers flew in formation, making skillful and graceful maneuvers in the air, in a spectacle which delighted the spectators in the stands.

After a long speech by the Emperor, who for the first time personally attended a military graduation ceremony, each graduate received his sword, a symbol of the courage required not to have given up during the four years of intensive training.

In these four years I, for one, had seen everything. More than fifty recruits had given up, some of them after the first weeks of tough training. I saw hard men weeping, and others getting crazy because they had been separated from their plugs. I saw three suicides and five soldiers shot to death as punishment for crimes they had committed. One new soldier committed suicide only because he got the smallest piece of meat at one of the meals. He shot his low potential laser gun three times into the mirror, and the rays rebounded into his head.

They were four difficult but marvelous years of my life. I made true friends and mortal enemies.

At the end of the ceremony, something unusual happened: the sword which would be handed to me by my immediate superior, was given to me by the Emperor himself, as a reward for my having been the 'model student' in the tests, one who established a record which would be difficult to break. Never had a mere cadet received such honor to meet our Emperor.

My sword was different from the other ones: a katana made of solid gold, with a handle in the shape of a serpent dragon carved in jade. I remember each word of the Emperor. He told me to march towards him, and all the battalion, including the general at the time, saluted. When I reached him, I kneeled, bowing my head, and held up my arms to receive it. He didn't give it to me immediately. He lightly touched my shoulders, one at a time, with the golden blade, and returned it to its sheath, saying:

'A man should never stop searching for knowledge. He should never stop extending his frontiers. You must become the greatest soldier we have ever had. I hereby give you the Sword of the Jade Dragon, which represents knowledge and supreme courage. Here and now I promote you to captain, if you agree to one condition of mine.'

I had no words to express myself to the greatest of authorities, chosen to be leader by our God. Feeling unworthy, I made a great effort to ask him what his condition was.

'What do you intend to study, young man?' he asked me. 'What career do you intend to follow, in addition to becoming a leader in my army?'

'If Your Majesty permits, I'd like to study Mechatronic Engineering' I replied, still looking down, not daring to look directly to him.

'It's a good choice' he said. 'You are now a first-year student in the Engineering school.'

I was still kneeling, looking down with my arms held out, when he finally gave me the sword, making his condition:

'After graduating in Engineering, you will work in the imperial laboratories and will learn Advanced Genetics in order to join my research group.'

I agreed, and six years later, already a major, the youngest in the army, I found myself in the Palace research laboratories. While I learned the concepts of Genetics, I was given complex DNA tests, and my molecular structure was reevaluated, in order to discover improvements for the establishment of the new infantry. I was something rare for the Hatis, a being who had been successfully created to learn and obey orders.

Let me try to explain:

As far as I know, I belong to a traditional Hati family. My father was a machine operator, and my mother a cook, in a luxury shelter. The registers confirm that I have an older sister, but I never had permission to meet her. I'm the second child of my parents, the product of an illegal pregnancy, as, according to the Hati laws, it's forbidden for couples to have more than one child.

As a choice given by the authorities, my parents decided to donate me to the Empire, and I spent all my childhood in the Palace laboratories, living like a guinea pig. A number of experiments were carried out on me. My genetic structure was enhanced, which helped me to become the perfect model soldier.

When I entered the army, I was a learning machine and got the best marks, both in theoretical and physical subjects. I was the top cadet in the Academy, the fittest and the best hu-tae-mui fighter in the Hive.

After entering the imperial laboratories, I became an apprentice geneticist and led a small study group. During the period I worked in the laboratories, my group had just one aim:

> *To design a living moving being by using a completely genetic vegetable structure.*

After many years of failures and frustrated attempts, we managed to make an important step: using advanced genetics, my group developed an animal cell with chloroplast receivers. This made it possible for us to develop a small insect which was able to fly and manufacture its own food, using a process which was similar to photosynthesis, that is, it consumed just water and sun as energy.

The 'bee-plant', as we called it, was a plant which could move, had a survival instinct, and possessed the same senses as the animal whose DNA had been extracted — the bee. The point of the project was to make an initial step before testing the new cell structure on our human guinea pigs, the illegally born babies who had been given us by the Empire.

We wanted to build a humanoid being who would be able to speak, reason and work machines, without the need to eat, as it would take its energy from the water and sun. It would be a mass produced being obedient and tolerant of atmospheric radiation and which would reproduce in an asexual way.

If we managed to complete the research, the problems of the lack of food in the Hive would be solved as people would receive the new genetic structure in their cells, and birth control would no longer be necessary. Other Hives could now be built, the Empire would grow once again, and we would no longer need our jetpacks, as research in Advanced Genetics would eventually even give us real wings!

I was forty-one when I was promoted to General. I now left the laboratory and was head of the High-Command. We had a couple of baby twins, Flautz and Flouts, who had been incubated with the new plant-animal cell structure when I named my substitute as project leader; but he was unable to develop it, and the project halted.

However, that year, as commander of the armed forces, many things happened to me. I got to know the human side of the Emperor, who was now my only superior in the Hive. I was maximum authority after him. Never, in the history of the Hive, had we had a general who was only forty-one years old.

I now regularly visited the Palace to discuss with the Emperor combat strategy, politics, and how the inter-plug could help us to control the population. The Emperor became a friend, and during my ten years as general, in 188 AE, I witnessed the Inauguration of the New Emperor, who also became a friend.

Interestingly, both Emperors thought and acted in similar ways, and as I visited the Palace almost every day, I was one of the few to notice this.

One day, shortly before I was retired, the present Emperor asked me to carry out a final task. The communication apparatus in the Palace was being repaired, and so I couldn't be announced. The room was dark, and the Emperor was alone, speaking to someone on his private videophone. It was somebody from outside, who was speaking in a strange language, and who also did not communicate by the inter-plug. At that time, I did not know how to speak Myra or even the language of the Banjins, but afterwards I discovered that the dialogue was in neither of these languages.

I spent a long time listening to them. The shape on the video screen seemed to be anxious from the seriousness with which it was speaking. The shape must have seen me, and it immediately went out on the screen. The Emperor then looked at me, somewhat worried, but didn't notice that I had recorded the conversation in my plug.

I still don't know what language they were using, and so I have no idea what was discussed.

The Emperor was angry and told me off for having entered unannounced. He then crossed his arms and explained why he had called for me.

He wanted me to lead a group of engineers who would attempt to improve the inter-plug signals in order to use them to control our airships from a long-distance.

The Hati engineers had always tried to find a way to guide our airships by remote control, but this had never been possible. In order to do this, it is necessary that the operator receives images in real time from the cabin of the airship, and this would only be possible with the help of satellites, but our satellites are unable to reach the regions affected by the blot which covers on the maps.

We hoped that by improving the inter-plug signals we would be able to take over the control of the airships. By controlling unmanned airships, which would obey signals coming from the plugs, we could fight a battle against the Myras without losing a single soldier. We would then be able to locate, invade and destroy the Myra Colony without a single Hati soldier being killed.

A number of months afterwards, when I was discussing the problems of the project with the Emperor in the Palace, he told me that some time before, the former generals had built a complex secret arsenal, which was protected in an underwater base, in the depths of the old Asia Sea. This arsenal was made up of intelligent weapons and hundreds of war airships, which had been developed to function by inter-plug signals.

The only problem was that the former leader of the project had died before finishing it, and even after fifty years of attempts, nobody had managed to put control the airships from the arsenal. And this was my last task with the engineers: to continue the project and to find a way of entering the navigation system of the airships through the inter-plug signals.

The Emperor invited me to enter his private rooms, opened the confidential files of the project, showed them to me, and saved a copy so I could examine them later. I therefore had access to all the details of the technology of the arsenal, even though I had never been there.

While I was studying the documents in my cell, I noticed something that the engineers had never realized: the signal receptors in the airships were on the same frequency as those of the human connectors, when they receive inter-plug signals. This made me suspicious of the real intentions the Emperor had for this project.

One day, when the Emperor was out of the Palace, I went into his private rooms and entered his confidential files. I found a number of files he had hidden from me, in which I saw that there was a secret plan behind the project. Once the signal capable of controlling the airships was developed, the intention of the Emperor was to also manipulate his people by liberating the full inter-plug access to civilians. The Hatis would thus receive both the signals emitted by the plugs and would be controlled by them. This plan was called 'Willpower Control Project', or 'WCP'.

When the project was finished, the Emperor intended to enslave his own people in order to put them at the front line in the battles against the Myras. As they would be mass-controlled by the inter-plug signals, our infantry soldiers would not be able to defend themselves and would be easily defeated by the Myras. The Hati civilization would be destroyed, and its people would be substituted by the new autotrophic beings, the plant-men who had been designed while I was working in the research laboratories.

With the fall of the Hati Empire, the Myras would believe in their victory and return to living on the surface of the land. It would then be easier to exterminate them by using the unmanned airships from the secret arsenal. In the future, there would only be the dominant Hati race, the generation of plant-men who would be able to fly like real bees.

The eventual aim of the Project would be to establish a slave civilization which would be absolutely obedient and would need no food. A new Era and a new Empire would arise.

In order to conclude his plan, the Emperor needed me to finish the last part of his project. Theoretically, if we managed to develop a signal to control the airships from the arsenal, the Empire could also use it to manipulate its own population.

This was the perfect plan in order to dominate willpower. The new society would be perfect, just like a society of insects, and I couldn't allow this to happen. I could not allow them to finish with the little that remained of free human will.

After much thought, I took a difficult decision: I saved the progress of the project in my personal files, to which only I had access, and I destroyed all of its confidential files. I set fire to the documents, deleted the files from the computers, and exterminated the living proof, killing all the team of engineers who were involved in the project. This was an extremely serious crime, even for a general, for which I would have to pay with my life.

However, I was not worried about dying, as long as I could save both Myras and Hatis from extinction. As a Buddhist, I always believed that one day there might be peace between the races and that my sacrifice would be rewarded in another life.

The Emperor was furious and accused me of treason, the worst of all crimes. However, he could not have me killed. If I died, fifty years of research would die with me, and the war airship fleet, the most complex arsenal which had even been built, would have to be forgotten forever.

The Ministry of Justice decided that there were two alternatives for me: solitary confinement or to return the copy of the documents to the Empire. As I refused to hand them over, making them believe that I had destroyed them, I was imprisoned in the solitary wing of our jail.

Although my sentence was for life, I did not spend much time in prison. After a few years, the number of prisoners passed the maximum capacity of the jail, and the law says that when this happens, the prisoners are obliged to take part in an event called 'The Battle of the Convicts', which people believed was an imperial tactic to prevent crimes, but that became reality for the unbelievers.

The Battle is a bloody spectacle in which all the prisoners are released into the main stadium in the Hive, and they fight each other until there is a single survivor, who gains his freedom and is expelled from the city.

As I was an expert master of hu-tae-mui, I managed to win the Battle after two days fighting, and as foreseen, I was sent into exile and expelled from the Hive.

I lost my rank of General, my Hati citizenship, my uniform, my equipment, and was released into the desert with just my personal plug and survival pouch.

I left Sumeru and began my solitary journey through the desert. One hot morning, I lit a fire and heated a strip of metal, injecting it into the holes in my connector. I carefully managed to melt the transmitter of my internal tracker, and from that moment I could no longer be located by the Hatis.

I remember that my time in the desert was very difficult. I ate little, killing small animals I found, and drinking water from the Olin. When I was very weak and thought I might die, I saw in the distance the ruins of a lost city. I went towards them with the last of my strength.

When I entered the ruins, I was made prisoner by the Banjins who lived there. They tried to make me go through their hanging ritual, but I had come so far that I wasn't going to die there.

At the moment of my execution, I freed myself from my rope and killed the warriors who guarded me. I then impaled the former leader of the tribe on his own spear . . . and here I am, the leader of the Kuata-Noans for almost forty years . . . this is my story, the story of how a General who was made prisoner and expelled from his society, for having acted against the Emperor's plans.

I did everything for peace. But this peace is far from becoming a reality, and it won't come without a struggle . . . I think you know the rest."

Hanara stopped. The valley no longer echoed his voice and was silent. His words had greatly impressed the small crowd of listeners, no one more than Miku, who had been waiting nearly eighteen years to hear them.

They were all sitting around a warm fire, in a stony valley, protected by steep slopes and tropical trees, seven kilometers from the eastern coast.

The Islands of the Painted Balerias were an archipelago made up of a main island in the center and various other small islands surrounding it. The main island, where the tribe had landed, was nearly twenty-four kilometers wide and thirty-three long. The hunters were now a third of the way along it, and had not discovered any signs of intelligent life.

The rest of the land had been explored from the air, by Hanara in his old Hati vehicle, and by Tork and Poko riding Buba and Bubu. As the Islands were far from any continent, the reptatiles were now released, and, to the misfortune of the small animals on the island, they finally learned how to hunt alone.

Although he had brought a number of uranium rocks, Hanara realized that there was no deposit of uranium on the Islands. The rocks would not last forever, and so the vehicle could not be used very much.

The large boat in which the tribe had arrived was anchored to the bed of the Tetis, and on the beach there was a small fleet of rafts, ready to take them to the boat in case they needed to escape.

The pasture for the few bigbugs they had brought was now ready, and the soil was being ploughed for planting. The Noans slowly got used to their new life, which was not so different from their former life. They were only sorry they had not moved before as it was now proved that the feared atmospheric radiation was no more than a myth.

At night, the fire was the only light in the valley, where the natives had pitched their tents. From the tops of the rocks, they could see the surroundings of the Island, and so it was not necessary to build observation towers.

In the middle of the valley, before the fire which was beginning to go out, Hanara's mental clock told him that it was now half past one in the morning. The majority of Noans were now asleep, but many of them, especially the young ones, were still awake around the fire to hear his stories.

"So now we finally know why you were thrown out of the Hive" said Miku in admiration. "I never realized that the Emperor's plans could be so cruel. I must apologize to you if I ever thought badly of you in the past."

Hanara nodded, sucking on his pipe.

"I always thought you were a superior kind of man" said Miku. "Now I understand that this superiority is because of the fact your genes were modified when you were born. By the way, if I may ask you, how old are you?"

"I'm exactly ninety-two" said Hanara, proudly. "But according to the geneticists, my cell structure will be renewed until I am more than a hundred and fifty . . ."

"I'm impressed" she said.

Kliver was sitting next to Miku and listening. His face muscles were paralyzed, he was unable to speak, and never stopped drooling. But he was conscious and was able to make a number of gestures to express himself, though he could not move his fingers.

He had woken up out of the coma after traveling for two weeks on the boat. His return to consciousness was celebrated, and the happy mood continued when they saw the Islands on the horizon.

Kliver needed to be carried everywhere. He could not yet move his legs and might not ever be able to walk again, not even with the help of crutches. Hanara believed that with appropriate treatment and physical exercise, it would be possible to recover the use of his limbs, but this would take years, unless they had access to the most modern Hati physio-therapy apparatuses.

"If you had proof of what you told us, we could warn the Hati people about the Emperor's plans and try to bring the two races together in a peace agreement," said Tork, sitting beside Poko.

"That was my intention" said Hanara. "But only you are able to do this, my boy. That is why you were born. You are the chosen one of the Spirit of Sakyamuni. As a mixed-race Myra-Hati, the prophecy is now complete. People will listen to you . . . now about the proofs, yes, I do have proof. It is in my files. But in order to use them, we need something which is inside the Imperial Palace in the Hive. In order to act against the Emperor's plans, we must take over his secret arsenal, and to do this, we need the access card in order to open the underwater base, in the depths of the Asia Sea, where the arsenal is located.

With the proofs and the arsenal in our hands, the Emperor will have no power against us. We need the card, and also the maps. The access card will be useless if we do not know where the base is located. I've neither seen nor visited it. But accord-ing to the confidential documents, I know its blueprints design, and I know it exists."

"So let's try to get the card" said Tork, with enthusiasm. "We'll enter the Palace and get the card. Let's do this. As soon as possible. And if we get into the Hive, we'll try to rescue my brothers, if they are there. We can leave this week."

"It's not so simple, my young apprentice" said Hanara. "The Hive is under watch. We need to act when the people are vul-nerable, being entertained at a spectacle, and not worried about the security of the city . . ."

"And when will this be?"

"The ideal moment to act will be at the next official hu-tae-mui championship. They will all be watching, most of them on the inter-plug, and security will be lower. If we act during the championship, there will be a chance of getting in without being seen."

"It seems the perfect plan. When will the next championship take place?"

"They take place every five years, whether in war times or not. If my calculations are correct, the next championship will be in exactly one year and three months."

"Oh, really?" ask Tork, sadly. "Do we have to wait so long?"

"Don't be disappointed. This will give us plenty of time to finish your training. In addition, I need to carry out some changes to the vehicle, which will also take time. We need to transform it into a mini-submarine so we can travel under the waters of the Tetis, as this is the only way we will avoid the Hati satellites, as the blot on the maps don't appears over the regions near Sumeru.

The easiest way to get into the Hive is through the ducts which suck water in to supply the reservoirs. We can enter them under water, along the coast on the south of Kafria. The only problem will be to get through the distillation plants, which are enormous filters to separate the salt of the sea water through ebullition. This could be dangerous as, if we fail, we'll be boiled alive!

We shall need waterproof suits and oxygen cylinders. With the resources we have, we'll have to improvise . . ."

"I'll help you with what you need, Granddad", said Tork.

"I'll also help", offered Poko.

"I was sure you'd both help me . . . . tomorrow we'll begin. We'll get up early and begin to get the vehicle ready. Today it's been quite enough to tell you all my story. It's now late, and we have to go to bed. We have a lot of work to do."

"Maybe we should also make a calendar, Granddad, so we can count the days", suggested Tork.

"You're right", said Hanara, putting out his pipe. "Do that tomorrow. Now go to bed."

The people around the fire got up and returned to their tents, laying down in hammocks, which on the Islands were excellent substitutes for beds.

"Good night, Granddad", said Tork.

Hanara stood up proudly, deeply breathing the not contaminated warm evening air. He put out what remained of the fire and went the main tent, which was away from the others. A sentry, who was getting ready to take over the watch, greeted him before he went on duty.

Tork, before going to bed, went back to the center of the valley to think about things. He kicked some sand onto the cinders of the fire and crouched down. He remained there for almost half an hour and finally returned to his tent, shortly after seeing Bubu flying low with a large piece of meat between his teeth. He smiled. He closed the curtains inside his tent and took off his shoes. Kliver and Miku were still awake, laying in separate hammocks.

"Good night, Dad. Good night, Mom", he said, thinking how good it was to say goodnight to his parents, who, in spite of so many problems, were still together and hopeful.

And thinking about his missing brothers, his fingers put out the lantern he was carrying, and the sparkle of his eyes, half Myra, half Hati, could no longer be seen.

To be continued . . .

ABOUT THE AUTHOR
FABIO EVANGELISTA

Fábio Evangelista was born in Marília, a town of 300,000 inhabitants in the state of São Paulo, Brazil. At the age of thirteen, he had the idea of telling the story of MYRA-HATI, though not in book form; rather as a comic's story. The project was sidelined for some time, as Evangelista started studying biomedicine. At the age of nineteen, Evangelista abandoned his course and joined the police force of his state. Unable to adjust to the military lifestyle, he quit eight months later. Unemployment, and lack of options, made him lapse into a depressive state, which lasted more than eight months. It was then he found writing a pleasurable way to recover from emotional distress. After writing some short stories, Evangelista decided to resume his former project of MYRA-HATI and started writing the saga once more from a more mature point of view.

Recently, Evangelista has begun to study philosophy at the São Paulo State University (UNESP). He intends to improve his knowledge of history and the evolution of human thought in order to apply these understandings to future stories.

Donnaink Publications, L.L.C.
www.donnaink.org
Publisher
www.donnaink.org

For more information: bulk orders and/or marketing and
promotions contact the Special Markets Division of Donnaink
Publications, L.L.C. at special_markets@donnaink.org and/or
http://www.donnaink.org.

ZENCON ART OF
ZEN CONSULTANCY

PR & Marketing
www.zenconartofzen.com

www.ingramcontent.com/pod-product-compliance
Lightning Source LLC
Chambersburg PA
CBHW011400010726
47495CB00009B/2715